W9-CPF-058

DISCARDED

THE
MAGDALENE
SCROLLS

NOVELS BY BARBARA WOOD

HOUNDS AND JACKALS

CURSE THIS HOUSE

THE MAGDALENE SCROLLS

"THE MAGDALENE SCROLLS"

∙∙◆━━◆>◉<◆━━◆∙∙

by Barbara Wood

Doubleday & Company, Inc.
Garden City, New York   1978

All of the characters in this book are fictitious, and any
resemblance to actual persons, living or dead, is purely
coincidental

ISBN: 0-385-13550-5
Library of Congress Catalog Card Number 77–16854

Copyright © 1978 by Barbara Wood
All Rights Reserved
Printed in the United States of America
First Edition

This book is dedicated to Dr. William Robertson
a good friend,
a good neurosurgeon,
and a great sculptor

I wish also to thank Margie Dillenburg for her
support, her patience, and her comic relief.

THE
MAGDALENE
SCROLLS

CHAPTER ONE

⚬⟶⟶⟶◆⟩⊙⟨◉⟶⟵⟵⟵⚬

Beware to the heathen and to the evil-intending Jew who would disturb the contents of these jars, for the Curse of Moses shall be upon him; and he shall be cursed in the city and in the field, and cursed will be the fruit of his body and of his land; and the Lord will smite him with a severe burning, inflict him with madness and blindness, and pursue him with mildew for ever and ever.

What is this? Benjamin Messer wondered. A curse? He stopped reading the papyrus, baffled.

Scanning the ancient handwriting, he absently scratched his head. Is it possible? he thought again in bewilderment. A curse?

Those words, having caught Ben totally by surprise, made him pause a moment to wonder if he was reading them wrong. But no . . . The writing was clear enough. No room for doubt.

"The Curse of Moses shall be upon him . . ."

Ben sat back in his chair, decidedly perplexed by what he had just read. Staring down at the two-thousand-year-old writing that shone harshly beneath the glare of his high-intensity lamp, the young paleographer considered again the circumstances that had brought him to this moment: the unexpected late-night knock upon his door; the mailman in the dripping-wet raincoat; the damp envelope bearing the stamps of Israel; signing for the special-delivery letter; bringing the envelope back to his den; opening it with anticipation and excitement; and finally reading the first line.

It had been such a surprise—those first few words—that Ben now sat staring at the papyrus fragment as though seeing it for the first time.

What could it mean, this curse? What had John Weatherby sent him? The accompanying letter had explained about the discovery of some ancient scrolls on the shore of the Sea of Galilee. "Possibly even bigger than the Dead Sea Scrolls," the old archaeologist Weatherby had said.

Ben Messer now frowned down at the Aramaic script before him. But no . . . Not the Dead Sea Scrolls. Not biblical texts or religious writings. But a curse. The Curse of Moses.

It had surprised him, this opening statement. It had not been what he had been expecting. Somewhat taken aback, Ben now leaned forward again and continued to read further:

> I am a Jew. And before I pass from this life into the Next, I must unburden my troubled soul before God and all men. What I have done, I have done of my own will; I do not claim to have been the victim of Fate or circumstance. Freely do I confess that I, David ben Jonah, am solely answerable for what I did, and that my progeny are innocent of my crimes. It is not for my seed to bear the stigma of their father's misdoings. Neither are they to judge me. For that is up to God alone.
>
> I have arrived at this wretched state by my own hand. I must speak now of the things I have wrought. And then, by the mercy of the Lord God, I will find peace at last in oblivion.

Benjamin straightened up and rubbed his eyes. Well, this was getting even more interesting. In those last few lines he had come across two more surprises, ones that now made him go back over the scroll to be certain of his translation. One surprise had been the unhoped-for ease in reading the papyrus. Normally it would be a challenge. Most ancient writings abbreviated words and left out vowels, because they were really only prompts for someone who had already memorized the content, thus making translation difficult for the modern paleographer. But not this one. And the second had been the realization that the scroll was not the religious text Ben had been prepared for.

But then, what is it? thought Ben as he wiped his glasses, replaced them on his nose and leaned forward again. What on earth has John Weatherby found!

I have but one other reason for writing this down before I die, and may the Lord God have mercy on me, but it is a greater need than what I stated above. It is, namely, that I write so that my son may understand. He must be made aware of the facts of the events which took place and also my reasoning behind them. He will have heard stories of what happened that day. I want him to know the truth.

I'll be damned! whispered Ben. John Weatherby, I don't think you know what you've unearthed! My God, this is more than just an archaeological discovery. More than just some nicely preserved scrolls for the museum. It looks like you've uncovered someone's last confession. And one that carries a curse with it as well!

Ben shook his head. This is incredible . . .

Therefore, these words are for your eyes, my son, wherever you are. My friends have known me to be a meticulous man, and I shall be true to my nature in this, my final act. These papers will be preserved for you, my son, as your inheritance, for I have little else to give you. Once, I could have bequeathed you a great fortune, but that is all gone now, and in this darkest hour I can leave you only my conscience.

While I know it will not be long before we are united again upon Zion in the New Israel, I shall nonetheless strive to hide these scrolls as if they were going to rest for eternity. You will find them soon, I am certain, and yet it would be the poorest tragedy were they to perish before your eyes befell them. For this reason am I calling upon the Protection of Moses to keep them safe.

The Protection of Moses? echoed Ben's mind. He glanced up again at the top of the papyrus, reread the first few lines, and vaguely recognized the curse that was found in the Old Testament.

John Weatherby, in his letter accompanying the photographs of the scrolls he had unearthed, had said that it appeared he and his team had come across an archaeological discovery of tremendous importance. But it seemed, Ben realized now, that old Dr. Weatherby had not been aware of just exactly what he had found.

Ben Messer, whose job it was to translate the scrolls, had expected religious texts—excerpts from the Bible. Like the Dead Sea Scrolls. But this? Some sort of a diary? And a curse?

He was stunned. Just what the hell *was* this?

> I pray now, my son, to the God of Abraham that He lead you to the hiding place of this pauper's treasure. I pray with all my heart and strength and with greater desperation than praying for His mercy upon my soul that one day soon, my dearest son, you will read these words.
>
> Do not judge me, for that alone is God's privilege. Rather think of me in your trying hours and remember that I loved you above all else. And when our Master appears at the gates of Jerusalem, search the faces of those clustered in his wake, and, with God's benevolence, you will see the face of your father among them.

Benjamin fell back in his chair with a look of amazement on his face. This was absolutely incredible! My God, Weatherby, you were only half right. Valuable scrolls, yes. An archaeological discovery that will "rock the civilized world," yes. But you also have something else here.

Ben felt a flutter of excitement. Something more . . .

Needing to stretch his tall, lean body back into circulation, the thirty-six-year-old paleographer stood, strode to the windows and pressed his forehead to the glass. Aside from his own immediate reflection—the horn-rimmed glasses, blond hair and smooth face— and aside from the dim image of the den behind him, he saw the bright lights of West Los Angeles twinkle back at him.

It was nighttime outside. The rain had stopped, leaving a gentle mist to hang in the air. It was a cold November evening in Los Angeles, but Ben had been unaware of it. As always when translating an ancient text, Dr. Benjamin Messer had lost himself for a while in the alphabet and syntax of authors long dead.

Author unknown and nameless.

Except for this one.

He turned slowly and stared for a while at his desk. A halo glow from the reading lamp illuminated a small area, leaving the rest of the room in darkness.

Except for this one, his mind echoed.

How astonishing, he thought, to have found some scrolls that are written by an ordinary man, instead of a priest, and that appear to be a personal letter of some sort, instead of the usual religious speeches. Is it possible? And if John Weatherby has indeed found the long-lost writings of an ordinary man who lived two thousand years ago, how high does that rank the discovery? Certainly "way up there." It belongs with Tutankhamen's tomb, surely, and Schliemann's Troy. Because if they *are* the personal words of a common citizen who is writing for personal reasons, then these scrolls are the very first of their kind in all of history!

Ben strode back to the desk and looked down. On the desk top a sleek black cat named Poppaea Sabina was inspecting this latest work. The glossy photo, sharp and contrasting, was one of three Ben had received by special delivery that evening. They were pictures of a scroll that was currently undergoing reconstruction and preservation under the auspices of the Israeli government. Each photo was a section of an entire scroll, the three making up one completed scroll. More were to come, Ben had been told, more sections of more scrolls. And each picture was an exact reproduction of its subject, with nothing altered and no reduction in size. Were it not for the smoothness and sheen of the glossies, Dr. Messer might be gazing at the actual papyrus fragments.

He sat down again, gently depositing Poppaea on the floor, and began translating where he had left off.

> Hear, O Israel, the Lord our God, the Lord is One God. Blessed art Thou, O Lord, Our God, King of the Universe, Who remembers the covenant, is faithful to His covenant, and keeps His promise; Who does good unto the undeserving and Who has also rendered all good unto me.

He smiled at what he had translated: the Sh'ma and a traditional benediction. Both in Hebrew. "*Barukh Attah Adonai Eloheinu Melekh ha-Olam.*" This was more like what Ben was used to. Sacred texts, lists of laws, proverbs and eschatology. David ben Jonah, whoever he was, had been an extremely pious Jew (he had not even dared write the name of God, but had written instead the tetragrammaton YHWH) and had wanted to make sure there was no mistake about it. He was also, Ben noted as he rechecked his translation, a highly educated man.

When the phone rang, Ben jumped, tossed his pen high in the air and answered it breathlessly as if he had been running.

"Ben?" came Angie's voice over the wire. "Did you just get in?"

"No." He grinned. "I was sitting here at the desk."

"Benjamin Messer, I'm too hungry to have a sense of humor. Tell me something, are you coming by or not?"

"Coming by?" He looked at his watch. "Jesus! It's eight o'clock."

"I know," she said dryly.

"God, I'm sorry. I must be half an hour—"

"*An hour* late." She sighed mockingly. "Mother always said paleographers were never on time."

"Your mother said that?"

Angie laughed. She had all the patience in the world when it came to Ben, the man she was engaged to. He was so reliable in all else that when it came to his punctuality—or lack of it—she was quite forgiving.

"Working on the Codex?" she asked.

"No." He frowned now, suddenly remembering his first duty. Upon receiving Dr. Weatherby's photographs from Israel, Ben had set aside the Egyptian Codex he had been hard at work on. "Something else . . ."

"Going to tell me?"

He hesitated. In one of his letters John Weatherby had asked Ben not to talk to anyone about this project. It was still in the hush-hush stages and nowhere near the moment of public announcement. Weatherby didn't want certain colleagues to hear of it just yet.

"I'll tell you at dinner. Give me ten minutes."

When he hung up, Ben Messer shrugged; Angie certainly wasn't part of the rest of the world. It would be all right for her to know.

As he slipped the photographs back into their envelope, he paused again to gaze at the square Aramaic script. There it was, in plain black and white. The voice of a man centuries dead. A man whose knife had sharpened the end of the writing reed, whose hands had smoothed the papyrus before him, whose saliva had wet the cakes to make ink. Here were his words, the thoughts he had felt compelled to record before dying.

Ben fell to staring for a long time. As if mesmerized by the ancient script, he stood rooted before his desk, the glossy photos suspended in mid-air.

John Weatherby had been right. If more David ben Jonah scrolls were found, this could be a discovery to rock the civilized world.

"Why?" asked Angie as she poured more wine into his glass.

Ben did not answer immediately. His eyes were leading his mind into a picaresque odyssey through the flames in the fireplace. In the hot glare he saw before him again the handwriting of David ben Jonah, and he recalled how, earlier that evening, it had shocked him to discover that the scroll had been written by a private citizen and in common language. Ben had been all set to translate a religious text, maybe the Book of Daniel or Ruth, and instead had gotten the surprise of his life.

"Ben?" said Angie quietly. She had seen him like this once before, at the Shrine of the Book in Israel, where, the year before, as two tourists, they had stood before the impressive fountain exhibit of the famous Isaiah Scroll from the Dead Sea. His life's one true love—cracked paper and faded ink—seemed to turn Ben into himself, make him lose contact with reality.

"Ben?"

"Hm?" He snapped out of it. "Oh, I'm sorry. Drifting, I guess."

"You were telling me about copies of a scroll you received tonight from Israel. You said Dr. Weatherby had sent them and that they gave evidence of being a discovery of great importance. Why? Are they from the Dead Sea?"

Ben smiled and took a sip of wine. Angie's knowledge of ancient manuscripts was the layman's: at best, the Dead Sea Scrolls. Maybe Tacitus, too. But then again, Angie was a fashion model and had no need of such information. Tall, willowy and strikingly beautiful, Benjamin Messer's fiancée had only the barest idea of what he did for a living.

"No, they're not from the Dead Sea." He and Angie were sitting on the floor, remnants of a dinner still on the table, and tasting good wine before a fire. Ben turned slightly onto his side to get a better look at her and hesitated, before answering, to enjoy her lovely face.

"They were found under what appears to be the ruins of an ancient dwelling of some sort—maybe a house—in a place called Khirbet Migdal. Does that mean anything to you?"

She shook her head. Firelight turned her hair into polished bronze.

"Well, about six months ago John Weatherby spoke to me of procuring, finally, permission from the Israeli government to conduct a dig in the region of Galilee. Weatherby's main interest, as I'm sure I've told you, is the first three centuries of our era. That would include ancient Rome and its fall, the destruction of Jerusalem, the rise of Christianity, etc. Anyway, by piecing together one lead and another, John had a strong hunch about one area of excavation, which I won't go into, and presented his case to the Israelis. Then he went five months ago with an archaeological group from California, set up camp near this Khirbet Migdal and commenced to dig."

Ben stopped at this point, sipped more wine and rearranged himself a little more comfortably. "I won't go into the progress he made —needless to say, it was worthy. However, what he was originally looking for—a Second Century synagogue—never turned up. He had been wrong. But accidentally, he came across something else, something of such initial importance that he called me from Jerusalem two months ago. He had found a cache of scrolls, he said, so hermetically sealed and buried as to have kept them in excellent preservation. Normally, we're not so lucky as that."

"But that one we saw, the Isaiah Scroll—"

"The Dead Sea is a phenomenally dry area, hence the Scrolls survived the usual deterioration caused by humidity. It's the same with Egyptian tomb papyri. But around Galilee, where the air is more humid, the longevity of such perishables as wood and paper is practically nil. In archaeological terms, of course."

"Yet Dr. Weatherby found some?"

"Yes," said Ben incredulously. "Apparently so."

Now Angie, her imagination ignited, also took to staring into the fire. "Just how old are these scrolls?"

"We don't know yet, for certain. The final say is up to me and two other translators. Weatherby was able, by chemical analysis, to estimate the age of the pottery containing the scrolls, but not too accurately. Within a century or two. The papyrus and ink were also analyzed, and that, too, was inconclusive. The final narrowing down is up to me and, as I said, two other guys."

"Why did he choose you?"

"There're three of us working separately: one in Detroit and one in London. Those two other guys are also receiving copies and working the same way I am. Translators usually work in teams, but Weatherby likes us to work separately and without collaboration because he thinks we will come up with more accurate translations that way. And he chose us three because, I guess, we can keep a secret."

"Why? What's the secret?"

"Well, internal politics mostly. Sometimes it's just a good idea to keep a fantastic discovery under wraps for a while, until you have it all prepared and ready to take to the public. It could fall under attack and then you'd have to be ready to defend it. In our line of work, there are always petty jealousies." Ben didn't want to go any further. Angie wouldn't understand. No one outside the field would, really, because it was not easy to explain. No matter how perfect your reputation, how honest your methods, there was always someone to dispute you. Even the Dead Sea Scrolls had provoked controversy among scholars worldwide. Scientists were just like that.

"You still haven't told me what's so special about these particular scrolls."

"Well, for one thing, they are the first of their kind ever found by anybody, anywhere. All other ancient scrolls around the world today in all the museums and universities are all of the same nature: religious. And they were all written by priests and monks. The average citizen of ancient times just never wrote things down, the way you or I might, and because of that never before has there ever been found anything like Weatherby's scrolls. You know, a regular guy writing regular words."

"What sort of words?"

"It looks like a letter or a diary of some sort. He says he has a confession to make."

"So because these scrolls are the only ones of their kind, that's what will make them famous?"

"That and, of course"—his eyes creased in a grin—"the Curse."

"Curse?"

"It's kind of romantic in a way, finding a cache of ancient scrolls that have a curse on them. Weatherby told me about it over the phone. It seems that the old Jew who wrote the scrolls, David ben Jonah, was determined to keep his precious scrolls safe and so called upon an ancient curse. The Curse of Moses."

"The Curse of Moses!"

"It's from Deuteronomy. Chapter Twenty-eight. There's a whole string of terrible curses. Like being visited with a severe burning and being pursued by mildew forever. I guess the old Jew had really wanted to protect those scrolls. He must have figured that was enough to scare anybody off."

"Well, it didn't scare Weatherby off."

Ben laughed. "I doubt the Curse has much power left after two thousand years. But if Weatherby starts mildewing—"

"Don't talk like that." Angie rubbed her arms. "Brrr. It gives me the creeps."

They both returned to staring into the fire, and Angie, recalling the yellowed parchment they had seen in the Shrine of the Book, asked, "Why were the Dead Sea Scrolls so fantastic a discovery?"

"Because they proved the validity of the Bible. And that's no small thing."

"Then isn't that more important than what Weatherby's scrolls have to say?"

Ben shook his head. "Not from the historian's standpoint. We've got enough Bible texts to tell us what we need to know about the development of the Bible over the centuries. What we don't have is enough information on what daily life was like back in those times. Religious scrolls, like the ones from the Dead Sea, only talk about prophecies and religious creeds, but they don't tell us anything about the times in which they were written or the men who wrote them. Now Weatherby's scrolls, on the other hand— Good God!" he blurted suddenly. "A personal diary from the Second or Third Century! Think of the blanks it could fill in!"

"What if they're older? Like the First Century."

Ben shrugged. "It's possible, but too soon to tell. Weatherby opts for late Second Century. Radiocarbon can't narrow it down any more for us. In the end, it's up to my analysis of the writing style that'll tell us when David ben Jonah lived. And mine, dear Angie, is not an exact science. From what I've read so far, old David ben Jonah could have lived at any time within a three-century period."

A far-off look came over Angie's face. Something had just occurred to her. "But the First Century would be the most fantastic, wouldn't it?"

"Of course. Aside from the Dead Sea Scrolls, the Bar-Kokba letters and the Masada Scrolls, no other Aramaic writing from the time of Christ is known to exist."

"Do you suppose *he*'s mentioned?"

"Who?"

"Jesus."

"Oh. Well, I don't . . ." Ben looked away from her. To him the phrase "during the time of Christ" was only an instrument of historical measure. It was easier than saying "from 4 B.C.E. to around 70 C.E." or "post-Augustan and pre-Flavian." It was just a shorthand way of designating that particular period in history. Ben had his own theory about the man people called Christ. And it differed from the norm.

"So it's by the handwriting you'll be able to figure out when it was written?"

"I hope to. Writing styles changed through the centuries. The handwriting itself, the alphabet used and the language are my three standards of measurement. I'll be comparing Weatherby's scrolls to others that we have today, like the ones from Masada, and see how the writing style matches. Now, according to the chemical analysis of the papyrus itself, we have a hypothetical date of 40 C.E. with a margin of two hundred years—which means the papyrus was manufactured between 160 B.C.E. and 240 C.E."

"What's C.E.?"

"It stands for Common Era. It means the same as A.D. Archaeologists and theologians use it. Anyway, about the dating. Radiocarbon works well with prehistoric skulls, where such a wide margin doesn't really matter. But when you're talking about a year that took place just two thousand years ago, then a two-hundred-year margin is practically no help at all. But it's a base to start on. Then we try to place a date on the depth of the dirt they were found in, with older layers being underneath and more recent years lying on top. Like geological layers. But even after all this, we still have to turn to the writing itself for the final date. And so far, Angie, our ancient Jew is writing in a hand similar to those of the Dead Sea Scrolls, which could put him anywhere from a hundred years before Christ to two hundred years after."

"Maybe this David will say something in his writing to give you an exact date, like a name or an event or something."

Ben stared at Angie with the glass halfway to his lips. This was something that had not occurred to him. And yet, why couldn't it be possible? Surely the first fragment had already proved that these Migdal Scrolls were different from any other kind so far. It was possible. *Anything* was possible . . .

"I don't know, Angie," he said slowly. "For him to give us a date . . . that would be too much to hope for."

She shrugged. "From the way you talk, just the scrolls themselves were too much to hope for, and yet there they are."

Ben stared at her for a second time. Angie's ability to so casually accept even the most bizarre events never failed to amaze him. And yet, maybe it wasn't so much her casual acceptance of them as her casual *dismissal* of them, he considered now as he studied her detached expression. Her ability to accept everything, whether the time of day or news of a disaster, with the same objectivity. Angie was not a woman of passions. She had never exhibited anything near a paroxysm, and indeed seemed to pride herself on being a most unilinear person. Hers was the capability of instantaneous recovery. A favorite story told by her friends was Angie's reaction to the assassination of John Kennedy. The very hour it had happened, shocking all the world, her only comment had been "Well, life's a bitch."

"Yes, scrolls like these are too much to hope for. As a matter of fact, they are every archaeologist's dream. But still . . ." Ben's voice died away. There were so many ifs. Dr. Weatherby had only referred to "Scrolls" in his letters. Yet he never mentioned the number. How many were there? How many had old David ben Jonah been able to write before passing from "this world into the Next"? And moreover, what was it he had so desperately needed to get off his chest and onto paper?

Sitting with Angie in front of the fire and sipping light wine, Ben began to drift into a world of questions and imaginings—questions that had not, until now, occurred to him.

Yes, indeed, what was it that had so urgently driven the old Jew to begin to commit his life to paper? What had happened that was so important that he had done what so few men of his own time did: write his mind with ink and pen? And furthermore, to then package those Scrolls as carefully as the monks of the Dead Sea had theirs, religious texts for posterity—*his* words for his son to read?

And then that bizarre curse! The Scrolls must have something important to say if old David had gone to such lengths to protect them.

Ben shifted from this wandering, chimerical thought back to the actual "find" itself. He knew from experience that it would not be long before news of this leaked out, and once that happened the world would snap to attention. The publicity would be staggering. His name, Dr. Benjamin Messer, would become inextricably linked with the discovery, and he would find himself suddenly in a limelight he had often dreamed of. There would be books published, television interviews, nationwide tours; there would be prestige and fame and recognition and—

The fire crackled and flames exploded with hot brilliance. Somewhere nearby someone breathed softly. Ben felt his face grow increasingly warm, either from the fire without or from the fire within. As his mind grew lazier and more undisciplined, random thoughts now introduced themselves, and by chance, John Weatherby's letters came to mind.

The first had only been a quick note, telling Ben of some "remarkable discovery" Weatherby had made.

So, Ben had thought upon reading that note just ten weeks earlier, Weatherby's found that Second Century synagogue. Well, good for him. But then there had come that phone call from Jerusalem, John Weatherby sounding as if he spoke with his head in a bucket, and talking about a cache of scrolls he had found, and saying that he was going to have Ben date and translate them for him. That had been two months ago.

The next communication had come four weeks later in the form of a long letter. A chronicle of the "dig" from its inception up to the finding of the Scrolls; a detailed description of the excavation site and particularly of Level VI; a list of artifacts found alongside the jars—household utensils, coins, bits of pottery; and then a description of the jars and the Scrolls themselves.

Next had come a report of the findings of the Institute of Nuclear

Studies at the University of Chicago, the results of the radiocarbon tests and a fixing of the date of the coins as being 70 C.E.

But at the end, three pages of scientific data had only been able to point to the broad spectrum of three hundred years, and had not been able to narrow it any more than that.

Which was why the Scrolls had been sent to Ben Messer. To determine the year in which they had been written, and also what they said.

"Ben?"

"Hm?" He slowly opened his eyes.

"Falling asleep?" Angie's voice was softly persuasive.

"Just thinking . . ."

"About what?"

"Oh . . ." Ben sighed. He felt euphoric. His mind meandered. "Something just came into my head. Something that didn't occur to me earlier."

"What's that?"

"That David's father had the same name as my own father."

"How do you know that?"

"It's in his name, David ben Jonah. *Ben*, in Aramaic, means 'son of.' So his father's name was Jonah. It just so happens that my father's name was Jonah, too . . ."

The wine was making him heady. For some reason, the Scrolls suddenly seemed more important at this point than they had before.

But then, he hadn't started reading them before tonight.

"Do you think there will be more?"

"I hope so. I pray to God there are."

Angie looked at him sideways. "I didn't think you knew how to pray, Ben."

"All right, that's enough." She had often teased him as being the most devout atheist she knew. Him, Benjamin Messer, son of a rabbi.

They slowly rose together now and clung to one another in that sweet twilight of wine and fire. Angie might not be passionate spiritually, but physically she was satisfying enough for the most eager of sexual appetites—which Ben was suddenly, quickly developing.

"Forget the past," she whispered against his ear. "Come back to the present. Come back to me."

They didn't bother going into the bedroom, for the shag rug in front of the fireplace was delicious enough. And for a short while Angie made Ben forget the enigma of a two-thousand-year-old alphabet.

Later, dressing before a fireplace of glowing embers, Ben felt himself sobering fast. There was the Alexandria Codex waiting to be translated—an apocryphal letter attributed to the evangelist Mark—and of course, the third photo of Weatherby's Scroll to read. And tomorrow he had classes.

"Stay the night," she urged softly.

"Sorry, my love, but neither rain nor sleet nor foxy lady shall stay the paleographer from his appointed translations. That's Herodotus."

"That's silly."

"Really? Was he Greek or Roman? Marcus Tullius Silly."

Angie grabbed his sweater and flung it against him. "Benjamin Messer, get out!"

He laughed and stuck his tongue out at her. Angie's auburn hair fell over her face in a little-girl way while her eyes flashed seductively at him. She was fun to be with. Knew nothing about ancient history, but fun to be with. And he loved her for it.

"*Ciao*, baby, as they say on TV." And he left, skipping down the stairs two at a time.

The jaunty mood, however, soon dissipated in the chill air as he drove down Wilshire Boulevard. A rock station on the radio was playing either Cat Stevens or Neal Young, he couldn't tell which. Ben was the sort of "out of it" person who could say his favorite singer was Olivia Elton John and get away with it.

But he was not really paying attention to the music because the pressing problem of the Scrolls came back to plague him. When, indeed, were they written? Second or Third Century would not be nearly so dramatic as First Century. Nor would the *latter* First Century have as much impact as the *early* First Century.

Ben recklessly parked his car in the underground garage and bounded up the stairs to his apartment.

What if? What if they *had* been written in the early part of the

First Century? There might even be some mention, some clue, some shred of evidence either supporting or disproving the existence of a man everyone calls Jesus Christ!

David Ben Jonah, thought Ben as he fumbled with his door key, what years did you live in and what is it that's so important for you to tell me?

❊

When he got inside, Ben first made himself a cup of rich dark coffee, opened a can of sardines for Poppaea, then seated himself back at his desk. The glow from his reading lamp created a small enclave against the black night beyond its borders, making a limitless cavern of his apartment. The sphere of light was only ever invaded occasionally by Poppaea, who, in her interminable curiosity, paid brief visits to the desk top and, seeing nothing of note, always departed to nocturnal rounds of the other rooms.

Tonight, while Ben spread the photographs before him again, she hopped silently up, stalked among the books, ashtray, empty glasses, and, reeking of sardines, gave a cursory sniff at one of the pictures, then jumped to the floor.

Free from the effects of Angie's wine, Ben sat at last staring at the third segment of papyrus. Almost willfully he brought a scene back to his mind, one of himself and Dr. John Weatherby seated in the latter's Pacific Palisades home six months before, and considering all aspects of the project the older man was about to embark upon.

Weatherby, gray, robust and speaking animatedly, had many times expressed his theory about a Second Century synagogue being buried somewhere near Khirbet Migdal in Israel. In his living room on that night six months ago, John Weatherby had told Ben, "As you know, the official register of the Department of Antiquities of Israel lists over twenty-seven hundred and fifty known sites within the pre-1967 borders. In 1970 there were at least twenty-five large-scale excavations going on within the eight thousand square miles of Israel, making it easily the most archaeologically active area in the world. And I intend to get a piece of that pie. My permit is bound to come through. Then I will be off to Migdal with my spade and bucket like a kid going to the seashore."

Ben gazed long at the third photograph, at the informal cursive style so unlike that of religious texts, and thought to himself: so,

David ben Jonah, you buried your precious testament in the earth of Khirbet Migdal and John Weatherby came by and dug it up.

But, of course, you didn't know it as Migdal back then. In your day the town was called Magdala. Famous for its fish, its hippodrome, and a woman named Mary. The Magdalena.

CHAPTER TWO

⌁⌁⌁

The third fragment was not so easily read as the first two, for at places the edges of the papyrus were torn and sentences aborted in mid-word. In several spots the ink had run into the grain and the writing was thus smeared. Also, because the major part of this fragment was so far a lengthy prayer and benediction, the old Jew had switched from Aramaic to Hebrew, and also to the practice of omitting vowels. Ben worked all through the night, laboring over fine shades of meaning and trying to fill in the incomprehensible areas.

Added to this was a mild disappointment. Although he was used to translating prayers and religious tracts—indeed, it was his profession—Ben had allowed himself to hope that the Migdal Scrolls would be of a completely different nature from any previously found. And yet now, with dawn only a short time away, Benjamin Messer was beginning to believe that all the old Jew had "left" his son after all was the usual Hebrew legacy—sacred words.

A second, paler disappointment to Ben was his inability to exactly pinpoint the period of David's handwriting. Some clues were evident —the absence of ligatures connecting the letters (a trait dropped by the mid-First Century), the familiar square Aramaic script, the Hebrew letter alef so characteristically like a backwards N—these clues were there and yet not nearly enough to pinpoint conclusively a specific period.

There was more to translate yet, a few lines left, but Ben was too tired to attempt them. His ten o'clock class would be expecting to go over their test, and his two o'clock class was going to be an involved discussion period. He would have to be prepared for both.

So with a mixture of reluctance and relief he returned the photos once again to their envelope and decided to save them for the weekend, by which time he would have to have finished with the Alexandria Codex.

Benjamin Messer was a professor of Near Eastern studies at the University of California at Los Angeles and taught three classes: Ancient and Modern Hebrew, Illuminated Hebrew Manuscripts and the Languages of Archaeology. When not involved with the translation of an ancient papyrus or inscription, he taught the rudiments of his specialty to anyone interested.

Having managed well enough with the morning class, he was beginning to feel the effects of a sleepless night during the afternoon session. This was his Ancient and Modern Hebrew class, comprised of sixteen postgraduate students who sat about him in a semicircle and all of whom, on this Tuesday afternoon, could not help but notice a certain distraction in their professor.

"Dr. Messer, don't you feel that the development of the oral tradition has had more effect upon the evolution of the language than the written?" This was asked by a person in bottle-thick glasses; he was a linguistics major and a devotee of Esperanto.

Ben looked at him as if for the first time. Their discussion today was the dynamics of Hebrew evolution, which was to say, which external factors aided in language change over the centuries. Ben had not been giving honest attention. He had found himself drifting several times, thinking of the Scroll from Magdala.

"Why should this be so, Mr. Harris? Do you believe the oral tradition to have been more important to the Jews than the written one?"

"I think so. Especially during the Diaspora. It was the oral tradition that kept them going when their scrolls were unattainable."

"I disagree," said another student. This was Judy Golden, a student of comparative religion. "We're still living in a Diaspora and it is the *written* word that keeps us united over the miles."

"Actually, you're both correct. Neither of these traditions, oral or written, can be treated solely by itself." He glanced up at the clock. The class seemed to be dragging today.

"Okay, now we're discussing this afternoon the changes that have evolved in written and oral Hebrew over the centuries and the exter-

nal factors that caused those changes. Does anybody have any ideas
on this? How about the effects of the Diaspora upon written Hebrew? Miss Golden?"

She gave him a brief smile. "Before the Talmud, Jews had to rely
upon their Hebrew scrolls and upon memory. But in Hellenistic
times, when Jews got away from learning Hebrew, so many of them
could not read the Torah. That was when the Septuagint was born—
the Five Books of Moses written in Greek—so that Jews all over the
Roman Empire could then read their sacred books. But I don't think
the Septuagint *changed* Hebrew at that time; it did away with it altogether."

Benjamin Messer let his eyebrows go up for an instant. She had
made an excellent point which he had not expected to hear. As she
spoke, he quickly rooted about in his memory for a fact or two about
her. Judy Golden, transferred from Berkeley, age twenty-six, and
majoring in comparative religion. She was a quiet girl with intense
brown eyes and long black hair; the symbol of Zionism hung about
her neck on a chain.

"You're quite right," said Ben after she was finished. "The Septuagint actually gave rise to two opposing conditions. On the one
hand, it brought the sacred books to Jews who could not speak Hebrew, but on the other, it profaned the Word of God by being in a
heathen tongue. Here again is a good example of how inseparable
the Hebrew language is from the Hebrew religion. In order to study
the one, you must study the other."

Another surreptitious glance at the clock. Could he recall when a
class had dragged on so? "Moving along, then," he said as he added
another word on the board: Masorah. Then a date: Fourth Century
C.E.

"It seems the first Masorete was Dosa ben Eleazar . . ."

And all the time he lectured and discussed, he had to force his
mind upon the issue, for in his lack of sleep, thoughts of the
Magdalene Scrolls kept filtering back.

He was relieved when, one hour later, the class was over for a couple of days. The assignment for Friday was: the development of
Mishnaic Hebrew and examples of differences between it and modern Hebrew. He also made the announcement that he would not be

keeping his usual office hours over the next couple of weeks, so that special appointments would have to be made.

Ben was little refreshed by the cool evening that met him outside the building. Nearly five o'clock and with the sun about to set, the campus was quiet and almost deserted in this period between day and evening classes. The few memos that went through his mind as he jogged down the steps—send off a report to Randall on his Codex, call Angie before six, stop by cleaners on way home—were interrupted by a voice at his side.

"Dr. Messer? Excuse me?"

He stopped on the last step and looked down. Judy Golden was almost a foot shorter than he and seemed even more so in her flat sandals. She was a small girl, and shapely. Her full black hair blew about in the late-afternoon breeze. "Excuse me, are you in a hurry?"

"No, not at all." He was, but he was also curious about what she had to say. Since the beginning of the quarter he had heard few words from the quiet girl.

"I just wanted to tell you that I like your use of Common Era instead of Anno Domini."

"I beg your pardon?"

"Fourth Century C.E. You wrote it on the board."

"Oh yes, yes . . ."

"I was surprised to see it. Especially coming from you. Well, I mean, I just wanted to let you know what I thought of it. That linguistics major, Glen Harris, asked me on the way out of the classroom what it meant—"

Ben frowned. "What do you mean, especially coming from me?"

Judy reddened and stepped away from him. "That was a dumb thing to say. I'm sorry, it just slipped out—"

"Oh, that's all right." He made up a smile. "But what did you mean?"

Her flush deepened. "Well, I mean, someone told me you're German. You were born in Germany, they said."

"Oh. That. Well, I was . . . but . . ." Ben started to walk slowly again in his original direction and Judy fell into step beside him. "The use of C.E. doesn't connote a theological opinion. It's like saying 'Ms.' If I were to call you Ms. Golden, it wouldn't necessarily mean I'm a women's libber."

"Still, you don't see it much, c.e." She had to take twice as many steps to keep up with his stride.

"Yes, I suppose." Ben had never really thought about it. Among Jewish historians and scholars, the use of a.d. to designate the modern era had been dropped (for it implied an agreement with its meaning) in favor of the use of c.e.—Common Era, which was a more objective designation, but meaning really the same thing. "What does my being German have to do with anything?"

"Well, it's a Jewish invention."

For an instant, his face showed mild surprise. Then he let out a little laugh and said, "Oh, I get it. Well, I guess it's really all right, then, because I'm also Jewish."

Judy Golden stopped short. "You are?"

He looked down at her, a mixture of perplexity and amusement. "What's the matter? Oh, wait, don't tell me. I don't *look* Jewish, is that what you're thinking?"

"Oh no," said Judy in embarrassment. "It's a wonder I can still walk having both feet in my mouth. That's exactly what I was thinking. And you know, I really hate that sort of thing myself."

They resumed walking toward the nearest parking structure. "That explains it," she said.

"Explains what?"

"The c.e."

"I'm afraid not. I use it because it's an objective designation and doesn't state a personal belief. I use it out of neutrality, not out of a *disavowal* of the faith that is meant by the words Anno Domini— the Year of Our Lord. Besides which, a lot of literature I read nowadays makes use of it, and many of my colleagues have taken to using it. The Jews don't have the monopoly. Just because you say c.e. instead of a.d. doesn't mean you're a Zionist."

Her hand automatically went to her necklace.

"You know," said Ben as they neared the parking structure, "you speak Hebrew like a native. Ever been to Israel?"

"No, but I'd like to someday."

They stopped at the entrance. Behind them was an orange sky growing red, and in front a lavender sky growing purple. Ben waited politely for the girl to say more, which he hoped very much she wouldn't, and finally said, "Someone like you, with your interest in religion and Hebrew and Judaic heritage, ought to sell everything she owns and get a one-way ticket to Israel."

"I've tried a couple of times, but my plans always went awry. It's hard to hang onto money. Anyway, thanks for your time, Dr. Messer. Good night."

"Good night."

The Codex glared accusingly up at him as, glass of wine in one hand and unlit pipe in the other, Ben stared back down at it. Dr. Joseph Randall had sent it (or rather this photostatic copy) to him two weeks before for more precise translation. It had been found in a Coptic monastery in the desert near Alexandria and was now in the Egyptian Museum in Cairo. It was a Greek manuscript bearing many of the characteristics found in the Codex Vaticanus, a Fourth Century copy of the Septuagint compiled in Egypt. Randall's papyrus, titled "Epistle of Mark," contained many inaccuracies and, although irrefutably written many centuries ago, was most likely bogus.

Ben set down his pipe and finished off the wine. On the stereo was Bach's Toccata and Fugue in D Minor, playing softly and subliminally. It often helped him to concentrate.

The Third and Fourth Centuries were rife with forgeries, many of them supposed Letters and Acts of the Apostles. This one must have been held in high reverence for centuries before being left behind when the monks deserted the monastery, because the evangelist Mark was said to have started the Egyptian Christian Church nineteen hundred years ago. This is what the Copts believed.

"If there was a St. Mark at all," murmured Ben. He was having difficulty concentrating. The wine hadn't helped, and Bach was only getting irritating. Also, he had forgotten to stop by the cleaners on his way home.

The Codex was a long work and not meticulously written. Some words were nebulous, making entire sentences vague and meaningless. He referred to several texts for comparisons and found himself forcing his mind to stay on the issue. When, a short while into the evening, Poppaea Sabina jumped up to survey the desk top, Ben picked her up and began stroking her.

"You're quite right, my hirsute she-devil. A job worth doing is worth doing well. And I'm not doing it well."

He stood with her cradled in his arms, feeling the little purring motor against his chest, and went to sit in one of the two easy chairs in his living room. Ben's was a nice apartment, north of Wilshire and therefore expensive, but it was large and quiet and private. The furnishings were his own: he believed in comfort. A living room with plush rugs, objets d'art and furniture that reached up to embrace you. A den made up of leather and dark wood and shelves upon shelves of books. Kitchen and bedroom, private entrance and a balcony. Ben enjoyed his apartment and frequently found it a place for retreat.

Yet he was not so relaxed tonight. "It's that old Jew," he said to Poppaea, who was nuzzling his neck. "David ben Jonah is far more interesting than that counterfeit letter by Mark. At least we know David really lived."

Ben rested his head against the back of the chair and stared at the ceiling. At least, he thought distantly, I'd sooner believe in the existence of David ben Jonah than in a saint named Mark who supposedly wrote the Gospel. Benjamin Messer conceded that a Roman Jew named John Marcus probably did exist in Palestine in the First Century, and that he was probably involved with Zealot activities. After all, who in Judea at that time wasn't? But that he was the author of the first and shortest Gospel was highly suspect. After all, the Gospel According to St. Mark didn't even exist in any sort of complete form earlier than the Fourth Century. What then, other than faith, proved Mark's Gospel to be any more "genuine" than, say, the Epistle of Mark now sitting on Ben's desk?

Faith.

Ben removed his glasses, which felt uncommonly heavy, and put them on the small end table by his arm. What is faith anyway, and how do you measure it? That the New Testament is found no earlier than the year 300 doesn't faze the faith of how many millions of Christians. That the story of a virgin birth, of countless miracles and of bodily resurrection after death comes down to us in manuscripts centuries later than their supposed occurrence, and that its authorship is dubious to say the least, doesn't seem to interfere with the firm belief of millions. That's faith for you.

For the most fleeting moment Ben thought of his mother, Rosa

Messer, who had mercifully died years before, and just as quickly put the memory from his mind. It served no good purpose to think of her now, just as Ben had long ago stopped trying to search the few memories from his infancy for a fragment of his father, Rabbi Jonah Messer. He had died before Ben ever got to know him.

That had been at Majdanek. A place in Poland where Jews had gone.

Ben let the phone ring three times before he got up to answer it.

"How's it going?" asked Angie. She always expressed an interest in his latest project, and whether or not it was a genuine interest did not matter.

"Slowly," he said. "Well, actually, it isn't going at all."

"Have you eaten?"

"No. Not hungry."

"Want to come over?"

He paused over the phone. God, it would be nice to relax at her place. Sit in front of that fire and forget ancient manuscripts for a while. And make love.

"I'd really like to, Angie, but I promised Randall. God, it's a bitch, this one."

"The other day you called it a challenge."

Ben laughed. His fiancée had a remarkable gift for cheering a person up. "Same thing. Yeh, it's a challenge." His eyes strayed back to the desk and settled, not upon the copy of Randall's Codex, but rather upon the manila envelope which contained Weatherby's three photographs.

This was what was really nibbling at him. Not the Alexandria Codex or his promise to Joe Randall. It was the three fragments of a scroll unearthed recently at Khirbet Migdal, and the last few lines as yet untranslated.

"Angie, I'm going to take a nap, then get up and put my mind to work. I promised Randall I'd have my best translation to him in two weeks. You understand."

"Of course. And listen, if you get grumblies in your tumbly, call me and I'll bring over a casserole."

He continued to stand by the phone after he had hung up, unaware of Poppaea Sabina entwining herself between his legs. She alternately purred and meowed, stretching her sleek body against his calves as a seductive reminder of her presence. But Ben was oblivious. He was thinking of the Magdalene Scroll. In all his career he had never before come across anything like this. And if more were coming from Weatherby, and if David ben Jonah had something interesting to say, then Ben Messer would be involved in one of the greatest historical discoveries ever made.

He couldn't stand it any longer. The suspense was too much. Curiosity overwhelmed him. To heck with his duty to Joe Randall and that Alexandria Codex. David ben Jonah had more to say, and Ben wanted to know what it was.

These blessings upon you, my son, so that as you read my words you will remember that you are a Jew, a son of the Covenant and a member of God's Chosen People. As I am a Jew, as my father was a Jew, so are you a Jew. Never forget this, my son.

Now it is time for me to tell you what no father should tell his son, yet told it must be—the shame and the horror of my deed—for this is my final confession.

Ben leaned closer to the photograph and refocused his high-intensity lamp. He was near the bottom of the papyrus now, and the deciphering became increasingly difficult.

Jerusalem is gone now. We are scattered all over Judea and Galilee, many of us into the desert. I have returned to Magdala, the place of my birth, so that it will also be the place of my death. If you look for me at all, you will look here. And in looking, will hopefully find these scrolls.

Ben blinked incredulously at what he'd just read. It stunned him, left him motionless. He rubbed his eyes, bent even closer and read more carefully. *Jerusalem is gone now.* It was too fantastic! Those four words, *Jerusalem is gone now,* could mean only one thing: that the words were written in the year 70, or just after!

"Good God!" he cried aloud. "I don't believe it!" Ben stood suddenly and sent his chair over backward. Below him, at arm's length, shiny and glary under the lamp, David ben Jonah's nineteen-hundred-year-old words shouted out across the ages.

"Good God . . ." he whispered again. Then he righted his chair, sat upon its edge and placed his fingers along the borders of the photograph.

For a long time Ben sat silently over the Scroll, disciplining his mind to calm his racing heart. But to no avail. This was more than he had hoped for, more than he had *dreamed* of. David ben Jonah had just dated his own words for posterity, as surely as if he had written the year in bold red ink.

The excitement made Ben's head swim. He had to let Weatherby know at once. This was too fantastic to believe. The scholarly world would be standing up and taking notice of this one, applauding John Weatherby and praising Benjamin Messer. There would be books and lectures and interviews . . .

Ben began to calm down. While the shock was subsiding, his passion became curtailed by intellectual training. He must first make certain of what he had translated. Then he must get a cable off to Weatherby. Then he would have to go over the previous two photographs and be certain the translation was letter-perfect.

In his excitement, Ben picked up Poppaea, brought her face close to his and murmured, "I don't see how you can be so cool and calm. Unless, of course, you don't care that David ben Jonah has just told us he was writing approximately forty years after the death of Jesus. Which would only mean one thing"—his eyes went back to the Scroll—"that David had probably lived in Jerusalem the same time as Jesus."

As Ben stopped speaking and heard his last words hang in the air, another thought occurred to him, one which made him drop Poppaea and stare down at the Scroll. This new thought, so sudden, so unexpected, made him shiver slightly. Because it was not a comfortable idea.

Ben forced his eyes away from the papyrus and gazed into the darkness at the periphery of the room. No, he didn't like this new idea at all.

The sudden thought that David's curse . . . the Curse of Moses . . . might have something to do with that other Galilean. And that David had a crime to confess . . .

Benjamin trembled as the cold breath of premonition blew through the room.

CHAPTER THREE

❖

Angie cleared away the dinner dishes and tidied up the kitchen while Ben played musical chairs in the living room.

First he sat in the easy chair, his fingers strumming the arm, then he got up and squatted on the ottoman. A minute later he got up and sat at one end of the couch and soon rose to sit at the other. After a brief rest, he walked about before sitting on the piano bench, and when Angie reappeared from the kitchen, he was back in the original easy chair.

"I don't think we should go to the show tonight," she said.

"Why not?"

"Well, it's usually polite to remain seated during the movie, and . . ." She swept her arm in an arc about the room.

Ben smiled and stretched his legs before him. "Sorry. Guess I'm restless."

Angie sat upon the arm of the chair and ran her fingers through Ben's luxurious blond hair. He was probably not so handsome as he was extremely pleasant to look at—a charming face and sinewy body. He gave almost an athletic appearance, so that one would never really suspect, looking at him, that all his time was divided between the classroom and his den.

"I'll be glad when you hear from Weatherby again."

"So will I. David ben Jonah had no right to leave me hanging like that."

Angie watched Benjamin's face closely and recognized the mask of mental involvement. She thought of how excited he had been, calling her up two nights ago and babbling incoherently into the phone. He had rattled on about Jerusalem being destroyed, and for an instant she had thought the Arabs had launched a nuclear attack. But then he had said something about "time of Christ" and Angie had realized, with relief, that the excitement was over the Scrolls.

She had sat up with him all that night, as he had gone over and over that third photograph. "There was only one occasion in all of history when Jerusalem was totally destroyed. It occurred in 70 C.E. and sent Jews scattering everywhere. Obviously David had been part of that final disaster and had fled to his home town to hide. I'm positive my conclusion is correct. I'm sure I haven't missed something." Then he had picked up the photograph once more to run his eyes wildly over it. "See? See here? There's no mistake about that word. And this short sentence here—" He had muttered something in a harsh, alien tongue. "There can't be any doubt as to what it says. And it also means Weatherby was off by almost two hundred years. Angie!"

He had then gone on to explain to her the bizarre phenomenon of *total destruction* of a city and the deaths of almost all its inhabitants due to the siege of Roman armies. The Jews had been rebellious toward Rome for years. Revolutionaries had been frequently seen nailed to crosses. And when revolt finally broke out, referred to by historians as the First Revolt, it took five bloody years for Rome to put an end to it.

"You see, we believe the Dead Sea Scrolls came to be put in those caves because of imminent danger of Roman soldiers. The Essene monks who hid the jars of scrolls planned to come back for them someday. The scrolls of Masada were found among ruination caused by the legions, who burned the fortress after capturing it. And the letters of Simon bar-Kokba, the last revolutionary leader in 135 C.E., were hidden in the caves of Judea's wilderness after the final, total vanquishing of Jewish patriots. And now David ben Jonah, driven back to Magdala by Roman troops . . . Do you see how it all fits into that last, tragic picture?"

Angie had nodded and suppressed a yawn. Ben had then gone on to explain how the fall of Jerusalem had caused the end of the state of Israel for centuries. "Until 1948. It took them that long to get back what they had so desperately fought to keep nineteen hundred years ago."

Afterward, Ben had slumped into a deep sleep from which he had not stirred. Angie had called UCLA that morning to cancel his one class of the day, and that afternoon the two of them had gotten a cable off to Weatherby in Galilee. By Friday morning, Ben had been a lot calmer and a great deal more coherent, placing events in their right perspective. He conducted his two Friday classes as usual, and had even held office hours for three of his students.

He reflected on this now as he sat in the easy chair with Angie's cool arm about his neck and her fingers in his hair. The first two appointments had been students from his Illuminated Hebrew Manuscripts class, but the third student had been Judy Golden, and it was to this meeting that he now gave passing thought.

"I want to change the subject of my term paper, Dr. Messer." She had sat on the other chair in his tiny office with her arms cradling a mountain of books. Her sleek black hair hung straight over her shoulders and, framing her face, made it seem unusually pale.

It had struck Ben, as she spoke, how different she was from Angie, and then it had struck him as odd to be making the observation.

"Won't that be difficult for you? I imagine your research is done by now and the outline underway."

"That's true, they are. But I lost interest. Well"—she gazed at him steadily—"not exactly lost interest. What I did was get more interested in something else. I know how you frown on changing term papers in midstream, but I think I could do the second one more justice."

Ben reached for his pipe. "Do you mind?"

Judy shook her head. Actually she did mind, she very much hated having her face smoked in, but after all, this was his office and she was here more or less to ask a favor.

Ben made a ritual of lighting his pipe—from start to finish it took a minute or two—and he never liked to talk at the same time. When he was through, viewing her through a gray wall, he said, "I'm supposed to counsel you against such a step, but you'll obviously be happier and your records show you're a good student. So let me make a note of it." He pulled open a ratty three-by-five card file, withdrew one card, scratched something out and then held the pen above it. He raised his eyebrows expectantly.

"The new title will be 'The Hebrew of Elieser Ben-Yehuda.'"

Ben wrote it down, replaced the card and puffed more smoke out of his pipe. "It doesn't seem an easy subject, although apropos. Your first one was a good one: 'Language of the Ashkenazim.'"

"But it was too limiting, too narrow. And possibly not as relevant to the theme of the course. What Ben-Yehuda did for Hebrew is heard on Israeli radio and read in Tel Aviv newspapers today."

"It seems a terribly ambitious work. Will you have time?"

Judy grinned. "More than enough."

Ben puffed thoughtfully on his pipe. "What do you plan to write your master's thesis on?"

"Now *that* I'm sure of. I've always been interested in isolated religious sects that have escaped the outside influence of historical and major religious forces."

"Like the Samaritans?"

"Yes, like them, only I was thinking of researching an aspect of the Copts. Possibly their origins."

"Indeed? Somehow I thought you'd choose something closer to home."

"Why? What do you think I am, Dr. Messer, a professional Jew?"

Ben stared at her for a second, then threw back his head and laughed. Strangely enough, that was exactly his impression of Judy Golden—daughter of Israel, fierce Zionist.

"I'm not even an Orthodox Jew," she said in amusement. "Sorry to disappoint you. I cook meals on the Sabbath."

"You do?" He remembered the Saturday rituals and restrictions. They made him smile now. It had been a long time since he had given any thought to those dreary Sabbaths so long ago. And oddly enough, he realized belatedly as he sat before Judy Golden, his utterance of the words "I'm Jewish" to her two days before had been the first time in twenty-three years. It hadn't surprised him at the moment of saying it, but it puzzled him now in the presence of this girl.

"The Copts are an interesting group," he heard himself say, "tracing their church back to St. Mark as they do, and having resisted the tremendous pressures of Islam. Their museum in the south of Cairo is quite unique."

"I can imagine."

His pipe was dying, so he knocked it empty in the cheap glass ashtray. "By coincidence, I'm translating a recently found Codex from the Alexandria area. An old deserted monastery was found, dating around, oh, Sixteenth, Seventeenth Century at its last occupation."

"Really!"

"I'll be glad to show it to you sometime."

"Oh, that would be—"

"I'll try to remember to bring it with me. Maybe next week." He glanced at his watch. His mail delivery would have come and gone by now. He wanted to get home. There might be something from Weatherby, another Scroll perhaps . . . "It's not the original, you understand, but a good photostatic copy. The real one is being preserved under glass in Cairo. Now, if you will excuse me . . ."

There was a loud crack in the fireplace, a few sparks flew, and Ben came back to the present. Angie was no longer hovering over him, but brushing her hair in front of a mirror. He watched her as she did so, her bronze hair reflecting the fire's glow. They had agreed to get married between quarters, and the next break was still weeks away. She was going to sell her furniture and move into his apartment. The only reason they didn't live together now was the fact of his work. He needed privacy, quiet and solitude.

"Maybe you'll get something tomorrow," she said, seeing his face behind her in the mirror.

"I hope so." That afternoon, following his brief talk with Judy Golden, he had rushed home to a crushingly empty mailbox. "The next Scroll might possibly be even more earthshaking."

Ben felt his face regroup into a frown. So how was getting married going to change anything? What circumstances would be altered so that his current privacy would still be insured once Angie moved in? She had promised not to interfere with his work or come into his den while he was translating, and yet once in a while, on nights like these, he felt tiny doubts prickle his mind. Angie was insisting they go to the movies. It was for his own good, she said, to get him to relax a little and forget the Scrolls.

Ben wasn't sure he wanted to.

By Monday morning he felt normal again. A good deal of solitude and reflection over the weekened had helped him to put things in proper perspective. After all, he was a scientist, not a romanticist. Just because the first three fragments had been in such good condition and had had such explosive words to offer, was no indication that the rest of the cache in the Migdal ruins would produce anything of the same. He must be prepared for disappointment. Not build his hopes up.

All through Saturday and Sunday he had been able to work on the Alexandria Codex and had sent off a worthy progress report to Randall.

His calm exterior and scientific detachment were shattered, however, on Monday afternoon when, as he opened his mailbox, a battered envelope bearing the stamps of Israel fell out into his hands.

He was surprised to find his palms sweating as he enacted a small ritual before addressing the task. "I'm more excited than I thought," Ben said to himself. Then he laughed a little. He knew what it was all about. "No one had heard of Howard Carter before Tutankhamen's tomb! And no one's heard of Benjamin Messer yet!"

He went about and extinguished all lights except the one on his desk: his favorite atmosphere for translating. Then he placed a few records on the stereo (Bach and Chopin), set very low. Poured the necessary wine, made sure the pipe tobacco was in emergency reach and solemnly took his place at the desk.

He wiped his palms down his pants. Ben was a man known for his happy-go-lucky character and pleasant humor. He smiled a lot and laughed a lot and tried not to take things too seriously. When it came to his passion for ancient manuscripts, however, the levity always quickly died away. He respected the unknown men whose words he labored over. He honored their ideals, their dedication and the piety with which they had written their sacred words. Ben esteemed these faceless and nameless men and even held them in a little awe. For the most part he did not agree with them, with their religious beliefs and national zeal; their creeds were not his, and yet he admired them for their devoutness and steadfastness and always, before starting a new text, took a moment to remember the forgotten man who had written it.

The photos (four this time) were sealed in an inner envelope, on top of which was clipped a badly typed letter from John Weatherby. This Ben read first.

The old archaeologist spoke in clipped sentences of the news of the "find" spreading and of the excitement being generated. He spoke of four more jars being found, of the deplorable state of two of the Scrolls, and of his own hectic pace as he rushed back and forth between Jerusalem and the site. He had ended with "We were sorry to see Scroll Number Four so badly damaged. And when we all saw that, because of a crack in the jar, Scroll Number Three had been reduced to a lump of tar, we were all certain the Curse of Moses was upon us!"

Ben smiled wryly at this last. There were not a few people, newspapermen in particular, who would not seize upon old David's curse and sensationalize it. Look what they had done with Tut's curse! He shook his head. The Curse of Moses indeed!

And then what, when Weatherby receives my cable, which he probably has by now. So everyone knows the years David wrote in, and once *that* leaks out, there'll be no more peace ever again.

Ben paused to envision a headline. SCROLL FROM JESUS' DAY FOUND IN GALILEE. That would be enough to cause a worldwide stampede. Just mention First Century and Galilee and you have mass hysteria on your hands. And add to it an ancient curse . . .

Ben finally undid the clasp and gently slid out the four photographs. A number had been pinned in the upper-right-hand corner of each one to indicate sequence. They were stacked in the order they were meant to be read.

He replaced the other three and kept the first. Lying on the desk top under his high-intensity lamp, it showed to be a picture of tattered papyrus pressed flat against a neutral background. At once he recognized the handwriting of David ben Jonah. This fragment was sixteen by twenty centimeters, in relatively good condition and written in Aramaic.

> It is good for a man to know his father, and you will know me only by the facts I give you. Know then, my son, that your father was born David, son of Jonah ben Ezekiel and his good wife Ruth, of the tribe of Benjamin, in the city of Magdala. It was the 20th year of Imperator Tiberius Claudius Nero, in the consulship of Paulus Fabius Persicus and Lucius Vitellius, Id. December, and in the 38th year of Herod Antipas, Tetrarch of Galilee and of Perea.

"Good God!" whispered Ben in amazement. "David ben Jonah, will you never cease to amaze me?"

He put his pen down and massaged his temples. A slight headache was beginning to form and he knew it was from mounting tension and excitement. He stared again in disbelief at that first paragraph. Its implications were staggering.

The fact that David had been a stickler for dates was probably going to be his greatest gift to mankind. Not that he might have anything else really earth-shattering to say. It was the fact that he was creating fixed standards for an otherwise uncertain science. Other manuscripts in museums all over the world with only guess-work dates might now be compared with David's alphabet and script and be fixed more accurately in time. By his own admission, the old Jew had confirmed the official title of Herod and his years as compared with those of Tiberius. In those few lines, David ben Jonah intimated a larger Magdala than had been previously suspected. He also revealed himself to be something of a worldly man, educated and probably scholarly, although not Hellenized.

Was that possible? Ben absently cleaned his glasses on a shirttail. Could such a worldly Jew as this escape the influence of his Hellenistic environment and still maintain his Jewishness? Considering Hillel and Gamaliel, yes. Considering Saul of Tarsus, yes.

Ben froze suddenly. As his eyes roamed over the lines he had translated, making sure of his figures, he stopped at the year of Emperor Tiberius. The twentieth year. Tiberius reigned for nearly twenty-three years from 14 C.E. to 37 C.E. That would mean David ben Jonah had been born in the year 34 C.E. on the thirteenth of December.

Born in 34 C.E. and wrote the Scrolls around 70 C.E. That made him around thirty-six years old.

Ben felt his headache increase. "He's no older than I am!" he whispered. "He's the *same age!*"

Not knowing why this revelation should have such an impact on him, Ben Messer slowly withdrew from his desk and wandered into the darkness of the living room. He sank into the easy chair and threw his feet up on the ottoman. Then he closed his eyes to let the headache subside.

A young David ben Jonah instead of an old one suddenly, for some unknown reason, changed everything. From the beginning, Ben had imagined a gray-bearded old patriarch laboring with arthritic hands over his precious Scrolls. It seemed only appropriate. It was always the pious old sages that found a certain fanaticism in writing things down.

But David ben Jonah, it seemed, was actually a robust young Jew, no older than Benjamin himself, and driven by some mysterious resolve to put his life story on paper.

Then why is he going to die soon? thought Ben. He had pictured the Jew on his old-age deathbed. This was totally different. How does a man of thirty-six know he's soon going to die?

On an impulse Ben strode back to the desk and sat before the Scroll again. He squinted over each word and letter. No, there was no doubt about it. David ben Jonah was born two years after the traditional crucifixion date of Jesus.

Without a moment's hesitation, Ben proceeded to translate the rest of the first photograph.

> My father—your grandfather, whom you never knew—was a fisherman by trade. He trawled by night for shoals on Lake Galilee and hung his nets to dry by day. Ours was a blest family —five boys and four girls—and we all helped my father in his work.

This was the end of the first fragment, so Ben rechecked his translation, replaced the photograph in the envelope and withdrew the second fragment. As he was about to begin it, the phone rang.

"Damn!" he whispered, slamming his pen down.

"Ben, darling," came Angie's voice. "I've been waiting for you to call."

"I got another envelope from Weatherby this afternoon. An entire Scroll in four segments. Sorry I didn't get a chance to call. Did we have a date?"

While she spoke, his eyes remained riveted to the first word of photograph number two. It said: Mary.

"A date? Come on, Ben. Since when do you and I need a date? Listen, I'm cooking a roast—"

"I can't, Angie. Not tonight."

Silence.

"I'm sorry, love, I really am." And he was. For a brief second Ben thought of chucking the Scrolls for a while and relaxing over at Angie's. The sound of her voice always came across as a delicious lure.

"I miss you, sweetheart," she said softly.

Ben sighed and was about to capitulate when his eye caught the name Mary again at the top of the Scroll.

"Really, Angie, I can't. I promised Weatherby."

"And what about Joe Randall?"

Of course. He had forgotten the Codex.

"And what about me?" Her voice was gentle, compelling. "Don't you have a promise to me? Ben, you're at school all day and translating all night. What does that leave for us?"

"I'm sorry," he said again, feebly.

"Will it take you long?"

"I can't say. Probably not. Want me to come over afterward?"

"I'd like that. Doesn't matter the hour. Don't rush. I know how important the Scrolls are. Okay?"

"Okay. See you later."

He addressed the second photograph. The first line read: Mary and Sarah and Rachel and Ruth were my sisters.

The next two photographs went quickly, for they were just lists of names and family genealogies. Three of David's sisters were married and lived in different parts of Syria-Palestine. One died of a hemorrhage at age twelve. His four brothers, all older, were: Moses, Saul, Simon and Judas, in that order. The three eldest married and remained in Magdala. Judas, the next youngest, died during one of the many freak storms on the lake.

> We were not an impoverished family and thanked God every day for His bounty and blessing. My father was a pious man and observed the Law as the best of Jews. He went to the synagogue to talk with the learned men, and he read the Scriptures every day. Yet he was not a worldly man. He lived by a basic truth, and that was: "For the Lord knoweth the way of the righteous, but the way of the ungodly shall perish."

Ben's head jerked slightly. Those last words—which he had not so much read as *heard*—suddenly struck him with such an echo of familiarity that they caused him to fall back in his chair.

"I'll be damned," he murmured in disbelief. How long had it been? How many years since he had heard those same words, spoken over and over again until they had become the companion of his childhood? Hearing the words now, after so many years, springing from the dimmest reaches of his memory, caused Ben's eyes to moisten. And a familiar voice, one he had long forgotten, now sounded oddly distant and close by at the same time: "Benjy, always remember what your father taught you, that God knows who the righteous are, and that the ungodly will perish."

His father's favorite quote, but one which was unfamiliar to most people—the first Psalm—had been one of the most familiar features of Ben's boyhood, for his mother had had the habit of repeating it at least once a day. It had been his father's basic philosophy, and Rosa Messer had seen to it that her son would be inculcated with it.

Except that Ben had not given those words one thought in over twenty years.

Until now.

Ben Messer blinked down at the Aramaic script and felt a bittersweet nostalgia engulf him. Such a shock to come across these same words now, how strange to have this long-dead Jew speaking them to him now and triggering remembrances of times long past.

Two Jonahs, one who died two thousand years ago and one who died thirty years ago, both living by the same philosophy, the same obscure lesson from Psalms.

Ben stared for some time, briefly suffering the long-buried memories David had accidentally exhumed. He relived them for only a moment and then, wishing for them no more, forced the past back into the shadows.

Ben smiled ruefully. The shock had knocked him off balance, had made him for the moment forget the work that lay before him. For one second he had been the helpless victim of David's power, the power to bring back the past. So now he shook his head and forced himself to resume the translation.

> Once he took us all to Jerusalem for Passover, and although he cried to look upon the Temple and to hear the blast of the shofar, he was content to return to his simple life on the lakeside.
>
> My boyhood days were serene and tranquil, marred only once, when I was nine years old. It was the same boating accident on the lake which caused the death of my brother Judas. I had broken my leg, and although it mended straight, it left me with a limp which has stayed with me to this very day.

When my brothers reached their maturity, they joined our father in his trade, yet I did not. I believe that all his life my father had intended something else for me, his youngest son. I had often caught him staring at me upon different occasions with an odd expression on his face. And I suppose it was for his secret reasons that I came to be sent away from Magdala at the age of thirteen to study at the feet of the wise men in Jerusalem.

And this, my son, is where it really all began.

CHAPTER FOUR

There was a pounding in his ears, loud and annoying. He rolled his head from side to side, and found it ached terribly. The pounding continued a little more, then it stopped and was followed by a rattling, jingling sound. Ben moaned. He felt awful.

There was the sound of a door opening and closing. Soft footsteps across the carpet. At once a cloud of fragrance enveloped him and then the sweetness of a gentle voice. "Ben?"

He moaned louder.

"Ben, sweetheart. Are you all right?"

With great effort he opened his eyes and saw Angie, concerned and loving, kneeling at his side. He tried to speak, but his mouth felt like it was lined with rabbit fur. Then he wondered why he was lying on the couch and why his head was killing him so.

"I knocked and knocked and finally used my own key. Ben, what's the matter? Why are you sleeping with your clothes on?"

First he managed "Huh?" then "Oh God . . ." and finally "Time?"

"It's almost noon. I called and called, but you didn't answer your phone. Are you ill?"

He looked at her foggily one more time, then his eyes focused and he said, "Almost noon! Oh no!" Then he sat bolt upright. "My class!"

"Professor Cox called me this morning, wanting to know where you were. I told him you were terribly ill and bedridden. Now I see I wasn't far off the truth. What happened?"

"I had a test all prepared for them . . ."

"He canceled the class. It's all right."

"But I missed them last Thursday, too. I've got to pull myself together." He swung his feet over the edge and held his head in his hands. "Wow, I feel crummy. Make me some coffee?"

"Sure." The floral fragrance disappeared as Angie headed for the kitchen. "What happened to you, love?"

"I translated the entire Scroll last night, and then . . . and then . . ." Ben rubbed his eyes. And then what? What was wrong with him? Why couldn't he remember what had happened after finishing the Scroll? Why was there a blank in his mind for the hours between the Scroll and Angie's finding him on the couch? "God . . ." he murmured into his hands. "I feel awful. What on earth got into me last night!" Louder, to Angie, he said, "Must have been awfully tired, I guess."

He then went into the bathroom, where he took a cold shower, cleaned himself up and emerged in a fresh change of clothes, thinking all the while of the strange loss of memory that had accompanied that last translation. He recalled only an uncanny compulsion that had overcome him, that had *forced* him, despite his extreme fatigue, to keep on working until he dropped from exhaustion. An almost unearthly drive that he had not been able to control . . .

Angie was sitting at the dining table with the steaming coffee already poured, watching him as he walked toward her.

"Sorry to have worried you, Angie. I'm not usually a heavy sleeper."

"I know you're not. Here, drink it black. Say, Ben, why were you limping just now? Did you hurt your leg?"

He looked at her in mild astonishment. "Why, Angie, I've always limped. You knew that." He frowned for some reason. "Ever since that boating accident on the lake . . ."

She stared at him for a minute, then, shrugging it off, said, "Anyway, I have a great idea. Let's go for a drive along the coast. I don't have any assignments, and it's a beautiful day."

Automatically his face turned toward the den, where, under the beam of a high-intensity lamp, last night's work lay like a hurricane aftermath. Again, there came memories of the eerie atmosphere that had engulfed him as he had worked. The unexpected echo of his mother's voice uttering words once so familiar but for so long forgotten. Jonah's life motto: the first Psalm.

Jonah Messer / Jonah ben Ezekiel.

"I don't think so . . ."

"I waited up for you till two last night."

He did not respond, continuing to stare at the den.

Angie caressed his hands with her long, cool fingers. "You're working too hard. Come on, let's go for a drive. I thought you always liked that. It relaxes you."

"Not today. I don't want to be relaxed." Ben cast a quick glance at the clock. "Mail delivery is in two hours. I want to be here."

"We'll be back in time."

"Angie," he said as he stood, leaving the coffee untouched. "You don't understand. I can't leave my work right now."

"Why not? I thought you said you'd translated it."

"I did. But—" But what? What could he tell her? How could he explain this sudden compulsion to remain near the Scrolls, to read over and over again David's words, this growing anxiousness for the next Scroll to come. "It's just that . . ."

"Come on, Ben. Let's go."

"No, you don't understand."

"Well then, tell me about it and maybe I will."

"Come on, Angie! You haven't even asked me what the second Scroll said! Jesus Christ, a fantastic thing like this and you're not even interested!"

She gaped at him in stunned silence.

Ben was at once contrite. He thrust his hands into his pockets and frowned down at the floor. "Oh, Angie," he muttered.

In an instant she was on her feet and had her arms about him. He returned the embrace and they stood locked for some time. "It's all right," she murmured softly. "It's all right. In my own way, I do understand."

Her body, pressing against his, was getting the message across more than her words. Ben found himself kissing her mouth, her cheeks, her neck. His gestures were hurried and hard, as if he made love out of desperation. He held Angie so tight that she couldn't breathe, and his actions betrayed a man driven by blind needs.

Suddenly, ironically, the phone rang.

"Shit," whispered Ben. "Stay right there, Angie, I'll get rid of whoever it is."

She smiled dreamily and wandered to the couch, where she sank down. She kicked off her shoes and started to unbutton her dress.

It was a bad overseas connection with lots of static and echo, but the voice on the other end was unmistakably John Weatherby's.

"I can't tell you what a commotion your cable caused at the camp!" he shouted over the wire. "Your news was followed three hours later by a cable from Dave Marshall in London. We all concur, Ben. The year seventy! We broke out a bottle of wine to celebrate! I hope you did the same. Listen, Ben, I've got great news. We've found four more jars!"

"What!" He felt his knees go funny. "Four more! Oh God!"

"Do you have Scroll Four yet? I sent it by registered mail last Sunday. I told you Number Three was hopelessly deteriorated. A lump of tar. Four is bad but still readable. Ben, you still there?"

Four more jars, he thought wildly. So David ben Jonah had had time to write even more! "John, I can't stand it! It's too exciting for words!"

"You're telling me! We've got news people crawling all over the site. Some of the biggest names in Israel have come by to inspect. Ben, this could be it."

"It already is it, John!" Ben found himself shouting into the phone. He was alive, his body charged with electricity. It was a new "high" he had never experienced before. "Keep sending those Scrolls, John!"

"And, Ben, you wouldn't believe the excitement in the camp! We've had trouble with the local workers. When they heard about the Curse of Moses, they all took off into the night. We had to hire a fresh crew from Jerusalem."

"The Curse of Moses . . ." Ben started to say, his voice dying.

The line crackled and roared, sounding like ocean waves and a thousand voices talking at once. "I've got to get back to the dig, Ben. I came into Jerusalem to call you and send off another set of photographs. Good ones this time."

When he hung up, Ben found he was shivering with excitement, his heart feeling as if it might burst. His mind became a turmoil of rushing thoughts.

The Curse of Moses, said his mind over and over again. It prickled his brain, left a funny taste in his mouth. Somehow, David's curse no longer seemed quaint and amusing. Although Ben had smiled at it once, he did not this time; for some reason the Curse of Moses seemed suddenly very unfunny.

"Ben? Was that Dr. Weatherby?"

Why a curse, David, and why such a horrible one? What is it you have written in your Scrolls that is so precious and so valuable that you were driven to place the most powerful of spells upon them, that they might be kept safe?

"Ben?"

The Lord will smite you with a burning and a blindness and a madness and with mildew.

"Ben!"

He turned distant eyes to her. Angie was now fully dressed, purse in hand.

"I'll be getting another Scroll any minute now," he heard himself say. "It'll be headline news. Don't know how long Weatherby can keep the lid on, especially once word of the Curse is spread . . ."

"Well, I'm in the way and I promised I wouldn't be. So I'll just move along. Ben?"

"Maybe I'll come by tonight . . ."

"Of course." She kissed him on the cheek and left.

Ben wasted no time in tidying up the mess on his desk and getting ready for the next Scroll. He moved with erratic gestures, his body so energized he felt unable to control it.

Then he drove to UCLA, where he explained to Professor Cox about the circumstances of illness which had happened to cause the cancellation of two Illuminated Manuscripts sessions. And assured him it wouldn't happen again.

Ben lastly went to his office, did some hasty paper work and then hurried across campus to where his car was parked. He was not far from the Student Union when he ran into Judy Golden.

"Hi, Dr. Messer," she said, as if pleased to see him.

"Hi." He stopped out of politeness, but was anxious to get going. "Classes today?"

"No. I came to do some research in the library." She held up a book spine for him to read.

"*Coptic Exegesis*," he read. "Sounds stimulating."

"Not really. On cold evenings I actually prefer to curl up with a Gothic romance. But this was the closest thing the library had, so . . ." She shrugged.

"Hope it tells you what you want to know." He tried to unobtrusively inch away.

"I stopped by your Manuscripts class this morning but it had been canceled."

"Yes—"

"I thought you might have brought that Codex with you . . ." Judy paused hopefully. "But I guess you didn't."

"No. I completely forgot."

Her disappointment showed on her face.

"I'll try to remember tomorrow. I've got a lot on my mind lately—"

"Oh sure." She suddenly appeared awkward. She drew her books even closer to her chest and said with a small laugh, "I don't want to be pushy or anything."

Well, you damn well are, he thought.

"There's no pressing need for me to see it right away. It's just that, well, it excites me, the thought of seeing a Coptic manuscript that hasn't been translated yet. I mean, that's not even in any books yet anywhere. It would be like being in on a special secret. I must sound freaky."

He tried to match her smile. For an instant he was reminded a little of his own college days, and how scroll fragments had excited him so. His friends—biology majors and math majors—had all kidded him about his "egghead" interests. People didn't use that term any more. Today it was "freak."

"I'll never remember to bring it," he finally confessed to her. "Especially if I can't even remember to get myself to school in the morning."

"What?"

"Private joke. I tell you what." He took a small spiral notebook out of his pocket and jotted something down on it. "Would you object to stopping by my apartment for it sometime? I'll give you the Codex itself and my translation so far, and you can keep them for a week. Here's the address. Would you mind?"

"Would I mind!"

Ben could empathize. Would *I* mind getting another Magdalene Scroll? "I mean, about stopping by the apartment. If you do, I'll just have to try to remember to bring the Codex to school."

"No, this is fine. When's a good time?"

"I'm home most evenings."

"Well, thanks a lot then."

"You're welcome. Good night."

Ben was glad to be away from her and heading for home again. Judy Golden was an enthusiast who, at the moment, was a little difficult to put up with. Maybe it was the clashing of his own electricity against hers: two exuberant people giving off energy. To be receptive to something like that you had to be neutral. Which Ben, at the moment, was not.

The mailbox was empty.

Ben thought he would die on the spot. It was empty, and the mailman had been by.

Angie would say, "Life's a bitch," but all Ben could do was mutter "damn damn damn" all the way up the stairs. Inside his apartment he did not know what to do with himself. Records didn't help. Wine tasted flat. And food never even entered his mind. So he paced.

Ben paced for an hour.

Judy Golden knocked on his door at exactly seven o'clock, and Ben, thinking it to be Angie, flung it open.

"Hi," said the Jewish girl. She was still dressed in blue jeans and sandals, but now wore a bulky sweater over her T-shirt. "You're going to say I didn't waste any time."

"You didn't waste any time."

"Have I interrupted something?"

"No, not at all. Come in a second, and I'll get the Codex. If I can remember where I put it."

He disappeared into the den, leaving Judy to stand and stare around the apartment. The only light came from a streetlamp which shone through the curtains. She followed Ben into the den.

He was lifting first this stack of books, then that. "I put the damn thing down somewhere and I can't remember."

Judy smiled and strolled toward his desk. "I'm like that. Hop from one project to another. It's not that I have a short attention span, it's just that I have a short attention span."

As he continued to search about, Judy casually eyed the photographs spread out on the desk, and without even thinking, unconsciously read the second one. Then she quickly read the whole "page" before it really occurred to her what the photograph was. Then she stepped closer and murmured the top line: "*Barukh Attah Adonai Eloheinu Melekh ha-Olam.*" When she saw that none of the others were in Hebrew but Aramaic, a language she recognized but did not know, Judy frowned heavily. "These are interesting photographs, Dr. Messer."

"Aha!" He whipped an envelope out from under a heavy volume. "I knew it wasn't far. Now then, the Codex and my notes are inside. What? Oh, the photographs." He looked down at them. "Yes . . . they're something special . . ."

"May I ask what they are? They look fascinating."

"Fascinating is one word, yes." He gave a small laugh and handed her the Codex. "They're some ancient scrolls I'm translating."

"Oh. You know, they don't look familiar. But I could be wrong."

"Why, do you know something about ancient scrolls?"

"Only what I come across in my major. The second one I can read because it's in Hebrew. Are they all prayers like this one?"

"No . . ." he said slowly. "No, they're not. They're more like . . . well, I can't really explain what they are."

"No, I'm sure I've never seen them before."

"Well," he said, his mouth jerking in a smile, "that's because no one's seen them before. At least, not for nineteen hundred years."

She stared back at him as the meaning of his words sank in, and when they reached an impact, she whispered, "Do you mean they've just been found?"

"Well, yes."

Her eyes grew wide. "In Israel?"

"In . . . Israel."

Judy took in a deep breath, then let it out as she gasped, "Dr. Messer!"

"Yes, well, it is rather an interesting find." Ben was trying to keep himself calm. Judy was becoming excited, he could see it, he could feel it. Her eyes stretched wide and her voice was strained. Seeing her reaction only ignited Ben all the more.

"But I haven't heard anything about it!"

"It's not in the news yet. They were found just a few weeks ago, and it's still in the hush-hush stages."

Judy turned to the photographs, the Codex suddenly unimportant and forgotten in her hand. The expression on her face moved Ben, for it revealed the girl's thoughts, her emotions over what he had just said, and they remarkably matched his own.

"Say," he said on an impulse. "Would you like to read them? I mean, my translation?"

She looked up at him in disbelief. "Can I?"

"Sure. It's still something of a secret yet, if you know what I mean, but I think it's all right if you . . ." Ben wasn't certain his mouth was uttering words he really wanted to say, because even as he took Judy and his notebook of translations into the living room, he was regretting his rashness. There were colleagues of his, other professors and specialists in this field, who might be some of Judy's instructors. She could mention a word to them . . .

Her face betrayed nothing as she sat cross-legged on the couch, reading his translation. Her face was fixed over the pages; not once did her expression change. Her breathing was slow and shallow; her posture bent and relaxed, with that long black hair falling forward over her shoulders.

So, he thought as he watched her, she's not impressed.

But when Judy Golden finally looked up from the notebook, her eyes said everything her face had not.

"There aren't words to describe this," she said softly.

"Yeh." He forced a laugh. "I know what you mean." If ever Ben had been the precise, objective scientist in handling scrolls, he was not that now. There was something about Judy Golden that affected his composure. Her reaction wasn't like Angie's—Angie who could take or leave the Scrolls. No, this girl with the slanting star of Zion about her neck was acting every bit the way Ben felt.

He no longer regretted having shown them to her.

"Let me tell you about the place where they were found." Ben briefly described the excavation site at Khirbet Migdal, told about John Weatherby's quest for an ancient synagogue, and finally the accidental discovery of the "library."

"Storing precious scrolls in jars was, as you know, common practice in ancient Israel. Only, up till now, they've all been of a religious nature. Obviously David ben Jonah considered his Scrolls as important as any Scriptures."

"Well, of course! He had desperately wanted his son to read them." She gazed ahead of herself. "I wonder why."

"So do I."

"It makes me sad."

"What does?"

"The fact that David's son never found them."

Ben stared at Judy Golden. Her round face was pale in the light of the one lamp, her hair so much darker and richer. "I had never thought of that, but I suppose you're right. Two of the jars—the most intact ones—bore his mark where they had been sealed, which means they hadn't been opened. Besides, if his son *had* read them, he wouldn't have sealed them back up and buried them again, would he? I guess you're right. His son . . . the one person he was so desperate to communicate with . . . to tell his confession to . . ."

"It's sad. We aren't the people he intended these for."

Ben stood abruptly and went around the room lighting more lamps, flooding the room with brightness. It was silly to get emotional about a drama that had ended two thousand years ago. What's the use in grieving for someone who's been dead for twenty centuries? "Would you like some coffee?" But *why* didn't your son get to the Scrolls, David? What happened to him? "It's only instant."

"Instant is all I'm used to, thanks."

My God, David, did you know, in the last split second before your eyes closed in death, that your son would never read the Scrolls after all? And did you die knowing that all this was in vain?

He moved mechanically about the kitchen—running the water, plugging in this, spooning out that—and when he emerged, he found Judy once again engrossed in reading the translation.

He set the cups down on the glass-topped coffee table, along with spoons, cream and sugar.

No, he thought sadly, we're not the ones who are supposed to be reading this. It was your son, whoever he was and whatever happened to him . . .

"I guess my handwriting is pretty bad," he heard himself say.

"It's all right."

"I wish I could type. Never learned. I don't know how I'm going to send all this to John Weatherby."

"I'd be glad to type it for you, Dr. Messer. In fact, it would be an honor."

He saw the pride in her deep brown eyes, the ingenuousness and sincerity, and offered her a smile. Unlike their chance meeting that afternoon, this encounter with Judy Golden was quite relaxing. Ben was surprised to find himself speaking freely to her about the Scrolls.

"And think of the years," she said, "C.E. 34 to C.E. 70! What a chunk of history to stumble across! Imagine what he might say in the rest of the Scrolls!" She looked down at the scrawl across Ben's notepaper. "But I wonder . . ."

"What?"

"I wonder how he knew he was going to die. I mean, he doesn't seem to be in prison. I wonder if he's ill. Or do you suppose—" She lifted her eyes to him. "Could he be planning suicide?"

Ben closed his eyes. Oh, David. Was your crime so bad?

"This is interesting here. I wonder what it means."

He opened his eyes. She was pointing halfway down the page.

" 'The Master at the gates of Jerusalem' . . ."

"And here. 'You will see the face of your father—' Dr. Messer, do you suppose David was—waiting for the Messiah?"

"It's possible." Ben squinted at his own handwriting.

"Could he even have been a—"

"Don't say it."

"Why not?"

"Because it's corny."

"Why would David being a Christian be corny?"

"Because the odds are just too astronomical. You know yourself that the First Century was rife with budding new religions and weird sects. Jesus wasn't the only one around at the time who drew a fanatical following. Just because he is worshipped by millions today, doesn't mean he was then."

"But still, David was a Jew living in Jerusalem."

"In a city of hundreds of thousands there were at least a hundred popular sects at that time. I really don't think it is likely. The odds are just as favorable for finding a Rechabite, or an Essene or a Zealot. Which David more likely was."

Judy gave a little shrug. She kept on reading. "Here's a coincidence. He's a member of the tribe of Benjamin."

"So?"

Judy raised her head. "Aren't you a Benjaminite also?"

"I don't think my family ever knew what tribe it belonged to. I think the name Benjamin came from an uncle I was named for."

They sat in silence for some time longer, sipping their coffee, when Judy, looking at her wristwatch, finally said, "I should be going, Dr. Messer."

They stood and faced one another a little awkwardly, although neither of them knew why. Ben looked down at Judy with a feeling of having spent an intimate hour with her, of having shown her private things, of having shared with her something he couldn't share with anyone else. And the thought of it now suddenly made him feel uncomfortable.

As they walked to the door, she said, "Let me know if you want me to do the typing for you."

"I'll keep it in mind."

She paused as he opened the door, turning to look up at him with a faint smile. "Will you let me know when you get another Scroll from Israel?"

"Of course. The minute I receive it."

They parted on this note as Ben closed the door behind her and listened to her footsteps fade away down the hall.

Without giving the scantest thought to his next move, Ben decided in an instant to go over to Angie's and spend the night there. After all, there was nothing more to do tonight, and the apartment now seemed somehow cold and empty. Putting out some cat food for Poppaea, who had gone into seclusion when the visitor was there, Ben then went around and turned out all the lights.

At the desk he looked down and saw that Judy had forgotten the Codex.

He was just warming up his car motor in the subterranean garage when a neighbor—the bachelor musician who lived next door—appeared suddenly before him. He waved his arms, then came around to the driver's window.

"Hey, man," he said, leaning on Ben's car. "How's it going?"

"Okay. Haven't seen you around lately."

"Haven't been around. Just got back this morning. Listen, I was just on my way out when I saw you here, so I thought I'd grab you while I can." He fished into his jacket pocket and withdrew a small piece of yellow paper. "Found this in my mailbox tonight. Mailman put it in there by mistake. It's for you."

"Oh." Ben took the paper and looked at it.

"Thought it might be important," said the neighbor. "Mailman must have come by with a registered letter for you this afternoon and you weren't home. Says on the slip you can pick it up at the post office tomorrow between nine and five."

"Yeh. Say, thanks a lot."

"Sure." The musician straightened up from the car, gave a casual wave and strolled away.

Ben stared at the return address indicated on the yellow slip.

Jerusalem.

CHAPTER FIVE

··>··—◆>◎<◆—··<··

The first class went fairly well, having consisted of an exercise in cryptography. Ben always enjoyed the challenges of hieroglyphics and cuneiform, and thought of the Languages of Archaeology class as his favorite. The two o'clock session, however, did not proceed as well. Having had other responsibilities on campus to attend to between the two classes, and being nervous about being late or slighting his duties as a professor, because of his recent absences, Ben had not been able to pick up his registered package at the post office. Since Ancient and Modern Hebrew was a two-hour class that frequently ran over, Ben was particularly apprehensive about getting out on time.

Today's subject was "Language of the Ashkenazim," and as luck would have it, every class member seemed singularly interested in it and desirous of drawing out the discussion.

Added to Ben's disquiet was the presence of Judy Golden, who, although she barely looked at him and hardly spoke, was unsettling to him. And he didn't know why.

She was bent over a piece of paper and scribbling notes while her long hair fell forward and obliterated her face. Ever since their conversation last night, their brief sharing of David ben Jonah, she had been on his mind. He couldn't shake it, couldn't explain it.

"Dr. Messer, do you think maybe the revival of Hebrew has played a part in the decline of Yiddish?"

He looked at the student who had asked the question. Before Ben could reply, another student said, "You're going on the presumption that Yiddish is declining. I don't happen to think it is."

Their words faded as Ben fell into his thoughts once again. Yes, the presence of Judy Golden affected him for some reason. She had read David's words, she knew about the Magdalene Scrolls. She knew as much about David as Ben did, and possibly there lay the problem: Judy was no longer an outsider. She was a physical reminder, perhaps even the personification of Ben's experience with the Scrolls. He looked at her now and the memories came rushing back: the horrible crime David had committed, the painful need to confess, his father's lifelong philosophy embodied in the first Psalm, the Curse of Moses and the unbearable but inescapable fact that David's son had never found the Scrolls.

After Judy had left last night, Ben had gone to Angie's. They had devoured an exotic meal, watched a movie on cable TV, made love twice and slept through the alarm this morning. And all night long Ben had been able to drive the Scrolls from his mind, had filled himself with Angie until there was no room left for David. And he had slept dreamlessly.

But now, knowing that another letter from Weatherby awaited him at the post office, and seeing Judy Golden bent over her work, Ben could not keep visions of Magdala from creeping back.

He looked up at the clock. It was four, and the class gave every indication of going on for quite a while longer. He patiently granted them fifteen minutes—answering questions, writing comparisons of Hebrew and Yiddish on the board and trying to draw it all to a close.

"I think we've beaten the subject to death," he said at last, ignoring two raised hands. It was four-fifteen. It would take at least twenty minutes to get off campus and to the post office—half an hour if traffic was unusually bad. The margin was too close for comfort. "If you think of any more questions we can pick them up on Friday."

He watched Judy Golden as she continued to write, seemingly lost in her work. He wondered briefly what she was so involved in, if she had had any difficulty putting David ben Jonah out of her mind, then he quickly dismissed it. Last night he had promised to keep her apprised of the Scroll situation and let her know when new ones arrived. He decided now that he would not.

Ben gathered up his pipe and briefcase and made a hasty exit. He did not get far before he was stopped in the hallway by Stan Freeman, a professor of Eastern philosophies and a long-time friend. Their fields were related, they were the same age, and had other interests in common. The few times Ben had gone fishing in the mountains, he had gone with Stan.

"Hi, guy!" said his friend enthusiastically. "Long time no see! What've you been up to?"

"The usual no good, Stan."

"Haven't seen you around much. Angie keeping you busy?"

"Well, yes. I also have an Egyptian Codex to translate."

"No kidding. I'd like to see it." Stan paused, waiting for Ben to say something, but when he didn't, added with a short laugh, "I see you're finally going bohemian on us!"

"What?"

Stan pointed down. "The sandals. You know, in all the years you and I have been friends, I've never seen you wear sandals. You always said they made a person look like a phony liberal. In fact, as I recall, you really hated them. Those are nice. Where'd you get them?"

Ben looked down. The sandals, which he had purchased that morning, were of rough leather and rope: primitive and unrefined. "I got them in Westwood. I felt like a change." In fleeting irritation, Ben thought: What's the big deal about my wearing sandals all of a sudden?

Judy Golden swept by at that moment, her shoulders curled over a burden of books, and disappeared around a corner.

"Listen, Stan. I'm in a big hurry." Ben inched away from him

"Oh, sure. Say, when's the big day?"

"Big day?"

"The wedding! You and Angie. Remember?"

"Oh. Quarter break. I'll let you know. If you play your cards right, you can be my best man." Ben had decided in the last second to catch Judy Golden and give her the Codex, which he had remembered to bring with him. He wanted to give it to her now, here on campus, and thus remove any excuse she could possibly have for dropping by the apartment later on. "I've really got to go, Stan. I'll call you. Okay?"

"Sure. See ya."

He had to search through the late-afternoon crowd as he stepped out of the building and into the sunset. Then he saw her, moving at a fast pace in the direction of the library. He looked at his watch. Four twenty-five. There was time.

"Miss Golden!" he called, hurrying to catch up with her.

She seemed not to hear. Judy walked remarkably fast for one so short, her black hair flying out behind.

"Miss Golden!"

Finally she looked over her shoulder. Then she stopped and turned to him.

"I forgot to give you this in class today," he said as he fumbled with the clasps of his briefcase. "You left it behind last night."

Her eyes were on his face.

"Here." He pulled out the manila envelope and handed it to her.

As she took it, Judy's eyes continued to watch his face. "Oh. The Codex. Thank you."

Ben gave her a halfhearted smile. I won't tell her, he said to himself. We'll just let last night go and not bring up the subject of the Scrolls ever again.

"I'd like it back in a week or so, if you don't mind. The last few lines are a bugger to translate and I commited myself to a specific deadline."

"Oh, sure." She seemed hesitant. "Dr. Messer, may I say something?"

He stuck his cold pipe into his mouth. "Go ahead."

"I don't happen to agree that Yiddish is dying out. I think that maybe its sphere of usage is shifting and that its value in Jewish life has changed, but I don't think it's dying out."

Ben stared down at the girl and felt himself smile. "You're entitled to your opinion, of course. Possibly only a worldwide survey could give us the answer, and until then all we can do is speculate. Your guess is as good as mine."

She nodded. "I grew up with Yiddish. It was the only language my mother ever knew. And when I was a kid, that's all we spoke at home. Maybe it has some sentimental value to me. Anyway, thanks for bringing the Codex. I appreciate it."

"Sure." Ben watched her as she gave a little wave and turned around. Then, on an impulse, he said suddenly, "Oh, by the way—"

"Yes?"

"I think I've received another Scroll from Magdala."

The wine was warm and bitter and annoying as it sat in the glass in his hand. Bach's Toccata and Fugue in D Minor came out as a cacophony. The smoke from the pipe clogged the air in noxious fumes. So Ben impatiently got up, snapped off the stereo, emptied his pipe into the ashtray and dumped the wine down the kitchen sink. Then he returned to his desk and sat down once again.

The aftertaste of a pastrami sandwich filled his mouth as a reminder that he had not so much *eaten* his dinner as shoveled it down his throat like a distasteful duty to be gotten out of the way. Which is what it had been. Ben had been hungry, yet he had not wanted to bother eating. And now, with a lump in his stomach and a bad taste in his mouth, he was sorry he had been so hasty.

Once again, the familiar bad typing of Dr. John Weatherby glared up at him in the high-intensity light.

A short note about Scroll Number Four, which had been found in bad condition and which had had to be photographed under infrared in order to see the writing, and also mention of Scroll Number Three, which had been reduced to a lump of tar due to a crack in the jar. That was all.

Ben shook his head sadly over the two photographs which confronted him. They were going to be a challenge. The edges looked as if wild dogs had ravaged them. The centers looked like Swiss cheese. Whole paragraphs were gone entirely. Many words were indiscernible.

Ben felt personally cheated, as if this had been done to him on purpose. First Scroll Three lost forever, and now this.

He slammed his fist on the desk.

Somewhere in the shadows lurked Poppaea Sabina, having slept all day and now starting her nocturnal rounds. She knew when to leave her master alone and so kept a discreet distance from him. The noise of the fist on the desk sent her into the bedroom for a lonely vigil into the night.

"David ben Jonah," said Ben over the photographs. "If you want me to read your words, if you have chosen me to read the confession that your son was not able to read, then don't make it quite so difficult for me."

He got up and went into the kitchen for a fresh glass of wine, came back to the desk, relit his pipe and began the arduous labor of translating Scroll Four.

> And so it was that I, David ben Jonah, in my fourteenth year, completed my studies with Rabbi Joseph ben Simon. Those three years were good ones, and I shall always look back upon them in loving remembrance of days of youth and innocence. Saul remained my dearest friend, and so it was that he and I together sought the counsel of Rabbi Eleazar ben Azariah, then one of the most famous and illustrious teachers in all of Israel.

This part had gone surprisingly well. But then again, upon further examination, it was obviously the clearest section in either photograph. The rest was not going to be as easy.

In the margins of his translation, Ben made some notations. "Scroll Three obviously description of early schooling and first years in Jerusalem. David in tutelage of Rabbi Joseph, probably with a number of other boys. Can only guess at subject of education—probably Torah, recitations, mnemonics, prayers, etc. Doubt he had any analysis of the Law. Probable education of average middle-class youth. Fourteen the age of apprenticeship and maturity. Friend Saul probably mentioned in Scroll Three and circumstances of their meeting."

Ben put down his pen and rubbed his eyes. The lost third Scroll was very annoying indeed. And the blank spaces coming up in this one were also exasperating. He felt impatient and irritable.

Impulsively he stood and walked to a window, looking out. Something was disturbing him. Generally a man to sit down at his work and commence at once with it, tonight he was just the opposite. He could not read David's words without becoming restless, almost agitated.

In the next moment Judy Golden came to his mind. Why had he so rashly blurted the news of the fourth Scroll to her, especially after having sworn to himself he would allow her no more confidences? Certainly she had not dragged it out of him, pressed him for it. Indeed, he had been the one to run after her, detain her for a minute. So why had he after all, as she was walking away from him, suddenly told her about the Scroll?

Ben paced the floor for a while, limping slightly. Other things were disturbing him, too. He was becoming unreasonably impatient for future Scrolls to arrive. He loathed the time it took for them to get there. And he envied John Weatherby to be right there on the scene, finding the jars just as David ben Jonah had left them.

Ben's mental deliberations were interrupted by the ringing of the telephone, which he at first chose to ignore, but then decided to answer after all.

"Hi, love," came Angie's soft voice. "Am I interrupting anything?"

"I was just in the middle of a new translation."

"Oh?"

"I got the fourth Scroll from Weatherby today. It's a hard one."

Angie gave a little laugh. "I don't know if I should be happy for you or feel sorry for you."

"Why?"

"Happy that you have a new Scroll but sorry it's a hard one." She paused. "Ben?"

"Yes?"

"You sound so distant. You all right?"

"I'm fine. Just thinking."

"Want to come over?"

"Not tonight. I'm in the middle of it and want to finish it."

"Of course," she murmured. "I understand. Still, if you get hungry or lonely . . . I'm here."

"Thanks." He was about to say goodbye when he changed his mind and said instead, "Angie?"

"Yes, love."

"Don't you want to know what the fourth Scroll is about?"

There was silence at the other end.

"Well, anyway," he went on, "it's rather boring really, just about David ben Jonah's schooling in Jerusalem. G'night, Angie."

With an index finger he pressed down the receiver button, then, listening to be sure their connection was broken, Benjamin Messer did something he had never before done in his whole life: he left the phone off the hook.

. . . Doctors of Law. We knew it would take years of hard labor, many sacrifices, and that only a few ever succeed. Saul and I chose Rabbi Eleazar . . . the greatest teacher in Judea

. . . [*ink smeared*] . . . his fame. We strived for the very highest. We knew that were we to survive his tutelage, we would be men of esteem. And yet, so many youths approached him while so few were chosen. Saul and I were determined. It would bring the greatest honor to my family were I to strive for and succeed in becoming a pupil of the great Eleazar.

I was fearful of failing. I knew many youths who had approached Eleazar and had been turned down. Yet Saul was confident. Saul . . . proud and happy boy, with laughing eyes and . . . mouth. He assured me daily that we had been the best pupils of Rabbi Joseph. And I was heartened. Yet when I heard of the numbers approaching Eleazar for instruction, I became saddened again. For this reason . . . [*large gap in papyrus*] . . . with Saul. For the Feast of Unleavened Bread we . . . [*handwriting illegible*] . . . and I lay fearful into the nights.

But Saul seemed not to fear. He also had many friends, for his was the ability to tell funny stories and make people laugh. I admired Saul for his quick wit and carefree manner, and often wished I could be as social and outspoken as he and earn friends quickly. We often went together . . . [*papyrus torn*] . . . and prayed in the Temple together. Saul and I were closer than my brothers and I had been, and were quick to one another's aid. In Jerusalem he was all the family I had, he was my only friend, and I loved him deeply. Had the occasion ever arisen, I would gladly have laid down my life for Saul.

At the end of the first photograph, Benjamin took off his glasses, gently placed them on the desk top and massaged his eyes. Then he stared unconsciously at the thick Aramaic script as it looked under infrared, and felt himself go back over the years to a school in New York City which he had attended and where he had been fast friends with a boy named Solomon Liebowitz.

The yeshiva had been in Brooklyn and Ben had been fourteen years old, carrying books in Hebrew and Yiddish as he trudged through the slushy snow. He and Solomon always walked the long way around to the yeshiva, for the direct route went through a Catholic neighborhood where certain bullies were always out to taunt them. Once, the no-necked teen-agers of Polish immigrants had grabbed Ben's yarmulke, thrown it to the ground and stomped on it, and then had laughed at his tears.

But they had not been the tears of sorrow or of anger, but of frustration. The goyim had had no way of knowing how badly Ben had wanted to go out of the house without his skullcap and how much he had longed to go to the public school, where he could be like other children.

And once Solomon, so much taller and bulkier than Ben, had lashed out at the goyim bullies in defense of Ben and had caused several noses to be bloodied. Running away, the sons of the Polish immigrants had shouted over their shoulders, "We'll teach you! You killers of Jesus! We'll teach you!"

And so Ben and Solomon had from then on taken the long route to the yeshiva.

There was a lump in Ben's throat. He pushed away from the desk and stared at his hands. He had not thought of Solomon Liebowitz in many years—not since Ben had left New York for California and Solomon had made the decision to enter the rabbinate. In the seven years that they had been neighbors and best friends, Ben had loved Solomon as if he were his own brother, and had spent most of his teen-age years with him. But then the time of separation had come —the time to make men's decisions and go the way of men. Their childhoods were at an end, Solomon Liebowitz and Benjamin Messer could no longer continue their adventures among the streets of Brooklyn like two soldiers of fortune. The time had come to face reality.

Ben had chosen science, and Solomon, God.

There was a timid, almost apologetic tapping at the door. At first Ben did not hear it, and then, hearing it, turned in its direction. Poppaea Sabina was nowhere about and so not up to her occasional trick of scratching at the door. When the tapping became a little louder, Ben realized someone was knocking.

He glanced at the phone—off the hook—then whispered, "Damn," thinking the intruder to be Angie.

Capitulating, he opened the door and was surprised to find Judy Golden standing on the other side. Her hair, so familiarly straight and blue-black shiny, partially obliterated a Kurt Vonnegut T-shirt. A shoulder bag hung over her shoulder. There was a manila envelope in her hands.

"Hello, Dr. Messer," she said, smiling. "I hope I'm not disturbing you."

"Well, to be honest, you are. What can I do for you?"

Without a word she held out the envelope.

"So soon?" he said with raised eyebrows. "You can't have had it more than two hours."

"Four hours, Dr. Messer. It's past eight o'clock."

"Is it?"

"And I . . ." She seemed oddly reticent. "I debated about coming here, or waiting until Friday's class. But I'm so anxious to read the Codex, and you had mentioned a deadline on it. So I gave in."

"I don't understand."

She held the envelope farther out. "It's empty."

"What!" Ben tore it open and couldn't believe his eyes. "Oh, for God's sake! Come in. Come in!"

Judy smiled and relaxed by visible degrees. "I really don't want to disturb you, but I—"

"I know," he cut her off. With Judy trailing behind, Ben strode into the den and surveyed the mounting mess. Texts of ancient Aramaic scrolls, Hebrew apocrypha and volumes relating to Semitic writings were spread about and mingling with pastrami crumbs, a withered pickle rind, a stale pipe and three half-empty glasses of wine. Typical bachelor's nest, he thought as he tried to remember where he had last seen the Codex. This girl must think I'm a real slob.

"Be with you in a minute," he mumbled as he started lifting up books. Some were opened to photos of yellowed papyrus fragments, others to tables and charts of alphabetical comparisons and still others to lengthy texts. All aids in helping Ben to extract the very finest translations from the David ben Jonah Scrolls.

While he rummaged, Judy stared at the two photographs spread out on the desk next to Ben's notebook. This must be the new Scroll, she thought in excitement, and tried to move closer without being obvious.

But Ben turned around all of a sudden, throwing up his hands in exasperation and saying, "It'll take me all night to look through this mess—" He stopped when he saw her looking at the photos.

"That's all right," she said quickly. "I can wait. I'm sorry I disturbed you."

The room was entirely dark except for the high-intensity lamp and its small sphere of illumination. This was the way Ben worked best; it helped him to concentrate. Yet in the dim shadows now, as he watched Judy Golden's face, he wished it were a little lighter so he could read her expression.

Suddenly understanding, he said, "You really could have waited till Friday. Or you could have met me at my ten o'clock class tomorrow. Or left a message at my office."

"Yes," she said in a small voice. "I know."

Ben looked down at the photographs of Scroll Four. "This one isn't as well preserved as the first two," he said matter-of-factly. "Weatherby said it appears that the roof of the ancient house must have fallen in at one point centuries ago, damaging some of the Scrolls. As you know, once the outside air gets to it, papyrus literally turns into a sticky, tarry substance that's worth nothing. In fact, Scroll Three was lost altogether like that."

Judy hesitated, seemed to weigh her words. "Dr. Messer?"

"Yes?"

"What does it say?"

He looked again at the girl's face; the pale skin and the wide dark eyes and the long black hair. She was not beautiful like Angie, but there was something to her face that was lacking in Angie's, a quality that Ben liked. But he didn't know what it was.

"What does it say?" he repeated. Then he thought of Solomon Liebowitz and their days together as Jews back in Brooklyn. How long ago, how dream-like that seemed now. As if it had never really happened.

"Come here." Ben picked up his notebook and handed it to Judy. She took it and read it under the small lamp. She read the translation, the notes in the margin, the spaces in between. She read it and reread it. Then she put the notebook down and looked up at Ben. "Thank you," she murmured.

"I'm sorry it isn't neater."

"It's fine. Just fine."

"My handwriting—" Ben shook his head.

Judy looked down at the photograph and concentrated her gaze upon it. "David ben Jonah was a real human being," she said. "He might have lived only yesterday, for all the passage of time means. We might almost have known him."

Ben gave a little laugh. "I'm beginning to feel I know him already."

"I hope there are more Scrolls to come."

"There are. Four more, to be exact."

Judy snapped her head up. "Four more! Dr. Messer!"

"Yeh, I know—" He turned sharply and walked out of the den, turning on lights as he went. "Care for some wine?" he called over his shoulder.

"Only if it's cheap wine," she replied, following him into the living room.

"Oh, you can be sure of that. Have a seat. I'll be right with you."

Ben busied himself in the kitchen, a room which was of late growing messy and cluttered. Usually a neat man and one to clean up after himself, Ben had these last few days let the kitchen fall into disarray. It almost looked like the den. Finding two clean glasses, he poured the wine and came back into the living room. He found Judy Golden on the couch stroking Poppaea Sabina.

"I didn't know you had a cat," she said, taking the wine. "Thanks."

"I usually don't when I have a visitor. Poppaea hates people and so never comes out to make friends. Even my fiancée never sees her. But then, Angie's allergic to cats."

"That's too bad. This one's a doll."

Ben stared in amazement as his otherwise temperamental and stuck-up cat curled herself into Judy's lap and closed her eyes in contentment.

"Did you know your phone's off the hook?"

"Yeh, I did that on purpose. I didn't want to be disturbed."

"Oh, great. Now if there was only a way you could take your door off the hook . . ."

He laughed softly. "Don't worry. Anyway, I've never done it before. I really don't believe in it. Someone might try to get hold of me in an emergency."

"I agree. Thanks for the wine."

"Is it cheap enough for you?"

"If it cost you more than eighty-nine cents, then it's too expensive for me."

Ben laughed again. He felt strangely relaxed with her now. The mood of this afternoon's class—the way she had unsettled him—was now forgotten.

"Why did you name her Poppaea?" she asked, stroking the cat.

Ben shrugged. He had never really thought about it. The name had just come naturally when he had gotten her as a kitten two years before.

"Is that Poppaea Sabina?" Judy went on.

"As a matter of fact, yes."

"Wife of Emperor Nero. Lived around 65 c.e., I think. Interesting name for a cat."

"She's a seductive, willful, arrogant and spoiled little bitch."

"And you love her."

"And I love her."

They both sipped their wine for a while, listening to the darkness beyond the periphery of light. Judy let her gaze trail around the apartment, admiring its furnishings, recognizing the quality of them. She thought she read the mark of Benjamin Messer in them, an extension of his easygoing, liberal, Southern California personality. Then a thought entered her mind, a sudden burning curiosity that she debated for a moment about breaching.

She looked at the man at her side, at his pleasant and attractive face, at his uncombed blond hair, at his body that reminded her of a swimmer's. Then she surprised herself a little by asking in a subdued voice, "Are you a practicing Jew?"

Her frankness caught him off guard. "I beg your pardon?"

"I'm sorry. It's none of my business, but I'm always curious about people's religious beliefs. That was impolite of me."

Ben looked away from her, feeling his defenses going up. "It's no secret. No, I don't practice Judaism any more. I haven't for many years."

"Why?"

He stared back at her, wondering again what strange impulse had caused him to tell her about the fourth Scroll. And why he had offered her wine, and why he was willing to sit with her now instead of showing her the door.

"Judaism isn't the answer for me, that's all."

Their eyes held for an instant—locked in a gaze that, for that moment, seemed to have been created for the purpose of bridging a space. Then Ben looked away and slowly turned the wineglass in his hands. He was beginning to feel extremely uncomfortable.

"Well." Judy lifted the cat out of her lap and stood. "You must be anxious to get into the next photograph."

Ben also stood, towering above her. "I'll try to remember the Codex—"

"That's all right." She flung her hair off her shoulders, causing it to fall down her back and past her waist. Then she picked up her shoulder bag.

They walked to the door together, where Ben paused before opening it. He said, "I'll let you know what David has to say."

She gave him a brief, quizzical look, then said, "Thank you for the wine."

"Good night."

Sitting at his desk, he reread the first photograph. Then he went right on to translate the second one.

It was not easy for us to have audience with Rabbi Eleazar. Many days Saul and I sat in the courtyard of the Temple only to . . . [*tear in papyrus*] . . . We sat with other youths, beneath the sun, our legs crossed and our buttocks aching. We were many times hungry and exhausted, but dared not move. One by one our waiting group diminished . . . [*edge broken off here*] . . . Saul and I. After a week of waiting to meet with Rabbi Eleazar, we were summoned into his circle on the porch.

My throat was dry and my legs weak, yet I showed no fear before the great man. I humbled myself at his feet . . . [*illegible sentence*] . . . while Saul remained proudly standing. The eyes of Eleazar were like those of an eagle. They pierced me through as if to see what was on the other side of my body. I was afraid and yet I clung fast to my determination. It was not within my power to smile, and yet Saul did.

Rabbi Eleazar said to Saul: Why would you become a scribe? And Saul replied: "And all the people gathered themselves together as one man into the street that was before the water gate; and they spake unto Ezra the scribe to bring the book of the Law of Moses, which the Lord had commanded to Israel. And

Ezra the priest brought the Law before the congregation both of men and women, and all that could hear with understanding, upon the first day of the seventh month." Saul said: Rabbi Eleazar, I would become as Ezra and Nehemiah before me.

Then Rabbi Eleazar turned to me and said: Why would you become a scribe? And I could not at first reply, for so perfect had been Saul's answer that I felt inferior beside him. Then I swallowed the hurtful lump in my throat and said: I would like to know, Master, wherefrom came Cain's wife if not created by the Lord.

Rabbi Eleazar gave me a look of surprise and turned to his disciples. He said to them: What manner of neophyte is this that answers a question with a question? And they all laughed.

Feeling angry and humiliated, I said to Eleazar: If I had no questions, Master, then a poor scribe I would make. And if I already had all the answers, then what need would I have of you?

A second time Eleazar was surprised. So he said to me: Which do you hold more sacred, the Law or the Temple of God?

And I replied: The study of the Torah is a greater deed than even the building of the Temple.

Rabbi Eleazar dismissed Saul and me from his presence on the porch and I fought back the tears of bitterness and frustration. I said to Saul: He gave me not half a chance to prove myself as worthy of his teaching. Now I must go to a lesser rabbi and learn only half.

I cried that night alone in my room; the first tears I had shed since leaving Magdala three years before. I had striven for the highest summit and I had failed.

[*The papyrus was torn right across from margin to margin at this point, obliterating about four lines. The last line read:*] The next day Saul and I received word that we were to commence our studies with Rabbi Eleazar.

CHAPTER SIX

⊷⊶⊷◈⊶⊷

Ben felt tremendously exhilarated. He rose early, showered and shaved, ate a large breakfast and used the time before class to tidy up the apartment. There were at least fifteen glasses to gather up and put in the dishwasher. All the ashtrays were overflowing. Poppaea's litter box needed changing. He opened the windows to let the breeze clear out the stale air. And last of all, Ben straightened up the den, replacing books on shelves, emptying the stuffed wastebasket, clearing off crumbs and ashes and ring stains from the desk top. As he worked, he hummed.

Ben had not felt so great in a long time. It was as though he had just inherited a lot of money or just been told he was going to live a hundred years. The electricity which charged his body sent him singing around the apartment and leaving order and cleanliness in his wake.

When Angie knocked at the door at nine o'clock he greeted her with an embrace, a ravaging kiss and a stream of apologies for the night before.

"It was a bitch," he said, drawing her inside. "The fourth Scroll was a real bitch, but I managed to translate it last night and earn myself eight hours of sleep. I haven't felt this good in weeks!"

Angie beamed. "I'm glad. You know, your line was busy for a long time."

"And so, my love, I have a surprise for you. On Saturday morning, dawnish, you and I are going to get into my car and drive down to San Diego for two fun-filled, rollicking days."

"Oh, Ben, that sounds great."

"We'll go to the Zoo, we'll go to Sea World, we'll eat at Boom Trenchard's Flare Path, and we'll make love all night long." He kissed her long and hard on the mouth. "Or . . . maybe we won't get to those other things and just make love for two days."

She giggled into his neck. "Silly!"

Ben held her out at arm's length, drinking in her beauty, the sweetness of her perfume, the excitement of her nearness. He felt so much in love at that moment he thought he might explode. "So what brought you by this morning?"

"Your line was busy."

"What? Oh!" He snapped his fingers. "I took the phone off the hook last night so I wouldn't be disturbed."

"By who? Me?"

"Hey . . ."

"Oh, it's all right."

"Hey, I have an idea! Ride with me to school, wait an hour, and I'll buy you the most fantastic lunch your pretty head can imagine."

"Sounds great."

They went to school together and Angie strolled the campus while Ben lectured his Illuminated Hebrew Manuscripts class, giving them also profuse apologies for having missed the last two sessions. And as he did so, Angie walked the paths of UCLA's rambling grounds, feeling happier than she had in a long time. It was good to see Ben this way, after that period of preoccupation with those Scrolls. He was himself again.

At least, that was what Angie preferred to think, for although she had noticed his new sandals and the slight limp in his walk, and although his speech had sounded odd to her this morning—sort of stilted and awkward—she had chosen to bury them all and put them out of her mind. Ben was just tired, that was all.

After class, they drove up the coast to a favorite restaurant that was built into the sea cliff and actually hung out over the waves.

They made love in the afternoon, went for a drive in the mountains at sunset and had dinner and a movie in Hollywood.

In all that time, Ben felt closer to Angie than he ever had before. She had the gift of laughter and humor that made him forget everything else existed. She was beautiful to look upon and exciting to hold. The entire day was perfect. From the moment of his rising in that strangely uplifted mood, to his passionate good-night kiss with Angie at midnight. It had been a fairy-tale day. One to remember for a long time.

"We'll get a place on Hotel Circle," he promised Angie before leaving her. "And we can go down to Tijuana if you like."

She had come alive under his attention. If Angie were beautiful all other times, she actually glowed now. She felt radiant and happy, and knew she had found the perfect man to spend the rest of her life with.

At midnight, a little drunk and very tired, they both laughed softly in her doorway. "Let's do this again," Ben whispered.

"Every day, my love, every day."

And he left her feeling as if he had sojourned a while in paradise.

The mood remained with him during the drive home and continued to charge Ben with excitement as he entered the apartment. For the entire day, from sunrise until now, it had not once occurred to him to inquire into the reasons for this "high." He never once wondered what it was that had caused such a mood of elation and joy.

And, of course, not for a second had he given the barest thought to David ben Jonah.

The next morning was quite different. Whatever it was that had made him so elated the day before was gone this Friday morning, leaving him in pretty much the state of mind he had been in the past week.

During their phone conversation on Tuesday, John Weatherby had said he was in Jerusalem to give Ben a call and to "send off another set of photographs. Good ones this time." That meant they would be arriving any day—Monday at the outside. Ben was anxious to get the next Scroll.

He was barely able to concentrate on his Languages of Archaeology class, and had an even more difficult time faking his way through Ancient and Modern Hebrew. The post office was on his mind. If the next Scroll was registered, then he would have to take the slip to the post office before five and raise a row to get his letter.

Otherwise, it would be Monday before he could claim it and that would make for a miserable weekend.

Ben was surprised to find Judy Golden absent from class. Although her presence had become unsettling to him, her absence was even more unnerving. And this time he had even remembered to bring the Codex.

After wrapping up the class early, Ben rushed home and found a yellow slip in his mailbox. A registered letter from Israel could be claimed at the post office on Monday between nine and five.

He wasted no time. Ben was at the post office and asking to speak to the postmaster at four forty-five. In five minutes he had drawn considerable attention to himself, was allowed to wait for his carrier to return after five and was begrudgingly given his envelope with a reminder that this was against the rules.

He was back in his apartment fifteen minutes later, spreading an area on his desk, sequestering Poppaea in the bedroom and building himself up for the next installment of David ben Jonah's life. As he sat down, Ben glanced up at the telephone and, with less reserve than he had felt the last time, took the receiver off the hook. Then he sat back down at the desk, wiped his perspiring palms down his pants and proceeded to open the envelope.

In it was a letter from John Weatherby.

Something about the entire Knesseth coming out to the excavation site; the Prime Minister; the American Ambassador; the famous Yigael Yadin himself. Descriptions of the ghastly working conditions —unpredictable weather, invading insects, lousy food and cold nights. And John Weatherby, at the end of it all, wishing the blessings of God upon all the dedicated workers and volunteers of his archaeological team.

Ben tossed the letter aside and tore open the inner envelope. Three photos fell out.

One was a candid shot of Dr. John Weatherby bent over his portable typewriter. His shirt sleeves were rolled up and his wire-rimmed glasses were perched on the tip of his nose. He was seated at a card table before the opening of a tent.

The second one was of Dr. Weatherby, his wife Helena and Professor Yigael Yadin—all three posed at the rim of the excavation site. Their smiles were like those of sweepstakes winners. Their clothes dusty and sweat-stained.

The last photo was of the site itself—considerably farther along than the first picture of it Ben had received. Cardboard placards indicated the different levels, and a roped-off section appeared to be the cache of the famous jars. The scene was populated by a variety of people—from leathery old scientists to vigorous young students all dressed in khaki and bent over their labors.

Ben looked in the envelope again. There were no more photos. Slamming the whole bundle onto the desk top, he swore, and drove his fingers through his hair.

So he still had to wait for Scroll Five to come! Another twenty-four hours of wondering, of pacing, of waiting for David to speak to him again . . .

Poppaea Sabina was making angry noises at the bedroom door, so he let her out. Together they slumped onto the couch in the living room and sat in the darkness of the night. Poppaea sulked from lack of attention. Ben pouted like a disappointed child.

After half an hour of trying to cope with this unbelievable letdown, Ben decided to be sensible about it and take the disappointment with calm. He also decided to go back over Scroll Four, since it had been so difficult to read, and make certain he had committed no errors.

After two hours of working at his desk, making minor corrections here and there, Ben came to a startling revelation of his own.

When he finished the last line of the second photograph, he felt oddly happy and elated. He jumped up from his desk and sang his way into the kitchen, where he started to decant himself a glass of wine. In mid-pour, however, the sound of his own whistling caused Ben to stop what he was doing, put glass and bottle down and frown at the vacant wall before him.

Why on earth was he suddenly so happy?

He went to the kitchen doorway and stood so that he could just see across the living room and into the den. At the end of light he could barely discern the corner of his desk and back of his swivel chair. On the desk top, appearing as a sliver of white from Ben's position, was his notebook of translations.

Ben stood at the kitchen door for a long time, staring across the silent apartment. He stared across the shadows and across the emptiness and began to feel a weird sensation come over him. Gooseflesh crept over his skin, causing the hairs on his arms and neck to rise. An eerie coldness filled the room.

Then he knew.

Walking slowly back to the den and standing a few feet from the desk, he looked first at the photograph of the battered papyrus, and then at the translation he had written.

The words "The next day Saul and I received word that we were to commence our studies with Rabbi Eleazar" came back to him.

And he knew.

They had given him immense joy.

"It was as if it had happened to *me*," he whispered to the photograph. "That's why I was in such a good mood yesterday. It was as though *I* had been the one to get accepted to Rabbi Eleazar's school."

Ben screwed his eyes tight as a strange chill swept over him. He rubbed his hands over his arms, feeling their clamminess, and shivered uncontrollably. The joy of yesterday had not been my own, he thought, it had been David's joy. David's joy . . .

Ben opened his eyes and gazed down again at the Aramaic words, and a feeling of having crossed a bridge, of having come to a point of no return, made him shudder.

Trying to shake off this sensation, a sensation which smacked of premonition, he forced a laugh and said out loud, "I guess I'm cracking up."

But his voice sounded tinny, the laugh almost a rattle. "Oh, David," he murmured with a shiver. "What are you doing to me?"

This was not the first time Ben was awakened by a knocking at his door. And it was not going to be the last. Struggling to get his eyes open and to orient himself to time and place, Ben could not imagine who would be wanting him at such an odd hour. But then again, Ben had no idea what time of day or night it was.

He swung out of bed and plodded barefoot into the living room in time to see Angie come in and close the door behind her. She was dressed in a denim pantsuit and had her hair artistically bound up in a scarf. "Hi, love," she said brightly, and dropped her overnight case on the coffee table.

"Hi," he said in a fog.

She kissed him on one cheek, patted him on the other and started toward the kitchen. "Something tells me we're not going to start on time this morning."

"What?" he mumbled. "Start what?"

Angie paused at the kitchen door. "San Diego, remember? You're going to make a fallen lady out of me this weekend. You promised." Then she went into the kitchen and started rattling about. "I hope you're not going to make something of the rain predictions," he heard her call out. "Because it'll just be a good excuse to stay in a motel room for forty-eight hours!"

Standing in the center of the living room, Ben said to himself, "San Diego?"

Angie poked her head around the door. "Want breakfast here or on the road?"

"Well, I—"

"Good idea. Coffee here and a meal on the way. That's how I like it. Maybe in San Juan Capistrano. There's a delightful Spanish-style café near the Mission . . ." More rattling sounds came from the kitchen, then Angie finally emerged. "There. Take but a minute to percolate. Go shower and it'll be ready when you get out."

"Angie—"

She paused before a mirror to inspect her coiffure. "Hm?"

"Angie, we can't go."

Her hands froze in mid-air. "What do you mean?"

"I mean that I might get the fifth Scroll today."

Angie slowly dropped her hands and turned to face him. "So?"

He took a step toward her, his hands outstretched. "I want to be here when it comes."

"Won't the mailman put it in the box?"

"No. The Scrolls are coming registered. If I'm not here to sign for them, then I'll have to wait till Monday."

Her voice grew cool. "So?"

"Come on, Angie. Try to understand."

She took a deep breath and let it out slowly. "I've been counting on this trip."

"I know—"

"You've gone away before when manuscripts were being delivered. You even let that Codex from Egypt sit at the post office three days before you got around to picking it up. You're more reliable claiming your dry cleaning. What's so different about these Scrolls?"

"Jesus Christ, Angie!" he exploded. "You know goddamn well what's so different!"

"Hey," she said evenly. "Don't shout at me. I'm in the same room. All right, all right. The Scrolls mean a lot. And they're different from anything you've ever received before. But you said the fifth Scroll only *might* come today. Can you take the chance that it won't and go to San Diego with me?"

Ben shook his head.

"It's not fair, you know, to disappoint me like this. You've never done that before."

"I'm sorry," he said weakly.

"All right. I'll try to understand. Well, you're just going to have to make this devastating disappointment up to me."

"Listen, Angie," he spoke hurriedly. "If I don't get the Scroll today, there's no reason why we can't go to San Diego tomorrow morning and spend the day."

She regarded him sadly, lovingly. "Is this what it will be like married to a paleographer?"

"I wouldn't know. I've never been married to one."

She laughed and kissed his cheek. The aroma of brewing coffee started to permeate the air. "Go shower and get dressed. I might as well wait for the Scroll with you, and if it doesn't come with this afternoon's mail delivery, then we can go to San Diego tonight. How about that?"

Ben took a very long shower, aware of the fact that he was mildly reluctant to join Angie's company. Although he couldn't explain it, indeed he didn't even understand it himself, there was a desperate need to be alone until the fifth Scroll arrived. Almost as if he needed to prepare himself for David once again.

They sat in silence over the coffee, Angie making frequent glances out the window for rain, and Ben thinking about the next Scroll.

As he stirred his black coffee, his mind wandered back over the years and the miles until before him was a face he had not envisioned in a very long time: the big nose and long-lashed eyes of Solomon Liebowitz. Now there had been a handsome youth, so bold and brawny with the face of acuity. He had curly black hair and darkish skin and a sensuous, voluptuous mouth. People had often kidded the two boys about their appearance: one a swarthy Semite and the other a pale, blue-eyed towhead. In appearance they were as different as night and day, but in mentality and outlook they had been a true pair. They had both harbored imaginations beyond extremes, traveling about Brooklyn together like Roland and Olivier. In yeshiva they had been excellent students, rivaling one another for the praise of their teachers. They frequently spent the night together, studied together and, later, dated girls together.

Such a surprise it had been, after leaving the yeshiva and being on their own, that they had gone such opposite ways.

"Ben?"

He focused on Angie.

"Ben? You haven't heard a word I've said. Thinking about the Scrolls?"

He nodded.

"Want to tell me about them?" Angie tipped her head to one side.

Ben could not pinpoint why he was irritable with Angie this morning. Possibly it was her forcing an interest in the Scrolls to make him feel better. The look in her eyes said: It will pass; little Ben will get over it and then we can go play.

"They're really dry," he said, looking away from her. In the morning light, overcast though it was outside, it struck Ben that Angie was wearing too much makeup. And that damned perfume of hers was spoiling his coffee.

"Try me."

"Oh, for God's sake, Angie, don't humor me." He shoved his chair back and stood up, hands in his pockets. A faint drizzle was starting to spot the window.

"What's the matter with you, Ben? I've never seen you like this. One minute you're fine and happy, the next minute you're cranky and irritable. I've never seen you so unpredictable before."

"I'm sorry," he muttered, striding away from her. Jesus! he thought. All I want is to be left alone! Alone to think. And you come in here with your fairy costume and kindergarten voice and—

"I'm getting more and more caught up in these Scrolls, Angie. I can't help it. They're . . . they're . . ." What? They're what? Starting to control me?

He smelled her perfume coming. Then he felt her slender hands on his shoulders. "Let me read what you've got so far."

Ben turned around to regard her. Oh, Angie love, he thought unhappily. I know you're trying to understand. I know you're going along with this for my sake. Only don't—

"May I?"

"Sure, why not? Have a seat."

She kicked off her shoes and sank onto the couch, drawing her feet up under her. When he handed her the notebook, she flipped through the pages and said, "Wow, so much!"

Then he wandered back to the dining room and picked up his coffee. It tasted better now.

After a considerable length of time, Angie tossed the notebook on the coffee table and said, "That was interesting."

Ben stared at her.

"I think you've done a great job. I hope Weatherby is generous with you."

Ben's eyes widened incredulously. "What do you think of David ben Jonah."

"What do I think of him? Oh . . ." She shrugged. "Nothing, really. Now if he mentions Jesus, then you will really have something big."

Ben put his coffee cup down. "Angie," he said in a lower voice, his words coming carefully. "David ben Jonah . . . when you read his words . . . doesn't he make you *feel* something?"

She tilted her head to one side. "What do you mean?"

"Well—" He wiped his moist palms down his pants. "Like, when I read his words, I get involved in them. You know what I mean? I'm drawn into them. I can't tear myself away. It's like he's really talking to *me* . . ."

"Ben—"

He shot to his feet and started pacing the floor, his limp noticeable. Can it only be me? he thought wildly. Am I the only one who gets these feelings when I read David's words? What is it? *What's causing it?*

This is ridiculous! Look at her. How can she be so damned detached about the whole thing, while I become a nervous wreck!

"Ben, what's wrong?"

He ignored her. His thoughts were flying. Jonah the father of David, and Jonah Messer the father of Ben, both saying: "Remember that the Lord knoweth the way of the righteous, but the way of the ungodly shall perish." You are a Benjaminite. The Curse of Moses upon you, and the Lord will inflict you with a madness—

"Ben!"

He stopped suddenly. "Angie, I want to be alone for a while."

"No!" She flew to her feet. "Don't send me away."

Ben backed away, feeling closed in.

"The mail won't be here for hours," she said. "Let's go for a drive and forget all about this for a while—"

"No!" he shouted. "Goddamnit, Angie, all you ever want me to do is 'get away' from my work. 'Forget about it for a while.' 'Escape from it.' Has it ever occurred to you that I might want to be very much involved in it?"

"I see," she said evenly.

"No, you don't. And I don't blame you. I just want to be alone."

"I won't disturb you."

He walked away from her under the pretense of inspecting the thermostat. "It's cold in here," he said quietly. Yes, you will disturb me. You can't sit for longer than five minutes without a conversation going.

Ben turned to Angie in amazement. She sat on the couch like the cover of a glamour magazine—her high cheekbones rouged, her lips and spiky nails blood red. How strange that he was thinking such things of her just now, when they had never before occurred to him. And yet they were no less true.

That beautiful woman poised on the couch with her cameo face and wild auburn hair was the dream mate of any man. She laughed a lot, dressed exquisitely, had a milky body and always created an attentive conversation. Ben had always enjoyed having other men stare at her wherever they went. Angie on his arm was like a medal on his lapel.

And yet, gazing at her now as if—in a way—for the first time, Ben started thinking thoughts that had never been there before.

"I won't disturb you," she repeated.

"And what will you do? While I'm sitting in the dark and listening to Bach, what will you be doing?"

"Oh, Ben." She regarded him with impatience. "All right. I'll go. If that's what you really want. I'll come by in the morning. Okay?" She picked up her overnight case. "And please don't take your phone off the hook. You did it again last night, didn't you, because I called and called and got a busy signal."

"I won't do it again."

She hesitated before the open door as if undecided what to say next. "I really think the Scrolls are interesting, Ben."

"Good."

"But you must keep in mind that I'm not familiar with Jewish things."

"You're familiar with me, aren't you?"

"Benjamin Messer!" Angie was genuinely surprised. "That's the first time I've ever heard you admit you're a Jew! You're usually trying so hard to deny it."

"Not to deny it, my love, to forget it. There's a difference."

Ben paced for the rest of the morning and all afternoon. He remembered to feed Poppaea. Managed a few "acrosses" of the L.A. *Times* puzzle. Listened to some records, threw a cheese sandwich down his throat and paced some more. The postman should soon be at the door.

He had gone through almost an entire pack of pipe tobacco when, at four o'clock exactly, he decided to go down to the mailboxes. He had waited for the knock at the door, to have to sign for a registered package, and when none had come, he wondered if the mailman had already been by.

He had.

There was fresh mail in the other boxes, a gas bill in his own and new magazines in the bin. But no little yellow slip.

Ben had not realized how anxiously he had awaited the fifth Scroll until it had not come. And now he was positively crushed. While a mild rain fell from a metallic sky and washed off the sidewalks of West Los Angeles, Ben stood like an idiot staring at mailboxes. There was nothing worse in all the world than getting your hopes up for something and then not getting it. He thought he was going to cry.

"I can't stand it. I can't stand it," he muttered over and over again as he went back up to his apartment. Why weren't the Scrolls coming faster? Why did he have to go through this agonized waiting?

Back upstairs Ben turned up the heat, poured a large glass of wine and settled down on the sofa. Within minutes Poppaea was on his lap, purring and kneading his stomach as if letting him know she was glad of his company.

"I don't know what's getting into me, Poppaea," he murmured gently to her. "I've never been like this before. It's becoming an obsession. Why? What's causing it? Is it David? How can someone who's been dead for two thousand years have such control over me?"

He sipped the wine slowly and felt the temperature of the room rise. He became swaddled in a blanket of warmth; a sleepy, cozy envelope that made him relax and put his head back.

Almost at once, his days with Solomon Liebowitz came flooding back. It was as though they had been bottled up behind a door for many years until now, for some reason unknown to Ben, a key was found that opened that door. And memories which Ben had long forgotten tumbled about in his mind.

There were other pictures, too, not as pleasant as the ones of the yeshiva and Solomon. They were flashes of his boyhood in Germany, of his immigration to the United States, of the painful growing up under his mother's care.

Ben had had no brothers or sisters. Nor a father. It had only been himself and his mother for as far back as he could remember. And his mother—his sole parent and companion at home—had been a difficult person to bear.

Then another vision flashed briefly in his mind. Her wrist. His mother's wrist. There was something wrong with it. She always wore long sleeves to hide it. But one day little Ben had caught sight of it and, pointing, had said, "What's that, Mama?"

A look of horror had crossed Rosa's face. She had slapped her hand over the mutilation and fled from the room. And she had cried for hours after that and long into the night.

When Ben was thirteen years old, on the day of his Bar Mitzvah, his mother had rolled up her sleeve to show the wrist to him. "Because now you are a man," she had said in Yiddish. "Because now you should know about such things."

And she had shown him the speckled scars made by the bites of wild dogs at the place called Majdanek.

When the phone rang, Ben bolted upright, sending Poppaea flying. He stumbled on sleeping feet and rubbed his face before answering. To his surprise, he wiped away a tear from his cheek.

"Hi, love. Well, what's the verdict."

For an instant he did not know who it was, then he said dully, "No Scroll, Angie."

"Far out," she whispered. "San Diego then?"

"Yeh . . . San Diego. But tomorrow morning. I'm too tired now."

"Great. I'll see you then. Bye-bye, sweetheart."

His lips formed the word "goodbye," but no voice came out. Ben stood by the phone for a long time, staring as if hypnotized. Then he gradually came around and realized he must have slept for a while on the couch. It was nearly seven o'clock.

There was only one thing he wanted to do now, and that was drive those memories from his mind. To forget the terror and anguish of the concentration camp. To obliterate the sadness of his boyhood home. And to put Rabbi Solomon Liebowitz back behind the locked door. It served no good purpose to dredge up the past. It only made one miserable and brought forth tears.

Turning on a lot of lights and starting a Beethoven record, Ben achieved some success in driving out the gloom and silence. However, when the faces of his mother and Solomon threatened to linger, Ben arrived at an understanding with himself: he did not want to be alone.

He dialed three digits of Angie's number and then hung up. Thinking for a minute, he next went to the kitchen and pulled out the telephone directory on the off chance that she might be listed. Surprisingly, she was. That is, if the Judith Golden in the phone book was the same one.

"Hello?"

"Miss Golden?"

"This is Ben Messer."

A pause. "Well, hello. How are you?"

"Just fine. Listen, I know it's Saturday night and you probably have plans, but something's come up and I could use your help."

She was silent.

"It's the Scrolls," he went on less confidently. "Weatherby has asked me for a progress report, and I'm afraid if I were to try typing my notes it would take a week. I was wondering if—"

"I'd be glad to. Your typewriter or mine?"

"Well, actually I have a very good one. It's electric and—"

"Great! What time do you want me to come by?"

Ben sighed with relief. "Is half an hour too soon?"

"That's fine."

"I'll be glad to pay you for it."

"Not at all. Just let me share in the glory. And please be sure they spell my name right. See you in a while, Dr. Messer."

"Yes. And thank you."

After he hung up he was not sure he had done the right thing. In fact, he was not really sure *why* he had done it. He had acted on an impulse (he seemed to be doing that a lot lately) and it was too late to go back on it.

Ben wandered into the living room. It was a dichotomy he was going to have to resign himself to: the desire to be alone and yet needing company at the same time. Poppaea was not enough, and Angie was too much. Maybe Judy would fall somewhere in between. Somehow, with her typing away at the dining table and minding her own business and with Ben by himself in the den, maybe a reasonable balance could be struck.

In reasoning this out, however, Ben was not aware of one thing: that the need for Judy's company was far greater than his fear of being alone. And if he had seen this and delved into it, he would have found that typing the progress report was only an excuse to have Judy come over. There was, growing deep within him, in a hidden place that not even Ben knew about, a mysterious need to have Judy by his side. A part of Ben Messer that Ben Messer did not know existed craved the company of Judy Golden, so much so that it invented reasons and excuses for seeking her out.

But Ben knew none of this. All he could think was: I don't want to be alone.

In any case, Solomon Liebowitz was not going willingly back into his closet. And neither would Rosa Messer's voice be silent. "They tortured your father, Benjamin! They tortured him to death!"

Ben turned up the stereo—Beethoven's Seventh Symphony—and hummed along with it. He noisily washed out some cups in the kitchen and started a fresh pot of coffee.

"And what they did to me!" Rosa Messer's voice cried from the past. "A mother shouldn't tell her son. But I died back there with your father. I died back there because of what the Germans did to your father and what they did to me! I'm not alive any more, Benjamin! A woman shouldn't have to live through what I did! You're living with a dead woman, Benjamin!"

Judy Golden had to knock very loud in order to be heard.

Ben greeted her with forced enthusiasm. And to his surprise, she was very wet.

"It's pouring out!" she said. "Didn't you know?"

"No, I didn't. Anyway, the coffee is fresh. You timed it perfectly."

He helped her off with her bulky sweater and hung it in an open doorway so that it would dry more easily. Then he started for the kitchen, saying something over his shoulder as he did so.

"I can't hear you, Dr. Messer." Judy looked over at the stereo. "Wow," she whispered.

He came back at once and turned the volume down. "Sorry."

"Bet your neighbors love you."

"I have only one, to the left, and he's rarely home. Have a seat. You take it black, don't you?"

Judy fell into the luxurious couch and put her feet up on the ottoman. The record had now gone into the Second Movement—that slow, haunting melody which captivated even the most disinterested listener. Ben returned with the coffee and some wedges of cake he had taken earlier out of the freezer.

"I hope you had dinner. I didn't think—"

"Oh yes."

"You didn't break a date or anything to come . . ." His voice died. Judy was looking out of the corner of her eye in amusement.

"I'm not exactly a dater. I have enough with my books and Bruno, thanks."

"Bruno?"

"My roommate."

He picked up a piece of cake, got it almost to his mouth and dropped half in his lap. He looked momentarily stunned, then burst out laughing. As the two of them tried to pick all the crumbs off the white couch and white rug, Ben said, "With Bruno for a roommate, then I guess you don't need dates."

Judy looked up. "What?" Then she laughed even harder. "Oh, Dr. Messer! Bruno's a German shepherd dog!"

Ben said, "Oh," and laughed some more.

They quieted down after a few minutes and settled back to listen to the harmony of Beethoven on the stereo and the rain on the window. Ben allowed himself to put his head back and relax, and after a short passage of time, he forgot Judy Golden was there.

A myriad of notions passed through his mind as he did so, a predominant one being his love of German classical music after having discovered it in California. Back in Brooklyn he had never heard of Beethoven, or if he had it had been in connection with a malign, hateful thing. Nothing German was good in his youth; or rather, everything German was bad. Volkswagens, sauerkraut, Bach and glockenspiels were odious things. They carried the touch of death with them. They stunk of bestiality and evil.

Only Jewish was good. Jewish was perfect, holy and pure. And in between the two poles—the loathsome German and the sacred Jew—was the rest of the world. It had something to do with Rosa Messer's twisted plan of the world peoples and the order in which they ranked down from Jews to Germans. Nothing was lower than Germany, for that was just below hell.

"Dr. Messer?"

"Hm? Ha?" He snapped his head up.

"The record is over."

"So it is. Guess I was drifting. Say, listen, you can start typing whenever you want. I don't know how long it'll take you."

They both stood. Ben went into the den to get the typewriter, which stood in its case under his desk. As he did so, he paused to take the phone off the hook. A habit he was beginning to practice without thinking.

In the dining room, he lifted the typewriter out of its case, plugged it in and flicked the "on" switch. The machine hummed with life.

"Very nice," said Judy. "Mine is one of those old black and gold manuals that require brute force to depress one key. This is like dying and going to heaven."

He went back into the den and returned with typing paper, carbon paper and the notebook of translations. This last he spread open on the table and frowned down at the first page. "What a mess," he murmured. "Chicken scratch. Looks like you're going to have almost as tough a translating job as I did. And I accused David ben Jonah of being messy! Look at that!"

Judy smiled and sat before the typewriter, playing with the shift key. Ben leaned over her and frowned some more over his handwriting. "I went real fast here. Ran some words together. You know, David did that, too. Most frustrating thing in the world. He was an educated man and an excellent writer, but there were times when he got excited or in a hurry and wrote sloppily—like I did here. Well, that's one thing David and I have in common. Sometimes he ran words too closely together and it took me half an hour to decipher what he was saying. Even the most minor error can change the entire meaning of a sentence. Like, for instance—"

Ben picked up a pencil and scratched a string of letters at the top of the page: GODISNOWHERE

"This is English, of course, but it gives you an idea of the obstacles I encounter in translating David's Aramaic. Read it out loud."

Judy studied it for a second, then said, "God is nowhere."

"Are you sure? Look again. Mightn't it also say: God is now here?"

"Oh, I see what you mean."

"And that changes the meaning considerably. Anyway, if you have any problems with my chicken scratch, just holler. Those sections that you see angrily scratched out are places where I encountered just such illegibility in David's handwriting."

"I think this is going to be fun."

"If you need anything, the kitchen's right there and the bathroom is back through there. I'll be in the den, okay?"

"Fine. Enjoy yourself."

Ben was scanning his shelves for something relaxing to read when there was a knock at the door. It was the musician neighbor, drenched in a yellow plastic poncho.

"Hey, man," he said. "I've got something for you. I was downstairs this afternoon just as the mailman was about to slip another yellow one into your box. I figured you weren't home, and if it's registered then it must be important, so I signed for it." He withdrew the heavy envelope from under his arm. "Otherwise, you would have had to wait till Monday, right?"

Ben did not reply, but stared instead at the familiar handwriting and the Israeli stamps.

"Listen, I'm sorry I didn't bring it up sooner, but I was in a hurry to get somewhere when I signed for it. Okay?"

"What? Oh, fine. Just fine! I was home all afternoon waiting for this, but I guess I didn't hear the mailman knock. Say, thanks a lot! I owe you for this."

"Forget it. G'night."

Long after the door was closed, Ben continued to stand and gape down at the envelope. And his heart began to beat very fast.

CHAPTER SEVEN

❦━━◆❖◆━━❦

I approached my discipleship under Eleazar with great apprehension. It was not that I feared the years of hardship and sacrifice ahead of me, nor was I afraid of failing. What concerned me above all was my worthiness.

Rabbi Eleazar ben Azariah was one of the truly great and gifted men at Law, and he was a renowned teacher. As well, he was a member of the Sanhedrin, a Pharisee and a pious man. Eleazar lived simply and humbly, working at his trade as cheesemaker in order to support himself and his family. He clothed himself in the garb of a modest man, and wore tephillin no larger than those of his neighbors. Unlike certain of his colleagues who prayed aloud in the streets, Eleazar was a quiet man and spoke to God with his heart. He knew the letter of the Law better than any man, and he practiced the spirit of the Law through his wisdom and daily living.

And he was to be my teacher.

Like most rabbis, Eleazar kept twelve disciples about him always. We two were the youngest. Saul and I were given shelter in an unused storage shed behind his house so that we might be in his proximity always. Of the other ten, three lived in the homes of their fathers, three resided with relatives and four lodged in the very upper rooms of the rabbi's house. Eleazar's wife Ruth fed and clothed us in exchange for work. Since she had no daughters, the unlikely duty fell to me of filling the cisterns daily from the wells. It was Saul's duty to keep the old house in good repair. The other four pupils assisted Eleazar in his cheese shop when we were not at the Temple. We were to endure years of this bondage, living as the humblest servants and exacting no wage, for such was the price of becoming men of the Law.

In the beginning, as I lay upon my mat and stared up in the darkness of our tiny room, I allowed myself to cry. A great darkness lay before me, a gulf so wide and endless as to be terrifying, so that my boy's mind cried out: Am I worthy, Lord?

Above all, I missed Magdala. I dreamed of my father's house by the lake; of helping him to spread his nets beneath the hot sun; of hearing his gruff laughter. I missed the embrace of my mother; of the sweet smell of honey and barley about her; the way she would cry when she laughed too hard.

I missed the summer nights when we would all sit outside our house and eat fried fish and coarse bread and drink the milk of our one goat. Cooking fires illuminated every smiling face. The men talked low and the women hummed quietly in contentment. Before us stretched the black Lake of Galilee, which was our entire life. And behind us rolled the western hills, rolling on to a body of water so vast that it was called the Great Sea, and beyond that—the end of the world.

While Saul slumbered on his mat, I sobbed like a child out of loneliness. Father, I called out over the miles. Why did you send me here?

But mine was not the place to question. Mine was to be humble and to learn the Law of the Covenant even as Eleazar knew it. I would not settle for less. I would one day become a great rabbi and recite the Torah from my heart.

I would become like Eleazar.

Jerusalem grew smaller the older I grew. When, at eleven, in my sister's house, I first saw the city, it overwhelmed me. But as I grew in body and spirit, Jerusalem shrank. Why this is I do not know. But you have seen Jerusalem, my son, and know what I mean when I say it is the Center of the World. You have felt the press of its marketplace, heard the roar of its great population, smelled the many stinks of its gutters. You have also witnessed her splendors and felt the presence of the Lord about you.

Starting with the first day, and every day from then on, Saul and I rose before dawn, said our prayers, put bread and cheese in our belts and struck out to the Temple with Rabbi Eleazar. He spoke to us along the way. While much of the city was still asleep, we walked those cold streets with our cloaks pulled tightly about us, and discussed the Law. There was never a moment, in Eleazar's company, that we did not discuss the Law. And he would examine us. If we faltered he was stern with us. If we were perfect he smiled approvingly.

On the porch of the Temple, I often spied other boys eyeing us enviously. When Eleazar had accepted Saul and me, he had rejected thirty-seven others. I tried not to become proud because of this. Yet it was difficult. My teacher knew more about the Law than any other man, and someday I would be just like him.

Saul and I were not insignificant to him, although it might at first have seemed that way. The other boys were more advanced than we and seemed to earn his smile more frequently. And yet, as in the parable of the one lost sheep, Eleazar often left the other boys to give special instruction to us.

In time I lost my fears and no longer cried. Instead I faced my appointment with great determination. The task of drawing the water from the wells was my only ignominy. And I felt it had been a test. If I were weak in any spot, it was this, and had I shown it, Eleazar would have dismissed me. But painful though it was to perform a woman's job, I executed it unfailingly and earned, in some small way, Eleazar's respect.

And this was just about all we could earn, for as the rabbi gave us a roof and fed us, we had no need for money.

Yet there was one instance in which I needed money, and that was when I first desired to communicate with my father. I had been in the rabbi's house six months and wanted very much to tell my father in my own words what my new life was like.

Yet how was I to write a letter with no paper and no ink, and nothing to pay a letter carrier? I sought an opportunity.

Our cisterns were filled every afternoon, just before sunset, so that Eleazar's wife Ruth would have enough water for cooking and washing. It occurred to me one day that I might perform the same errand for another person and perhaps earn a small fee. My problem was this: all my time was taken up with my studies of the Law. All other time was devoted to prayer, eating and sleeping—all under Eleazar's eye. And so my opportunity had to come at the well. Which one day it did.

As I dipped my jar and drew it up, I watched the stiff labors of an old widow whom I had seen many times before. I knew her to be a woman alone, without family or friends, and though not poor she could not afford servants. So I approached her. And I said this: If I were to carry water to your cisterns for the period of a month, saving you the task, would you pay me a shekel?

To my great surprise, the widow gladly accepted. Her back ached and her joints were stiff, yet there was no one to draw water for her. And so we agreed.

Now what I had to do was fill the cisterns of my own house as well as hers in the same amount of time, for Rabbi Eleazar would not approve my taking time away from the Law of God.

This is what I did. I walked twice as fast and carried twice as much water. In the amount of time it had taken me to replenish our own water supply, I now replenished the widow's as well.

At first I tired greatly and found new soreness in my muscles. And the limp which had remained with me from my boyhood was at first a hindrance. But as days of this passed and as my body adapted, I found the chore not so difficult at all.

And in that time I did not believe Eleazar suspected.

After a month, the widow paid me not one shekel but two, and when I went to lie on my mat to sleep that night, I found a fresh sheet of papyrus upon it.

After another month, she gave me another two shekels, I found a reed pen on my bed.

After the third month, another two shekels, and a cake of black ink was upon my mat.

So I wrote the letter by moonlight and dispatched it the next afternoon with a letter carrier whom I had often seen near the well. That evening, after supper and after our prayers, Rabbi Eleazar called me aside for a private talk. It concerned me, for he had never done this before.

He said: David ben Jonah, did you send the letter off to your father today?

I replied: Yes, sir, and was surprised.

Did you think I was unaware of your plans? That the widow had not spoken to me? That I have not noticed the development of your arms?

Yes, sir, I replied shyly.

And tell me, David ben Jonah, who do you think put the papyrus and the pen and the ink upon your mat each night?

My only reply was: Are you angry with me, Rabbi?

I think Eleazar was stunned. Angry with you? Why, David ben Jonah, should I be angry with you when you are the only one among all my pupils who has strived so very hard to keep holy the Fifth Commandment of the Lord. You have honored your father and mother well.

Now Eleazar put his hands heavily upon my shoulders and I saw a deep affection in his eyes. And to achieve this feat, he said, you did not steal one minute from the Law.

I continued to draw the widow's water, and tucked my shekels away in a safe place. As we grew into our second and third years with Eleazar, as we moved out of the shed and up to the top floor, we were now given a small allowance which we were given every month. By now we needed new sandals and new cloaks, and so had little opportunity to save.

As we matured and left boyhood behind, the friendship between Saul and me became even closer and more intimate and more precious. We slept together, ate together and studied the Law together. I knew his every thought, and he knew mine. We kept no secrets from one another. And yet, people often remarked that we were as different as night is from day.

By his sixteenth year Saul was the tallest man I knew, towering above the heads of the priests and scribes when we gathered in the Temple. He had broad shoulders and a massive chest, with brawny arms and hands of incredible strength. His dark brown hair grew curly and wiry, and his beard was thicker and fuller than even Eleazar's. Many thought Saul to be far older than he was.

I, on the other hand, was slighter of build, though by no means weak. My arms were slender but sinewy, knotted with the muscles I had developed carrying the water. My body was the same, slender but strong, deceiving others who thought me to be a weakling because of my limp. My hair was black, blacker than the bottom of a well, and my eyes were as dark. Eleazar once told me I had the large, brooding eyes of a prophet or a poet, and then he shook his head sadly as if he knew something I did not. The hair on my head was long and wavy, falling just to my shoulders. The hair on my face, however, was spare, and comparing it with Saul's beard, I feared mine would never be so grand.

Eleazar's wife Ruth had often spoken of us as her handsome boys, and I think she liked us in a special way. We were never seen apart, Saul and I; he the loud and laughing one, myself quiet and withdrawn. She likened us to Kings Saul and David, and remarked that the day would arrive when princesses would be vying for our favors.

This embarrassed me, for, unlike Saul, who already had an eye for the maidens, I was too shy to even look upon one. As we walked through the streets in the morning or late afternoon, we frequently passed groups of young women at their marketing. They would smile at us and cast their eyes modestly down, yet I never failed to see one of them stare admiringly at Saul.

The time came when I no longer had to draw water from the well. I was both relieved and sad, for although I no longer had the humiliation of doing a woman's job, I nonetheless had my small source of income now denied me.

Saul did not seem to care about or need money, and he never saved his few shekels. I, on the other hand, recognized security in money and felt sure that the day would come when I would be glad of my frugality. This trait, of course, had a direct bearing upon what was to happen later, and had I not been endowed with such thinking, possibly the course of my history would have been greatly altered. And I would not today be sitting in Magdala writing this for you, my son. However, I was the way I was, and so the course of my destiny was to bring me to the Hour about which I must tell you.

But for now, let me relive those sweet days of youth in Jerusalem.

Upon my frugality, Eleazar once commented to me one day. He said: David ben Jonah, were I to send you into the streets to shovel the droppings of horses and donkeys, you would find a way to turn it into a profit-making venture. He said this half in amusement, half seriously.

You are one of my best pupils in the Law, he said, with your keen mind and shrewdness. And yet I sometimes wonder if you would not be more of an asset to Israel by becoming a banker or stockbroker.

This speculation had so horrified me that I was as stricken as if he had hit me.

Forgive me, David, he went on, but I only pay you a compliment and not an insult. If I do you an injury, it is inadvertent. But remember, my son, that there are other ways to serve God than by guarding His Law. Not all men are scribes, just as not all men are fishermen. And yet, each man in his way serves God in the way he knows best. You will become a Doctor of the Law and safeguard God's Law against the ravages of change.

He paused at this point and looked at me long. And yet . . . he said. But he never finished his thought.

So I had some silver hidden away and wore my sandals through and mended my own cloak as a woman might. When Saul purchased his third new pair of sandals, I took his old castoff ones from him and wore them another six months. He laughed at me for this, but I believe he secretly envied my ability to save money.

I was seventeen years old when I first met Rebekah.

Most other young men by this age were already married or betrothed, yet this could not be so for the rabbinic students, who must not steal one minute from study of the Law. As a consequence we gave little thought to marriage. The time would come when our teacher would deem us ready to go on our own and be teachers ourselves. And when that time came we would find a desirable woman and marry her. But just as we never knew when our teacher would set us free, so did we also never know when we would be able to marry. Because of this, we gave it little thought.

Or so I did until I met Rebekah. She was the daughter of Eleazar's brother who was a tent maker in Jerusalem. In my first three years of dwelling in the rabbi's house, I never met this girl. However, the day came when Eleazar's wife Ruth fell ill and was confined to her bed for many weeks. The rabbi's brother sent two of his daughters to help Eleazar, for he himself had none.

The day I met Rebekah was the day before the Sabbath, and she and her sister came to the house to cook the meals we would eat the next day. I will never forget that afternoon.

We all arrived early from the Temple with Eleazar: Saul and I, and the four other boys who lived with us. Rebekah and Rachel were at their labors cooking, hurrying to finish before sunset. I went immediately upstairs to wash and prepare for prayers, and noticed that Saul did not follow. After a brief wait, I went back down and to my surprise, found him in the kitchen.

Rebekah had uncommonly red hair and pale green eyes. I will never forget the way she blushed when Saul introduced us. Rachel, who was four years older and not as pretty, said hello to me and continued with her work. Saul and I paid as much attention to Rebekah as we could, confined of course by our awkwardness and inexperience. She was sixteen, a year younger than we.

Eleazar seemed not to mind our attentiveness to the girl and was, I think, amused. She stayed with us for the meal but had to return to her father's house afterward while Rachel remained to take care of Ruth.

Eleazar chose me to accompany Rebekah.

I have never in all my life—before that time and since—felt both uncomfortable and happy at the same time. Rebekah was a delightful girl, shy yet pleasing, with a funny little laugh I liked to hear. We said little as we walked through the dark streets, yet our silence was not so much awkward as expectant.

Once at her own house, which was full of children and light, she introduced me to her father, who was impressed that I should be a student of the Law. He invited me to stay, but I insisted upon going home—as much as it distressed me to leave Rebekah—for I did not want to miss evening studies with Eleazar.

Rachel remained with us for the whole time Ruth was ill, and I saw Rebekah many times after that.

CHAPTER EIGHT

Ben went straight to the bathroom and dashed ice-cold water on his face. Rubbing it dry with a rough towel, he went back to the den and looked at the clock. It was six-thirty. The sun had been up for half an hour.

The den was a disaster area. During his night of translating, Ben had dragged out every reference book he owned, had sweated over each word and letter David had written, had checked it and cross-checked it and had ended with books, papers and tobacco ashes strewn everywhere.

Rubbing his sore arm muscles, he limped into the kitchen to fix some instant coffee and noticed, passing through the dining room, that his typewriter was back again in its case on the table, and that a stack of paper was set neatly on top. His notebook and an impeccably typed copy were the only evidence of Judy Golden's having been there.

He looked out the window at the overcast sky. The sidewalks were still wet, the trees glistened in the after-rain. When had she left? When had she quietly finished her work and tiptoed out without a word?

Ben went into the kitchen. The two coffee cups and plates from the evening before had been washed and put away. The uneaten cake was neatly wrapped in cellophane and on a refrigerator shelf.

He didn't remember her leaving.

Half an hour later, as he sat on the couch with his coffee and the mess of Scroll Five's translation on his lap, Ben was startled by a knock at the door. Smiling, he rose and thought to himself: Okay, Miss Golden, you've come back to tell me what a lousy host and inconsiderate employer I am. How much for the typing? I'll pay you twice the amount.

To his surprise, it wasn't Judy.

"Angie!" he said.

"Hi, lover." She breezed in, planted a kiss on his cheek and raised her nose in the air. "Do I smell coffee?"

"It's instant," he said in confusion.

"That's fine with me." Angie turned to him, her face alive and smiling. "Hey, you haven't shaved yet. Am I too early?"

"For what?"

She laughed. "A comedian at this hour of the morning! You know, I tried calling you before I left, to be sure you were up, but your line was busy. Phone off the hook again? Naughty, naughty."

She turned and went off in the direction of the kitchen. As he watched her, the slender body in the tight yellow pants and flowery blouse, it suddenly struck him. "Oh God!" he whispered. And a sinking feeling came over him.

Ben went to stand in the doorway of the kitchen, watching Angie make some coffee, and wondered how to word his next phrase. All that came out was "Angie—"

It was enough. As she was about to spoon the instant into her cup, Angie hesitated, froze for one second, then put the jar down and turned fully to Ben. "What's wrong?"

"Angie, I didn't just get up. I've been up all night. I never went to bed."

"Why not?"

He explained about the neighbor signing for the Scroll and not bringing it up until later. Angie's face remained expressionless, her voice flat. "Why didn't you call me then?"

Ben was at a loss. "I was so excited. I guess I forgot . . ."

Angie looked down at the floor for a moment, visibly struggling with herself, and when she looked up at him again, there was a cryptic expression in her eyes. "You forgot. You forgot all about me."

"Yes," he said barely above a whisper.

"Okay." She started to tremble.

"Angie, I—"

"Ben, you may not believe this, but I'm trying to be very understanding. You see, it's not easy for me." With great effort she pushed past him and went blindly into the living room. "It was never like this, Ben," she said in a tight voice. "Always before, no matter how important an assignment, you always found time for me. But things are different now. *You're* different now. Why are you so unpredictable all of a sudden?"

He spread out his hands, helplessly.

Yes, Angie thought now objectively. Ben had changed. Gone was the even, predictable temperament she had always known. Gone was Ben's mellow nature, replaced now by a strange sort of irrationality, a fluctuating between two personalities, as though he weren't aware of it, had no control over it.

As though he were being manipulated.

She narrowed her eyes at him. What was out of place here, besides his erratic temperament? What physical aberrations? Oh yes, she had noticed them before, but she had been only too eager to overlook them, to ignore them. But now she didn't. This time Angie studied Ben with different eyes, seeing in him now the slight changes that had been gradually taking place.

The sudden preference for sandals. The limp in his walk. The stiltedness of his speech, sounding like a foreigner trying hard to speak correctly. None of these had been part of Ben Messer before the appearance of the Scrolls.

She wandered over to the couch and saw the pages of his translation spread out on it. "Is it a good Scroll?" she asked quietly.

"Yes. It's a long one. Would you like to read it?"

She swung around. There was anger in her face. "What is so important about David that he means more to you than I?"

"He doesn't, Angie."

"Yes, he does, Ben!" Her voice rose higher. "Because of him you forget me! You'd rather spend your time with him than with me." She became shrill. "One old dead Jew has suddenly got you so—"

"Jesus Christ, Angie!" shouted Ben.

"And don't say that! Why do you take in vain the name of someone you don't even believe in?"

"You don't believe in him either, Angie."

"How do you know!" She took a step toward him. "How do you know! Have you ever asked me? Have we ever talked about Jesus or God or beliefs?"

"Oh wow, this is a great time to bring up theology."

"Why not? No other time was ever good enough. You always managed to steer away from the subject as if you had a monopoly on religion. I know you're an atheist, Ben, but that doesn't mean everyone else is."

"For God's sake, Angie. What the hell does all that have to do with this morning?"

She looked down at the couch again and suddenly her anger subsided. A queer look came over her face as she gazed at the papers strewn everywhere. "I don't know, Ben," she said softly. "But there is a connection. I don't really know what's going on here, but it's something more than just an archaeological find. I can't put my finger on it. I can't even put it into words, but I get an odd feeling about all this. As though . . ." She finally raised her eyes to his. "As though you were becoming *obsessed* with David ben Jonah."

Ben regarded her for a moment, then forced a nervous laugh. "That's ridiculous and you know it."

"I don't know . . ."

"Listen, Angie," he spread out his hands again. "I'm tired. I'm so god-awful tired. Can't we just forget it today?" He absently massaged his right shoulder. "And I'm stiff. I've been hauling water for the— I mean, walking twice as fast and carrying twice—" He shook his head. "No, I mean—"

"Ben! What's wrong with you!"

"Goddamnit, Angie, I'm tired, that's all! I haven't had any sleep! I just want to be left alone!"

"But how could you *forget* all about me?"

Oh God, he thought, rubbing his hands over his face. I can't even remember last night! I don't remember Judy leaving. I don't remember translating the Scroll. There's a blank—

He looked up at her. "I'm sorry," he said defeatedly.

Angie fell back a step. "All right, then."

Ben reached out to her, walked toward her.

But Angie held up a hand, saying, "No, Ben. Not this time. I am hurt. Deeply hurt. I have to think this thing out. Answer me one thing. Do you plan to leave that Scroll alone for one day? Even a few hours?"

He frowned. "I can't, Angie. I can't . . . leave it . . ."

"Enough said. Maybe I'll come crawling back to you when all this is over and it's published in a book. Until then, I hope you and David are very happy together."

Ben felt the room swim about him. Through a whirlwind of thoughts he vaguely heard Angie stalk out of the room and slam the door behind her. He was exhausted, more tired than he knew, for the tension of sitting all night at the desk had completely drained him. He continued to stand in the center of the living room for a long time after Angie left, uncertain of what to do next, feeling suspended between realities.

Then, after calming himself down and trying to sort out his thoughts, Ben felt a great depression come over him. It began at the pit of his stomach—a sickly, hollow, *lonely* feeling that crept throughout his body and overwhelmed him in a paroxysm of sadness and depression. Suddenly, all he wanted to do was sleep. He wanted to crawl into a black hole and sleep through a night of foreverness.

Only, now it was day. Nearly eight o'clock and starkly light outside. He closed all the blinds and curtains in the apartment, methodically drew them together to block out the glaring daylight and the inescapable present. Then, without undressing even, he fell onto his bed and at once slid into unconsciousness.

The last dream was the most bizarre. The first had been the usual mélange of characters and whirlpool of events—of Angie and Judy Golden and Dr. Weatherby. He had gone from one twisted sequence to another, moving through a world of hazy faces and muffled voices. But at the end, close to the time of surfacing to consciousness, Ben experienced a most vivid and frightening dream.

He was walking down a strange street at an unknown hour of the night. There were no lights, no cars, or any distinguishing landmarks to tell him where he was. It was not so much the visual fright of it as the icy fear that gripped his mind—the incredible vastness of being alone, the loneliness of a man who had no family and no friends and who walked cold dark streets by himself.

All of a sudden, there was someone at his side. A pretty young girl with long red hair and green eyes. He was not startled by her unexpected appearance. They walked in silence for some length until Ben heard himself ask: Where are we?

"We are in Jerusalem," she replied.

"That's odd."

"Why?"

"It's not how I imagined it."

Then, strangely, the girl laughed. She had a high, ringing laugh as of a person insane. She said, "David, you don't have to *imagine* Jerusalem!"

"But I'm not David."

"How silly! Of course you are. Who else would you be?"

Before he could say any more, a queer feeling came over him. One of being watched, of being intently spied upon. His fear mounted. The girl at his side was a menace. She had no name, no identity, and yet he feared her.

"What's your name?" he asked with a tight throat.

"Rosa," she replied with peals of laughter.

"No!" he cried. "You're not Rosa!"

Her laughter echoed all about him. It came from everywhere, from all sides at once.

"What's so funny!" he shrieked at her.

"We're not alone," said the red-haired girl as she laughed. "*We're not alone!*"

The feeling of being watched grew to a maddening degree. All about him was darkness and cold and desolation. Yet he was certain he felt eyes upon him. "Where!" he shouted. "Where are they!"

The girl, laughing too hard to speak, pointed downward to the ground.

Ben looked down. He was standing barefoot on loosely packed earth. As he stared, the ground seemed to move. An uncanny sensation came over him. The earth moved and shifted, as if something were trying to come out.

"Oh God," he moaned, embracing himself in a shiver.

As if something were trying to come out.

"Oh, sweet Jesus, no!" he whispered.

The girl was gone. Ben stood alone on the trembling mound of earth. He felt as if he stood on the edge of creation, teetering upon a precipice of oblivion.

He did not want to look down. He knew what he would see, and that it would frighten him to death.

With eyes stretched wide and nearly out of their sockets, he gaped down at the earth.

Suddenly it broke open.

"*Oh God!*" he cried, sitting bolt upright.

A heavy sweat covered Ben's body, and the mangled bedspread was drenched. He had perspired right through his clothes and to the sheets below.

Ben's teeth chattered. His body trembled uncontrollably. "Oh God, oh God," he said over and over again.

The bedroom was dark and cold. The air was freezing. Beyond the curtains, against the windows could be heard a heavy November rain. In an instant he had all the lights on, and was turning the thermostat up. With jerky, erratic movements he stripped off his clothes and plunged into a hot shower, scalding his body under a fierce spray. He screwed his face into a frown as the water pummeled him, trying to push the vision of the nightmare from his mind.

Then he put on fresh clothes, toweled his hair dry and went straight to the kitchen for some black coffee. He turned on every light along the way.

At the sink, however, Ben finally stopped. There was no running from the memory, from the picture that had nearly scared him to death. All the moving and working and lights and coffee would not prevent that scene from having its way. Because now it was in the open. For years Ben had been able to push it into his subconscious, hide it under layers and layers of living. He had not thought of it in over sixteen years, but he thought of it now—the nightmare that had brought it out—and there was no longer a way to run from it.

Ben covered his face with his hands and let a sob escape his lips. Then slowly, as if approaching from a great distance, his mother's voice gradually came back to him.

She was saying, "Benjamin Messer, today you are thirteen years old. You are now a man. It is your duty to be the son your father wanted, because he died protecting you. I've never told you how your father died, Benjamin, only that it was at the hands of German beasts. Now you should know."

A tear fell between Ben's fingers as he stood at the kitchen sink reliving that scene of twenty-three years before. And he experienced the same sorrow, the same anguish as he had then.

"Benjamin," said Rosa Messer gravely. "You should know your father was killed by the Nazis. You should know he died defending Zion for Jews everywhere. He did not go as a lamb to his death like those at Auschwitz, but fighting like a lion of God. I watched, Benjamin, from behind a fence, as the German beasts took your father out of the compound, stripped him naked and forced him to dig a hole with a shovel. Then, Benjamin, the German beasts put your father into that hole and buried him alive."

Ben knew it had been a long time since he had eaten and yet the idea now of food was most repugnant to him. Able at least to drink coffee, he thickened it up with cream and sugar and downed two cups before he began to feel better.

The nightmare had had an incredible impact on him. Now it all came back to him, how twenty-three years ago, when his mother had first told him the truth of his father's death, Ben had started having these same nightmares. They were never exactly the same, except for that one aspect: the feeling of something moving beneath his feet. He had awakened to tears and severe sweat many times, and had even, on occasion, cried out in his sleep. It was not only the burial of his father that had made Ben's boyhood a horror, but also the other tales of Rosa's concentration camp experiences that she had felt so compelled to hound her child with. The long evenings of listening to the stories, of imagining the atrocities, of seeing his mother weep for hours on end; all this had made childhood a misery for Ben Messer, to the point of his having wished he had never been born a Jew.

The last time he had given thought to his father or Majdanek had been the last time he had sat and spoken with Solomon Liebowitz. He was nineteen years old then and it was the last time he had cried.

Ben reached for the scattered pages of translation and tried to put them in order.

It had hurt him to part with Solomon, for Solomon had been the one joy in his youth. A friend he had loved and confided in and depended upon. But at the same time Ben knew he had to escape the environment of his childhood and start fresh in new surroundings. The old Brooklyn streets were too heavy with memories. He had to run away from them.

His translation of Scroll Five was a long one—the longest Scroll yet—and consequently very disorderly. Lines were scratched out.

Some words written over other words. Marginal notes that ran into
the text. And at points a totally incomprehensible handwriting.

Ben looked at the phone, then at the clock. It was six-thirty. He
wondered if Judy Golden was home.

She was wet again, but grinning all the same. "It's good for me,"
she said as he hung up her sweater to dry. "I could park closer, but I
like to walk in the rain."

Judy again wore jeans and a T-shirt. Her hair was damp and clinging to her skull, giving her a drowned-kitten look. "Thanks for dropping everything and coming over," said Ben.

"Didn't have to drop a thing. I'm anxious to read the Scroll. And
you say it's the longest one yet?"

They went into the living room, where all the lights were on and
the air was warm. Against the rainy night, it was a very cozy atmosphere.

"This time I brewed real coffee for us," he said, heading for the
kitchen. Judy sank onto the couch, kicked off her boots and drew her
knees up to her chest, wrapping her arms about her legs. Ben
Messer's was a comfortable apartment, not at all like her own, which
was disorderly and untidy and occupied by an enormous dog. A
mouth-breather, at that. Judy had noisy neighbors on either side and
a ten-foot monster living overhead. She rarely had the peace and
quiet Ben so fortunately enjoyed.

He came in with the coffee and set it down on the low table. Sitting next to her, he pointed to the pile of papers by the tray and
said, "Scroll Five. In all its illegible glory."

She grinned. "You know, as I was leaving last night, I stood in the
doorway of your den and watched you work. Wow, you sure were
concentrating. I cleared my throat a few times and you didn't even
hear me. And your hand was writing a hundred miles an hour! It
must be an exciting Scroll."

"Read for yourself."

With coffee cup in one hand and the papers in her lap, Judy
started to read Scroll Five.

For a long time, the only sound to be heard was the heavy rain
dashing against the windows. Occasionally the heater could be heard

going on and off as the thermostat kept the atmosphere a perpetual temperature. And Judy's breathing, soft and low, while she read the Scroll.

Ben was close at her side, absently stroking Poppaea Sabina, who had claimed his lap. He couldn't take his eyes off Judy's face, wondering about her, wondering about his having called her.

As her large brown eyes went slowly across the lines of translation, Ben realized with fascination that she was at that very moment reliving a day back in ancient Jerusalem. And he wondered: Is this why I need her here? To share David's experiences?

In the heat and the silence of the apartment, with the autumn rain steadily pelting the windows, Ben came one step closer to understanding his need to have Judy Golden at his side. For in the heat and the silence, and drifting away on the distant sounds of the November rain, Ben Messer thought he heard a gentle whisper in the nether regions of his mind. And it said: *She's here because David wants her here.*

When Judy was finished, she did not make a move, but continued to stare down at the last line she had read. In her left hand, poised near her lips, was a cup of cool coffee. By her side sat Ben, hardly breathing, drifting in a twilight of his own.

Finally she broke the spell. "It's beautiful," she whispered.

Ben looked at her, trying to focus his eyes. What had he been thinking about? Something about David . . . Ben shook his head and saw Judy come into sharp focus. His mind had wandered. He couldn't remember what he had been thinking of. Something about David . . .

But it was gone now.

Ben cleared his throat. "Yes, it is beautiful. You know, I get sort of a strange feeling when I read David's words. Like . . . almost as if he's talking directly to me. Do you know what I mean? It's as though he might at any minute say, 'Now, Ben . . .'"

"Well, obviously you feel some sort of kinship with him. You do have some things in common. Same age, both Jews, both scholars of the Law . . ."

Her voice drifted from his consciousness. Ben's eyes wandered over the walls and came to rest on a watercolor of the Pyramids and the Nile. Another voice replaced Judy's now, coming from very far away and saying, "Benjy, your father always said that the Lord knows the way of the righteous, but the way of the ungodly shall perish."

Jonah Messer. Jonah ben Ezekiel.

Then he thought of Saul, so robust and brawny beside the gentle, poetic David. And he thought of Solomon Liebowitz, bloodying the noses of the Polish bullies.

Can it all be coincidence? he wondered in confusion. I don't understand. It seems too much—

Judy's voice came filtering back. "I'm sure you see a lot of yourself in David, and that's why his words mean so much."

He squinted at her, trying again to bring her face into focus. There was another thought now . . . strange . . . elusive . . . I see a lot of myself in David. I see a lot of David in myself. What did it mean? What does all this mean? The coincidences . . . David talking to me—

Judy leaned forward to put her coffee cup on the glass table, and the movement, the sound of it, snapped Ben out of his reverie. He shook his head a second time. Strange thoughts. Can't imagine what put them there. Must be too hot in here. Maybe I'm hungry.

"Would you like something to eat?"—startled by the loudness of his own voice.

"No, thanks. Bruno and I scarfed just before you called. The coffee's fine, thanks."

They continued to sit and listen to the soft patter of rain on the window behind them, imagining the cold bare trees and the shiny sidewalks, until Judy asked offhandedly, "Why did you become a paleographer?"

"What?"

"Why did you become a paleographer?"

"Why? Well . . ." He frowned as he searched for an answer. "No one's ever asked me that before. I don't really know. Just interested in it, I guess."

"All your life?"

"As far back as I can remember. As a boy, ancient manuscripts used to fascinate me." Ben picked up his cup and took a noisy sip. It was true. No one had ever asked him that before, and consequently he had never thought about it. Pondering it now, Ben had no idea why he had entered the field of paleography. "Just fell into it, I guess."

"It is interesting. But you've got to have patience, which I don't have. Did you have a lot of religious training as a child?"

"Yes."

"I didn't. My parents were Reform Jews. And even at that they weren't observers of any laws. I don't recall ever knowing the difference between Yom Kippur and Rosh Hoshanah." She sipped her coffee some more and deliberated over her next words. "Were you very little when you left Germany?"

"I was ten."

She regarded him with those large eyes that were so expressive and compelling, and Ben knew what she was thinking. It was a subject he had never broached with anyone, not even Angie, and he recognized himself dangerously close to entering upon it.

"Do you have any brothers or sisters?"

"No."

"You're lucky. I was one of five kids. Three brothers and a sister, and I was in the middle. God, what a madhouse. My father was a tailor, he owned his own shop, and could afford to keep us in comparative comfort. Rachel, my little sister, still lives with my parents. The others are all married. You know"—she let out a little laugh—"I so often wished I had been an only child. You were lucky."

"Well, I don't know," he said distantly. How many times had he, as a boy, wished for brothers and sisters? "Actually, I did have an older brother. But he died before I really knew him."

"That's too bad. Do you remember much about Germany?"

Ben let his gaze settle upon Judy, feeling strangely comfortable talking with her this way. He knew he was being drawn out, that by speaking of her own past he would feel at ease speaking about his own.

"You want to know what it was like to have been a Jew in Germany during the war," he said finally.

"Yes."

Ben looked thoughtfully at his hands. This seems to be the day for letting skeletons out of the closet, he thought. First Angie, then the nightmare, and now this. One revelation after another. "You know, I've never spoken to anyone about that period in my life. Not even my fiancée knows much about me before the age of twenty, and she's quite content to leave it that way. Why are you so interested?"

"It's just my nature, I guess. I like to know about people. What makes them tick. What makes a Jew stop being a Jew."

"How do you know I once really was one?"

"You said you had a religious childhood."

"Yes . . . I did say that, didn't I? All right, I'll give you that. I did leave Judaism. I wasn't just born into it and it ended there, like you. I was once a practicing Jew and then I willfully left it. In fact, it was more than that. I stalked away from it and slammed a door in its face. Satisfied?"

She shrugged her shoulders. "That's not very theological of you."

"Never said it was. Anyway . . ." His voice and eyes trailed away from Judy. "Maybe I just wasn't meant to be a Jew. God knows, I had enough training in childhood. Hebrew was as natural a tongue to me as Yiddish. I went to yeshiva and attended synagogue every Saturday. Then, when I was nineteen, I decided it just wasn't for me. And so I left it altogether."

"Are you an atheist now?"

Again he was caught off guard. "Boy, you don't hedge about asking personal questions, do you? Are *you* an atheist?"

"Not at all. I do cleave to Judaism in my own fashion."

"A Judaism of convenience."

"If you prefer."

"Yes, I'm an atheist. Does that surprise you?"

"In a way. Only because it seems weird to devote your life to studying religious writings without being religious yourself."

"Good God, Judy, you don't have to be a grasshopper to study entomology!"

She laughed. "That's true. But still, I'll bet you know the Torah better than any rabbi."

Ben's eyebrows flew up. Once before, somewhere in the hazy past, someone had said the same thing. He could not remember now who had said it, but it had generated the same reaction in his mind. Just as back then, Ben now found himself thinking: It is rather odd that I should know more about the Torah and Judaism than probably the local rabbi, and yet there is this profound difference . . .

What is religion, after all? It's more than knowing something, more than memorizing, than being an expert. It's *feeling* something.

And that feeling—usually called faith—was absent in Ben.

"So why atheism?" he heard Judy ask. "Why not give Christianity a try? Or Zen?"

"It wasn't Judaism I left, it was God. Some people don't need religion. It doesn't bring peace of mind to everyone, you know. To some people, religion can be a sorrow."

"Yes, I suppose . . ." Her eyes went back down to the stack of papers in her lap. "I wonder how it turns out for David. Do you suppose he became a great rabbi? Maybe even a member of the Sanhedrin?"

Ben also fell to staring at his sheets of translation. He pictured a seventeen-year-old Judean, with black wavy hair down to his shoulders and the brooding eyes of a prophet.

David, David, thought Ben. What is it you're trying to tell me? What horrible deed is coming up that you've taken the courage to confess, to seal in hidden jars, and then to protect with a powerful curse?

And that curse . . . Ben's eyes clouded over. Is it possible it really has some power? Could it possibly affect me? Is that why I'm having nightmares, why I'm losing sleep, why I fight with Angie and why I think David is taking over my life? Is it possible the Curse of Moses is working? . . .

"Dr. Messer?"

He looked at Judy. She had been talking and he hadn't heard.

"It's getting late, so I should get to the typing."

Why am I thinking such strange things? Why am I thinking thoughts I've never had before, as though someone else were putting them there . . . ?

"Yes, the typing . . ."

They stood together and stretched their legs. Ben looked at his watch and was startled by the lateness of the hour. Where had the time gone?

Judy typed late into the night, often pausing for as long as five minutes at a time, and while she did so Ben sat alone in the darkness of his den. The clickety-clack of the keys was not as disturbing as the periods of silence, so that, at one point when she seemed to have stopped altogether, Ben got up and peered around the doorway. Judy was seated at the typewriter, her chin in her hands, and staring off into space. After another minute, as if suddenly remembering herself, she resumed typing again.

Ben sat back in his chair and webbed his fingers behind his head. His mind strolled back over the events of Scroll Five, lingering a while with Rebekah, envisioning the lessons on the porch of the

Temple, writing that first letter to his father, being surprised that Eleazar had known about drawing the widow's water. Those were good days, back in Jerusalem, living in the rabbi's house. Ben wished he could go back to those years, for they were sweet memories—

"Dr. Messer?"

He dropped his hands and sat up. "Yes?"

"I finished it."

"Great." He got to his feet. "You know what? I'm suddenly hungry. Do you like pizza?"

"Well, yes—"

"Listen, I'm going to dash down the street and get us one, with everything on it. I don't think I've put anything in my stomach since, well, since I can't remember when." He headed for the coat closet. "It won't take me long, they're just down the street and they're pretty fast. I usually go to them when I have a lot of work to do. And I'll get a bottle of cheap wine to go with it. How's that?"

"Just fine."

After he left, Judy wandered about the apartment and inspected some of the art objects that were about. There was a preponderance of items from the Middle East, many archaeological artifacts, some tourist souvenirs, and the rest the usual expensive knickknacks found in better homes. As she stood before the watercolor of the Pyramids and the Nile, the phone rang.

Judy answered it without hesitation. "Hello?"

There was a brief silence on the other end and then the sound of hanging up.

As Judy walked away, the phone rang again. This time she answered it, "Dr. Messer's residence," but the party still hung up.

It did not ring a third time, and when Ben finally got home with the wine and the pizza and Judy told him about the calls, he merely shrugged and said, "If it's important they'll call back."

They spread out the carton on the coffee table, brought glasses and napkins from the kitchen and proceeded to dig in.

"You have some interesting things around your apartment," said Judy, licking strings of cheese off her fingers.

"All booty from my travels."

"I like that painting there."

"The Pyramids? Yes, it's one of my favorites. It brings back memories." He laughed to himself. "You know, there's a trick the camel drivers pull on you at the Pyramids. It's a tourist attraction to ride a camel around them and it only costs a few piasters. However, as you're jogging along atop the nasty beast and really enjoying yourself, the camel driver starts to hand you some spiel about how he's taken a liking to you and would like to give you an extra-long ride as a present from him to you. No one can flatter you like an Arab, so naturally you accept. The camel driver runs alongside as you bounce your way out into the desert, far enough away so that you can't be heard and the people around the Pyramids look like ants. Then the camel driver turns to you, while you're sitting atop his ill-tempered animal, and tells you it will cost five American dollars to get back."

"You're kidding! Did that happen to you?"

"It sure did. And I had to pay him, too, or risk getting stomped on by that beast of his. And it's a long walk back over the sand dunes."

"Did he get away with it?"

"Not at all. As soon as we got back I found a Tourist Policeman and reported the incident to him. He was very good about it and made the man give me my money back. The Tourist Police are everywhere in Egypt, and they can be quite helpful sometimes."

"I envy you. The closest I ever got to the East was a trip I made to Brooklyn last year. Have you ever been there?"

"You might say I have. I grew up there."

"You're kidding. Where's your Brooklyn accent?"

"I worked very hard to lose it."

"You sound like a Californian."

"Thank you."

"Why? Didn't you like Brooklyn?"

Ben put his wineglass down and wiped off his face and hands with a fresh napkin. He was full now and the wine was having an effect. He leaned back and gazed straight ahead. "It's hard to say. In a way I like Brooklyn, and in a way I don't."

"Painful memories?"

"Some of them. Not all of them." He was thinking of Solomon Liebowitz.

"Is that where your brother died?"

Ben slowly brought his face around so he could look at Judy. "My brother died in a concentration camp in Poland."

"Oh," she barely whispered.

"He was just a little boy and he starved to death. In fact, my father also died there."

"Where?"

He closed his eyes and rolled his head away. "It was called Majdanek, in Lublin, Poland. About a hundred twenty-five thousand Jews died there. Two of them were my father and brother."

"How did you escape it?" she asked softly.

"I don't really know. My father was very outspoken against the Nazis and fought them where he could. Before they came to our house, neighbors warned us and so my father was able to get me away with their help. I was taken into a sympathizer's home while my father and mother and brother were taken away. He hadn't had time to hide them as well."

"What happened to your mother?"

"She lived through it and got out in 1944 when the Soviets liberated them."

"Well . . ." Judy also put her glass down and quietly wiped her hands on a napkin. She knew that Ben Messer's confession to her had not been easy, that he would sooner not have told her, and because of it Judy felt a tremendous responsibility.

"I didn't lose any family in the war. I don't think any of us— cousins, aunts, uncles—were touched by it. I can only, in a very small way, sympathize with you."

"What the hell. It happened over thirty years ago."

"But still—"

"I was five when my mother was able to get me. We continued to stay with friends, who somehow helped her find a job. She was an excellent seamstress and was able, believe it or not, in those postwar days to find enough work to save up money. Five years later, when I was ten, we emigrated to America. My mother worked long exhausting hours to support us here. I can remember her sitting all day and all night by a single lamp with a pile of alterations by her feet. She was a skilled and conscientious worker and never lacked for customers. But the pay was low and the work long and hard. It made her prematurely old."

He turned to look at Judy again. There was moisture in his eyes. "That, and Majdanek."

Judy remained silent, recognizing that fresh wounds had been opened, and sat quietly until he chose to go on.

"Majdanek had made her sick and old. When we came to America she was thirty-three years old and everyone thought she was my grandmother. Growing up with her was an experience in itself. She talked incessantly of my father and brother, often as if they were still alive. It wasn't easy, the two of us alone in a strange country, and I suppose it helped her to keep sane by talking about her loved ones. She was a doting, overpowering mother. She smothered me with her love and concern. And I can't blame her. I was all she had."

Ben's face twisted in a sardonic smile. "I remember, I could never keep my shoelaces tied. What kid can? But it was a thing with her. She would become so upset by it and threatened to sew them shut right over my feet. 'David,' she would say, 'if you trip on these laces and break your neck, then I shall be all alone. Don't you love your mother?' Poor thing lived in constant fear of losing me. I'm surprised she even let me go to school."

"I can understand her feelings," Judy said softly. "But why did she call you David?"

"What?" He brought his head up. "She didn't. I meant Benjy. She called me Benjy."

Judy cleared her throat and moved to the edge of the couch. "It's late, and I have to be going."

"Oh, sure."

She stood up and looked around for her purse. "Thank you for the pizza," she said in a tight voice. "It was kind of you."

Ben went to retrieve her sweater, which was now warm and dry. As he helped her on with it, he said, "I'll let you know as soon as I get Scroll Six."

"Okay."

He opened the coat closet and withdrew his jacket. "I'll walk you to your car. There's no telling who is out there at this hour."

They went down the stairs and out onto the wet street in a somber silence. Judy kicked brown leaves with her feet as they walked, feeling as if she had spent longer than just an evening with Ben Messer. At her car, they stood in the gentle mist trying to say good night. It had not been a casual visit—a lot had been said, a lot laid bare. Now Judy Golden shared Ben's secrets; she no longer stood at the periphery of his life.

He was a head taller than she and so had to look down to smile at her. Droplets were gathering on his glasses, obscuring his vision, but he could see her smiling back. Between their eyes passed a special communication.

Finally she murmured, "Good night," and got into the car. He stood back as she warmed up the engine, and then waved as she pulled away. Watching her taillights disappear down the dark street, Ben whispered, "Shalom," and walked slowly back to his apartment.

CHAPTER NINE

••▸———◈▸◉◂◈———◂••

Ben felt awful when he awoke the next morning. Long after Judy had left, he had sat up and finished off the rest of the wine. Then he had held his face in his hands and cried for a long time. When it occurred to him, sometime after midnight, that he had not shed a tear in seventeen years and yet today he had cried twice, Ben drifted off into a sleep of bits and pieces. Bizarre dreams haunted him again. Scenarios in which he played varying roles: first himself, then David, then his dead father, then his dead brother. More and more frightening memories came rushing back. The more he remembered, the more that followed close behind. All the bottling up and storing away of his painful past was now suddenly for naught.

For some reason, Ben could no longer keep the past from coming back.

His ten o'clock class was a lecture on classical Greek as an aid to the archaeologist. Ben showed slides and spoke in a monotone. Most of the time he was not present. He kept thinking of David at Eleazar's feet on Solomon's porch; of David carrying the widow's water; of Eleazar's deep affection for his youngest pupil; of Rebekah . . .

Later, in his office, with the door closed and locked, Ben meditated amid a cloud of pipe smoke, oblivious of the passage of time and of present realities.

Twenty-two years ago, walking through the brown slush of Brooklyn, the teen-age sons of Polish immigrants had shouted at Ben and Solomon, "We'll get you, you Jesus killers!"

That night, as they ate a simple meal at the kitchen table, Ben had asked his mother what the Polish boys had meant. Rosa Messer had put her knife and fork down and looked wearily at her son. "The goyim worship a dead Jew, Benjamin, and they say we killed him."

"Where was this? In Poland?"

A dry smile had wrinkled her face. "No, Benjamin. In Poland it was the Jews who were killed by goyim. The man they talk about lived many centuries ago. Romans crucified him for speaking out against Caesar. But somehow"—she shook her head sadly—"over the years the story got distorted and the Jews were blamed instead."

Ben had never heard the Jesus story before, and wondered what there was about it that caused millions of Christians to believe in it. Rosa Messer's knowledge was sparse, and it was a slanted view. As Ben had no Gentile friends, and as his own friends were as ignorant of the tale, he had gone elsewhere for clarification.

"You should not taint yourself, Benjamin Messer, by listening to the goyim words," one of his yeshiva teachers had said. "It is enough to know that they profaned the Covenant of Abraham and established a false one of their own. The way to fight the lies of the goyim is to study the Torah and keep holy its laws."

Nowhere had Ben been able to satisfy his desire to know more about the Jesus of the Christians, and so he had decided to read their words for himself. In as hidden a corner as he could find, beyond the eyes of any Jews that might happen by, Ben had sat in the public library with the New Testament spread before him.

His teachers and rabbi had taught him that the way to defend the Torah against the goyim was to know it by heart, to practice its laws rigorously, and to avoid the contamination of Christian words. But this had not satisfied Ben, whose curiosity had driven him to committing a deed that would have horrified his elders. Ben had felt in his heart that, to defend the Torah against the goyim, one had to know what the goyim were saying and what they believed in. The enemy had also to be studied.

So Ben, in his curiosity and drive to understand what set Jews apart from Christians, had read the New Testament one wintry day.

There was a knocking at the door and a familiar voice. "Dr. Messer? Are you in there?"

He jumped up and opened the door to Judy Golden.

"Dr. Messer. It's two-fifteen. I took a chance that you might be here—"

"What?" He looked up at the clock. "Oh, Jesus Christ, where have I been?"

"Everyone is waiting in class—"

"Let's go." He grabbed his briefcase and they hurried off down the hall.

After profuse apologies to the students, Ben launched awkwardly into a lecture. He was totally unprepared for them, but was able, by his wit, to offer some semblance of an organized lesson. His eyes frequently rested on Judy Golden, who sat staring at him the whole time. And as he spoke, Ben was conscious of the time.

There would be a mail delivery soon. Scroll Six would arrive and be waiting at the post office for him to claim it with the yellow slip. Once again David ben Jonah would speak to him.

David ben Jonah. Ben had dreamed a lot about him last night. Had dreamed that he was David back in Jerusalem and walking the streets with Saul and Rebekah. He had dreamed of warm evenings in Magdala, with Rosa Messer frying fish over an open fire. He had many brothers and sisters in the dream and a happy childhood. So pleasant, in fact, had the dream of David ben Jonah been that, upon awakening this morning, Ben had been sad to find they were only dreams.

The class ended at last, after two hours of struggling with his attention span. It was not easy, for Ben found he once again slid into reveries about David or his mother or boyhood in Brooklyn. Ben had to put forth a real effort to remain in the present. And when it all finally came to an end, he seized his briefcase and rushed out before anyone else had even stood up.

So fourteen-year-old Benjamin Messer, in an attempt to understand why the goyim hated him without their even knowing him, had read the New Testament.

At first it had been very confusing, for the first four sections, called the Gospels, did not exactly agree. There seemed to be many discrepancies between them. The part called the acts of the Apostles had seemed an interesting story in history. But the subsequent letters that led to Revelations offered up no further information about the man named Jesus. And so Ben had to rely solely upon the four Gospels and could not, though he had earnestly tried, see in them the foundations for one of the largest religions in the world.

That Jesus had been a good Jew was obvious. That he was probably a rabbi was also apparent. But that the proceedings of his trial followed just as they were written seemed somehow incomprehensible. Something about it had seemed wrong to young Ben: the convening of the Sanhedrin at night, the matter of a Roman procurator appealing to a mob for his decision, and the punishment of crucifixion instead of death by stoning. He had read and reread those Gospels many times and began to know them by heart. At the core of them, Ben knew, was the genesis of anti-Semitism among Christians. For, according to these holy books, Jews were guilty of the murder of their Christ.

And yet it could not be so. Young Ben had been able, in a way, to feel the illogic of the trial and death sequence, but had not, in his inadequacy, been able to pinpoint the problems. It was not until years later, in college, that Ben had finally understood.

It was so simple, really. The Gospel account was full of errors and misrepresentations. First of all, there was the problem of the Sanhedrin—the Jewish high tribunal—convening at night, which it never did. Second, if the Jewish leaders accused and condemned Jesus of blasphemy (as they did in Mark 14:64), then the punishment would have been death by stoning. Third, it would seem Pilate's charge against him was a political one and not the same as that of the Sanhedrin (Mark 15:1-2). Fourth, a great deal was known of the character of Pilate from ancient historians, and that such a tough-minded and arrogant man should consult a Jewish mob in his decisions, that he should appear weak before them, was the height of ludicrousness. And the fifth point was that crucifixion was solely a Roman punishment, practiced only by Romans and for the crime of treason; and nailed to the gibbet above his head had been a description of Jesus' crime—claiming to be King of the Jews. Clearly an act of treason.

So the problem arises: how did it come about that the Jews put Jesus to death?

Ben sat in his car long after the motor was turned off and stared into the darkness of the parking garage. If one looked for the solution in the Gospels, it was not there, for they offered only illogical

Math 10:5 Jesus came only for the Jews.

and confusing contradictions. The answer was easily found, however, in comparing the Gospel account within the framework of history.

The Gospel of Mark was written shortly after the destruction of Jerusalem when there was fierce anti-Jewish feeling at Rome. Unable to convert Gentiles to the new Christianity if a Roman governor was the one to have killed their Messiah, Mark had simply shifted the blame from Pilate to the Jews, a simple solution to getting his Gospel accepted in Rome.

As Ben walked slowly away from the car, he shook his head sadly. So much for Jesus killers!

A scrap of paper was attached to the large battered envelope that fell out of his mailbox, and on it was jotted a hasty note from his neighbor. The mailman had been by again with another registered letter, and had been about to put a yellow claim slip in Ben's box when the musician had happened by. He had signed for it again.

Ben clutched the envelope with immense gratitude; he was going to buy that guy the most expensive bottle of wine he could find.

Then he rushed upstairs as fast as he could, dashed inside and into his den, where he fell into the chair and proceeded to tear open the envelope. On top was the usual badly typed note from Weatherby, and inside, another sealed envelope. It was thick and felt as if it contained many photographs. Tossing out Weatherby's note without even reading it, Ben tore the second envelope open and gently withdrew the pictures.

Before him was the familiar handwriting of David ben Jonah.

Rebekah was a shy and quiet girl, often timidly hiding behind her veil in my presence. I don't know when I first began to love her, but it was a growing, gradual thing. I do not know how Rebekah felt toward me, for she often cast her eyes down when I looked at her. I thought of her as a fragile, little bird, so delicate and precious. She had tiny hands and feet and small freckles on her face. And whenever she did look at me with those lovely pale green eyes, I thought I saw joy.

I should have been happy in my love for sweet Rebekah, yet I was not, for thoughts of her often made it difficult for me to concentrate on my studies. Eleazar noticed this and gave me wise counsel. But it was not easy to follow. I was seventeen and would have loved to take Rebekah to wife. Yet what had I to offer her? I was poor. As a student of the Law, I had to live modestly and take joy in the honor of attending upon the rabbi. My clothes were coarse and plain. Whenever I saw her, I tried to cover the frayed edges of my cloak or hide the places where I had sewn patches. Rebekah seemed not to mind my poverty, and yet I do not know if she would have been my bride under such circumstances.

There were several years before me yet under Rabbi Eleazar before I would be my own man, and even then, once a Doctor of the Law, it would take time to earn the money and prestige necessary to offer Rebekah.

I tell you all this, my son, because it has a direct bearing on what happened next—possibly the most crucial turning point in my life. And having caused that to occur, also inadvertently led to what happened later, the event which you must know the truth about, the real reason for my writing these scrolls.

But for now, I must tell you what my love for Rebekah coupled with my poverty caused to happen.

During our free time, which Eleazar now allowed us, Saul and I led a carefree life. One afternoon and evening each week we were free from our studies, and so we took to wandering the streets of Jerusalem, exploring the gardens beyond the city walls, or visiting the homes of friends. As we pushed our way through the press of the marketplace we smelled the pungent odors of exotic foods, of expensive perfumes, of tanned leather and of human sweat. We ogled at extraordinary sights; the slave market, the gates which saw daily the arrivals of foreigners, the beautiful Gentile women in carrying chairs, snake charmers, street musicians and the red-cloaked Roman soldiers.

Jerusalem with its many faces and voices and colors never ceased to entertain us. And yet, for the most part, my thoughts were of Rebekah. I visited with her as much as I could without scandalizing her, for we were not betrothed. And Eleazar said often to me: David ben Jonah, you must not let this infatuation take you away from the Law. If you ever once falter in your practice of God's Law, if you ever stray from it in such a way as to bring shame upon it, then it would be as if you had spat in the Sanctuary. For the Doctor of the Law is above all men in one respect: he is on this earth to protect Abraham's Covenant and to ensure that the Chosen People never stray from God. If, through your infatuation with Rebekah, you should let the people down, then you have let God down, and that is unpardonable.

But what can I do, Rabbi? She is ever in my thoughts. And when I sit near her I feel a strange weakness in my loins.

He replied: All men of God are tempted many times in their lives, and they must fight it. The keeping of God's Law is no easy task, and it is because of this that we are above other men. By our example, they will follow the Law. And the Law must come first, David. If you should abandon it for that girl, then it would be better if you had never been born.

So the struggle waged within me. There was no compromise. I must cleave to my studies and forget Rebekah. Yet I could not. And one night, my son, the flesh was victorious over my spirit.

Saul and I had eaten olives in one of the gardens beyond the walls, at the house of a man who lived alone and who enjoyed our company. When the sun started to set, he begged us to stay a while longer, for he was lonely, and so offered us some of his best wine. Saul and I had drunk very little of it in our lives, for Eleazar was forever reminding us of Noah's weakness. We stayed and drank some wine with him, intending to leave shortly. However, it seemed that once the wine warmed our blood, the resistance against more dwindled. And so we stayed and enjoyed the old olive merchant's wine.

When at last we left, I was quite heady and not in good control of myself. Saul, on the other hand, so large and brawny, seemed to have been little touched by it. We sang as we wound our way through Jerusalem's narrow streets, and came eventually, by chance, upon a notorious tavern. Neither of us had ever visited one before, so that our curiosity mounted as we stood outside its door, seeing the lights on the other side and hearing happy voices within. It was Saul who suggested we go inside and see, and I readily agreed.

At first we were a novelty, dressed poorly as we were and with our long black beards and side curls. Rarely seeing rabbinic students in their midst, the Gentiles asked us to sit with them and talk. They bought us mugs of unwatered wine, which we at first tried to refuse, but which we finally drank. As we did so, we stared openly at young girls who danced with their breasts bare and who let strange men freely touch them. Saul and I were astounded at this, and yet mesmerized at the same time. There were camel drivers in the crowded tavern, and Roman soldiers and other such men who had great knowledge of the world. They told us tales of strange people at the far ends of the earth, of sea monsters and mythical animals, and of faraway places that made our mouths hang open.

I don't know exactly when I met Salmonides; if he had been there all along or if he joined us later. All I recall is that at one point, in my stupor, I found him sitting next to me with a long white hand on my arm. He had a strange, ageless face with white hair and unfathomable blue eyes. He spoke Aramaic beautifully, as if it were his native tongue.

I must have been bemoaning my dilemma of Rebekah and poverty, for he said: There is one sure way to win a woman's heart, and that is through money. You need not give up your studies to secure the promise of marriage from her. You need only prove that, when the time of leaving school comes, you will be able to support her comfortably and respectably. Then she will agree to wait for you. I know this, for women are alike everywhere.

I tried hard to focus on his face, but could not. Through my haze I could hear Saul laughing with some men. Our table was laden with wine and cheese and pork sausages, all of which were so delectable that I stuffed myself on them. I was as drunk on the food as on the wine, and therefore paid little attention to what I said. I must have mentioned my small cache of money to Salmonides, for he went on to say: Money grows as do the cedar and the palm. Plant your shekels, my handsome Jew, and watch them sprout into mighty sesterces.

What are you? I asked. A sorcerer?

I am a stockbroker from Antioch in Syria. There is a fleet departing in a day from Joppa for Egypt. They will pick up great quantities of grain for Rome, and if all the ships make it to Ostia, the profits will be great.

What do you want of me?

The captain of these vessels needs financing to pay his crew. In return, he will share his profits. You, my friend, can buy a share of that profit now. Give me the money you have, and in six months I will give you in return a king's ransom.

And if the ships fail? I asked.

That is the chance all investors take. If they fail, as they sometimes do, then you will lose your money. On the other hand, if they make it to Ostia with the grain . . .

Had I been sober, my son, I would have laughed at the Greek and departed from him. But I was not. I was seventeen and drunk and desperate to win Rebekah.

I do not know at which point I left the tavern, but Saul must not have seen me, for he said later that he had not been aware of my absence. Whatever, I somehow found my way home to Eleazar's house, stumbled up to my room without waking anyone, unburied my small hoard of money and staggered back to the tavern. When I returned, the Greek had already drawn up a document of sorts, two copies of it, and although I did not read it, I readily affixed my seal to it. Salmonides took my money and gave me the piece of paper in return.

And that is all I remember of that evening.

Saul told me, the next day, that he had happened to look up and seen me asleep at a table where I sat alone. And so he had taken leave of the group with whom he had sat and had carried me home across his broad shoulders and had put me to bed. The next day was to be the worst of my life.

The shame was greater than any burden I had ever before carried. I humbled myself before Eleazar and poured my heart out to him. While I spoke, with my eyes to the floor, he listened in grave silence. He listened as I told him of my public drunkenness, of my keeping company with naked girls and disreputable Gentiles, of my having freely eaten pork and lastly of having turned all my money over to Salmonides.

When I was through, Eleazar sat in silence for only a moment, then he gave such a cry that it frightened me. He beat his breast and tore at his hair and cried out: What have I done to deserve this, O Lord? Where have I failed? Was this not the boy in whom I saw the most promise and who would have followed me as the greatest rabbi in Judea? What have I done to deserve this, O Lord?

Eleazar fell to his knees and made a great show of unhappiness. He blamed himself for my misdeed, claimed that he had not been a good enough teacher and cried that he had disappointed God by letting his best pupil go astray.

I wept with him also, wept until the tears soaked my sleeves and until I could cry no more. When all that came out of me were dry sobs, I looked at Eleazar and saw on his face how great his pain was.

You have contaminated God's Holy Law, he said grimly. David ben Jonah, by your own actions you have spat upon the Covenant of Abraham and shamed all Jews before God. Had I not taught you well? How is it that you could have strayed so and allowed yourself to sink so low?

Saul, who had not become drunk and who had refused the pork and who had not lost money to a Greek, was likewise in bad graces with Eleazar, and yet it was not the same. Eleazar had not prided in Saul as much as he had in me; he had not seen in Saul the successor to his own lofty office and the carrying on of his tradition. And so because of all of this, Saul was saved from being banished from the school.

It was not so with me. Eleazar looked upon my abominable sins as if they were personal affronts to himself. I had let *him* down, and I had dirtied the Law of God. There was to be no pardon for me.

Eleazar expelled me that day from his sight, and made a vow to never again think of me as his son. I gathered up my few poor possessions and went out into the street with no idea of where to go or what to do.

When Eleazar's door slammed behind me, it was as if God Himself had turned His back on me. Without Eleazar and the school, bearing this burden of shame, and knowing that I was no longer fit for Rebekah or to live among Jews, I contemplated taking my life.

Ben felt something on his cheek and, rubbing it, found a tear. The impact of David's words, the profound effect they had on him as he read them, astonished Ben. As if matching the ancient Jew's despair,

Ben felt sick inside, and horribly wretched. He had to go on. He had to read the last two fragments of Scroll Six. But his vision was blurred with tears, and his nose started to run. He needed a handkerchief.

Ben stood up from the desk, turned around and said, "Jesus Christ!"

Angie was standing in the doorway. "Hello, Ben," she said softly.

"Wow! Don't sneak up on me like that!" He put a hand on his chest.

"I'm sorry. But I knocked and knocked. Your car is downstairs, so I figured you were home. I let myself in with my key."

"How long have you been standing there?"

"Long enough to clear my throat a few times and get no response from you."

"Wow . . ." he said again, shaking his head. "For a while there I was back in Jerusalem . . ." Ben picked up the sheet of paper on which he had scratched his translation. "I don't even remember writing this. All I remember is being in Jerusalem . . ."

"Ben."

He turned to her.

"Ben, where were you last night?"

"Last night?" He rubbed his face. When was that, last night? How long ago? How many days, weeks ago— "Let me see . . . Last night. I was . . . here . . . Why?"

Angie turned away and wandered into the dark living room. A moonless night was shining through the open curtains, and all around was a chilly silence.

As Ben started to follow her, he felt himself drawn back to the den, and looking over his shoulder, saw the remaining untranslated portion of Scroll Six under the light. He was cold and hollow inside, depressed by David's words. He didn't want to tangle with Angie. He had to get back to Jerusalem.

"Ben." Angie spun around. "I called you last night, and a female voice answered the phone."

"What? That's impossible. You must have dialed the wrong number."

"She answered the phone: 'Dr. Messer's residence.' How many Dr. Messers do you suppose there are in West L.A.?"

"But that's silly, Angie—" He stopped short and frowned. "Wait a minute. I remember. That was Judy—"

"Judy!"

"Yeh. I went out for some pizza—"

"Judy who?" Angie's voice rose.

"A student of mine named Judy Golden who was over to do some typing for me."

"How nice."

"Oh, come off it, Angie. Jealousy doesn't become you. She did some typing for me and that's all there is to it. I don't have to account for my actions to you or anyone."

"That's right, you don't." Although he could not see her expression in the darkness, he could imagine it by the tone of her voice. She was trembling, trying to keep a hold on herself. Good old passionless, always-in-control Angie.

"Did you come over here for a fight? Is that it?"

"Ben, I came over because I love you. Can't you see that?"

"Don't get so melodramatic. I have one student over to do some typing for me and already we have to prove our love to one another. Jesus, Angie, can't you just believe me and leave it at that?"

A stunned silence fell over them. Angie was puzzled, perplexed. In the past, Ben had always been so predictable. She always knew how he would react and what he would say. Why were things so different now?

In a flat voice she said, "You've changed, Ben."

"And you have the gift of non sequitur." He laughed nervously. "If anyone has changed, doll, it's you. I never had to explain myself to you before. There was never a need of great protestations of love. What's gotten into you all of a sudden?"

She walked toward him, entering the small residue of light that came from the den, and as she did so, Ben was able to see the queer look in her eyes.

"It's not what's gotten into me," she said slowly. "It's what's gotten into *you*. Or rather . . ." Her eyes strayed from his face and settled on a point above his shoulder. "Rather . . . *who's* gotten into you." A small furrow appeared between her eyebrows as she frowned. "You haven't been the same since the discovery of those Scrolls. I've known you for almost three years, Ben, and I think I know you better than anyone else. But in the last few days you've been like a stranger. I'm losing you, Ben, I'm losing you fast, and I don't know how to get you back."

Seeing tears flood her eyes, Ben suddenly pulled Angie into his arms and pressed her face into his neck. An uncanny fear swept over him at that moment, and he felt as if he stood at the edge of a great, black abyss. He looked down but could see nothing but depths and depths of night. Clinging to Angie, he felt like a man drowning. He was a man suspended between sanity and insanity, between reality and nightmare, and Ben knew—in that moment—that even as he hung onto Angie for self-preservation, he knew he was sliding closer and closer toward the abyss.

"I don't know what it is, Angie," he murmured hurriedly into her perfumed hair. "I can't pull myself out of this Scroll business. It's almost as if . . . as if . . ."

She drew away and looked up at him with tears streaking down her cheeks. "Don't say it, Ben!"

"I have to, Angie. It's almost as if David ben Jonah were making a claim on me."

"No!" she cried. "You can get away from it. You can, Ben. Let me help you."

"But I don't want to, Angie. Can't you see that? From the very beginning, he's been slowly making a claim on me. *And now he's got me.* I don't want to run from him, Angie. He's here now and I can't escape him. *I must find out what it is he's trying to tell me.*"

The black abyss yawned before Ben, and he knew in the next instant he would fall.

"I'm no longer going to fight him, Angie. I must commit myself totally to David. The answer lies in those Scrolls, and I have to find it."

As Ben tumbled down into oblivion, leaving reality far behind him, he heard Angie's voice calling to him from a distance. "I love you, Ben. I love you so much I could die of it. But I'm losing you and I don't even know *to what.* If it were another woman—like that Judy person—then I would know how to fight back. But how can you fight *a ghost?*"

He turned away from her, feeling the magnetism of the remaining photographs. He had to get back to David.

"Please don't leave me!" she cried.

Ben was shocked by his actions. It was as if he had no control over his own body. For the first time in their relationship, Angie was exhibiting real emotion. The sight of her pale, trembling lips and mascara-streaked eyes startled him. He had never before known

Angie to make such a display. He had never known her even capable of it. And yet there she stood now, pleading with him, coming apart, and when it should have knocked Ben into sensibility, it did not.

"I can't help it, Angie," he heard himself say. "I can't explain what it is, but there's no longer any room in my life for anything but the Scrolls. I have to read David's words. He's reaching out to me."

"And I'm reaching out to you, Ben. My God, what's happening to you!"

But he had to walk away from her. He had left David ben Jonah on the brink of suicide, at the depths of misery and despair, and Ben had to get back to him. The need to read more and more of David's words was growing out of control. He was a prisoner of David's power.

As he sat again at his desk, turning his eyes to the Aramaic alphabet, Ben did not hear Angie quietly leave the apartment.

At the top of the next photograph was written: "Words cannot describe my wretchedness." David went on to depict his loneliness and despair as he wandered the streets of Jerusalem, without a friend, without a place to go, and—worst of all—abandoned by God. When he read the words "For one moment of weakness, I lost everything I had strived for; brought shame upon myself and my family; lost the woman I loved; and was abandoned by God. Can there have been a more wretched, despicable creature than I?" When he read these words, Ben put his head on his arms and wept. He cried as if he had been the one alone on the streets of Jerusalem without family or friend; as if he had been the one to shame his father's name and turn his loved ones against him; as if he, Ben Messer, had caused God's love to turn away from him.

It tore his heart and soul from his body, made him feel sick and cold and wretched. Taking David ben Jonah's sorrows upon himself, Benjamin Messer relived that abominable day of two thousand years ago.

And finally, unable to carry the burden of David's destitution any longer, Ben suddenly stood up and stumbled blindly to the phone. He dialed without thinking, and when she answered, he said in a voice not his own, "Judy, come over. I need you . . ."

CHAPTER TEN

◅━━◆━❉━◈━━▻

Words cannot describe my wretchedness. Was there ever before so miserable a creature as I, shamed among men? In my moment of drunkenness I had turned my back upon the Torah and had profaned its Laws. So now it was only just that God turned His back upon me. I wandered the streets like a dazed man, clutching my small bundle of possessions to me. I was in a state of shock and had no idea where to go. I could not further my family's shame by returning to Magdala, for I knew my father would turn me from his door. I dared not go to my sister's house and bring shame into her household. I had no money for an inn room, nor fare to travel outside of Judea. I had no skill, no trade with which to support myself. I could no longer look upon sweet Rebekah. And worst of all, I was abandoned by God. For one moment of weakness I lost everything I had strived for; brought shame upon myself and my family; lost the woman I loved; and was abandoned by God. Can there have been a more wretched, despicable creature than I?

All that remained to me were two choices: to stay in the city and beg for alms, or go out to the countryside and hope to earn some bread for field labor. Neither prospect was heartening, and I sorely wished I had never been born.

I walked all day and on past sunset, wandering strange streets and venturing into foreign parts of the city. When, at sunset, I was exhausted from walking, I chanced to rest at a well where several women were gathering the last of their water. Seeing them reminded me of the days I had spent filling Eleazar's cisterns and how, at the same time, I had devised a way to carry also the widow's water to her house. The shekels she had paid me were among those I had so foolishly given to Salmonides the night before. And their memory caused me bitter anguish.

As I sat at the edge of the well and gazed down, I saw the answer to my quandary at its murky bottom. To die would be so simple, so easy. Since there was no longer any reason for living, I would find escape in dying. And all I had to do was let go, fall . . .

But it was the voice of a woman nearby that stopped me from going any further. She had drawn her water and was ready to leave, yet lingered behind to watch me. She said: Good evening, brother, are you well? You look tired.

I glanced first over my shoulder to see who it was that she spoke to, and seeing no one, regarded her in surprise. She was an older woman, older possibly than my own mother, yet very handsome and well dressed.

She came closer to me. Are you well? she asked again.

Then I realized I had no cause to be surprised that she would speak to me, for, after all, how could she know of my shame?

I am not well, I replied. And I'm very tired.

Are you hungry, too? There was kindness in her voice.

So I said to her: Before you take pity on me, madam, it is fair I should warn you that I am a shamed man, an outcast among my own family. There is no man who will call me friend, no woman who will call me brother.

But she said: I am not interested in what you have done, only that you are tired and hungry. We have plenty of food in my house and a spare mat to sleep on. You are welcome to come with me.

I protested a second time: I am anathema, madam. You would take a cursed man into your home.

But she said: It is for God to judge you, not I.

And I protested a third time: Would you take a viper to your house?

And she smiled and said: Even the viper does not prey on its own kind.

Too weary to argue further, and lured by the offer of food, I went with the woman to her house. There I met several people who took me in as one of their own and shared bread with me. They were pious Jews who wore immaculate white robes and tephillin on their foreheads and wrists. That evening I was given a mat to sleep on, and the offer to remain as long as I wished. And not once, in all the time I was there, did they ask a single question of me.

I did not stay in Miriam's house for long—such was the good woman's name—for these were reverent people who prayed until their knees were hardened, and I felt that my presence tainted them. Not once did they wonder about the abomination I had committed, nor did they treat me as a stranger in any way, but seemed concerned only with my health. When, two days later, I announced that I must depart, they did not question me, but laid blessings upon me instead and put a few shekels in my purse.

Thus it was that I was given a new beginning in life, for once at the house of Miriam, I no longer considered the act of suicide. Although I by no means felt myself to be worthy before God or to even live among Jews, the few hours of rest and plates of good food had given me the strength and resolve to face my uncertain future.

On the day that I left Miriam's house, an idea came to me. With one shekel I purchased a new sheet of papyrus and went with it to the marketplace. Here I spread my cloak upon the dirt and, sitting upon it, called out to passers-by that I was a letter writer. The pay was meager and the hours of sitting long and strenuous, but this was the means by which I was able to survive in Jerusalem after my banishment from Eleazar's house. With Miriam's shekels I bought papyri, and with my education I wrote letters. So it was that, for the weeks that followed, I was able to secure a small room at a nearby inn and afford one meal a day.

And yet I remained wretched. I let my hair go unkempt and my clothes run to rags. I could never call any man my friend, nor look again upon the woman I loved. I would live out my life as a wretched letter writer amid the dung and flies of the marketplace, lose my identity and join the mass of faceless creatures who had also been abandoned by God.

One day, as I was sweating in the sun while dirt baked on my skin, I saw the hem of a familiar cloak come into view. Looking up, I could not believe my eyes, for it was Saul, and he was smiling down upon me.

Please go away, I cried at him, and tried to hide myself from his eyes. But Saul knelt in the dirt and regarded me gravely. He said: My dear brother, I have searched and searched this city for you. There has not been a day gone by that I have not studied the faces of those about me, hoping to glimpse my sweet David. How I have missed you!

When he would have embraced me, I pushed him away, saying: Do not contaminate yourself with my presence. Leave me alone and go your way. I have prayed that you had forgotten me and that my family thought me dead. Don't tell them, Saul, that you have found me!

His voice was heavy as he said: Indeed they think you are dead, for in three months no one has seen you or heard from you. We do not see you in the streets or meet you in the Temple for worship. It was only by chance today that I looked down and recognized my brother.

I cannot go to the Temple, Saul, for I would not profane God's holy ground. Tell me, what does my father think?

He was greatly saddened by what happened, David, and yet he prays daily that you come home to him.

Ironically, it was not my father's opinion that weighed heavily in my heart. And Eleazar? I asked.

The day you left, Eleazar tore his hair and put on the clothes of mourning. He wears them to this day, and has not once uttered your name. But listen, David, he prays twice as much now, and can be heard crying late into the night. Since you left it is a house of sadness we dwell in. David, I love you as my brother, I cannot live without you. Please come back!

Yet I knew I could not, for Eleazar was a proud man and I had tainted his Law.

Before Saul departed, I made him promise not to mention me or this visit to anyone; and to never come back. He gave me his promise.

A month went by before I was visited a second time. Rebekah, also having been searching the city for me, found me among the hawkers and donkeys and beggers, and she knelt before me to beg me to return. She said: I love you, David ben Jonah, and cannot bear to see you this way. Come to my house, my father will take you in.

Yet I knew I could not, for it was Eleazar I thought of, and he was a proud man and I had tainted his Law.

So torn apart had I been by Rebekah's visit and seeing the tears in her lovely eyes, so wretched had she made me feel, that I left my good spot in the marketplace and went to sit beyond the walls where I could not be found, but—alas—where the customers were fewer.

The day came when, as I sat in the dirt with flies buzzing about me and as I nibbled some hard cheese, a tall man stood before me in modest clothes. He stood with the sun at his back so that he was only a silhouette to me, and asked: What is your fee?

A shekel for the papyrus and writing, master, and two shekels for the leader of the caravan.

How far can you send a letter? he asked.

I am in contact with men who go as far as Damascus, as far Alexandria, and even to Rome. To send a letter beyond, as to Gaul or Britain, you must seek someone else.

My letter does not go that far, he said, and it is a very short one.

It will still be a shekel, master, I replied.

So be it. And he cleared his throat to dictate.

I spat upon my ink cake and mixed it with the tip of my pen. Then I poised my hand above the papyrus, ready to write.

This is to my son David who lives in Jerusalem, he said in a low voice. I want to say to him: My son, I have been wrong. I have been a vain and blasphemous man, taking God's judgment upon myself. It was not for me to judge you, but for God, and yet in my pride I did so. I loved you more than my own sons, for you were sharp-witted and expressed a unique passion for the Law. I was a selfish man, thinking only of how you would glorify my name once you entered the Temple as a scribe. When you committed the sins you did, I took them as a personal affront—not as an affront to God. And this was very wrong. I have been a weak and vain man and have caused my family to suffer through my selfish bitterness. And because of my indignation, I have caused you to stay away from the Temple and turn your back on God. Now I am asking you to come back to me, David, and forgive an old teacher his pride.

I gaped up at Eleazar in stunned silence. Silhouetted against the sun, he appeared thinner than before, and frail. His voice was tremulous, his eyes toward the sky.

When I would have kissed the hem of his robe, Eleazar reached down and brought me to my feet, and then we clasped as father and son might. He was so small in my arms, and now so short. I had never noticed Eleazar's physical stature before, or that I was taller than he.

You must come back to the Temple with me, he said with tears of joy in his eyes. And be my pupil again.

But I replied: I will return to the Temple with you, Rabbi, but only as a member of the congregation, not as your pupil. What has been done cannot be undone. That wretched night of my downfall six months ago opened my eyes and proved to me that I am not worthy to be a student of the Law. I ate pork and gazed upon the nakedness of young girls. I forgot all about God and Isarel in my greed for more money, and it can never be corrected. Saul is a good pupil, and he loves the Law. He would never allow himself the recklessness that I fell into, for he is a stronger man than I. Make him your best example, Eleazar, for that would be worthy of both of you.

He and I remained thus for a long time by the gate and cried upon one another's shoulders. Later, when we arrived home, there was much rejoicing among his family and the other pupils, and after I had changed into fresh clothes and washed the feet of everyone present, Rabbi Eleazar told us the story of the Prodigal son.

The next day I saw Rebekah.

Judy had to knock loudly several times before Ben opened the door. He was surprised to see her.

"Is there something wrong?" she asked. "Are you all right?"

"I . . . yes, I'm fine." He rubbed his forehead and frowned. "Is there something I can do for you?"

Judy was startled to see how haggard he was, how drawn and tired. "You telephoned me about an hour ago. You asked me to come over."

He raised his eyebrows. "I did?" Ben rubbed his forehead again. "I did . . . ?"

"Shall I come in?"

"Oh, sure! Sure!" He tried desperately to organize his thoughts as she swept past him and he closed the door behind her. Wasn't Angie here a minute ago?

"What time is it?" he asked thickly.

"It's ten o'clock, Dr. Messer. I came as quickly as I could . . ." Her voice trailed off. Judy saw the dark circles under his eyes, that his glasses were missing, that his blond hair was standing out from his head. "Don't you remember calling me?"

"I . . ." Ben massaged his temples. "Yes . . . now I do. But Angie was here. No, wait, she left. We had a fight and she left. But that was hours ago! Oh, Jesus."

Ben headed straight for the kitchen, where he started to fill the coffeepot with water. Feeling Judy's presence in the doorway and her eyes on him, he said, "I can't tell you how lost I got myself in this last Scroll. It's like I wasn't here at all, but drawn back two thousand years and reliving David's life . . ."

"You got another Scroll today?"

He looked up at Judy. It seemed ages since he had seen her in class at school. And yet it had only been that afternoon. So much had happened since then. David losing his money and falling into disgrace. Living like a beggar among the rabble of Jerusalem.

"Yes, I got Number Six today . . ."

"Is it—"

Ben looked down at his shaking hands. "Oh, Lord, what's happening to me! I can't believe I'm being so affected by those Scrolls, that I'm reacting this way. Jesus, I've got to get myself back together."

"Why don't you sit down, and I'll make the coffee?"

Ben left the kitchen and was gone for a few minutes. When he returned, he had in his hands the random papers on which he had written his translation. He stared down at them with a frown. "I don't remember writing this. So help me, Judy, I don't remember writing any of this. And yet here it is, Scroll Six, translated in its entirety."

She took the pages from him and glanced over the erratic hand-writing. It was only barely legible. "I've never gotten involved like that before," he went on. "Where I became so absorbed that I wasn't even aware of reading anything but actually *lived* the events I was reading about."

They took their coffee and the pages of translation and went to their usual places on the couch. Judy kicked off her shoes and curled her feet under her, making herself comfortable for the long, tedious reading. As she did so, Ben watched her. He felt a small sense of security with her at his side, like something he had never felt with Angie. Judy Golden had the remarkable capacity for truly understanding what he was going through, and Ben needed that now.

While she read, they hovered in a place between time and dimension. It was a moment of unreality because Ben knew at that moment, as her eyes took in the words he had written, that Judy was back in Jerusalem.

She let the papers fall in her lap as she gazed straight ahead and whispered, "That's fantastic . . . Utterly fantastic!"

Ben carefully picked up the pages and stacked them neatly on the coffee table. "Then you felt it, too?"

Judy turned to him. Her eyes were wide with imaginings. "Yes! How can you help but feel it! It's as though two thousand years doesn't exist at all between us."

"Did you see Jerusalem? Did you *feel* Jerusalem?"

Judy's eyes focused on the face of Benjamin Messer, and for a moment they flickered in perplexity. For the first time since she had started coming to visit him, she noticed something different about him.

"What do you see when you read these words?" she asked, watching his face closely.

"The same thing you see. The crowded streets of ancient Jerusalem, the mud-brick walls and towering buildings. I see a rainbow of foreigners in the busy marketplace. The refined streets of the Roman elite, the squalid quarter of the poor. I can hear the babble of many tongues and smell the smells of a thousand things. I feel the heat of the Judean sun upon my neck, and tread in the dust of Jerusalem's alleys."

While he spoke, Ben came alive. His face glowed and his gestures were animated. Judy listened to the excitement in his voice and watched the light behind his eyes, and slowly began to discern a hidden quality there . . . one which she had not seen before now.

By his motions and expressions, Ben Messer was talking like a man coming home after a long journey.

Judy picked up her cup and held it against her lips for a long time. The hot coffee aroma warmed her face and filled her nose with a delicious scent. And while she sat, half listening to Ben talk about Jerusalem, half reflecting on David ben Jonah's words, she came to the realization that the man sitting next to her had undergone some sort of change.

"What are you thinking about?" he asked suddenly.

Yes, definitely a change. His speech was somehow altered . . .

She said, "I was just imagining the picture you paint of Jerusalem. You certainly bring it to life."

"David has done it, not I. He makes me see things as they really are." He released a long sigh and then turned to smile at her. "You know what I like about you? You're a good listener. No, it's more than that. You're adaptable. You don't seem to care if there's a conversation going on or not. I could sit here in silence if I wanted and you'd sit patiently with me. And if I decided to talk, you'd listen. That's a rare quality, you know."

Judy looked away. She was not used to compliments. Flattery made her uncomfortable.

Ben fell to studying her profile for a moment, and wondered if he wasn't seeing her for the first time. Judy Golden was not exactly a pretty girl, but she had an interesting face. Large thoughtful eyes with long black lashes. A straight, sharp nose and small mouth. Sleek black hair that was always clean and shiny. Judy was a quiet, almost intriguing girl. And Ben was glad she was there.

"You know . . . I wonder . . ." His voice trailed off.

"What do you wonder?"

"If way, way back, my family does come from the Benjaminite tribe. Maybe that's why I was named Benjamin, and not for an uncle."

"It's possible. The tribes continue today in the Levis and Cohens and Reubens. If so, you're in good company. The first King of Israel, Saul, was a Benjaminite."

Ben nodded. "Saul . . ." he said slowly, picturing David's friend.

How similar their relationship was to his and Solomon's of long ago! The parallels were many: Solomon of larger stature than little Ben; Solomon of the free smiles and carefree manner that so easily won him friends; Solomon who had stayed in the rabbinic school while Ben had left it . . .

"So alike . . . so alike . . ." said Ben.

"I beg your pardon?"

"I was just thinking about a friend I had in my youth, a boy named Saul Liebowitz. Our relationship was a lot like that of David and Solomon." Ben suddenly shook his head. "No, I mean, it was David and Saul. Solomon was *my* friend."

Ben fell to staring at his hands, thinking about the decision David made to leave the study of the Law. He thought of his last visit with Solomon back in Brooklyn, when he had tried to express his need to get away from the orthodoxy.

"You know," he said aloud, but talking to himself, "back in those days, when I made the decision to come out to California and attend college, I had still intended to remain a Jew. I guess I was just fooling myself at the time. Or maybe I was afraid to be really honest with myself and my friends. But I had told Solomon that even though I was no longer interested in the rabbinate, I would still be a Jew. And yet that wasn't true. It was an act. Looking back, I can see now I had no intention of staying with Judaism. In fact, I couldn't get away from it fast enough."

He regarded Judy with clouded eyes. "You know something? I have always been secretly glad I don't look Jewish."

"Oh, please—"

"It's true. And none of my friends know I'm Jewish. It's like a skeleton in my closet. A rotten, moldering skeleton that seems to stink more and more. Oh God." He stood up abruptly and shoved his hands in his pockets. "This is insane! Listen to me, spilling out my deepest, darkest secrets to you again. I can imagine what you must be thinking."

"No, you can't," she said softly.

Ben looked down at her. There it was again, that strange need to have this girl at his side; a thin, fleeting concept that eluded his grasp so that he could not quite latch onto it and so understand the nature of this need. Hadn't he once sworn he wouldn't tell her about the next Scrolls? Hadn't he once before firmly decided to never again allow her these special confidences? Yet what was it, he wondered now, what nameless yearning overrode his rational process and caused him to repeatedly call her to his side?

Ben shook his head again. It was gone before he could seize upon it. It had something to do with David . . .

Ben strode away from her and took to pacing the floor in long strides. He walked back and forth in front of her like a lawyer before a jury, his mind already switching from one train of thought to another. It was uncontrollable, unpredictable, this rapid changing of moods. While Ben was not aware of it, others were, as was Judy, who watched his face melt from its previous preoccupation and now frown again into new thinking.

Something new now went on in Ben's mind and it showed on his face as something disturbing.

"You know, I've had the most unbelievable nightmares since I started translating the Scrolls. And during waking hours, I can't control my thoughts." He stopped where he was and stared.

She rose to face him. "Maybe the Scrolls remind you of things—"

"Of course they do!" he blurted. "Look at all the goddamn coincidences!"

"Well, there are a—"

"I know it sounds crazy, Judy, but I can't throw off the feeling that . . . that . . ." He started wildly at her, his mouth twisting over the next word.

"Throw off what feeling?" she whispered.

He attacked his lower lip as if trying to keep from speaking. Then he said, "The feeling that David ben Jonah *really is* speaking to me."

Judy's eyes flew open.

"I know it's crazy, but I believe it! It's as though David still existed, that he watches me as I'm translating."

Ben spun away and stalked up and down the room like a caged animal. "And what's worse, I have no control over it! No matter how hard I try, I can't get David out of my mind. I find myself thinking thoughts he might have had. I reminisce about Magdala as though it were my own childhood I was remembering. I daydream about Rebekah and summers in Jerusalem. I'm having losses of memory. I can't remember writing the translations. I frequently forget what time of day it is."

He suddenly stopped short. "You think it's crazy, don't you?"

"No, I don't."

"Then tell me what you think."

"Honestly?"

"Honestly."

"Well, I think that the Scrolls have in some way or another triggered off memories of your past. Memories you prefer to forget and that you have been able to keep buried until now. Maybe even guilt feelings—"

"Guilt!"

"You asked me to be honest. Yes, guilt."

"Over what?"

"The total rejection of your past and your heritage. As a boy you were inculcated with Judaic orthodoxy, and then all of a sudden you abandoned it. You went so far afield that you almost regard Jews as another species of animal instead of your own people. Haven't you ever wondered why you have this lifelong ambition to translate ancient sacred texts? You're searching for your own beginnings. By studying Hebrew manuscripts, maybe you seek your own lost Jewishness."

"Nonsense!"

"Well then, when you left Judaism, you didn't leave it entirely, did you? Instead you approach it from a different angle. Now you're the disinterested scientist reading the ancient texts, instead of the Talmudist. In a twisted sort of way, you've fulfilled the ambition your mother had for you—to become a rabbi. By doing what you're doing, you serve two identities at once—the Jew and the non-Jew."

"That's too farfetched. I study ancient manuscripts because I had a good start in it back in the yeshiva. I could have gone into another field, but that would have been wasting a good foundation. You still haven't answered my question: Guilt about what?"

"All right then, your mother maybe, if not Judaism itself."

"Oh God, my mother! You have no idea what it was like being raised by her! Being told every day that Jews are the saints of the world. That all goyim are evil. For Chrissake, the Jews don't have a monopoly on persecution. They weren't the only ones sent to concentration camps. Poles and Czechs and anyone the Germans felt were inferior were exterminated! Why do we have to be the goddamn suffering servants of God!"

This last Ben had shouted so forcefully that the veins in his neck and forehead bulged. Then he fell suddenly silent, breathing heavily and gazing at Judy. "I'm sorry," he whispered.

He walked back to the coach and slumped tiredly onto it. "I've never been like this before. David must be bringing out all the pent-up frustrations in me. I'm really sorry, Judy."

She sat next to him. "It's all right."

"No, it isn't." Ben took hold of her hands and held them tightly. "I call you up late at night and then shout at you like a madman. I really don't know what's gotten into me. I must be a madman, really."

Judy looked down at their hands and felt a strange warmth come over her.

"I'm obsessed," he said. "I know it. But I can't fight it. David won't let me."

Ben was tormented again by bizarre dreams and horrifying night-mares. Imprisoned in sleep, he was forced to witness the stark horror of the concentration camp, of his father's ignominious death, of his mother's tortures. All night long he was victimized by centuries of Jewish persecution. He looked upon medieval massacres and religious pogroms. He saw Jews slain in maniacal eruptions of Christian fervor.

At one point he awoke shivering, feverish and cold at the same time. His bedclothes were pulled out and twisted in knots. Staggering into the hall, Ben turned up the thermostat, then crawled back into bed, pulling the covers over him. He was sweating profusely and trembling so badly that the bed shook.

"Oh God," he groaned. "What's happening to me?"

When he sank to unconsciousness again, it was to suffer more nightmares. He saw himself standing on a gallows and looking down over a crowd of evil, jeering people. A faceless man stood at his side, who called out, "Do any of you speak for this man?"

And the people shouted back, "His blood be on us and on our children!"

As the hangman's noose was placed around his neck, Ben cried, "No, no, you've got it wrong! Matthew made that up in order to convert Romans to Christianity. The Jews weren't responsible!"

But the crowd shouted, "His blood be on us and on our children," again, and gestured their lust for his death.

Next to Ben's ear, the faceless man murmured, "Chapter Twenty-seven, verse twenty-five." Then the rope tightened and Ben felt the floor give way.

He shot up in bed with a cry stifled in his throat. He was dripping wet all over and the sheets were soaked.

"Centuries and centuries of suffering," he whispered into the darkness. "All because of that one line. Oh God, it could have been helped!" And he put his hands over his face and cried.

By dawn he was exhausted and felt as if he had not slept at all. Memories of the nightmares obsessed him as he tried to freshen up and prepare for the day. Beneath a hot, hard shower, he ruminated over the symbolism of his dreams and wondered why, after all these years, they should come back to him now.

He ignored the messy state of the apartment, ignored Poppaea's demand for food, and sat in a trance over a cup of sour coffee. Before him danced scenarios from the dreams—bizarre and uncanny sequences of death and multilation and bestiality. They sickened him, made him feel gray and cold inside. He felt as if he personally, for the period of one night, had suffered every pain and agony and debasement of every Jew in two thousand years of history.

"All because of one line in a book," he murmured over the coffee. "Why are you doing this to me, David? Why must I be forced to suffer this way?"

Before his flat, dull stare stood the image of David ben Jonah, a dark handsome Jew with heavy brooding eyes. He was not a solid specter, but a hazy diaphanous form like a desert mirage. Ben stared at him without emotion. Spoke without feeling. "If only I knew why you chose me, I might be able to take it. But I don't know, and I think I'm going insane."

Ben slowly rose to his feet and drifted into the living room. He lay down on the couch and folded his arms under his head. Possibly, in the light of day, he might be able to sleep better.

He did not. The instant he was asleep, the dreams started again. Just as vividly as if they were truly occurring. Ben was back in Brooklyn with his mother, and vomiting in the bathroom. She had started in on the concentration camp again—over and over again like a deranged woman. Recounting atrocities that fourteen-year-old Ben was incapable of handling. It was not the first time he had thrown up that way. And all the while, Rosa Messer wailing, "For your poor dead father you must become a rabbi, Benjamin. He died fighting for Jews. Now you have to take his place and fight the goyim."

That his mother had gone in some way insane at Majdanek, Ben always knew. And that with each passing year she became more and more unbalanced, Ben had also known. But why he himself had so violently reacted to her cries the way he had, why he had flung her precious Judaism in her face, he had never understood.

"You know, Benjy," said Solomon Liebowitz during their last visit. "You're just not clear on why you want to leave Judaism."

"I didn't say I was leaving it. I'll still be a Jew."

"But not Orthodox, Benjy, and that's no Jew at all. You've forsaken the Torah and the synagogue, Benjy, and I just don't understand why."

Ben had felt the twisted frustration inside. How could he explain to his best friend, let Solomon know that in order to get away from the unhappiness of his past, he also had to get away from Judaism? Because they were inextricably intertwined for Ben—Judaism and unhappiness.

"It'll kill your mother," said Solomon.

"She's suffered worse."

"Has she, Benjy? Has she?"

That final parting with Solomon had been one of the most painful moments in Ben's life. And now, as he agonized on the couch beneath an onslaught of nightmare after nightmare, all those painful memories of Rosa Messer and Solomon Liebowitz came flooding back.

In the final dream, Ben was confronted by David. The handsome Jew, bearded and finely dressed, said in Aramaic, "You're a Jew, Benjamin Messer, a member of the Chosen of God. It was wrong of you to forsake your people through your own cowardice. Your father died fighting for the dignity of Jews. And yet you would run from it as though it were an unclean thing."

"Why are you persecuting me!" cried Ben in his sleep.

"I do not persecute you. It is you who persecute yourself. Chapter Twenty-seven, verse twenty-five."

He awoke to the phone ringing. He answered it in a muddle. On the other end, Professor Cox's voice came out crisp and clear. It was afternoon, Ben had not shown up for his class. This was the third time. What was wrong?

Ben heard himself mumble an excuse about illness, then agreed to meet with Professor Cox in his office at five. If there were personal problems, if a substitute teacher was necessary, highly unlike you, Ben . . .

"Yes, yes. Thank you. See you at five."

Ben hung up and swung away from the phone. There was a small ache rumbling around in his head and an even larger one in his stomach. Without really thinking about it, he made his way into the kitchen and foraged for something to eat. Finding a can of soup, he emptied it in a pan, set the pan on the stove and wandered away.

He felt sicker than he ever had in his life. It transcended physical discomfort, for it was a nausea that had its roots in the pit of his soul. Ben felt diseased through and through, contaminated by the grisly nightmares he had just suffered.

Slumping back onto the couch, he stared in a daze. He was tired beyond belief. The clock on the opposite wall indicated another hour or so before mail delivery—another hour before he could be in Jerusalem again, living David's life, escaping from the present. A painful hour of waiting for the next Scroll, if there would be a next Scroll. Had Weatherby reached the end?

Ben rubbed his eyes with his fists. Last week sometime Weatherby had said they had discovered four more. When was that? Had Ben already read them?

"Oh God, please no," he whispered. "Don't let the Scrolls end before I've read them all. I have to know what David is trying to tell me. I have to know why he chose me."

The hour passed in a reverie of ancient Jerusalem. Closing his eyes and resting his head back, Ben felt himself gently drift into another world. In West Los Angeles a gray rain fell, but in Jerusalem it was hot and sunny. The streets were dusty, filled with the constant drone of flies. Dogs slept in bits of shade, and the alms beggars were nowhere to be seen. Ben was out walking with his friend David, walking toward the gate that led to the gardens beyond the city. They would follow the road to Bethany, cross over the Kedron and visit the old merchant on the Mount of Olives. Maybe they would drink some wine beneath the shade of an olive tree and quietly laugh away the idle hours. It was a good feeling, to pass an afternoon with David, and Ben was reluctant to give up the daydream.

He did so for only one reason. The mailman would be by soon.

Bounding suddenly to life, Ben dashed to the coat closet and yanked out a jacket. "Okay, David, my friend. Let's hope you haven't let me down."

He skipped down the stairs and came to a jarring halt in front of the bank of mailboxes. A quick inspection told him the delivery had not yet come, so he sat down on the cold, damp step and waited.

Fifteen minutes passed. Ben was beside himself with impatience. He took to pacing up and down the slick walkway, heedless of the drizzle that fell on him. The closer the moment drew, of reading the next Scroll, the more unbearable it became. And as he strode up and down, hands clasped behind his back, Ben was aware of the presence that stood by him.

It was David ben Jonah. And he was watching to see that the next Scroll arrived safely.

When the mailman walked up, Ben nearly attacked him.

"Messer? Apartment 302? Let me see." The man shuffled through the bundle in his cold hands. "Must be a check. Is that it? Seems the only people that hang around mailboxes are waiting for checks." He came to the end of the pile. "Nope. No letter for Messer. Sorry."

Ben nearly screamed. "It has to be there! Look again. A big brown envelope."

"Look, mister, you can see for yourself it ain't here."

"Oh, Christ, it has to be! How about in your bag? Look there!"

"Nothing in there for this address."

"It's registered!" he cried. "A registered envelope!"

The mailman held up a finger. "Oh, registered, you say. Yeh. I have one here for this building. The guy's never home to sign for it. Let me see . . ." He rummaged through a side pocket of his leather bag. "Here it is. Well, I'll be damned. It's for you all right. Want to sign here, please?"

Ben took the stairs two and three at a time, almost killing himself to get inside. Once in the apartment, leaning against the door, he breathed heavily and stared down at the envelope. A surge of excitement went through his body. A mixture of joy and apprehension and exuberance made him shiver.

Looking down at the familiar hand of Weatherby, Ben whispered, "David. Oh . . . David . . ."

CHAPTER ELEVEN

⋯≻⊶⊙⊷⋯⋅≺⋯

While Eleazar insisted I continue to live in his house, I could not. This was a home of good people, of pious Jews, and I no longer felt as one of them. In my own way, I had to reconcile with God, and on my own forge a new life for myself. When Eleazar offered me apprenticeship in his cheese shop, I refused. When my father asked me to come back to Magdala and operate my own fishing boat, I refused.

One day, I went out of the city and to the house of the olive merchant whose wine I had drunk with Saul. I told him all that had happened in these six months. And I offered him a proposition. Since he was a widower without children, and had an orchard and olive press to maintain, I would work for him at a wage far below the standard of any laborer. He was glad of my offer, for he had a small affection for me and remembered the times I had filled in his loneliness. But he would not pay me a slave's wage. Whatever I had done, I had done. The sins of the past were gone. We would not look back.

And so it was that I sorrowfully left the house of Eleazar and went to stay in the humble quarters of the olive merchant. I saw Rebekah seldom, but I dreamed of her every night. Once, when we were alone together and I dared take her hands in mine, I swore my love to her, and promised that the day would come when I would be a fit husband. But until that time I had to prove myself to God and all men. I had to become fit to live among Jews again.

I saw Saul frequently. He came to the olive press and ate cheese and bread with me. His words of Eleazar and the school caused a great pain in my heart, and it was as though a knife twisted in my breast. And yet I would not have him be silent, for to hear of these things was my punishment. The time would come when Saul would receive the title of Doctor of the Law, and walk with his head high among men. I envied him for it, and I loved him for it.

And I continued to regard Eleazar as my own father. He alone did I love above all men, for he was wise and just and merciful. On my own I continued to study the Law, for I knew that the Law was the means for Jews to inherit the earth, and when I had questions I would go into the city and sit at Eleazar's feet and listen to his exhortations.

I was sad and happy at the same time. I sweated beneath the sun in the olive orchard and ate fish and cheese at night. The evenings were soft and gentle, and my thoughts were often of sweet Rebekah. Possibly, I could have been content like this for the rest of my life, but it was not to be so.

I tell you this, my son, so that you will know that the greatest of our plans are easily scattered in the wind. God alone plans our destiny, it is not in our control. There is a saying that life is like a river, always moving, and that you cannot dip your hand into the same place twice.

Once again, my life was to change. Something occurred which was but another step toward the inevitable hour that I must soon tell you about. The crime which I ultimately committed, that you have no doubt by now heard about, was the end result of many such detours and changes in my life. None of my planning, none of my power, could have kept me from acting out that Final Hour.

Just as my life was altered when my father sent me from Magdala to study in Jerusalem, just as I fell from grace and was expelled from the school, so did a third incident yet put me on the road again to my Destiny.

I was bringing oil from our press to be sold in the market-place. Five donkeys laden with jars, and myself on foot, waited patiently in the line that slowly wove itself through the Gennath Gate. And as I stood idly in the sun, I chanced to look up and spy a familiar face in the crowd.

It was Salmonides the Greek.

There was a rapid knocking at the door. "Christ!" shouted Ben as he flew to his feet. He flung open the door. "Judy!"

"Hi, I was just—"

"Am I glad to see you!" Ben seized her by the hand and pulled her inside. "He's found Salmonides!"

"What?"

"David found Salmonides! Come on, we can read it together!" He dragged Judy into the den and beamed at her with a grin that spread from ear to ear. "Can you believe that? What do you think David's going to do? I hope he beats the Greek shit out of him!"

"Wait a minute—" She pulled her hand back.

Ben stopped when he saw the seriousness of her expression. Next he noticed the folded newspaper in her hand. "What's that?"

"You haven't seen it yet?"

"Seen it! Seen what?"

With some trepidation Judy opened out the newspaper and extended it to Ben. He stared incredulously at the front-page headline. It read:

JESUS SCROLLS FOUND?

"What the—" He snatched it out of her hand. "*Jesus Scrolls!* What the hell kind of a joke is this!"

"It's not a joke—"

"Jesus Scrolls! *Jesus Scrolls!* Oh, for Chrissake!" He held the paper out at arm's length, stared at it, then fell backward into his chair. "Jesus Scrolls Found! And with a question mark yet! God, it's so cheap!"

Beneath the headline was a UPI photograph of Dr. John Weatherby standing at the lip of the excavation site, cradling one of the large jars in his arms. The caption read: "Archaeologist Dr. John Weatherby of Southern California holds a jar which contained one of the Scrolls found at Khirbet Migdal."

Ben gazed at the newspaper as if he had been struck by lightning. His eyes held the classic look of disbelief.

"Read the story," said Judy. She cleared a space on the desk top and sat on the edge. Her face was pale and sad; she hated to have brought this news to him.

"This is disastrous," murmured Ben. "I just don't believe it!"

"Well, it was bound to happen. You can't expect something like this to remain a secret for long."

Ben read from the article. "Listen to this: 'That this is going to be bigger than the Dead Sea Scrolls was intimated today by an archaeologist at the scene who said, "This is going to be bigger than the Dead Sea Scrolls."'" Ben looked up at Judy. "Christ, what kind of journalism is that?" He continued to read. "Dr. Weatherby deferred comment on the content of the Scrolls, saying that the text would be made public when the work of translating had been completed. The Scrolls are currently being translated by three paleographic experts in America and Britain. So far, one can only speculate as to what they have found."

Ben threw the paper to the floor. "Speculate, yes, but for God's sake— *Jesus Scrolls!*"

"It sells papers, Ben—"

"I know it sells papers. You're telling me? That's why the headline doesn't read: DAVID BEN JONAH SCROLLS FOUND. Who's ever heard of David ben Jonah? Everyone's heard of Jesus. Oh, for God's sake. Did you read how they seized upon such names as Galilee and Magdala? 'Time of Christ.' What the hell did Jesus do that made him so goddamned important!"

Judy was dismayed to see Ben so upset. She knew the pain it caused him, the prostituting of his precious Scrolls. Dragging David ben Jonah before the public like a freak. It hurt her, too, in a smaller way.

"Next they'll be making a Hollywood movie out of it," he went on. "With a couple of sex idols playing David and Rebekah. Madison Avenue will turn out T-shirts and bumper stickers. They'll capitalize on it as much as they can. "Oh, Judy . . ." He shook his head as if he were going to cry. "I can't bear for them to do that to David. They won't understand him. Not like we do."

"I know."

After Ben calmed a little, he retrieved the paper off the floor and scanned it again. What an ignominious spectacle the press was going to make of this. They would seize upon the small minutiae and blow them all out of proportion. The fact that the author of the Scrolls was a gentle, pious Jew who had a private confession to make to his only son would be ignored. Instead they would play up the Galilee angle, throw out words like Magdala and "Time of Christ."

"It sells papers, all right," he whispered sadly. "I guess Weatherby had no choice."

"I'm sure he didn't."

"Look at this." He tapped the page with a finger. "They mention the Curse. The Curse of Moses, as though it were some goddamn quaint laughable gimmick. You'll see, tomorrow's headline will be something about the Curse. They'll manage to find someone who's been hurt or fallen sick during the excavation, and blame it on the Curse. Oh, David, *how can they do this to you!*"

Ben looked up at Judy wearily. "I can't take this. I had an awful night last night. It was the worst of my life. I honestly thought I was dying."

"More nightmares?"

He nodded.

When she was about to say something else, the phone rang. Ben seemed not to hear it. On the fifth ring, Judy picked it up and said, "Hello?"

It was Professor Cox.

Judy put her hand over the phone. "He says you had a five o'clock appointment."

Ben looked at his watch. "Ohmygod. I can't go. Not now. Listen, tell him . . . tell him there's been a death in the family and that I'm grief-stricken and I'll be going out of town and will need a substitute for my classes."

Judy stared at him with her mouth open.

"Go on. Tell him that. Tell him I'll get in touch with him in a few days and that I'm really sorry."

She hesitated again, uncertain of what to do. Finally, really having no choice, Judy gave Professor Cox her best rendition of what Ben had said, hung up and stared at him again.

"What's wrong?"

"Your classes—"

"I can't go to them, Judy. Not now. You know that. I can't leave David alone for a minute—or rather . . . he won't leave me alone. He's haunting me, obsessing me and won't give me respite until I've read his entire story."

Without another thought, Ben turned away from her and addressed the next papyrus fragment. As he started to read, Judy watched him closely, scrutinized the dark circles under his eyes, the deep lines etched around his mouth. Ben had aged in the last few days, he had aged very much.

Finally, after some deliberation, she laid a gentle hand on his shoulder and said, "Ben?" He did not seem to hear. "Ben?"

"Hm?" He looked up.

"When was the last time you ate?"

"Ate? I don't know. Not long ago, I guess. Just last . . . just last . . ." His eyebrows knotted in a frown. "I don't remember."

"No wonder you have nightmares. You're starving yourself to death. I'm going to see if I can concoct something for you in the kitchen."

"Yes, yes. That would be fine."

As she left the den, Judy noticed that the apartment was very warm. Turning down the thermostat, she glanced into the bedroom and saw the devastation he had made of the bed, and a trail of dirty clothes leading to the bedroom. In the living room, the pages of Scroll Six's translation were strewn about, pillows lay everywhere, half-empty coffee cups and overflowing ashtrays. The kitchen was worse. There was even a cold pan of uncooked soup on the stove.

Huddled in one corner was Poppaea Sabina, glaring angrily and distrustfully at Judy. She had sought refuge from the shouting and yelling, and was sulking over an empty food dish.

Before all else, Judy fed the cat. Next she cleaned the litter box, which was as overflowing as the ashtrays. And next set about to try to put some sort of meal together. But the cupboards were barren.

When she heard the phone ring again, she froze. There were three rings and then Ben's muffled voice. In the next moment she heard him shout, "Leave me alone!" which was followed by a crash.

Judy ran into the den to find Ben once again quietly reading the Scroll. "What happened?" she asked breathlessly.

"Nothing."

"But what was—" The question was answered before she finished asking it. Against the opposite wall and on the floor lay the telephone where Ben had flung it after ripping it out of the wall.

"Saves taking it off the hook all the time," murmured Judy as she left the den and returned to the kitchen.

Fully knowing that even the most sumptuous feast would not entice Ben into eating right now, Judy decided to save the soup for later. In the meantime, not wanting to disturb his sojourn with Scroll Seven, she busied herself with cleaning up the apartment.

When an hour had passed and not a sound had come from the den, she ventured to look inside. Ben was still bent over the papyrus, his right hand scribbling away in the notebook, his eyes glued to the Aramaic. But there was something else to the portrait he struck, something which fascinated Judy and drew her inside. Standing only inches from him, Judy held her eyes on Ben's face and was mystified by what she saw.

His features were strained in an odd pose, one which emanated an otherworldliness. He appeared transfixed, like a man undergoing a deep spiritual revelation. The pallid skin was drawn taut over his skull, making visible the blue veins at his temple and neck. His mouth was a tight thin line, white and bloodless. Ben's blue eyes, fixed and glazed, seemed unusually bright, as if on fire, and very like the eyes of a fever victim.

He hardly breathed. He didn't move at all. The only sound to be heard was the scratching of his pen on the paper as his hand scribbled out illegible lines. Never once did he look at the notebook, or move in any way from the papyrus. He was a man frozen in time, trapped in another dimension and another world. Judy had never seen anything like it before and could only marvel at it.

After a while—she had no idea how long she stood and watched him—she left the den and went to sit in the living room. At once Poppaea was up in her lap, purring gratefully and ready for attention. Judy smiled down at the cat. Poor Poppaea Sabina had no idea what was happening to her master.

"I have no idea either," whispered Judy as the cat pressed her face into Judy's long hair. "I've only known him for a short while, but I can tell he's changed. Or maybe changing. Has it already happened, or is it still happening? And then again . . . is *what* happening?"

When Ben emerged from the den, he had the face of a man who had just undergone a spiritual transfiguration. He was not quite the same man who had sat down two hours before to finish reading the Scroll, although the changes were subtle. It was as though—Judy found herself thinking—each time he read a Scroll he changed a little.

"I'm glad you're still here," he said.

As though with the reading of each Scroll, a little of Ben Messer was lost and a little of *something else* was put in its place.

"I couldn't leave without reading Scroll Seven," she said quietly. Yes, there were changes, all right. The alterations in his speech were now even more pronounced.

He took a seat opposite her, sitting on the coffee table, and gazed at her with his brilliant blue eyes. "Thank you for standing by me in this."

"Are you ready for something to eat now?"

"Not yet. Read this first." He handed her the papers on which he had scrawled the translation. "My handwriting is getting worse."

As she took them from him and glanced over them, she saw him open his mouth to say something else.

"What is it?"

Ben was hesitant. "There's a new development in this Scroll, Judy. One that I fear is going to cause trouble."

"Trouble?"

He heaved a sigh. "I don't know how David thinks we're going to react to it, but all I can say is it will be disaster if the newspapers get hold of it. There'll be a stampede to Magdala."

Then Ben did a curious thing. As soon as he said it, he turned his head to one side, as if listening to someone. His eyes were fixed on the wall behind Judy, but they seemed focused on something. Ben smiled and shook his head.

"David won't give any hint about what's in the next Scroll."

"David?"

"I guess we'll have to learn things the hard way."

Judy shuddered involuntarily. Ben's voice had a peculiar edge to it, and it made her feel suddenly cold.

"Anyway, read what I've written and tell me what you think."

Even while I stared at Salmonides, I could find no voice to call out, so stunned was I. That evening of eight months before, the night of my shameful downfall, seemed now to me as a dream. I had never expected to see the unscrupulous Greek again; indeed I had destroyed the contract I had so foolishly bought from him with all my money. To see him standing at the Gennath Gate, as real as if I had met him only yesterday, struck me so dumb that I could not speak.

Nor did I have to. To my great surprise, as soon as Salmonides caught sight of me, his face lit up and he approached me as if we were long-lost friends.

Hail, master! he shouted to me, arms outstretched.

I reflexively fell back a step.

Forgive me, master, he said. In my joy to see you I had forgotten what a devout Jew you are and that the touch of a Gentile is loathsome to you. But, by the gods, I am glad to see you!

Why? I asked stupidly.

Why? Because I have searched this city over for you, master. I bring you good news and profits.

What? I said, still not comprehending.

The ships arrived safely in Ostia with not a grain lost. The shekels you planted have indeed grown into sesterces.

I was again struck dumb. Not only had Salmonides kept true to our bargain, but he was anxious to pay me as well. He had it in mind that I might right away enter into a second investment and so had been anxious to find me. Leaving my donkeys in the care of a friend, I went with Salmonides to the street of bankers, where, upon his written order, he received two hundred denarii. We went from there to the money-changers at the Temple, where, under the keen eye of my Greek companion, the Roman coins were weighed, inspected and exchanged for two hundred Syrian zuzim. Five of these I gave to Salmonides, who immediately, with an apologetic shrug, exchanged them for drachmas.

From here we went to a food shop, where we sat in the shade and discussed the economics of the Empire. That I was ignorant of such matters was greatly apparent to Salmonides, yet he was patient with me.

He said: You have a rare quality, my young master, which a man as astute as myself can easily see. You have a quick mind and an agility with figures. See how easily you grasp the concepts of finance that I throw at you. Most men are slow and become quickly bored. But you are sharply interested in what I say and retain it with ease. You are in the wrong profession, my young master. You should study banking, not the Law.

So I went on to tell Salmonides what happened after the night of my shame and he was surprised that Eleazar had been so hard on me.

Even more so, he said, you are unduly harsh with yourself. What young man does not spend such a night as you did? Indeed, many times over. And was your crime so great—a little drunkenness? You should visit Rome if you want to see real sin.

But I held up my hand. It is not the same for Jews, I said, for we are God's Chosen People. Since we must set an example for the rest of the world, then we must be zealous in our observance of the Law. What leaders would we be if we, too, gave in to drunkenness and whoring and shameful acts?

Salmonides was skeptical, I knew, like so many Gentiles, but that is because they do not yet believe that God has chosen us to inherit the earth.

In the course of that afternoon, I gave Salmonides one hundred zuzim and entered into another contract with him. This was toward the purchase of a crop of barley, soon to be harvested. If the crop was fruitful, I would sell it at a profit. If the crop proved barren, then my money was lost. For this reason I only gave him half, and saved the other half against future need.

That night I questioned Eleazar about the ethics and morality of my profit. Can it be as honest as money earned through labor? I asked. And he replied that I was laboring all the same, if not with my hands then with my mind. The money was not illicitly gained. And it was not gotten from other Jews. For these reasons my actions were justified.

The next morning I returned again to the city for the purpose of a single errand. In the eight months that had passed since my shame, I had not for a moment forgotten the woman named Miriam whom I had met by the well and who had brought me home to feed me and give me haven. Eight months ago, out of piety and love for fellow man, she had sent me away with a full belly and with coins in my pocket. She had also diverted me from the path of suicide. Today I would go back to her house with repayment.

She recognized me at once and drew me inside. One of the many women who lived in this house washed my feet and gave me bread and cheese. When I expressed amazement at this treatment, Miriam said: We always welcome a returning brother.

Am I your brother? I asked.

And for reply, she kissed my cheek.

When I gave her the purse of twenty-five zuzims she accepted it modestly and said it would go to the feeding of many.

Have you such a large family? I asked, for her house was inhabited by many people.

She replied: All who await the return of the Master are my family.

When I would have questioned her further, she stayed me and begged that I remain a while, for at such time there would come a man who would answer my questions.

And so it was that a fourth time my life took a turn. I waited in the house of Miriam until the time a man named Simon came home.

Judy dropped the papers and looked squarely at Ben. She said nothing, made no move, uttered no sound. All communication was in her eyes.

"We can't keep this from the press, can we?" he said in futility.

"Once this is out—"

"Oh God!" he cried suddenly. "Why does it have to be? Why did this have to come up?" Ben jumped to his feet and clenched his fists. "Is this part of your plan, David! Don't you see how it's tormenting me?"

Ben fell silent and stared at the wall opposite. He was breathing heavily. There was something frenzied about his eyes, a mixture of confusion and anger. Then, after a moment of glaring at the blank wall, Ben suddenly let his head fall down so that he stood in the attitude of prayer—or of remorse.

When he finally straightened up and brought himself to look at Judy, he said in a thick voice, "I can see him . . . but you can't."

Judy stared back, suspended.

"Yes, he's here, all right. David ben Jonah. He's actually been here for some time, only I wasn't aware of it until yesterday. He didn't reveal himself until he was sure I would understand why he's here."

Judy's eyes ran over the blank wall, trying to see the phantom that only Ben Messer could see. "How could he be—"

"I don't know, Judy. It's still not clear to me. All I know is that the spirit of David ben Jonah is here at my side and that for some reason"—his voice grew strangled—"for some reason he has come back to *haunt* me."

Judy flew to her feet. "But why should he!"

"I don't know." Ben's voice dropped low. He spoke in a flat, even tone. "For some reason, David wants me to know his story. He wants me to know what happened to him. How do I know? Maybe it's the Curse of Moses. Maybe it's because his son never read the Scrolls. How do I know? All I know is, he has chosen me."

Oh, Ben, thought Judy frantically. It's not the Curse, it's not his son, it's not David at all! Can't you see that? It's your own past that's haunting you!

Ben's eyes held Judy's for an interminable length of time, staring across the silence and into her eyes as if he were, for the moment, hypnotized. Outside, sounds of traffic passed on the street, a bicycle bell rang, voices of children calling to one another. But neither Ben nor Judy heard these things, for they belonged to another time, and in another reality.

Finally, in a soft voice, Ben said, "You believe me, don't you?"

She held her breath for only a second, then she whispered, "Yes, I do."

He sighed as if a heavy burden had been lifted from his shoulders. "Thank God for you," he said as he sank onto the couch. I guess that's why you're here, he thought as she sat next to him, because David knew I would need you.

Trying to appear calm and not show her alarm, Judy picked up the sheets of translation and read a few lines out loud. She wanted to bring Ben back to sanity, tried to break the unshakable spell. "I wonder what the newspapers will do when they read this."

"Well," said Ben, speaking mechanically. "Miriam and Simon were common names in ancient Israel. There is nothing to indicate that they are Mary and Peter."

"But the kiss on the cheek. That was only an early Christian practice, other Jews didn't do it."

"Yes . . . I know. The Epistles of Paul. So you're thinking that this Miriam is the same Mary whose house was the center of the Nazarene Church in Jerusalem; the mother of Mark."

"Why not?"

"Because it's ridiculous. For God's sake, the Scrolls of a follower of Jesus—" Ben brushed a hand across his face. "The odds against it are, well . . . I refuse to believe we have an original Christian document on our hands."

That's irony for you, thought Judy. You refuse to believe that, and yet you're convinced you're being haunted by a man two thousand years dead.

She studied Ben's face. No, the spell would not be broken. He could not be drawn out of his preoccupation. Wherever his mind had planted itself, it wanted to stay there, and for reasons known only to itself.

"Let me heat that soup up now."

He did not reply.

"Ben, why did you have me say that to Professor Cox?"

"Because I don't want to go to school until this thing is over. David won't let me. I have to stay here."

"I see."

This was an unsettling idea: Ben barricading himself from the world, withdrawing and withdrawing until one day he would never be brought back to the present.

It was almost as if he were afraid that contact with reality would snap the slender thread that joined him to David.

CHAPTER TWELVE

The obsession grew. Everywhere Ben turned, there was David ben Jonah. The ancient Jew stood at the periphery of his dreams, looking on like a disinterested spectator. As Ben battled the past again in bizarre nightmares of Majdanek and his childhood in Brooklyn, David ben Jonah stood idly by as if measuring the limits of Ben's endurance.

"Why the dreams!" murmured Ben the next morning, again unrested and haggard. "Why must I suffer these dreams? Is it not enough that, after all these years, my past is back with me, that I'm not able to push it out of my mind any more? I don't understand why I must have these violent nightmares!"

He plodded about the apartment on heavy feet, the nebulous specter of David at his side. Ben did not feel like eating. Nor did he feel like doing anything except read the next Scroll. It would not be there until four o'clock that afternoon, and Ben dreaded the hours of waiting.

Thinking it might help him to sleep, Ben poured himself a large glass of wine, drank it down without a breath and lay down on the couch in exhaustion.

Judy did not have to knock on the door this time, for to her surprise it was standing ajar. It was eight o'clock in the evening, Ben's car was in its parking space, but there were no lights on in the apartment.

She cautiously poked her head inside. "Ben? Are you awake? It's me."

Her only response was silence.

"Ben?" She stepped all the way in and quietly closed the door behind her.

The apartment was dark and chilly. In the air was a distinctly perceptible odor of alcohol. Judy widened her eyes, straining to see. When something warm suddenly touched her leg, she gasped.

"Oh, Poppaea!" she said. "You startled me." Picking up the cat, Judy went farther into the apartment.

She found Ben unconscious on the living-room floor. An empty bottle of wine and an empty bottle of scotch lay nearby. A glass was on its side, spilling out a crimson stain on the rug.

Kneeling at his side, Judy said softly, "Ben? Ben, wake up." She shook his shoulder.

"Hm? Wha?" His head lolled from side to side.

"Ben, it's me, Judy. Are you all right?"

"All right . . ." he mumbled. "'Sallright . . ."

"Ben, wake up. It's late. Come on."

He lifted an unsteady hand and dropped it on his forehead. "Feel awful . . ." he mumbled. "Dying . . ."

"Hey," she whispered. "No, you're not. But you've got to get up. What a mess you made!"

Finally he opened his eyes and tried to look at her. "It was David's fault, you know," he slurred. "He drove me to this. I waited by the mailbox for two hours, and the Scroll didn't come! He did it on purpose. He's watching me, Judy. All the time. No matter what I do, that goddamn Jew is always there."

"Please get up."

"Oh, what's the use. No Scroll. How'm I gonna make it through tonight and tomorrow?"

"You will. I'll help you. Come on." She slid an arm under his shoulders and helped him to a sitting position. As she did so, Ben looked at her face so close to his and murmured, "You know, I didn't used to think you were pretty. But now I do."

"Thanks. Do you think you can stand?"

He clasped his head with his hands and cried, "David ben Jonah, you're a rotten bum! Yes . . . I think I can stand."

Judy grunted as she lifted Ben to his feet, noticing as she did so that the back of his shirt was soaked in wine. With almost no effort she was able to lead him to the bathroom, where, flicking on the bright light, she gave him firm orders to get into the shower. Oddly enough, he did not protest, but proceeded to obey obsequiously. As he started to undress, Judy turned on the water, and then left him alone. In the bedroom she found a complete change of clothes, passed it through the bathroom door and shouted, "Take your time!" Then she went back to the living room and cleaned it up as best she could.

When Ben emerged half an hour later, he looked somewhat better. He didn't say a word as he came over to the couch, sat down and started to drink the strong coffee she had set out for him. An interval of five long minutes passed before he finally looked at her.

"I'm sorry," he said softly.

"I know."

"I just don't know what's happening to me. I've never done anything like that before. I just don't know."

As he sat shaking his head, Judy tried to imagine what he was going through. She saw the aged face and the paleness and the stubble of a beard, and wondered what it must be like for a man to suddenly have his identity ripped out of him and be left with nothing in its place. Nothing, that is, but horrifying memories.

"I remember," he said thickly. "I remember how my mother and I used to sit in the dark every Shabbas, and how she would say to me over and over again, 'Benjy, your purpose in this life is to be a leader among Jews. The only reason for your existence is to become a great rabbi and teach Jews how to use the Torah as a shield.'"

He forced a dry laugh. "She had always wanted to go to Eretz Israel, but she had come to the United States instead. She was always talking about going to Israel one day with her son the famous rabbi." He gazed thoughtfully into his black coffee. "I sure made a mess of the rug, didn't I?"

Judy looked over at the large wine stain that bruised the carpet. "Shampoo should get it out."

"That's all right, 'cause I really don't care." Ben turned his blue eyes to Judy and she saw how heavy with concern they were. "I don't question it any more. It just simply happened. Who knows why? Maybe it's the Curse of Moses. But I don't care. David is here next to me right now, listening to what I'm saying to you. I don't know what he's waiting for, but I suppose that when it happens, I'll know."

Ben drank some more coffee, his gaze again on the rug stain. Finally, putting his cup down, he released a long and weighty sigh and said, "Oh, David . . . David." Tears filled his eyes. "What happened to you all those years ago? How did you die? And how did you know you were going to die? You once contemplated taking your own life when you couldn't bear to go on. Is that what happened in the end? Did you hope to find solace in suicide?"

Judy reached over and laid her hand on top of his. They sat thus, staring, for a very long time.

She returned the next day in the early afternoon. Having left Ben's apartment at midnight, having seen to it that he was going to sleep for a while, she went home and worked on arrangements to have someone take care of her dog Bruno. Judy had some small intuition that the time would come when she would be away from home for a long time.

Then she attended her two morning classes at UCLA, stopped at a supermarket and walked through Ben's front door at three o'clock. To her surprise, he was not in.

The bed had been carefully made, the living room somewhat tidied, and washed coffee cups in the kitchen. In the den, however, Judy encountered the familiar chaos. On the cluttered desk top lay the mail that had arrived the day before, and among it was an unopened letter from Joe Randall, the man who awaited a translation of the Alexandria Codex.

There was also a piece of flowered notepaper lying atop all the debris, and on it was a brief letter written in a feminine hand. It was from Angie. She had an offer of a modeling job back in Boston; she was thinking of accepting it. It would mean being away for a while. If Ben wanted to talk about it, she would be home until tomorrow night; after that she was leaving.

A piece of cellophane tape on the reverse indicated that Ben must have found the note taped to his door.

Judy gave Poppaea some food, put the rest of the groceries away and went quietly to the place where she knew she would find Ben.

"Hi," she said, coming down the stairs.

He was sitting on the bottom step, holding vigil over the mailboxes. "Hi," he said dully.

"Sleep any better last night?"

"No. I was tormented by the same horrors. The vision of the earth moving under my feet. Mass murders and persecutions. God, why is David doing it to me!"

"I saw the letter from Randall. Aren't you interested in the Codex any more?" Ben shook his head.

Judy sat next to him and nodded. Neither was she. "And the note from Angie?"

Ben did not reply.

The mailman came forty-five minutes later, and when Ben signed for the envelope, he flew back up the stairs, leaving Judy far behind. Ripping open the envelope as he bounded into the apartment, Ben pulled out the photographs and threw the rest on the floor.

When Judy came into the den, she found him sweeping a space on the desk top with one move of his arm, sending everything crashing to the floor. Then he sat down at once to read the Scroll. His face was red with fire, his eyes wide and protruding. He licked his lips as if he were about to devour a feast.

Judy picked up a piece of paper from the floor. "It's a letter from Weatherby. Want to read it?"

He violently shook his head. With a pen working rapidly on a clean sheet of paper, Ben had already begun.

"He says there's only one more Scroll after this."

"Good, good," he said impatiently, writing. "That means this will all be over tomorrow."

"And he says . . ." Judy stopped herself short. In the next instant she decided not to tell Ben the rest of the letter, not just yet, because now he was deliriously happy and back again where he so desperately wanted to be.

Simon was one of those pious ascetics who inhabit a community by the Sea of Salt, not far from Jericho. He wore an immaculate white robe and practiced those remarkable feats of healing that the Essenes are known for. I was at once impressed with him, for although his voice was soft and his speech measured, his words were weighty and all that he said carried great worth.

When Miriam introduced us, Simon kissed my cheek and explained that this was their greeting, which meant: Peace be with you, brother.

He then washed his hands and feet and broke bread with me.

In Jerusalem it is not rare to see men belonging to various sects of religious piety, from the extreme Nazarites who follow Samson's example, to the sword-carrying Zealots who nourish the Torah with the blood of Israel's enemies. And yet, in my years in Jerusalem, so involved had I been with Eleazar and our study of the Law, I had never once had the occasion to converse with one of the noble Essenes.

We await the Final Hour, Simon said to me, which will be upon us at any moment. And while some of my brothers remain at the monastery in the desert and in other isolated communities, I and my friends go out among the people and preach the Second Coming.

He went on to explain the philosophy of their sect, which was, namely, to keep pure God's Law and to be ritually pure for the return of the next King of Israel. To Simon and his many friends, that return was imminent, pressingly so, and would be upon us before we knew it.

He spoke with clarity and intelligence, and exhibited an extraordinary knowledge of the Law and the Prophets.

Are you a rabbi? I asked him.

I am only a member of the Poor, the Sons of Light who will inherit the earth.

Most Jews await the time when God will send His agent to establish the supremacy of Israel over all other nations. And Simon was no exception. In many ways, he reminded me of Eleazar, who was a Pharisee and who was also awaiting the Messiah.

Yet they differed in this respect: while Eleazar spoke of an age yet to come, Simon claimed to have already met the new King.

Where is he? I asked. What is his name?

He is away, preparing. His name is of no consequence. But he is of royal blood, the last of the Hasmonean line and a descendant of David. You will know him when he returns.

Simon and I conversed late into the night, and I left the

house of Miriam in the Upper City with mixed feelings. I could not bring myself to accept Simon's prophecy—that our kingdom would come any day now—and yet he had spoken so convincingly that I was unable to think of anything else in the days that followed.

Eleazar surprised me by discounting the beliefs of Simon. He said: The monks are good men and keep the Law pure. But in their zeal to see the Kingdom of Israel established again they have become fanatics. They are hasty men, David, and err in their predictions. Everyone knows that no blood of the Hasmonean line remains, for the last was executed years ago by Rome.

Can there have been another, hidden? I asked.

If a rightful claimant to the throne were alive today, we would know of him, for all Jews would rally to his support. As I say, the last was crucified just before you were born.

I believed Eleazar, and yet while Simon's words did not convince me, they intrigued me, and I found myself returning to the house of Miriam.

One evening I took Rebekah with me and she was at once converted. Simon convinced my love that the Messiah had already walked among us and that he would return again.

I asked Simon: If he was here once, why did he leave?

Because he came the first time to herald his own coming. He came to give us time to prepare. When next he walks the streets of Jerusalem he will come as God's agent, and all those who are not prepared will fall at the wayside.

Where did he go? I asked.

And here was the astounding answer Simon gave me. He said: Our master was killed on a Roman tree and was raised to life again by God, to prove that he was indeed our new king.

While Rebekah fully accepted this and joined the new sect which called itself the Poor, I could not. And so a second time I conferred with Eleazar.

He said: These men are misguided, David. Their leader did not die on the tree, for he hung there but a few hours. Everyone knows that death on the cross takes days. He was taken away by men in white robes, whom ignorant witnesses called angels, and was taken to their monastery by the Sea of Salt. You have seen the wonders they perform in healing, as they have done for a hundred years, and that their name Essene means healer. I do not doubt their leader is alive today and in the desert.

They are fanatics, David, who are desperate to overthrow the yoke of Roman oppression and are clinging blindly to a miracle that never took place.

A second time Eleazar convinced me and I went away thinking Simon a good Jew, but a misguided one.

For the Feast of Unleavened Bread, instead of joining Eleazar and his family, which had been my custom, I took Rebekah and the olive merchant for whom I worked to the house of Miriam. I did this for two reasons: it was Rebekah's wish, and I was curious about the ritual observance of religious men who had forsaken Temple worship.

At the onset, there was little difference and Simon recited the Four Questions during the First Seder. But then the feast changed and became the traditional "love feast" of the Essenes, which they have practiced for a hundred years, and in which bread and wine are shared in expectation of the day it would be shared with the new King of Israel. While their Passover was essentially the same as that of any good Jew, it differed in the aspect of the symbolic Messiah in our midst.

A third time I approached Eleazar, and I sensed he was becoming impatient with me. I told him: This man Simon spoke of the prophecies of Isaiah and Jeremiah and told how their Master was the fulfillment of those prophecies. But Eleazar said: They use Isaiah to prove their false preachings. The Messiah of Israel has not yet come, for we are not yet worthy.

But they are trying to be worthy, I argued, and are trying to help others to enter a state of purity. These are exceptional Jews, Rabbi, perhaps we should listen.

Now Eleazar became angry. They are not as strict in their observance of the Law as I am, and yet I am still not worthy to receive the Messiah.

For the first time I noted a strain of pride in his humility, as though Eleazar were vain about his humbleness.

But they are truly modest men, I replied, and faultless as Jews. They do not live only *by* the Law, Eleazar, but rather *for* the Law, and that is how God would have it.

Eleazar fell silent at this point, and this was how I left him that day.

From then on I continued to visit the house of Miriam until one day I, too, became convinced. As part of my initiation into the Poor, I was fully immersed in a pool of water. They called it baptism, and they had practiced it for over a century. While I did not become an Essene, or wear white robes or learn their art of healing, I was brought into the Poor and called brother by one and all. At the same time I agreed to share my worldly goods with my new brothers and sisters, to help them in any hour of need and to keep myself pure within the Law so that I would be prepared when the Master returned.

And this, my son, is how I entered into the New Covenant and joined the most pious of Jews. Not a day went by that I did not wonder at my worthiness.

The time came when Salmonides sought me out again to pay me the profits of the barley crop. I gave him a handsome fee, shared the wealth with Miriam and the Poor, gave some to the olive merchant for whom I worked and invested a portion, on Salmonides' sage advice, into a caravan bound for Damascus.

When, two months later, the olive merchant died and bequeathed all his estate to me, whom he "loved as a son," I suddenly found myself a modestly well-to-do man.

And so it was that I felt myself now fit to take Rebekah to wife.

She sat under the canopy in the house of Miriam while all our new friends gathered and feasted and wished us well. The Master was coming soon, perhaps tomorrow, and I wanted Rebekah at my side. As man and wife we would hail the new King at the gates of Jerusalem.

Eleazar would speak to me no more. It was as if I had disappeared and no longer existed. In his eyes, I had committed a terrible affront to God, but in my eyes I was becoming pure before

God. Eleazar was a conservative rabbi, one who lived in the past and for the old Laws. He could not be made to see that these were indeed the Last Days prophesied by Isaiah and Daniel, and that while the old world needed the old Law, a New Age required a new Law. This was the New Covenant—the New Testament, which did not abolish the Torah but which fulfilled it. Rather than abandoning the Law of the Books of Moses, we were all the more zealous in their observance. Yet we did two things: we no longer considered the Temple to be necessary to keeping holy the Lord's Covenant, for we now worshipped in our own homes; and we now kept a second day holy as well as the Sabbath—one on which we held our Essenic love feast and sat to listen to Simon or one of the Twelve speak of the coming King.

It pained me to part with Eleazar, but it was a different sort of pain than that which had driven me to consider taking my life two years before. On that dark day, Eleazar had expelled me in disgrace. This time I left him for a mission holier than his.

I remained friends with Saul. While he did not in the slightest agree with my new belief—since he was still under Eleazar's influence—he respected my right to observe it. And I promised Saul that, even though he would not become a member of the Poor, on the day our Master returned to Jerusalem, I would speak for him and be witness to his worthiness.

All this took place sixteen years before the time which I must yet tell you about. And even though they far preceded the Day which must be told to you, they bear heavily on the events that took place. Indeed, without all of this that went on before, that Day of Infamy would never have taken place.

One more turn in my life was to occur that forever set me on the road to my inevitable destiny. And I think now, my son, that even with all else that had gone on before, if this one thing could have been averted, I might not now be sitting in this place in Magdala, awaiting my final hour.

But there was no way it could have been averted, for we as simple men cannot see into the future. And so I had no way of knowing that on one particular summer night, as I sat in my own house among my olive trees, my destiny was to be permanently fixed.

For on that night, Saul brought Sarah to me.

They finished the Scroll at midnight, with Judy reading Ben's translation as he wrote it down. She had drawn up a chair and was sitting next to him, anxiously bent over the notebook. When the last line was written, Ben dropped his pen and seized his wrist in sudden awareness of writer's cramp.

After a while, he and Judy turned to look at one another, their faces illuminated by the harsh high-intensity lamp. For the first time the two had spent an evening in ancient Jerusalem together, and the realization of this—that Judy had shared the same experiences at the same time—caused Ben to feel closer to her than he ever had before.

"I was right," he whispered finally. "David was an educated and wealthy man. From the start I knew this. His wealth will increase, I just know it. In the next Scroll he'll be telling us about bigger and bigger profits . . ."

Ben eased himself back in the chair, wincing with the pain of lower-back strain. "Didn't you say something . . . a letter from Weatherby? Something about the next Scroll being the last one?"

Judy did not reply. The moment was too beautiful, too fragile to speak now of bad news.

"Then that'll be the last of it. David will reveal what horrible thing he did and that'll be the end of his story. And then he'll go away from me and leave me in peace."

As Ben spoke, Judy felt her stomach begin to tighten. A horrible foreboding gripped her, dispelling the euphoria she had been in since visiting ancient Jerusalem. An intuition that things were about to get much, much worse.

"Let me make some coffee," she said at last. "I guess we should eat something."

"I'm not hungry," said Ben without feeling.

"You're losing weight."

"Am I?" They both slowly got to their feet and hesitated a moment over the last photograph. It was difficult to tear themselves away from Jerusalem, away from Jews who loved one another, away from the kiss of peace and tranquil summer evenings.

"And you were thin in the first place," Judy said. Then she took his hand. "Come on."

She led him into the living room, left him there and went on into the kitchen. But she could not move. Standing before the sink, almost hovering over it, Judy could not make her muscles respond. In her mind she imagined the handsome face of David and the sweetness of Rebekah. It was almost as if she knew them personally. She pictured the gathering at Miriam's house, the sharing of the Essenic wine and bread, the accumulated hope of better days to come.

When she felt his presence in the doorway, Judy looked up at Ben. They stared into each other's eyes.

Then Ben said quietly, "David was a Christian, wasn't he?"

"I guess so."

He turned abruptly away and went back into the living room.

Following him, Judy said, "What's wrong with that? Why can't you just accept the possibility—"

"Oh, it's not that, Judy. It's because of something else. Something I haven't told you about."

She waited on his words. The apartment was dark and cold, but neither had the inclination to turn on the heater or any lights. "What else could it be?" she whispered.

"There were hundreds of weird cults flourishing at that time."

"But none that a devout Jew like David would join. What about the leader that was crucified by Rome and then believed to have risen from the dead? And who were the Twelve David mentioned?"

"All right. So he was a Christian. Or, more properly, a Nazarene, as we call them. 'Christians' were in Rome and Antioch. Nazarenes were only in Jerusalem. There was a difference, you know."

"I think I know something of it. A Jerusalem Church and a Rome Church." Judy sat on the couch next to Ben. She sat close to him, almost leaning against him, and spoke in subdued tones. "After the destruction of Jerusalem, only the Rome Church survived."

"That's it, basically. So . . . David was one of them."

"What's so bad about that? Actually, I think it's great. These Scrolls will fill in so much history, prove so many theories to be true, and refute others. They will clarify the dim beginnings of the Church. Think of the enlightenment, Ben, what's wrong with that?"

"Nothing" was all he said.

Judy deliberated a moment. "What are you afraid of? That these Scrolls might prove the existence of a man you had long held to be fictional?"

Ben turned suddenly to her. "Oh no! Not at all! And I never

thought Jesus was fictional, because surely there had to be some basis for the Gospels. No, Jesus lived, but he wasn't what everyone says he was. He was just an itinerant Jew who had charisma. But even so, David isn't going to tell us anything we don't already know. There is no doubt that there was a Messianic movement before 70 c.e. and that the Essenes and Zealots might have been involved. David has confirmed that, nothing more."

"Then what's disturbing you, Ben?"

"What's disturbing me?" He looked away from her and sighed heavily. "When I was fourteen years old, I suffered from an insatiable curiosity. I also had a bad habit of questioning everything. My mother and my teachers referred to the Torah as a shield against the contamination of the goyim. But what sort of contamination? I wondered. And why did they call us Jesus killers? Well, one thing led to another, until I could not stop myself from trying to find out what it was that separated us from the goyim. Oh, I knew that we had the Torah and they didn't. But that wasn't enough for little Benjamin Messer. I wanted to know what it was the Christians had, if not the Torah, and what was so evil about it."

They sat in the dark for several long minutes, Ben reliving the terrifying past, and Judy waiting patiently for him to continue.

"I started going to the library to read the New Testament. It intrigued me. I didn't believe it at all, but it intrigued me. I read it over and over, searching for some clue that would let me know what it was that made people believe in it. I did this as long as I could until finally, out of recklessness, I brought a copy home. I had it hidden in my room for over a week before my mother found it. And, Judy . . ." He paused. "She beat the shit out of me. I mean, she thrashed me within a millimeter of my life. I don't even remember half the things she said to me, so frightened I was for my life. But she was like a crazy woman. She was a raving lunatic. As if the horror stories of the concentration camp hadn't been enough, as if the glorification of my father's heroism hadn't been enough, now she had to beat the shit out of me in order to knock some Judaism into me. Oh, Jesus!"

Ben doubled up and rested his forehead on his knees. "Heroism. Oh, for Chrissake! Why does everyone condemn the Auschwitz Jews for having gone to their deaths like sheep? What the hell should they have done? What *could* they have done? So my heroic father spat in an SS officer's face and called Hitler a *Schwein* and was sentenced to be buried alive. And because she was the wife of this 'heroic' Jew, my mother had had wild dogs set on her. Oh, Christ, what kind of heroism is that!"

Judy laid her hand on Ben's back and waited while he cried in the darkness. Then she said softly, "That was over thirty years ago, Ben."

"Oh yes." He straightened up, wiping his cheeks. "And David ben Jonah lived *two thousand years ago*, but look at him standing there. *Look at him!*"

Judy squinted into the fathomless dark of the room. "I don't see him, Ben."

"No, of course you don't. He only lets me see him. Just like you can't hear my mother tell me what a filthy little bastard I am for reading the goyim Bible. What could I tell her? How could I explain to her that in reading the Bible of the goyim I saw their *weakness*, not their strength."

Ben wiped his nose and calmed himself down. "If I was going to fight an enemy, I had to know something about *them*. I had to know who I was fighting. But my mother didn't see that. It didn't occur to her that I was *trying* to be a good Jew, that I wanted to become the rabbi she saw in me. But it just didn't work. She tried too hard. Something inside me snapped that night. As I lay in my bed, too crippled to cry, I felt as if my eyes were open for the first time. And, Judy . . . that night as I lay in my bed, I saw what Judaism can do to a person. I saw how it had slaughtered millions of Jews all through history, how it had exterminated countless millions of Jews in Nazi concentration camps, how it had destroyed my father, how it had tortured my mother. We were all miserable because we were Jews. It wasn't the Christians who were at fault. It was us—ourselves. *We* were the problem. And the only way to escape the misery and torture and insanity of being a Jew was simply to stop being a Jew."

"Ben . . ."

"I know what you're thinking," he said. "You're thinking that my mother wasn't the only crazy one in the family. Perhaps not. But at least I'm happy in my lunacy."

"Are you?"

"At least I was until a few days ago. From the moment I left the past behind seventeen years ago I have been happy. And it's because I wasn't a Jew. What would it have been like if I had gone on as she wished?"

"I don't know, Ben." Judy stood all of a sudden and turned on some lights. "Tell me why you're upset David was a Christian. I still don't see why it bothers you."

"Because," he started, also rising from the couch, "because until now I felt a kinship to David. In the Scrolls he is now nineteen years old, and until I was nineteen years old I was still a good practicing Jew. Now he has upset all that. He has entered into the very conflict that started all my trouble long ago—the quandary of Christian versus Jew. Good guys and bad guys. One pure, one contaminated. I sought a reconciliation of that little perplexity when I was fourteen years old and nearly got killed for it. Now David, my sweet David, has actually *joined* them. Only now he's a Jew *and* a Christian at the same time."

"But in David's day, Christians *were* Jews, no different."

"Little comfort."

"Can I feed you something now?"

"Yes . . ." Ben started to pace the floor.

When Judy reached the kitchen door, she stopped and turned. "By the way," she said carefully. "About the next Scroll . . ."

He stopped pacing and stood in the middle of the living room with his shoulders slumped forward. "Thank God for the next Scroll." He wearily shook his head. "Being the last one, it should end all my worries, answer all our questions. And then all this will be over. God, I can't . . . wait . . ."

"Ben—"

"What?" The caution in her voice alarmed him. "It *is* the last Scroll, is it not?"

"Well, yes. The next one we get will be the last one. But not because it was the last one David wrote . . ."

"What do you mean?"

Her heart started to pound. "It's the last one Weatherby will send. The *real* last one, the last one David wrote, could not be salvaged. It was just a lump of tar."

CHAPTER THIRTEEN

Ben read Weatherby's letter for the tenth time, but nothing changed. The news was still bad. Like Scroll Number Three, the jar of Number Ten had been badly damaged, thus allowing the elements to get to the papyrus. Two thousand years of decay had done its job. The last Scroll was lost.

No more tears could be shed. It was the worst day of Ben's life. The night before, after Judy had broken the news to him, Ben had flown into such a violent rage that he had smashed things against the wall and had sent Judy running out of the apartment in fear. Then he had sunk into a deep dreamless sleep, almost a coma, and had awakened this morning feeling as if, for a while, he had dwelt among the realm of the dead.

So David's last Scroll was gone forever and there was no way of finding out what had been written on it. That meant that everything was riding on Scroll Nine. Ben prayed desperately that it was a long and undamaged papyrus and that David had said enough on it to fill in the mystery. Otherwise . . .

Ben stared at the ghost that stood before him, the ghost of David ben Jonah.

Otherwise . . . *he might never leave.* He might not understand that the last Scroll would never come and therefore go on haunting Ben forever.

Judy knocked timidly on the door, and when Ben opened it, he at once drew her into his arms and gently kissed her forehead. "I'm sorry about last night," he murmured against her hair. "I am so deeply, profoundly sorry. Throwing things at you, carrying on. I don't know what—"

"Never mind, Ben," she said, her face buried against his chest. The night had been a bad one for her, too. And the decision to return had taken a great deal of courage. But love had helped her overcome her fear.

"I wouldn't have hurt you," he said.

"Wait." She placed her fingertips on his mouth. "Don't talk about it. We won't ever mention it again. All right?"

He nodded dumbly.

"I came over to wait for the next Scroll with you."

She fixed them both some lunch, which they ate without once speaking, and then together they sought to straighten up the den. A lot of translation sheets lay about everywhere. They had to be gathered up, put in order and then typed for Weatherby. The fact that he was probably receiving up-to-date translations from the other two paleographers had not occurred to them. Indeed, the fact that a large team of archaeologists was at work on the real papyrus sheets themselves in Jerusalem also did not enter their minds. For Ben and Judy this was a personal encounter, one that involved only themselves and David, so that the fact of hundreds of other people at work on the Magdalene Scrolls simply vanished from their thoughts.

Ben insisted they go downstairs at two o'clock, even though mail delivery was always reliably at four. They sat on the steps in anticipation and each prayed, for different reasons, that this last Scroll would come today.

When it arrived, Ben almost passed out with tension. He shook so badly that Judy had to sign the receipt, and then had to help Ben upstairs and into the apartment.

"You're sweating," she said once inside. "And it was cold out there."

"I thought it would never come. I thought it would never come."

"It's here now. The last Scroll. Let's read it, Ben."

No letter accompanied the photographs, and to Ben's limitless joy, a quick scan of them showed the papyrus to be lengthy and in fairly good condition.

"These broken edges here, we can probably guess rather accurately at what was written there. It's when whole chunks are missing. Now, let's read it. Oh God . . . I thought it would never come." He blindly grabbed for her hand and squeezed it tightly. "Pray, Judy. Pray that this Scroll will end it all."

I hope so, she thought desperately. God, how I hope so.

Rebekah and I had been married for one month, enjoying the bliss and discoveries of the newly wed. She was a sweet, adoring wife, like a quiet child in my arms, and thanked God daily for her fortune. I, likewise, expressed contentment to the Lord and thought that I could go on like this forever, with demure Rebekah at my side and our olive trees always bearing fruit.

But then one evening, after we had been married a month, Saul came by to visit us and to join us in supper. I had invited him several days before, and he had said that when he came he would have a surprise for us.

The surprise was this: Saul was betrothed. And he brought his future wife with him.

My son, I had no way of preparing for that moment. No man does. Just as one day it will happen to you, so it happened to me that night as I opened my door to my friend.

I was speechless from the very start. It was as if I had been struck by lightning. Sarah's eyes met mine, and in an instant they pierced me through and split my soul asunder. I cannot begin to describe my feelings at that moment, for there are no words sufficient. In that very instant, as Saul greeted us and proudly showed off his betrothed, I fell in love with Sarah. And as her eyes delved into mine, as her expression froze and her mouth fell partly open, I knew that Sarah had fallen in love with me.

Such is what we hear in myth and legend, and yet we never expect it to pass our way. But it smote me, my son, and struck with such force that I knew even then, in that fleeting moment, that my life was never to be the same again.

Neither Saul nor Rebekah saw what happened between us. I washed my friend's hands and feet and shared a skin of watered wine with him as Sarah and Rebekah went to work in the kitchen. And all the while, as Saul prattled on about news in the city, I was deaf and blind to him. I could think only of Sarah, the vision of beauty and mystery that comes to men only in dreams.

I felt awkward that evening, but Saul and Rebekah did not notice. As we ate we talked and laughed and enjoyed the company of good friendship. I feared to look at Sarah, for I knew that if I did I would become a pillar of fire. Once or twice our eyes met, and we were at once frozen in time and space. She gazed boldly at me, her moist lips slightly parted, as if trying to say something without speaking it.

When at last Saul and Sarah left, I was numb all over. That night I did not touch Rebekah, but pretended to sleep. And all through the darkest hours the vision was ever before me: Sarah's wide, probing eyes; her full mouth; her sleek black hair and graceful body. She was more than a beauty, she was a mythical maiden that had come to torment me.

For days afterward I could not put Sarah out of my mind. I paid little attention to my work and often had to be spoken to twice. If Rebekah noticed this, she never said so. But then Rebekah was a quiet and obedient wife and never would have questioned my actions.

One day I could take it no more. Instead of having my steward go to the bankers as was my practice, I went instead and left him behind to oversee the orchard. I donned my finest tunic and best cloak, rubbed fragrance into my beard and set off into Jerusalem with my heart high.

Saul was near the end of his studies and therefore no longer dwelling in Eleazar's house. He was back again with his father and would reside here with his new wife until such time as he could afford his own home.

Saul was not at first home, but I was received warmly by his family. When he finally returned from the Temple a while later, he was happy to see me and did not, in his zeal, notice a shadow of disappointment pass across my face. Sarah was not with him.

And what had I expected? Surely she would not be in his company with any frequency until they were wed. I had to devise another way.

What I came to was this: I invited the two of them for supper again on the night of the Sabbath and asked them to stay over through the next day.

I said: Rebekah is lonely in that house by the orchard, for she rarely sees young women of her own age. She would enjoy Sarah's company for that time.

And Saul readily accepted.

My son, I practiced deceit and used my best friend to my own ends, and yet, in my ardent desire to look upon Sarah once again, none of this entered my mind. A man driven by love, by a consuming passion, is not a rational man. In my mind, I thought I was arranging something special for Rebekah.

When Saul and Sarah arrived before sunset, I was beside myself. I stood to watch them come up the path, I heard Sarah's laughter ring out among the trees, I saw her magnificent hair catch the sunlight as it flew in the breeze. Once at our threshold, however, she was modest and veiled once again. Yet her dark eyes flashed at me and I felt my legs go weak.

No one can explain the feeling of love, where it comes from, why it exists, what causes it to happen at certain times. One only knows that it is the sublimest of emotions.

Thy lips, O my love, drop as the honeycomb; honey and milk are under thy tongue; and the smell of thy garments is like the smell of Lebanon.

I know a little of how Solomon felt when he wrote that song, for in the presence of Sarah I was weak, on fire, and consumed with a desire to hold her.

The next day Saul returned to the city to attend at the Temple, but I did not, for it was the day after and not the Sabbath which we of the Poor set aside for worship. And so I offered to escort Sarah around my orchard, that she might see all that I own and feel the morning air of the hillside. Rebekah preferred to stay inside, and so we went, Sarah and I, out among my olive trees.

At first we did not speak, there was a strange silence between us. But as we strolled under the branches and delighted in the warmth of the day, I knew that Sarah felt the same as I.

Eventually we came to the last of the trees and were able to stand at the edge of a beautiful vista. The blood-red anemone was in bloom, brightening the countryside with their radiance. The air was full of the smell of Aleppo pine, and white lilies lay about in the grass like sleeping doves.

Finally, I could stand it no more, and I told Sarah what was in my heart. I confessed that I did not feel guilty, that I was a new husband and yet could not think of my wife, and that the fire which consumed me was beyond my mortal control.

To my surprise and delight, Sarah spoke the same words, that from the moment of our first meeting she had been restless and felt an ache in her heart.

How can it be? she asked. Is it possible that such a love can blossom in an instant? Can two people merely look at one another and become helplessly entrapped in a passion so great that all the waters of Siloam cannot cool it?

I told her that it must be so, since it happened to us. I would have kissed her then, but some small sanity remained to me. In the Fifth Book of Moses it states that a man must rejoice with his bride for one year. I was not following this commandment to the fullest. And I am a man of the Law.

We spoke quietly on the hilltop, and when a gentle breeze lifted away Sarah's veil to set her hair free, I thought my heart would cry out in a voice of its own.

I have a great love for Saul. In my eight years in Jerusalem since leaving Magdala, Saul had been my brother and my friend. Before God, there is nothing I would not do for him. So it was for this reason and no other that I refrained from approaching Sarah. My love for Saul was the staying power over my love for his betrothed. I am a man of loyalties.

I am also a man of the Law, and yet, ironically, it was not the Law that held me in check that day. I knew that the punishment of taking another man's fiancée to bed was stoning—stoning to death; also, that if a girl did not go to her husband as a virgin and he discovered this on the wedding night, she could be stoned to death. As strict and forbidding as the Laws of the Fifth Book of Moses are, it was my friendship with Saul that was my willpower.

In the days that followed, I was a different man. When Salmonides reported to me with yet more profits and to tell me that the gods were favorable to me, his words fell upon a deafmute. Within my breast there was an ache that could not be assuaged. My love for Sarah increased with every hour.

Rebekah and I continued to visit our friends at the house of

Miriam in the Upper City, and because they were pious Jews, I tried my hardest to be attentive.

I have not yet mentioned Jacob to you, whom you know. Now I will speak about him.

Jacob was a Nazarite, a man of the firmest convictions and of the strongest vows. At Simon's side, he helped in the leadership of the Poor. These were busy days for them, since they were anxious to increase their membership before the Master returned. Jacob often said: We were instructed to go and gather up the lost sheep of Israel and preach to them that the Kingdom is at hand.

For this reason, Simon and his followers went about the country preaching their New Covenant and heralding the Return of our King. It would not be long before the prophecies of old would be fulfilled and Israel raised up to be the rightful ruler of the world. For this to take place, all Jews had to be prepared, and it was the task of Simon and Jacob to organize the missions and to see that all houses of Israel were reached.

I once asked them: Where do you go, brothers?

And Jacob replied: We are to go into every city of Israel and speak with every Jew there. We were instructed to avoid the way of the Gentiles and not enter the city of the Samaritans. For the Kingdom at hand is for Jews alone.

At this point there arose an argument. Simon and Jacob received letters from their brothers in Antioch who were preaching to Jews, and they told of another man, one Saul of Tarsus, who claimed to have spoken with the Master on the Damascus Road and who was given instruction to preach to the Gentiles.

But Simon and Jacob, being the overseers of the Poor in all matters, counseled them strongly against going among the uncircumcised, for unless they became Jews as we were—that is, if they suffered the rite of circumcision—and promised to keep holy the Torah, the Gentiles might not enter the New Covenant.

A second argument arose also at this point, one which was not at first serious, but which in later years grew to outsized proportions. You know that Simon was the Master's best friend and his first disciple. You know also that Jacob was the Master's brother. Because of this, a small dissension arose. Simon and

Jacob vied for absolute supremacy over the Poor. If they disagreed on any point, a heated debate sprang up, and each would claim the right to have the final say-so. This was not a major problem at first, but later, as Simon and Jacob began to drift apart in their views, the struggle for topmost leadership of the Poor grew in intensity.

And so it was at that time that Simon and Jacob were busy men. The day of the Return was almost upon us. It could be tomorrow, and they feared to have reached not enough Jews before our Master came through the gates as King. Simon and Jacob fought the idea of allowing Gentiles into the group, and they vied with each other for absolute control of the community.

This was also a time, sadly, when we began to take to the sword. Zealots all over Galilee and Judea were creating more and more political unrest with our Roman overlords, and we feared that a great conflict might occur before our Master returned.

Simon said: Our Lord told us: Whosoever does not have a sword must sell his coat and buy one.

These were not dangerous times, my son, as happened later, which you know about. These were but the small seeds of unrest, a few ill winds blowing about. When the boiling pot finally erupted, you were witness to it.

My love for Sarah grew. I could not control it. When Saul was finally deemed fit to teach the Law himself, and when Eleazar conferred the title of Rabbi upon him, Saul decided upon the date of his wedding. And it ravaged my soul as if by hungry lions.

Rebekah was as excited as if she were the bride, and spent many days in preparation with Sarah. They came frequently to our house, she and Saul, for we were their best friends, and I was like a sick puppy. I pined for her. I longed for her as I had never before longed for a woman. My love flared into passion and then into lust, and no matter how much I sweated beneath the sun in my orchard or prayed until my knees were callused, the intense desire to have Sarah only increased.

That she suffered as did I was apparent in her eyes. And once, when our hands accidentally touched, I saw a crimson flush in her cheeks. Long into the night I dreamed of her, I tossed and turned like a man in fever. And I prayed that when the day of her wedding came, I would be able to purge my body and soul of this obsession.

It happened that, one day, Rebekah went into Jerusalem to visit her mother and sisters while I remained at the olive press. I knew that Saul was already in the Temple, seeking pupils so that he might start his own school. My steward was in Jerusalem with the latest of our oil, and my few slaves were taking a siesta out of the sun.

And so it would seem that it was Fate that brought Sarah up the path that day. As though our stars had been inevitably linked long ago at the hours of our births. I stepped out of the shade and into the sunlight, scarcely believing my eyes. It was as if a vision approached me.

With a veil over her face and her eyes cast down, Sarah bid me good day and explained she had brought a basket of honey cakes for Rebekah and me. Ones which she had just baked and were yet warm.

When I told her that Rebekah was not home and that I was alone, Sarah raised her eyes to me, and my heart sang out to the hills.

Take a cake, she said, holding out the basket. They are made with honey and locust powder and the finest nuts.

But I could not eat. My mouth was dry and my throat had closed up. My heart raced as if I were a young boy.

Come sit in the shade, I said, and took the heavy basket from her.

We walked for a while, enjoying the heat of summer and the freshness of the air. We stopped occasionally to watch the birds or smell a flower.

It is so quiet here, said Sarah when we had walked a way. Not like the city, which is congested and always noisy. Here, among the trees, it is peaceful.

We decided to sit for a while in the shade of a pine, one which hung low with heavy branches and spread wide arms to embrace the sky. As we sat, I saw that we had gone out of view of the house.

Saul has one pupil now, Sarah said with her eyes on the

ground. She sat on her hip with her small feet modestly drawn under her. It is the son of a poor merchant who could not afford to send him to a better-known rabbi.

I said: All famous men had humble beginnings. The time will come when Saul is as sought-after as Eleazar.

Then we sat in silence for a while.

I asked her: When is the wedding day, Sarah?

In two months, for then Saul can purchase a small house in the city. It is a humble one, but it will be our own.

Two months, I thought. Will it be easier to fight this passion once she is a married woman, or will it make no difference?

As we watched some squirrels at play, Sarah laughed, causing her veil to fall back. Seeing her long black hair stream down her shoulders and breast increased my ardor.

Sarah, I said to her, it is difficult for me to be with you this way.

It is the same for me, she replied.

Saul is my best friend and my brother, I cannot betray him.

She whispered: I know.

And even so, I could not help myself. I trembled with the inner battle, fought desperately against the urge that came over me. And I could not help myself. On an impulse I gathered her sweet hair in my hands and kissed it.

There were tears in her eyes. Suddenly, in a strained voice, she said: Saul will never know.

I was struck as if by thunder. But, my love, I said, you must go to your husband as a virgin. The Law is clear. It is also clear that: if a man find a damsel in the city and she is betrothed to another man, and if he lie with her, then ye shall bring both out to the gate of the city and stone them with stones until they are dead.

I said: The Law is clear. It is not for myself that I fear, but for your sake, my love.

Her hand was on mine, and all loyalty to Saul dissipated. Sarah sat close to me, her small body shaking, her lips parted.

So I said: It also says in the Fifth Book of Moses that: if a man find a damsel in the *field* and she is betrothed to another man, and if he force her and lie with her, then the man *only* that lay with her shall die.

But Sarah said: No, my love! If we are caught, then we shall be punished together. Forget the Law and the city and the field. There is no way around it. We must take the chance. If we are found out, then it is just. If we are not found out, then we must forever live with our consciences.

No one saw us that day, we were never found out. For the moment, it was a glance into Paradise. But afterward, that evening and the days which followed, I was a man driven to despair. No lower creature existed than I, despicable in my deceit. I had betrayed my wife Rebekah, I had betrayed my best friend Saul, and I had betrayed God. There was no excusing the deed, nor did I try. I had stolen from my best friend what was rightfully his. I could never again look upon him without feeling the deepest shame.

Twice in my life now I had defiled the Torah. How could I expect to be counted among the Chosen when the Master returned, if I did not keep holy God's sacred Law? There would be a King upon Zion any day now, and I was no longer worthy.

In my anguish I went to Simon for counsel. I gave him no details but merely confessed that I had committed a criminal deed. I threw myself to my knees and asked his guidance. To my surprise, Simon said this: In seeking purification, you are purified, for God can see into your heart. If you are sincere in your contrition, then forgiveness comes at once. So I said: I am no fit Jew to receive the Messiah.

And Simon replied: Remember the parable of the wedding feast. Do not sit down in the best place, for it could happen that the host has invited someone more important than you and he might say to you, 'Please rise and give him this place.' Then you would be ashamed and have to sit in a lower place. Instead, when you are invited, go and sit in the lowest place so that your host can say to you, 'Come higher, friend, and sit up here.' This will honor you in the presence of the other guests. For everyone who makes himself great will be humbled. And whoever humbles himself will be made great.

I gave much thought to Simon's counsel, and while I felt he might be right, it did little to assuage my despair.

And then my sorrow was made manifold, for, even though I

had received the prize I had so longed for, and even though I felt miserable for it afterward, I still loved Sarah with all my heart and soul.

It made a change in me, my son. While Simon assured me that I was but nineteen years old and being too harsh with myself, and that I would in time learn to forgive myself, I was never able after that to feel secure in my worthiness before God. And so it was that I forced vows upon myself: to pray twice as often and twice as long as required by Law; to wear the tephillin about my wrist and forehead; to keep holy both the Old Covenant and the Essenic Covenant; and to redouble my efforts at becoming a worthy agent of this Messiah.

In this way alone was I able to live with myself. I continued to quietly and secretly love Sarah, but I also increased my devotion to Rebekah that she might not suffer because of my weakness. I remained steadfast to Saul, but was always awkward in his presence, and strived to avoid any contact with his wife.

I did not attend their wedding feast, but feigned illness and sent Rebekah with her mother and sisters. Once married, Saul and Sarah were too busy for the visiting they had done before. And I always found excuses to postpone their invitations to their house.

After this, Salmonides approached me with the suggestion that I purchase the neighboring farm, which was poor and profitless, and turn it into a lucrative one. I appreciated the diversion, and at once hired new help, purchased a larger olive press, and worked out a better system of irrigation. Salmonides was right, for the adjacent farm soon began paying for itself, and then brought in profits. While my olive trees bore plump fruit and my press produced the best oil, Salmonides continued to increase my earnings in investments and other enterprises.

Toward the beginning of the next year, after my twentieth birthday, a messenger came from the city with a letter from Saul. Sarah was going to give birth to their first child.

Eight days later, Rebekah and I were on hand for the circumcision. It was the first time I had looked upon Sarah since just before the wedding, and I was amazed at how easily my knees weakened and my heart raced at the sight of her. In her paleness and fragility—for the birth had been an arduous one—

she was as lovely as I remembered her, and as the *mohel* performed the operation and recited the words, I paid attention only to Sarah.

They named the boy Jonathan, for he was the son of Saul. I would be his uncle and he my nephew. We said special prayers for the new babe, and I secretly envied Saul. I as yet had no son of my own.

I made a blessing over Jonathan and wished him long life, and then silently—in my heart—I prayed that he survive until the Return of the Messiah so that he might grow to manhood in the true Kingdom of Israel.

Judy left Ben to go and fix some hamburgers in the kitchen. It was a mechanical task she performed, one without thinking, because even though her body was in this all-electric kitchen in the Twentieth Century, her mind was still back in ancient Jerusalem.

At his desk, Ben did not move. Having gotten so involved in reading the Scroll and experiencing the life of David ben Jonah, the jolt of coming to the end of the writing had left him hanging, floating in air.

This can't be, he thought vacantly. This can't be all there is.

Ben placed his hands, fingers spread, flat out on the photographs. He sat there immobilized, feeling the words of David ben Jonah beneath his palms, feeling the hot Jerusalem summer and the act of love beneath an Aleppo pine. He felt the noise and the press of Jerusalem's cosmopolitan market; smelled the fish imported from Capernaum and Magdala and Bethesda. Felt the silks from Damascus, the linen from Egypt, the ivory from India. He *felt* the exotic perfumes, the cries of the hawkers and tradesmen. *Felt* the clank of the Roman swords in sheaths as they marched by. *Felt* the dust and the animals and the heat and the sweat of Jerusalem—

"Oh God!" cried Ben, jumping to his feet.

In the next instant Judy was at his side, wiping her hands on a towel. "Ben, what is it?"

He stared down at his trembling fingertips. "Oh God," he whispered again.

"What happened?"

"David . . ." he began. "David was . . ."

She put an arm about his shoulders. "Come on, Ben, you're exhausted. I'll have dinner ready in a few minutes and then we can relax. How about a little wine in the meantime?"

She led him to the living room, past the purple stain in the rug and over to the couch. As soon as he sat down, Poppaea was in his lap, purring and rubbing against his chest. But Ben ignored the seductive cat. Instead he rested his head back on the couch, his mouth open, and stared at the ceiling.

What had happened just then in the den? That was something new, something different. It was as though David were—

"What do you take on your hamburger?" called Judy, popping her head around the kitchen door.

"Huh?" He snapped his head up. "Mustard . . ."

She made some sounds, then emerged in the next moment with a heavy tray. Placing it before him on the coffee table, she dropped a napkin in his lap and tore open a giant bag of potato chips. The hamburgers were thick and juicy.

"Come on now, you promised you'd eat."

"Did I . . . ?" He pushed Poppaea's nose away from his plate and brought the hamburger to his lips.

What was it David had tried to do back there in the den?

They ate for a little while in silence, breaking the monotony with an occasional crunch of a potato chip, until Ben, nearly finished, said, "What puzzles me is . . . David is still here."

"Why does it puzzle you?"

"I thought he would leave when I had nothing left to translate, but I guess I was wrong. What if he haunts me for the rest of my life, not knowing the last Scroll will never come?"

They finished the hamburgers, wiped off their hands and faces and leaned back with the wine. Poppaea browsed among the crumbs. "She's such a little bitch," said Ben. "Pretending to be high-class and finicky, but really a whore at heart."

"Like her namesake maybe."

The moment passed slowly, quietly, in thought. Then Ben said softly, "You know, he's looking at you. David is looking at you."

Judy's eyes darted up ahead of her and into the dim shadows across the room. She saw nothing but the shapes of furniture and plants and pictures on the walls. "Why, do you suppose?"

"I don't know. Maybe you remind him of Sarah."

She gave a little laugh. "Hardly!"

"Oh . . . I don't know . . ."

Nervously, Judy said, "So the Scrolls are finished."

"Yes, I guess so." Ben's face returned from its distant stare and molded into seriousness. "And I guess we've learned a lot." His voice was flat, totally without interest. "David's verified some of the sayings of Jesus, which ought to make everyone happy. Some of Simon's words. Jacob's quote. The parable of the wedding feast."

"You don't sound happy about it."

"I'm not. I don't care about anything except David and what on earth happened to him." Ben started to clench and unclench his fist.

Judy watched him in growing concern. She had become used to the unpredictable vacillations in his personality, and was able to recognize the signs that indicated a sudden change of mood was about to take place. But she did not like it. This instability alarmed her.

"What was the Big Crime he wanted to tell his son about? Was it the thing with Sarah?"

"It couldn't have been. In Scroll Eight he says his day of infamy wasn't to come for sixteen years yet. He only thought the incident with Sarah was instrumental in leading him to that day in 70 C.E."

Ben became more agitated. Judy saw that he was losing control again. "Which means that the last Scroll, the one we will never see, revealed the entire point of his writing the Scrolls in the first place, probably explained how and why he was going to die soon, and also filled in sixteen years of—"

"Ben!"

He was suddenly on his feet. "*I can't take it!* There's no way I can go on without knowing the rest of David's story. It'll drive me crazy. *He'll* drive me crazy!" And he pointed to the invisible Jew before him. "Do you think *he's* going to give me any peace now? Look at him! Look at him standing there staring at me! Why doesn't he talk? Why doesn't he move?" Ben's voice became loud and shrill. His body trembled violently. "For Chrissake!" he screamed. "Don't just stand there! *Do something!*"

Judy groped for Ben's hand, trying to pull him back down. "Please, Ben. Oh, Ben, please—"

"Look at him! Christ, I wish you could see him. If only I could fight him! If only I knew how to get to him! Jesus! He's driving me crazy!" Ben's hands curled up into fists. "Come on, you goddamned Jew! I dare you! Tell me what it is you're after!"

And in that instant Ben fell suddenly silent. He was breathing heavily and perspiring. His eyes were wide, bulging. The nervous actions of his fingers stopped. Ben looked as if he were a frame on a roll of movie film, frozen by the stopping of the projector.

Judy stared up at him, speechless.

And then, quietly, almost imperceptibly, his voice started to speak. And Ben was saying, "Wait a minute . . . I think I know now what it is you want . . ."

CHAPTER FOURTEEN

※──────◆>●<◆──────※

If Ben had heard of it happening to anyone else, he would have suggested they seek psychiatric help. But because it was happening to him, because he was the one experiencing it and actually feeling it, he believed it.

After Judy left, he stormed about the apartment like a man about to explode. He shouted incoherently, frequently in Yiddish, slammed his fist into his palm and threw books against the wall.

"That can't be the end of it!" he cried, out of control. "I haven't gone through all this, suffered all this, only to be left hanging. It isn't fair! It just isn't fair!"

Shortly after midnight he sank in exhaustion onto the bed, and spent a night of twilight existence. Never really in touch with reality, never really aware of the present, and yet never quite asleep either, he tossed and turned and labored beneath a parade of nightmares and illusions. The characters were all the familiar ones: Rosa Messer, Solomon Liebowitz, David and Saul and Sarah.

Twice he got up and roamed about the apartment without knowing it, searching for something he knew not. The dark shadows represented evil and horror to him, the cold empty rooms were the years of his life. When he spoke it was either in Yiddish or Aramaic or Hebrew. He twisted and turned on the bed, his body sweating small rivers, his face distorted in a sardonic grin. Many times his eyes were open, but he did not see. Or, if he saw, they were images that belonged to another time. Nazarenes gathered in a low-ceilinged room to wait for their Messiah to come back. Rosa Messer keeping one dim light bulb lit for Shabbas, while the rest of the house was dreary and depressing. Solomon Liebowitz entering the rabbinic university. David ben Jonah standing on the hilltop, waiting for Sarah.

When dawn came and forced its own light into the apartment, dispelling the shadows and the dark, Ben felt as if he had undergone a hundred tortures. Every muscle in his body was sore. There were bruises on his arms and legs. He found that he had vomited in bed and had lain in it.

Dragging himself about, muttering under his breath, Ben forced himself to bring some semblance of order back to his apartment. He had some vague notion of what he had suffered during the night, bits and pieces of the nightmares flashed in his memory, and he knew why it had happened.

"There's no stopping it now," he said as he remade the bed. "If I continue to fight it, it'll kill me and some morning I'll wake up dead. Why don't I just give in and save myself the pain and anguish?"

He was talking more for David's benefit than his own, because he wanted the Jew to know the conclusion he had reached.

"I'm no match for you," said Ben. "Being immortal, you have powers I cannot combat. Like the ability to bring my past back to life. It was you all along, wasn't it? It was you that started me remembering. Even before you showed yourself, you planted the little inescapable horrors in my mind. God, you're insidious, David ben Jonah."

After this, Ben decided to go for a walk and clear his head. The gray morning of West Los Angeles was cold and biting, yet Ben did not wear a jacket, for as he stepped outside and stood on the sidewalk, he was walking a dusty path that wound its way between aging olive trees. The air was warm and heavy, full of dust and buzzing flies. It felt good, because it was the path to the city, and in the city he could find diversion.

As he walked along Wilshire Boulevard, Ben nodded genially at the passers-by he met: farmers on their way to the marketplace, men of the Law on their way to the Temple, Roman soldiers patrolling the streets in pairs, groups of children on their way to school. He paused now and then to admire the handiwork of craftsmen who labored in their crowded stalls that opened out onto the narrow street. He stepped aside for the passing sedan chair of someone of wealth. It was such a good, free feeling to wander through the city at will, to sit by a well and eat the bread and cheese he had bought, to peruse the wares of a fabric merchant in search of a small gift for Rebekah.

His farm was large now and the investments he continued to wisely make were reaping good profits. David felt secure and content at this time of his life, waiting only for the day when Rebekah would give him a son, and then he would be truly a man "in the shade of his fig tree." And when that day came he would have a great feast under the olive trees and invite as many people as he could, and hire musicians so that everyone could sing and dance. It would be a day of great rejoicing, and David would be the happiest man on earth.

After several hours had passed, he decided to return to the farm and inspect the day's work. David was lucky to have such a trustworthy steward to oversee his slaves, and to have Salmonides, an honest Greek—so unusual a thing in this day and age.

David passed through the gate and started on the road to Bethany, from where he would turn off and head up the path to his home. Along the way he saw many people streaming into the city: farmers and craftsmen with items to sell; squads of Roman soldiers who put away their standards so that the image of Caesar would offend no one; the handsome centurion waving to him from his high-stepping horse, recognizing an influential Jew when he saw one; and foreigners from the far corners of the world. David never ceased to be amazed at the array of men God had created, each different, each speaking his own tongue, each colorfully garbed.

David climbed the path and looked forward to a cup of cool milk in the shade of a fig tree. Perhaps Rebekah had baked some honey cakes. It had been a good day.

When Ben stepped through his apartment door, he was instantly bewildered. Judy got up at once from the couch and came up to him. "I was worried. Where have you been?"

"Where have I . . . ?" Ben's face wrinkled in a frown. His eyes were perplexed, confused. "I . . . don't . . . know. What am I doing over here? I was in the bedroom . . ."

"No, you weren't. You were out. I let myself in when I got here, your door wasn't locked. I've been waiting three hours."

"Three hours—" He rubbed his forehead. "Oh, Christ! What time is it?"

"Nearly noon."

Then he began to remember. The cold gray sky of dawn, the absence of cars on the street, a hushed silence all about. And then suddenly, the crowded streets of Jerusalem. "Oh God," he groaned. "I must have been out for hours!"

"Where did you go?"

"I don't know. Christ, I don't even know."

"Come over here and sit down. Oh, Ben, you look like hell! When was the last time you shaved?"

He ran a hand over his chin. "I . . . don't . . . Judy! Judy, the most extraordinary thing happened!"

"Hey, calm down. You're shivering. Ben, I'm worried about you."

"Listen, I have to tell you about this morning. It's positively uncanny." His voice died to a whisper until he stared ahead with blank eyes. "Why . . . I must have been wandering the streets and talking to myself. Christ, I'm lucky I wasn't picked up."

"Ben—"

"I just can't get over what's happening to me."

"Ben, listen to me. I want you to eat something."

"Later."

"No! You're not well. Look at you, pale and shaky. Sunken eyes. For God's sake, you look awful."

"I can't get over what's happening to me."

"Don't ignore me, Ben. Look, I brought something to show you." In her desperation to snap him out of his bewildered state, Judy thrust the newspaper at him, which she had not planned to show him until later. But it worked. As soon as he saw the headline, Ben came around. He read the headline. "What the hell? Are they serious?"

"Read the story. I'm making you some coffee."

Ben scanned the front-page story, studied the pictures of the excavation site and then threw the paper down in disgust.

"Come on, Judy! They're reaching! You know they are!" He strode to the kitchen, leaned in the doorway and watched her fill the coffeepot and plug it in. "More yellow journalism. How the hell do they get away with question marks in headlines!" He glanced back at the paper sprawled on the floor, and from where he stood, could see the headline: Q DOCUMENT FOUND?

"They're really reaching!" he shouted. "How can Weatherby allow it?"

"I don't think he has any control over it, Ben."

He shook his head in disgust. Yes, they were really reaching. The reference in the headline was to a nonexistent document which Bible scholars generally believe was around in the period following Jesus' death and before the first Gospel was written. Due to certain clues found in Matthew, Mark and Luke, it was held that another collection of the sayings of Jesus must have been circulating among Nazarenes before Mark came out with his Gospel. That supposed collection of sayings was labeled "*Quelle*," or "source," by German scholars in the Nineteenth Century, and these days abbreviated to simply *Q*. No trace of that document has ever been found.

"Do people really think that's what Weatherby has?"

"Not people, Judy, newspapermen. And it's not what they think, it's what they want the public to think so they'll buy their goddamned newspapers. Just because he threw in a few quotes that might prove Jesus actually said them! I hardly think the Magdalene Scrolls were the basis for Matthew and Luke!"

Judy grinned. She was glad to see Ben himself again, the analytical historian. "You know," she said as the coffeepot began to percolate, "I doubt David even heard of the virgin birth or the nativity."

Ben folded his arms and leaned against the doorframe. "The mythology came much later. And Jesus had no intention of founding a worldwide church. Even Matthew, Chapter Ten, verse five, tells us that. If you asked David ben Jonah, he wouldn't know what a Christian was, or even a church. He and all the others waiting for Jesus to come back were pious Jews who observed Passover, fasted on Yom Kippur, refrained from pork and considered themselves the Chosen People of God. All the mythology and ritual came much later, when the Gentiles joined."

Judy unplugged the pot and poured two steaming cups of coffee. "Here. Let's go sit down. I really wish the last Scroll hadn't perished. Maybe it could have cleared up some of the things you just mentioned."

Ben kicked the newspaper with his foot before sitting down. "Q Document indeed! Pile of crap! What do they know?"

Judy drank her coffee slowly, savoringly. "Where David mentioned a monastery by the Sea of Salt, he was talking about Qumran, wasn't he?"

"The ancient name for the Dead Sea was Sea of Salt. In all likelihood, he personally knew the man who hid the Dead Sea Scrolls in those caves."

Judy shuddered involuntarily. "God, it's awesome. The whole thing is just overwhelming." She turned to Ben. "What are you going to do now? Write a book?"

But he remained silent. There was a queer expression on his face, one that troubled Judy. "It isn't over yet," he said distantly.

"What? How do you know?"

"It's a feeling I have. Judy, do you remember last night when you were in the kitchen and I suddenly cried out? And you came running in? I never told you what happened. It was the strangest thing . . ." Ben's eyes clouded over as he recalled the uncanny sensation of actually moving back in time. "I can't find words to describe it. It was just . . . weird! There I was, sitting at the desk with my hands spread out upon the photographs, when all of a sudden, I felt a change come over me. It was most bizarre. I had no control over it. I was fixed to the spot. And as I sat there, I began to feel . . . to feel . . ."

"To feel what, Ben?"

"To feel the air around me change. It turned into the air of another place and another time. Then I saw images before my eyes. Things I wouldn't normally imagine. They fluctuated, like a poor TV reception—now fuzzy, now sharp—until, all of a sudden, it was *all* in focus. All of it. And there I sat, amid the real smells and sounds and sights of Jerusalem. Judy, for one brief instant I was actually there in David's Jerusalem!"

She stared at him in disbelief. The expression on his face was wild, animated. His eyes were afire again. And his words, what he had just said . . .

Judy became worried. Ben was switching his moods too easily, was becoming more and more unstable.

"You don't believe me," he said flatly.

"No, I don't."

"But what I saw—"

"You've been to Israel before, Ben. You've seen Jerusalem many times. And you've read descriptions of what it was like in the past. It was your imagination!"

"No, no, it wasn't. And this morning. I walked the streets of West Los Angeles for five hours, and for every single second of that time I was back in Jerusalem. I was not imagining it!"

"Then what are you trying to tell me? That David is trying to take you back to Jerusalem with him?"

"No," said Ben quietly. "I'm not saying that at all. Last night I stood up to David ben Jonah and shouted at him. I clenched my fists and dared him to make a move. Well"—Ben raised his eyes to Judy—"David accepted my challenge. Now I know what he was doing here all this time. It wasn't to stand by while I translated his Scrolls, as I had thought. No, David had another reason for coming here and for standing and watching and waiting. He was waiting for the moment for me to break down, which I finally did last night."

"Why? What does he want?"

"He wants *me*, Judy. Or rather, he wants my body."

She involuntarily drew back from him, her eyes gaping incredulously. "No!" she whispered coarsely.

"Yes, it's true. David doesn't give a damn about me, Judy. He wants to inhabit my body so he can go back to Israel."

"Oh, Ben, this is insane!"

"Goddamnit, don't say that! There's nothing wrong with me!"

She saw the veins at his neck bulge out, saw spittle fly out of his mouth as he shouted. So she said, "Listen, Ben, it can't possibly be so. David wouldn't hurt you. He's . . . your friend."

"Oh, but don't you see? It doesn't hurt at all. It's actually very nice." Ben smiled flippantly. "He's shown me how pleasant it can be to go back to ancient Jerusalem."

Oh, dear God, thought Judy in a panic. "What will you do then?" she asked in a strangled voice.

"I don't know, Judy. I haven't given it that much thought. Maybe I'll leave the decision up to David."

"Do you mean— Do you mean you're going to let him . . . possess you?"

"Why not?"

Judy felt her stomach rise. "But, Ben, you're your own man! What will become of you if David takes over your mind? What will become of Benjamin Messer?"

"Benjamin Messer can go to hell for all I care, along with his lunatic mother and heroic father. You see, I experienced a lot of changes last night after you left."

"And?"

"David made me see what sort of a person I really was. What sort of a wretch Ben Messer really is, who forsook his mother and was ashamed of his father's memory. I was a rotten child from the start and a worse Jew."

"But, Ben, you can't help all that. The way you were raised—"

"I think I'll be happier with David."

She turned away from him and wrung her hands frantically. "What about me?"

"You? Well, of course, I'll take you with me."

Judy whipped around. Ben's blue eyes were clear and sharp. His face relaxed, dressed in an easy smile. He was like a man arranging a picnic in the country. "Take . . . me with you . . . ?"

"Certainly. It's what David would want, and it's certainly what I want." Ben reached out for her hand, gently cradled it in his and said softly, "You didn't think I would go without you, did you?"

Uncontrollably, tears sprang into her eyes. She had been in love with Ben for a while now, and was sick to despair to see what had happened to him. She decided there and then to never leave his side again. She would move into his apartment and see this thing out with him. And if there were no end to it . . .

Just then there was a knock at the door, and Judy felt Ben rise up from the couch. She did not see the person on the other side, but she heard his voice. "Overseas cable for Dr. Messer. We usually call them in, but your phone is out of order. Didja know that?"

"Yes, yes, thanks." Ben signed for the cable, tipped the messenger and closed the door slowly. "It's from Weatherby," he said.

"Probably been trying to phone you and can't. I bet he wants to know why you haven't sent him any translations."

"Yeh, you're right." Without opening it, Ben tossed the cable onto the coffee table. Then he picked up Judy's empty cup. "Want a refill?"

"Please. Heavy on the cream this time."

As Ben disappeared into the kitchen, Judy stared at the crumpled brown envelope on the coffee table. And a chilly feeling of foreboding came over her. No, she thought sadly. There's more to it than that. Or Weatherby would have just sent an ordinary letter.

With great apprehension she picked up the envelope and slit it open. When she read the brief message inside, her heart came to a complete standstill. "Oh God," she whispered, and began to tremble.

Her next quandary was how to tell the news to Ben. Or *if* to tell him at all. But then again, he would find out soon anyway, and for him to learn it this way was better.

Judy rose tiredly from the couch. She was unsure about her feelings at this moment, whether she was happy or sad or angry at the news. In a way, she was all three.

Ben came whistling into the living room, and when he saw Judy's face, stopped short. "What's the matter?"

"It's Weatherby," she said in a tight voice. "Oh, Ben—"

Quickly he placed the cups on the coffee table and reached for the cable.

Judy said, "I don't know whether to shout or laugh or cry, Ben. Dr. Weatherby has found three more Scrolls."

CHAPTER FIFTEEN

The days that it took for Number Eleven to get there were unbearable ones for Ben and Judy. It had taken her half an hour to rush home, pack a few things, leave Bruno in a neighbor's care and rush back. If the news of no more Scrolls had turned Ben into an unstable person, the news of now *three* more made him unbalanced altogether. She watched him as he switched back and forth between the three time periods. One moment he would be in the present—normal and chatty; the next, back in Brooklyn as a poor tormented boy; next, as David ben Jonah enjoying a meal of dried fish and cheese under an olive tree; and back to the present again, with no memory of the minutes before.

"I have no control over it!" he cried in despair that evening. "I can't fight it. When David takes over, he makes me see what he wants me to see!"

And when Ben got this way, Judy cradled him in her arms and rocked him until he was quiet.

That night she dissolved a sleeping pill in some warm wine and consequently gave him his first restful sleep in many days. After he was sound asleep in bed, his face placid and his respiration low, she made a bed for herself on the couch with a pillow and blanket, and lay awake a long time before also falling asleep.

The next morning, after a dreamless night, Ben seemed greatly improved. He took a shower, shaved and put on fresh clothes. Although he was outwardly cheerful, Judy saw the signs of agitation underneath—jerking hand movements, quick darting glances, a forced nervous laugh. She knew Ben was anxious to get the next Scroll, and she knew his anxiety would grow with each day.

She felt it, too. Another Scroll . . . Indeed, three more! So these would be the ones to fill in the blank sixteen years, tell of the growth of the Messiah movement and reveal the infamous deed David had committed for which he was going to die. Judy was anxious, too, desperate to have all this over with before Ben lost hold of his last fragment of sanity.

She kept him quiet on Sunday, involving him in discussions and going over all their translations. He would sit and stare for hours on end at the Aramaic writing on the papyrus, and Judy knew that he was two thousand years away from her, enjoying some tranquil day in the life of David ben Jonah. She did not even attempt to draw him out of that world, for he seemed so at peace with himself and so content. She decided that, for now, it was better to leave him alone in the quietude of David's day rather than bring him forward to the turbulent present. For when he was himself and existing in this reality, he was nervous and paced the floor. And if he slipped back to his childhood and relived the horrors of being with his crazed mother again, he would cry and rage in Yiddish and throw himself about.

So Judy left him in David's reverie, and hoped he would remain there until the next Scroll came.

On Monday there was a letter from Weatherby. Before it arrived, Ben stayed in the present for five hours without once slipping in time. He was clearheaded and in full control of his faculties. Aside from his great agitation, he was almost normal.

Judy had to keep him from attacking the mailman when he walked up, and then had to succor Ben after the tremendous disappointment. He stayed in the present long enough for Judy to read him the letter.

"He describes how they found the last three jars," she said, paraphrasing. "It seems that after they'd gotten used to the idea of there being no more Scrolls, the floor of the house fell in and some sort of ancient cistern or storage area beneath the house was revealed. In it were three more jars. Weatherby thinks that David must have run out of room in his original hiding place and so put the rest in here. Anyway, since then, Weatherby says, they've gone over the entire area with a fine-tooth comb and have come up with nothing else. He's certain that these really are the last Scrolls."

"Does he say what condition they're in, when he sent them?"

"No, but he says he's anxious to hear from you."

"Ha! That's a switch!" Ben turned on his heel and in that instant David abruptly took over. That phlegmatic stare which Judy had come to recognize as the ancient past fell over Ben's face like a curtain, and he wandered away from her without another word, gliding into the bedroom and falling onto the bed.

While he did so, Judy decided to fill her time constructively, and so set up the typewriter in the dining room, where she began copying the translations.

Scroll Number Eleven came the next day. Ben had been in torment all day long, pacing and nervous like a caged animal. Occasionally, from her spot at the dining table, Judy overheard Ben's argumentative colloquies with David, or with his mother. Sometimes she could hear him talking quietly with Saul about the differences between Eleazar's and Simon's teachings, in such a way that it appeared David was trying to convert Saul to Messianism. Occasionally Ben spoke to Solomon, murmuring that at times he wished he had gone ahead to the university with him and become a rabbi.

Judy heard Ben shouting at David, telling him to stay out of his body and to take his grisly nightmares with him. At other times she heard him sobbing and speaking in Yiddish, so she knew he was back with his mother again.

Witnessing the gradual breakdown of Ben's sanity had torn Judy apart. Twice, after hearing him scream about Majdanek, she had put her head on the typewriter and cried. But she could not interfere. The battle was Ben's. The search for identity was a lonely one, and she knew that her intervention would only bring a negative result.

When Scroll Eleven came, Ben snatched it out of the mailman's hands and dashed upstairs while Judy remained behind to sign for it and apologize for his behavior. When she reached the apartment, Ben was already at the desk and scribbling in his notebook.

When the actual moment of departure came, I was saddened, but up until then I had been excited and looking forward to my trip with much joy. The anticipation of such a journey always far outweighs the thought of leaving one's loved ones, or of the dangers inherent in such a trip, until the actual moment of embarkation, and then one remembers the months of loneliness that lay ahead.

Rebekah was quietly forlorn. Not once in all the time since my announcement to go had she expressed dismay, for Rebekah was a demure and obedient wife and knew that my decisions were for the best. And if she did harbor a reluctance to have me go, or an ill foreboding about the journey, she did not voice it. So respectful of my wish was Rebekah.

Yet there were many who did not hold their tongues. Saul was the most outspoken. Several times he had come to our house to sit with me for long hours in the evening and try to dissuade me from going. And I loved him all the more for it.

He said: You cross a great and treacherous sea, which often claims many lives. And if you survive the going over, then what is to prevent you from malicious attack in that sinful Babylon? And if by some bizarre chance you should live through your visit there, then there is the trip home, again on that treacherous sea!

You are an optimist, my brother, I said, and forced him to smile. Now, you know that I have financial interests there, and must travel at least once in my life to inspect them. I will have old Salmonides with me. He is a veteran traveler and wise to the treachery of your Babylon.

My other friends of the Poor were likewise against me. They were afraid that the Master would return while I was gone, and I knew this was a chance I had to take. But my old mentor Simon was in Rome, and I longed to see him again. And since I had heard so many outrageous tales about this city of a million inhabitants, I wanted to see it for myself.

Of everyone who tried to dissuade me, only one might have been successful. But my sweet Sarah maintained her silence. As accustomed as I was by now to being in close proximity with her, ever since she had joined the Poor, I still never failed to feel the familiar ache in my heart and weakness in my knees whenever her eyes met mine. It had been a long time since that afternoon on the hilltop, and yet I continued to love and desire her as if it had been only yesterday.

On the day of my departure, all my friends gathered. My wife stood at my side as our brothers and sisters of the Poor gave me the kiss of peace. Sarah also touched her lips to my cheek and whispered: The God of Abraham will protect you. Yet she did not raise her eyes to me. Saul, who still was not a member of the New Covenant and who did not believe the Messiah would return any day now, embraced me and let his tears run freely down his cheeks.

The last to bid me farewell was Jonathan, my favorite nephew, whom I loved dearly. He put his arms about my neck and expressed his wish that I would not go.

So I said to him: Jonathan, you are the eldest son of Saul, just like the eldest son of the first King of Israel. That Jonathan was a noted warrior and a brave man. Do you remember what David of old said of his best friend Jonathan? It is written that David said: Saul and Jonathan were lovely and pleasant in their lives. And thee, my brother Jonathan, thou hast been pleasant unto me; thy love to me was wonderful, passing the love of women!

Jonathan enjoyed these words and became less distressed. So I did not tell him that they had been the lamentations of David upon the slayings of Saul and Jonathan on Mount Gilboa. And because he was also a member of the Poor, since Sarah persisted to take him to the meetings despite Saul's disapproval, Jonathan gave me the kiss of peace.

Salmonides and I departed that day by caravan, and arrived at Joppa in the next week. From here we secured passage on a fine Phoenician ship bound for Crete. We fared the voyage well, hugging the coast all the way as we did. In a harbor not far from the town of Lasea, we were able to buy passage aboard a Roman vessel which was sturdy beneath its single heavy square sail. We were assured she could not be reefed in foul weather.

The season remained favorable and so we set out toward Rome. All along the way we were aided by gentle winds from the south, and while the Roman captain thanked his Capitoline deities for their help, and while Salmonides gave credit to his Greek gods, I alone knew that it was the work of the God of Abraham that made the journey so pleasant.

My first glimpse of Italy was at Rhegium, where we stopped to let off passengers and pick up new ones. And from there we traveled the coast to Ostia, the port of Rome.

We hired donkeys at this point and traveled a day's journey until we reached the city, on the eve of a holiday known as the Saturnalia. It was also, coincidentally, the Emperor's birthday.

I will not, in these brief scrolls, my son, go into the shocking sights that met my eyes as Salmonides and I entered the city. There is little time left to me now, and every hour that my pen is crossing this papyrus brings me that much closer to my death. I will not go into the licentious nature of Rome, or the startling behavior of its populace, let me only cleave to my own story and suffice it to say that Rome is truly a Babylon.

Salmonides and I took separate rooms at a respectable inn, and while I dispatched him as my agent to look into my financial holdings in Rome, I had but one purpose intended for myself: to see Simon.

You know, my son, that Simon had left Jerusalem several years before, but what you do not know and what you will not understand until you are a grown man is *why* Simon left Jerusalem. You will remember that I told you of the differences he held with Jacob and their struggle for supreme leadership of the Poor. As our membership grew and as each day passed and the Messiah did not return, the more Jacob challenged Simon for his leadership. His grounds were that he is the Master's brother.

And so it happened that Simon, the Master's best friend, finally succumbed to the pressure and left Jerusalem with his wife to preach about the coming of the Messiah in other cities. Why he went eventually to Rome, I do not know, except that it was possibly because of a growing Messianic community there, and he desired to help them.

In the days of my first conversion, I have told you, there was much consternation among the Twelve about a man named Saul of Tarsus, who, having had a vision of the Messiah on the Damascus road, claimed to have been ordained to convert Gentiles into the New Covenant. In time, having begun a large community of the Poor in Antioch, this Saul of Tarsus went to Rome on some criminal charge with the intention of pleading his case before Caesar. He was one of the ones responsible for converting many Jews in Rome to our beliefs, so that when I arrived in Rome on that fifteenth day of the Roman month of

December, it was not difficult for me to find the homes of men who, like myself, awaited the return of our Messiah.

I was received by them, given the kiss of peace and called brother. This was the first time I heard the word *Christian* and it greatly baffled me. My Jewish brethren in Rome also spoke of the Messiah by the name of Jesus, which is the Latinization of his name, and this also gave me pause.

When finally I was led to Simon, it was a reunion of embraces and many tears. I clasped the old man to me as if to never let go, and he let forth such a rush of Aramaic that I felt it must have tasted good on his tongue. Then we sat over a meal of sharp cheese and bread and olives and reminisced about the past.

He asked me: Has Jacob done a good job?

And I replied: Yes, for he is influential. We have thousands in our community now, all awaiting the return of the Master. With increased agitation against Rome, all agree that the Last Days are upon us and that these were the times the Master spoke of. He will be at the gates tomorrow.

Then I looked around me at the faces in our gathering, and saw the necklaces they wore, and I knew they were Gentiles. So I said: When the Master returns, the Kingdom of God in Israel will be established on Zion, and the Chosen People will rule the world.

Now Simon laid a hand upon me, saying: I know what is in your heart, my son, and I would like to dispel your dismay. When our Master left this earth thirty years ago and was reborn again, I was a young man and impatient for his Return. So I told everyone that it would be tomorrow. But now I am very old and somewhat prescient. I can see now that he had not intended to return until more faithful were prepared for him.

I said: All Jerusalem awaits him, Simon.

And he replied: They are only Jews. We cannot forsake the Gentiles.

This struck me as a blow, and I was speechless. Simon had so changed in our years of separation that he was no longer the same man. After a length, I was able to say: Do you mean that you preach of the Messiah here in Rome?

He said: I preach it to them and they believe.

But they are uncircumcised! I said.

Circumcision belongs to the Old Covenant, said Simon. We are brothers in the New Covenant.

And do they keep holy the Law of the Torah?

They do not.

Do they go to the synagogue or fast on the Day of Atonement?

They do not.

Do they abstain from eating the flesh of swine?

They do not.

I was horrified. Perhaps my shock was made manifold by having heard all this from Simon, who was once the most pious of Jews.

I asked him: What are the symbols they wear about their necks?

He said: It is the sign of the fish, the symbol of our brotherhood. It came from Antioch, where they speak Greek.

And you allow them to wear graven images?

There is no time to force our laws upon the Gentiles, for the Messiah will return at any moment. Maybe even as we speak, he is approaching the gates of the city. These good people believe in him, they have been saved. Had I insisted they first become Jews, they might not be prepared in time and fall to the wayside when the Kingdom of God is at hand.

But I was not mollified. So I said: Simon, in Judea countless Jews are preparing to fight Romans. Men who are your brothers are arming themselves for the battle which must come. And yet here you are, converting Romans. What happened? It is as though you and I were on opposite sides.

But we are not, he argued, for we are both on the side of God.

I could not agree with him. In Jerusalem, where Simon once preached, Jews were waiting for their King to come back. In Rome, Gentiles waited for someone they would not recognize.

Why do they call you Peter? I asked.

Because the Master once said I was so solid and reliable a friend that I was like a rock to him.

And they burn incense, which is a heathen thing.

It is because these men were once heathens, but now they worship God. This is their way of adoring him.

They do not worship God, I said bitterly, they have simply changed the names of their own gods. Each man will continue as before, having changed little. And in their hearts they will still be heathens. You even call your Lord's Day the Sun Day because that is what the Mithras followers call it.

He said: There are many of them among us. And we have won converts from Isis, from Baal, from Jupiter.

But I said: There was no conversion, Simon, for all they have done is exchanged new words for old. In the end, all of this is pagan.

We parted sadly and finally, forever. It was later that I learned Saul of Tarsus had changed his name to Paul, like Peter, in order to please the Romans. I also learned that few Jews in Rome had heard of the Messiah and that mostly uncircumcised pagans awaited him.

I cried very hard and lamented the day I had left Judea. As I sat in that stinking room at the inn, I longed for my olive trees and to feel the dirt of Israel beneath my feet. I saw Sarah's beautiful face before me, heard the voice of my beloved Saul and felt little Jonathan's arms about my neck. How I wished I had listened to them, for nothing came of my journey except pain and anguish.

We were to depart the next day for Ostia. Salmonides tried to persuade me to linger a while in Rome, insisting that I had judged it too quickly and too harshly. Yet I was deaf to his words. In Rome was hedonism and a disregard for God. I felt unclean. So I said to him: My home is Israel, for I am a Jew. There is Zion and the land promised to us by God. How can a Jew keep the Laws of the Torah among this sinful people?

Salmonides only shrugged and shook his head. In the nearly eleven years we had been friends, he still did not understand me.

It happened that, in the evening before sunset, I took a short walk on the street with Salmonides, for I was restless. There were great crowds on the streets, men and women of every type, speaking tongues I did not understand. Prostitutes called to me from doorways. Merchants pushed carts steeped with joints of pig and every cut of swine's flesh. There were statues all about and graven images on pillars and walls. It was a crowded, congested city, far worse than Jerusalem even during Passover.

At one point we felt ourselves suddenly caught in a surge as the crowd pressed together and moved forward. Salmonides and I tried to fight our way out but could not, so strong was the current. A great shout arose from the people, as if from one throat, and it was then that the mob suddenly split apart, like the Red Sea when parted by Moses, and my companion and I found ourselves at the very front with the street open before us, and the other half of the mob facing us across the way.

And this is what we saw: Cohorts of Roman soldiers, in bright red cloaks and shining armor, passed before us bearing the standards of Emperor Nero. Behind them there came a fanfare; rows of men blowing trumpets to the sky, making such a noise as to cause me to cover my ears. Following the fanfare was a regiment of the Praetorian Guard, the Emperor's personal bodyguard, stepping high and proud in arrogant vanity. And immediately behind them was the Emperor himself, driving a chariot of gold which was drawn by four magnificent horses. The twenty-six-year-old Imperator was thickset, had almost no neck and displayed a dense crop of red curls on his head. He smiled as he rode past and waved a thick arm at us. It fascinated me to actually look upon this young man who ruled the world. This young man who was nearly my own age.

After Nero had passed, there came a sight which I will not forget for a very long time. Steering her own chariot of two horses was the Emperor's wife, Poppaea Sabina.

She was without a doubt the most magnificent woman I have ever looked upon. Her sunlight-blond hair crowned her head and was fixed in place with tiny ribbons and jeweled pins. Her beautiful face, very like those I had seen on statues, was whiter than white, pale and delicate like porcelain, with eyes the color of the sky and lips a soft pink. She was shocking with her throat and one arm bare, but beautiful at the same time, standing so still in her chariot that one might think she was indeed a statue.

Her clothes were of pure silk, and of a lavender so vivid that I thought I could smell the fragrance.

A hush fell over the crowd as the Empress rode by, and as she passed just a short distance before me, I felt the breath catch in my throat. There could not be, in all the Empire, a woman more beautiful than she.

Close to my ear, I heard a voice murmur: She is as vain as the goddesses and has teeth like a viper.

It was Salmonides, who had seen the look of admiration on my face.

He said quietly, so that no one else could hear: She bathes every day in milk and rubs crocodile mucus on her hands. She acts the patrician, but at heart she is a whore. It is because of her that Nero shared the fate of Orestes and Oedipus.

I knew what Salmonides meant and shook the enchanting vision from my mind. He was right. Beautiful and alluring though she was, Poppaea was a seductive she-devil and destined to drive men to destruction.

I tell you all this, my son, so that you will know that nothing good comes from Rome. While on the surface it can be appealing and enticing, underneath it will be evil. And I also tell you all this, my son, so that you will choose the right path.

Those in Jerusalem are dead and gone now, as I write these words, and all who knew the Master when he lived have perished. But those in Rome still live, yet they never knew him. The man whom they call Messiah and whose return they await is a myth, he never lived, and they will wait forever.

But you, my son, are a Jew and must wait for the man who will return to proclaim the Kingdom of God on earth. He will come only to Jews, for he is the Messiah of the Jews.

Look not to Rome, therefore, for theirs is the path of falseness and oblivion.

It was midnight, and the only light burning was the one on Ben's desk. He and Judy sat close to one another, Ben writing down his translation and Judy reading as he did so, so that they experienced the events in David's life together and at the same time.

Neither spoke for a considerable length, but continued to stare at the last line Ben had written. They were suspended in time, caught in the twilight between dreams and reality, and seemed almost afraid to dispel the mood.

Finally, after an interminable silence, Ben said flatly, "This is fantastic." He spoke mechanically and without feeling. "This Scroll has the power of a fifty-megaton bomb, and when it's unleashed . . ." He continued to stare. There was a glassiness to his gaze, a peculiar distance that made Judy wonder: Who are you now, Ben?

Gradually, like a sleeper being aroused from a deep, deep slumber, Ben started to stir and show signs of life. He straightened his back and stretched with a groan. Then he looked at Judy and smiled weakly. "There're a lot of people who aren't going to like this Scroll. It certainly isn't anything the Vatican will applaud—one of the original Jesus followers condemning the Rome Church."

Then he let out a short, dry laugh and his expression turned bitter. "They'll want to destroy this Scroll, if not all of them. Destroy David . . ."

Judy finally forced herself to stand and found her legs shaky. "Come on, Ben, let's move into the living room. I need some coffee."

He did not respond.

"Ben?"

He was bending close to one of the photographs, squinting at a smeared word. Judy noticed he was not wearing his glasses, had not been all evening, so she picked them up and offered them to him.

Pushing her hand away, he said, "I don't need them."

"I see." She turned the heavy glasses over and over in her hands. "Who are you now?"

Ben looked up. "What?"

"Who are you? Who am I talking to, Ben or David?"

His expression was for an instant blank, then it grouped into a twisted frown. "I . . . I don't know—" He drove his fingers through his hair. "I don't know. I can't tell . . ."

"Come on, let me give you some coffee." Judy held out her hand and, to her surprise, Ben quietly took it. He followed her obsequiously into the living room and sank onto the couch, his face still puzzled. Judy turned on a few lights and went into the kitchen.

As he listened to sounds of running water and cupboards opening and closing, Ben continued to look about himself in confusion. He felt strangely odd—a peculiar way he had never felt before.

When Judy returned with the coffee and some doughnuts, she found Ben on the couch with his head buried in his hands. Sitting next to him and gently laying a hand on his back, Judy whispered, "What is it, Ben?"

He raised his face to hers and it startled her to see the fear and confusion in his eyes. "I feel strange," he said in a tight voice. "That Scroll . . . something about it . . ." Then he turned his head in the direction of the den and seemed to be piercing the wall with his gaze so that he could see the photos on the desk. "Poppaea Sabina . . ." he murmured, as if trying to understand.

"Ben, come on. Eat a doughnut and drink some coffee. You're going to have to snap out of it because I want something explained to me."

He returned his phlegmatic gaze to her. "And my glasses . . ."

Fighting the urge to scream and slap Ben into reality, Judy forced herself to calmly pour a cup of coffee and put it in Ben's hands. He drank it obediently, unthinkingly.

"There's something I don't understand about this Scroll," she said in a strong voice, attempting to draw him out of himself. "When was it written?"

He did not answer, but continued to drink and stare.

"Ben? When was the Scroll written?" She placed a hand on his arm. "What year did David go to Rome?"

Finally Ben's eyes met hers and slowly came into focus. "What?"

"The year David was in Rome. When was it? We have a gap between Scroll Nine and this one because we lost Scroll Ten. We've moved up in time. David was twenty in the last Scroll and Saul's son had just been born. Now they're all older—"

"Oh, well," said Ben matter-of-factly. "That's easy to figure. How old did David say the Emperor was?"

"Twenty-six."

"And what year was Nero born?"

"I don't know."

As if they had been discussing it all evening, Ben suddenly got up from the couch, strode into the den and emerged a minute later with a book. He was thumbing through it as he resumed his seat on the couch. "Nero . . . Nero . . . Nero . . ." he muttered as he flipped over the pages. "Here we are." His hand slapped the open page. "Born in the year 37 C.E."

Ben extended the book to Judy, which she took. It was open to a chapter titled "Lucius Domitius Ahenobarbus (Nero)" The first paragraph gave the Emperor's dates as 37 A.D. to 68 A.D.

"Just add twenty-six to thirty-seven and you have sixty-three. That was the year David was in Rome, 63 C.E. Which means Scroll Ten probably filled in those eight years. A lot must have happened in that time. Sarah's conversion to the Poor, increasing wealth for David. It doesn't seem, however, that Saul has joined the ranks of the Nazarenes. I wonder why . . ."

Judy looked at Ben quizzically. Suddenly, he seemed himself again, as if nothing had been wrong just minutes before. She watched him as he poured himself a second cup of coffee and proceed to devour a doughnut.

"Scroll Ten," he went on, talking with his mouth full, "filled in those missing years. I hate not to have them."

"But we still have seven years to go."

Ben nodded. He appeared calm now, relaxed and untroubled. Whatever had been on his mind a minute before was now gone and forgotten. "The next two Scrolls will fill in those seven years. And they'll reveal the abominable deed David committed. He'll also tell us why he's about to die."

Judy nodded thoughtfully and stared into her cup. She was having a hard time coping with Ben's arbitrary switches in personality. It was difficult to follow him, to know how to handle him, or what to expect next.

When he finally put his cup down and said, "I'm exhausted," she was profoundly relieved.

"I'm going to bed. Tomorrow is another day, another Scroll." Ben rose from the couch and stretched his tall lean body. Then he took a minute to look down at Judy, noticing how small she seemed. "Hey," he said softly, "it's late. Let's go to bed."

But she shook her head. Possibly the worst part about Ben's abrupt changes was his ignorance of them. She wanted to say, "What happened to you a few minutes ago? What is it that makes you lose your grip on reality?" But she didn't. She knew what he would say, how he would react. He would have no memory of the peculiar way he had acted after reading the Scroll. And it would be useless to try to explain it to him.

"I want to sit up for a while," she said distantly.

Ben reached down and rested his hand on top of her head. "You know," he said in a subdued voice, "I never thanked you for moving in with me. It's made all the difference, having you here."

Judy didn't look at him, didn't move. She felt his hand caress her hair for just a moment, then it withdrew, and she finally heard him leave the living room and close the bedroom door behind him.

Judy remained sitting for some time before she finally got up from the couch and drifted over to the window. The curtains were parted, letting in the cold darkness of midnight beyond and reflecting the lights inside the apartment. She saw also her own reflection in the glass, a poor imitation of her former self—a face too pale that had gone thin from worry. It was a blank, expressionless face that looked out at the sleeping city, and the eyes were dead and lifeless. Judy was at a complete loss for feelings, for motivations, for anything. The events of the past week had robbed her of all certainty and of all strength of character, leaving her now devoid of will. For Judy was, after all, only a puppet—like Ben—to be manipulated by the forces at work here.

And just what were those forces that wreaked havoc in this quiet West Los Angeles apartment? Were they powers of the supernatural, or were they no more than the energies of the two personalities involved?

She pressed her face against the cool glass. Why am I here? she wondered distantly. How was it that I came to be caught up in Ben Messer's private cataclysm? Was it meant to be?

It's almost as if the two of us had been brought together from the far parts of the universe to act out this bizarre play. But why? To what purpose?

Without thinking about it, Judy disengaged herself from the window and floated about the room extinguishing all lights. She loathed the light, she wanted obscurity. It was easier to get lost in darkness, easier to find oblivion.

When she returned to the window the reflections were gone and all she could see were the skeletal trees that lined the street and bent in the wind. It looked cold outside. Cold and forbidding.

How can wind *look* cold? she thought absently, her forehead once more against the pane. How can you evaluate something that's invisible? How can you *look* at wind?

It's like David ben Jonah. I can't see him, and yet . . .

Judy slowly turned away from the window and the leafless trees beyond and took to staring into the depths of the darkened apartment.

She couldn't see David and yet she knew he was there.

Her eyes strayed to where the bedroom door was and lingered there a while, reflecting upon the strange man who slept on the other side.

How phenomenally Benjamin Messer had changed these last three weeks! Such a crisis he was suffering! And why? Is it Judaism? Judy wondered as her eyes imagined dust and palm trees. Or is it simply a matter of identity? Or possibly . . . they are one and the same thing. A person was simply a Jew. Did Catholics feel the same way? Or was there something to being a Jew that was like no other experience—the Judaism and the identity being so inextricably entwined.

She stared vacantly, unaware of visions of sunbaked roads and crowded marketplaces that her itinerant mind was conjuring. Surely Benjamin Messer was not the only important factor here, or possibly even the central one. There was David ben Jonah. There was the long-suffering Rosa Messer. Her martyred rabbi husband. And there was Judy herself.

Thoughts now seemed to group themselves about a particular focus, for she began to go inward, away from the dried figs and rope sandals and white robes she was imagining, and more in the direction of a dark little circle at the center of her soul.

And what she saw there, as she stood at the very edge of that abyss —looking down—alarmed her. As if at the periphery of a vast, fathomless crater, Judy felt a great sense of emptiness overwhelm her. A loneliness beyond comprehension. A cold barrenness that made her suddenly feel like crying out in despair. The vast black crater, filled with an inky coldness and stretching to the boundaries of imagination, was at the very center of Judy's core. And it was a dead, anathema thing; no life grew there.

The darkness of the apartment, the midnight on the other side of the window and the formidable void in Judy's soul were all one and the same—they were the absence of light.

More visions flashed before her. Aleppo pines against a lavishly blue sky. The smell of nard in the air. A hot sun that beat down on dusty roads.

She turned away from them. Turned her back on the allure of ancient Jerusalem. It would be nice to escape to it, yes, to let go for just an instant and run to the past to avoid facing the present. Just as Ben was doing . . .

Judy looked again at the bedroom door and realized, in a fleeting moment of lucidity, that he was being abnormally quiet.

Forcing herself away from the revelations of her inner self and away from the brief glimpses into the past, she crossed the darkness and opened the bedroom door.

Ben was deeply, peacefully asleep on top of the bed. He was fully clothed, his body completely at rest, with slow, steady respirations. As Judy stepped cautiously nearer, she was able to barely see his face, and the expression it wore surprised her. With his face composed in the faintest trace of a smile, Ben appeared to be in a state of complete repose.

She stared incredulously at him. Except for the one night she had given him a sleeping pill, Ben had not known such peace. Nor had she ever before seen such a tranquil look on his face—awake or asleep—and as she gazed down at it now, Judy began to see a deeper, clearer character to that expression.

It was one of surrender. Complete surrender.

Judy brought her head up sharply and looked around the room. Something was wrong. Something was terribly wrong.

Disturbed, but not knowing why she should be, Judy made a silent exit from the bedroom, gently closed the door and returned to her vigil at the window. The glass felt good against her face, for she was uncommonly warm. The sky, she saw, was starless tonight, and stirring about amid turbulent clouds.

She should be happy that Ben slept so well. And yet she was not. His expression, so ominous . . .

As she watched the heavy clouds roll overhead, Judy thought: Why are you doing this to us? Why have you come here? And which are you, David ben Jonah, friend or enemy? Do you stand and watch over him to protect him, or are you waiting for that one moment of weakness—

"Oh God!" she whispered. Her hands flew to her mouth. "What's happening to me?"

Judy spun about, her eyes bulging as they strained to see in the darkness.

"To see what? What am I looking for? Am I, too, losing my sanity?"

As she stared wildly before her, more visions flashed in her mind. The dark apartment suddenly exploded with brightness, and she saw before her a green hillside covered with white lilies and red anemone. She saw the fig trees and olive trees and a boy tending a small herd of goats.

"Oh God, I want to help you, Ben," she whispered hoarsely. "I want to help you because I love you, but I don't know how. I don't know how to fight this thing. How can I fight a ghost!"

She smelled olive oil burning in a lamp and tasted sharp cheese on her tongue. "It is stronger than I am, Ben. Just as you finally gave in, so now am I succumbing . . ."

Tears fell down Judy's cheeks. Her entire body trembled. The great void at the center of her soul was reaching up to embrace the warmth and life of the ancient past.

A clap of thunder dispelled the vision. She was alone in the dark apartment again. Outside, rain began to pelt the window.

Judy turned to look out. More cracking thunder. A flash of lightning. And in the brief second of illumination, she saw the dome of the Temple and the grim walls of the Antonia Fortress.

"Where is the rain falling?" she whispered sadly. "Here or . . . or *there?*"

An immeasurable length of time passed as Judy remained transfixed at the window. She was lost in a quandary of questions to which there came no answers. There were no solutions to the problems her mind presented, just more and more puzzles. Having glimpsed the emptiness that was her life, Judy wondered what it was that had brought her to this incredible hour, suddenly questioning her entire existence.

And what was it that was making her mind see things it had never before imagined? Was she, too, in some small way, also beginning to give in to the power of the specter that was David ben Jonah?

Judy might have reached some conclusions had she not, at a point just before dawn, been suddenly interrupted. During that quiet hour before sunrise, as a gentle rain fell and she felt herself drawing near to the answers, something happened which caused her to freeze. There had been no sound, no noise or outward indication. The darkness had simply shifted around her. The air had changed, and she suddenly sensed there was something different. An uncanny foreboding made her turn around.

The bedroom door was open and Ben stood there unmoving, not speaking.

A cold chill swept Judy's body, and she shuddered involuntarily. Her eyes were wide, her mouth slightly open. An unknown intuition caused her to feel suddenly, strangely afraid.

Something had happened.

"Ben . . ." she whispered.

He took a few steps toward her, then reached down and turned on the light.

In that instant Judy knew the reason for her fear. And when she saw his eyes, she screamed.

She screamed for a very long time.

CHAPTER SIXTEEN

◄►─────◄►◄○►◄─────◄►

No other change had taken place, just his eyes—which had gone from pale blue to dark brown.

He stood before her, gazing almost compassionately with a smile on his lips. "Judith—" he said softly, compellingly.

When he took a step toward her, she fell back.

"Why are you afraid of me, Judith?"

"I . . ." She searched her mind for a response. There was none. All she could do was shake her head in astonishment and feel the pounding of her heart. The screams had made her throat hurt. And now, in the aftermath of the initial shock, her fear was giving way to bewilderment.

"How can you be afraid of me, after all this time?" he asked softly. "Judith—" Ben extended both hands, and again she recoiled. "Don't you know who I am?"

"Who . . . are you?"

"I am David," he said with a reassuring smile.

"No!" said Judy, violently shaking her head. "Don't say that!"

"But it is true."

"Where's Ben!"

"Ben? Why, he never existed. There never was a Benjamin Messer—"

"Oh God," whimpered Judy. Tears sprang in her eyes, causing the image before her to swim. "I want Ben to come back. Oh God, what's happened?"

His expression changed to one of concern. "Please, I do not mean to frighten you. Do not back away from me, Judith. I need you."

"Oh, Ben," she cried. As the tears fell, she fought back the sobs. "What . . . happened to your eyes?"

He paused for a moment, thinking, then said with a smile, "It is interesting, is it not, that they should change? I cannot explain it to you, but I suppose it has an important significance."

Judy continued to stare wildly at the man before her, expecting at any moment to wake up from the nightmare.

He went on: "There never was a Benjamin Messer, for I have always been David ben Jonah. I have been asleep for so many years. The Scrolls awoke me to myself, reminded me of who I was, and now I have come back to live again. Do you understand?"

No, it wasn't just his eyes, Judy was beginning to realize. They were the only physical change in him, yes, but there was another, more subtle alteration that she was now beginning to discern.

It was his manner, his attitude. Calm and self-assured, this man was not the same nervous, anxiety-ridden man who had said good night to her just hours before. This stranger with the blond hair and dark brown eyes was completely relaxed and self-confident. He stood casually and spoke in a tone that revealed a man completely at ease and certain of himself.

"I know it must be hard for you," he was saying, "and that it will take time for you to get used to me. Until now you have only thought of me as a ghost."

Also, he spoke with the barest trace of an accent. German? Hebrew?

"Is Ben coming back?" she asked in a whisper.

"He cannot come back, because he never existed. You see, when I was Benjamin I thought at first that David was haunting me. Then I thought David was trying to *possess* me. But I was wrong. For I *was* David all along. It was Benjamin who never existed."

Feeling suddenly sick to her stomach, Judy turned abruptly away from him and clutched her abdomen.

"Why do you reject me?" he asked, almost pleading.

"I . . . I don't reject you," she heard herself say. "I refuse to believe you."

"But you will in time. You see, this explains so much. Last night, as we were reading the Scroll . . ." He walked casually past her and took a seat on the couch. "As we read the Scroll, it occurred to me that there was something odd about the Poppaea Sabina passage. Do you remember?"

Finding it hard to speak, Judy whispered, "I remember."

"There was something about it I could not pinpoint. Of course, now I know what it was. Poppaea Sabina was the name of my cat, and that is how I came to name her, for the Empress. When I bought the cat two years ago, she reminded me of Nero's wife, whom I had seen pass in her chariot."

Judy screwed her eyes tightly. "No," she barely whispered.

"And when you offered me those glasses, I did not need them any more, for even last night I was no longer Ben. I saw how you were worrying about my state, but there was no cause for alarm, dear Judith, since that was just the final stage of my becoming myself."

She opened her eyes and stared at him as if he were a monster.

"Please come sit by me."

"No."

He tilted his head to one side and studied her in concern. "Are you ill?"

"No."

"Please do not shun me. I had not meant to hurt you. I had thought you would be happy."

As he was shaking his head sadly, a small black shape emerged from the kitchen doorway, regarding the man on the couch with cautious eyes and widely dilated pupils. Poppaea took a few experimental steps toward him, and when he leaned forward to encourage her, she arched her back and hissed at him.

But Ben only laughed softly. "It is because I am a stranger to her now. In time she will come to know me and then we will be friends."

Judy gaped at the cat in disbelief. Poppaea's fur stood out on end, her ears flattened back. In the next instant, as if frightened, she darted back into the kitchen and could be heard scrambling into a small space.

"She will learn in time," Ben's gentle voice was saying. "And so will you, dearest Judith."

She raised her eyes to him again and saw a sweetly sad smile on his face. His whole attitude, his entire being seemed to be one of apology, of asking to be forgiven and to be accepted. And when she saw him thus reaching, Judy felt her heart go out to him.

"I'm afraid of you," she said at last.

"But you must not be. I would never harm you."

"I don't know what you are. I don't know what you'll be tomorrow, or even in the next hour. And that frightens me."

"But it is all over, Judith, can't you see? No more struggle for identity, no more trying to find myself. The agony that Benjamin went through—the nightmares and the tears and the torments— were all the pangs of my birth. It was necessary that he, that I suffer all that in order that I should be born again. All that is in the past, my dearest Judith, for I am now one with myself and at peace with myself. I was hoping you would understand."

She studied him for a moment longer, then cautiously, carefully approached the couch. Sitting on the edge, as far from him as possible, Judy continued to keep her eyes on him. Eventually the wave of nausea subsided and the turbulence began to die. The first shock was over, and now the bewilderment was also fading away. In its place Judy felt uncertainty, a perplexity over what to do next.

When he reached out his hand, as though offering a gift, Judy took it and felt herself calm even more.

He smiled reassuringly at her, emanating an air of complete control and confidence. His touch was warm and gentle, his voice comforting. "What has changed, has changed and there can be no going back. What was yesterday will never return. Benjamin Messer no longer lives. I was not happy in that life. But in this, I am."

Judy felt his fingers squeeze her hand and draw on it a little. She resisted at first, but finally gave in and let him bring her close to him on the couch. He had both arms about her, but lightly, as if afraid of breaking her, and was speaking softly. "You cannot possibly have liked me as Ben, for he was a troubled man. He was a man who denied his past and his heritage and who always tried to be something he was not. Benjamin Messer was but one manifestation of my personality, and I am sorry you were witness to it. Now that I am David ben Jonah . . ." He drew her against him and buried her face in his neck. "But now that I am David ben Jonah at last, dear Judith, possibly you can find it in your heart to love me."

When she awoke, she was in bed. Although fully clothed, she was under the covers and her shoes stood neatly by the bed. A comfortingly bright day flooded through the window, glistening remnant raindrops on the panes. Through the tree branches could be seen white clouds and scraps of blue sky. And through the open door, Judy could hear sounds of someone moving about in the next room.

Her mind began to race. Although all the unhappy events of the night before came back in a single rush, there was no memory of going to bed or falling asleep. The last thing she remembered was sitting on the couch with Ben's arms about her and listening to a gentle voice speaking compellingly of love.

She was hesitant to rise. She was fearful of what she might find in the other room. Ben's insanity could fly in any direction, his instability could be toppled by the slightest provocation. And yet reluctant though she was to confront him, Judy was at the same time desirious of staying by his side and watching over him. It was an irreconcilable dichotomy: the impulse to flee from this madhouse and the wish to help Ben through the crisis.

As she quietly rose and stole softly into the bathroom, avoiding seeing him and being seen, Judy tried to make a decision as to her next move.

Under the cool pray of the shower, however, the sinister aspects of the night before seemed to dissipate in favor of a more analytical attitude. As her sleepiness wore off, and as the effects of her fright from last night gradually went away, Judy began to feel better able to handle the situation.

After all, Ben—in his new state as David—had given no indication of tendencies toward violence. And if he were to maintain this current frame of personality, at least until the last Scroll was read, then she would be able to cope with it.

What happens after the last Scroll has come and gone, she had no idea. Nor did she care. For now, she and Ben were going to somehow live through another day.

He looked up as she came into the room, and broke into a broad grin. "Good morning, Judith. Are you feeling better?"

"Yes, thank you." She studied him cautiously.

"You fell asleep in my arms and so I carried you to bed. You are so light, it was like lifting a child."

As he spoke, Judy became fascinated. The man before her, except for the brown eyes, was Benjamin Messer in every way. Only, it wasn't . . .

He came toward her and took hold of her hand. Then he led her to the dining table.

No, this man was definitely different. While he looked exactly like Ben Messer, his whole attitude was different. The gestures and mannerisms belonged to someone else; the affectations were totally changed. This man seemed older, more mature, and strikingly self-confident. He was a man in full control of himself and one used to being in command.

He sat her down at the table before a cup of steaming coffee and a plate of eggs and buttered toast. Sitting opposite her, he said, "I have already eaten. Please, you will feel better."

Judy soon discovered a hidden appetite and quickly devoured the breakfast and two cups of coffee. While she ate, the unsettling gaze of Ben/David was ever on her, not leaving her for a moment, and that slight, secretive smile was always on his lips. Twice she started to speak, and each time he held up a hand, saying, "Eat first. Later we will talk." And she obeyed.

Afterward, they went together into the living room, which, to Judy's surprise, had been meticulously cleaned up. Even the wine spot on the carpet seemed paler, and everywhere was neat, dusted and orderly. Without having to look, she suspected the den and kitchen were the same.

When they sat on the couch, Ben said, "Now then, you feel better. You are no longer uncomfortable with me?"

"I don't know," she said uncertainly. "Are you . . . ?"

He laughed warmly. "Yes, I am still David. I told you last night that Ben was gone and would never return. But I can see that it will take time to convince you of this. That is all right, for I am a patient man."

Judy relaxed back into the couch, feeling better for having eaten, and considered her next words. "If you are David ben Jonah," she said warily, "then what does the next Scroll say?"

He grinned even wider. "You are testing me, Judith. That is a sign of faithlessness, and I want you to have faith in me. Do you?"

"You're avoiding my question."

"And you mine."

Judy shifted about to face him squarely. "I don't want to play word games with you, Ben. I am only trying to understand what's happened. You say you're now David reincarnated. Is that correct?"

"If you are comfortable with that term, yes. But it is more than a reincarnation, more than a rebirth, for, you see, I was never really away. I have been here all the time as Benjamin Messer."

"I see . . ."

"I do not think you do."

"Well, I'm trying." She sat back and regarded him a little more.

Yes, this new personality was definitely easier to deal with. Benjamin Messer, in his other state, had been a difficult man to handle. When he was himself, he was tormented by his past. When he was possessed by David, he was quiet and withdrawn. But this new condition, this state of actually being the ancient Jew, was almost a pleasant one, for he appeared rational, communicated well and seemed stable enough.

If he suffered no sudden slips in time or lapses in memory, if he suffered no explosions of rage, as Ben had had to suffer before, then possibly this new development was for the better. At least for now.

"What is going to happen?" she asked quietly.

"That is something I do not know. The future is as unknown to me as it is to you."

"But surely you can't go on as Ben Messer."

"And why not? It has served me well thus far. I can continue to use the identity a while longer until my intentions become clear to me. But whatever, dear Judith"—he reached out for her hand—"they will include you."

Oh, Ben, cried her mind in confusion. I want you to always include me! And I love you more than I can say. But what are you now? *Who* are you? And who will you be tomorrow?

"Why do you have that look of sadness, Judith?"

She averted her face. "Because I loved Ben."

"But I am the same man."

"No," she said quickly. "No, you're not."

"Then . . ." His voice dropped down. "Can't you find it in your heart to love me also?"

She brought herself abruptly about. His expression was one of longing, of gentle sorrow. She felt his fingertips caress her cheek, heard his tender voice. In her eyes it was Ben who sought awkwardly to make love to her, but in her heart she knew it was another man. In his struggle for identity, Ben had somehow lost the battle and had in some strange way seized upon the identity of the Jew in the

Scrolls. For whatever unspoken needs, for whatever arcane reasons, Ben had decided to become David, simply because he was no longer strong enough to exist as Ben.

"I want you back," whispered Judy in a last effort to reach him. "Send David back where he belongs, Ben, and come back to me."

But the man who continued to smile enigmatically at her, whose brooding dark eyes looked lovingly upon her, was not Benjamin Messer.

It was inconceivable that another Scroll would arrive this afternoon, and yet it did. Number Twelve came in the usual registered envelope and required the usual signature. But this time it was received differently. Instead of the excitement and agitation Ben had exhibited upon receipt of each of the previous Scrolls, Number Twelve was met with calmness and quiet joy.

He took his time going up the stairs and entering the apartment. Moved carefully about preparing his notebook and pen and adjusting the light. The pipe rack and tobacco pouch and ashtray had been removed from the desk and were out of sight—no longer necessary.

Poppaea Sabina, having been curled up on the swivel chair, arched her back and spat at Ben when he came near. Then she sprang off the chair and darted out of the room. Ben only shook his head.

Judy hesitated in the doorway, watching him slowly get ready to translate the next Scroll. This was not the Ben she knew before, who by now would have had the photographs out, the envelope on the floor, and the first words translated before his buttocks touched the chair.

When he looked up and saw her lingering, he said, "Are you not interested?"

"Yes, I am—"

"Well, come then, and sit next to me. Read as I write. We will relive these days of my life together."

When she drew up a chair and sat next to him, Judy murmured, "Don't you already know what this is going to say?"

But he did not reply.

Scroll Number Twelve was in poor condition. Comprised of six fragments, the edges were chewed, there were holes in the center and sections of undecipherable writing. But what remained was still a great portion and very informative.

I came home to a troubled Judea. My countrymen were growing less and less able to tolerate the presence of our Roman overlords, and I saw signs of agitation everywhere. Salmonides and I were both shocked to see so many crucifixes along the Joppa road, and marveled that the Zealot movement had grown so in our absence. We also saw many more Roman legions on the roads than there had been before, many of them heavily armed and freshly outfitted from Rome, so that we knew we had returned to troubled times.

But after an absence of so many months, it felt good to be among my friends and embrace my loved ones again. They were all gathered at my house: Saul and Sarah and little Jonathan; Rebekah and our friends of the Poor; and even Jacob, who stood apart from the rest in his white robes and ascetic silence.

Saul washed my feet as I entered and I saw that there were tears in his eyes. He said: Truly this is a day of days that has brought my brother home. We missed you, David, and prayed every day for your safe sojourn in Babylon.

I saw that he wore his best clothes and had put aside his teaching of the Law to spend this day with me.

Then Rebekah embraced me and kissed me and let her tears run freely onto my shoulder. If there was trouble in her heart, she did not speak of it, nor did she remind me of the loneliness she had suffered in my absence. Rebekah was a good wife and knew that what I had done had had to be done.

So I held her from me at arm's length and said: There will be no more journeys to Rome, my dearest, for I have seen enough.

The next to greet me was little Jonathan, whose excitement was boundless. He hugged me and kissed my cheeks and prattled without a breath about all the things I had missed while I was gone. And I laughed to hear him and to look upon him, because I loved little Jonathan dearly. He had Saul's gift for making friends easily and he had his mother's beautiful face. But deep in my heart I knew that I loved Jonathan to an extreme because I had, as yet, no child of my own and was despairing of it.

When Sarah came up to welcome me home, my legs weakened and my heart cried out, for she was yet the one woman I loved above all else, and it had been her image I had seen before me on the endless nights out at sea. Since joining the Poor and spending time in the company of Miriam and the other women who waited for the Messiah, Sarah had grown even lovelier and more radiant. Her faith in God and her belief in the return of the Kingdom of Israel had given her a special inner beauty and a tranquillity that shone in her eyes.

We had never again, since that day in the orchard, spoken of love. But there are ways of communicating other than by words, and I saw it that day on her face and in her eyes, that she loved me still.

Jacob, the leader of the Poor, waited until all had greeted me before himself approaching me with the kiss of peace. Then he said: Brother, it caused us great anguish to have you away in Babylon while we knew at any time the Kingdom of God was at hand. Yeshua will be at the gates of Jerusalem perhaps tomorrow, and we feared you would still be away on that Glorious Day. But now you are back and will not miss the Second Coming.

Jacob's fierce eyes penetrated my soul, and I saw in his gaze the firm belief in the imminent return of his brother. His hands clutched my arms and he spoke not another word, but on his face I read his thoughts.

He was telling me that indeed these were the Last Days the Prophets had spoken of, for everywhere there was unrest and agitation. These were the visions of Isaiah and Jeremiah and Daniel: the times when the Abomination of Desolation will occur and the Kingdom of Zion be restored.

In my absence, my vineyards and olive presses had made me an even wealthier man, so that my holdings exceeded even those of many old aristocratic families in Jerusalem. All this I credited to my friend Salmonides, who did not age with the years and whose keenness never dulled. He remained honest and faithful to me, extracting only the fee that was his due, and accumulating a small fortune for himself. When I praised him he argued, saying that it was I who was the shrewd one and that he was only my agent. Whatever, as I grew to an age when most men are proud of a small shop or are content with a fishing boat, the wealth of David ben Jonah became known and I was an influential man.

Being a member of the Poor, I shared a great deal of my wealth with the enormous congregation that was rapidly increasing in size. Besides Jacob and the Twelve, other followers were now preaching in the cities and in the countryside about the Kingdom that was to come and the Master who was to return. And when Jews everywhere saw the swords of the Romans and saw the Zealots hanging upon crosses, they knew in their hearts that these were indeed the Last Days.

So our ranks grew phenomenally, until we numbered in the tens of thousands.

And while the communion of bread and wine was celebrated in many houses in Jerusalem, while more and more Jews underwent baptism and adopted the creed of the New Covenant, my friend and brother Saul remained yet on the outside.

In many ways, our discussions reminded me of those I had had with Eleazar years ago, when Simon was persuading me. For now it was Simon's words I quoted to Saul, and his arguments echoed Eleazar.

The time has not yet come, said Saul, for God to re-establish the Kingdom of Israel. What you have read in the Book of Daniel you have misinterpreted. That time is a long way off yet before the Messiah of Israel appears among us.

Then I quoted Isaiah to him, and Esdras and Jeremiah, thinking my interpretation of the prophecies to be correct.

But these are the Last Days, my brother Saul, for you can see it everywhere. There is revolution in the air.

Saul only shook his head. And so it was in the time of the Maccabees, he said. Yet no Messiah came.

And I replied: But these are worse times.

And so our arguments went. Saul was a good rabbi and much sought after in the Temple. He was a pious Jew and knew the letter of the Law better than any man. And it saddened me that he did not believe in the return of our Master. For that was going to be a Glorious Day and Zion would be established again.

It came to pass that we heard news of the Fire at Rome which destroyed much of the city and caused disease and famine. And we also heard that our old friend and brother Simon had been executed in the arena for being suspect in the setting of that Fire.

We of the Poor gathered in Miriam's house and said prayers and sang psalms in memory of the man who had once been the Master's best friend, and who had been the first to recognize him as the Messiah.

And we also prayed that night because we knew somehow that the death of Simon—who had changed his name to Peter —and of his friend Paul was but the heralding of the Last Days. Now that Yeshua's best friend had been martyred for his sake, just as had Stephen and Jacob ben Zebedee, so now would our Master have to return to his people and lead them to victory against the oppressor.

But there were worse times yet to come.

Many of those among the Poor were Zealots. Such men now took to arming themselves. Even among the Essenes, who had been pacifists in the past, swords were taken up, for they believed that the struggle between Light and Darkness was at hand.

They said: The Messiah of Israel is almost at the gates, and we will not be found unprepared. He went away that we may preach the news and spread the word; but now he is on the road that approaches the city and we must be ready to fight for Zion.

While I did not agree with this and did not take up a sword, I did not deny my brethren the right to arm themselves. For these were the Last Days.

Ironically, Saul now carried a sword with him, for he heard the reports of insurrections all around Galilee and Syria; from Dan to Beersheba, Jews were beginning to stand up to the oppression of Rome.

Late into the night, we of the Poor gathered in our homes for

the bread and wine and to listen for the trumpets that would
announce the arrival of the Messiah. And on those nights I
watched Sarah, her head bent in prayer, her arms about Jonathan, and I rejoiced that she was so faithful.

In the spring of the following year, Procurator Gessius Florus
violated the Temple Treasury.
We never had an hour of peace again.

Judy stared at the erratic handwriting in the notebook and could
not remember having read it. Ben had spent the entire evening and
late into the night deciphering the Aramaic script, and Judy had
read each word as he had written it down. But now, with no more
papyrus to be read and the last line translated, she found herself staring at the notepaper as if for the first time.

Ben, also, seemed to be staring in perplexity at what he had just
written. His pen remained poised over the page, his hand ready to
write more. But the end of the sixth fragment had come abruptly,
leaving both him and Judy dangling in the air.

It was some moments before they began to rouse themselves from
their suspended animation, and it was Judy who made the first
move. Suddenly aware of a terribly aching back and painful joints,
she slowly extricated herself from the position she had been so long
in, and looked up at the clock.

It was just past midnight, and she stared at the illuminated dial
for several minutes before she realized what she was seeing.

"My God," she murmured, writhing stiffly. "We've sat here for
eight hours!" Then she looked at Ben.

He was still hanging over the last photograph, his body frozen in
an attitude of waiting. The pen still hovered over the notebook, his
eyes still staring at the last line of Aramaic. A fine sweat had broken
out on his forehead and was now trickling down his temples and
onto his neck. His shirt was soaked through with perspiration, and his
skin had blanched to an uncommon whiteness.

"Ben," said Judy quietly. "Ben, it's over. That's the end of the
Scroll."

When he did not respond, she gently lifted the pen from his
fingers and took a firm hold of his hand. "Ben? Can you hear me?"

Finally he turned his head to face her. The brown eyes were all the darker for the total dilation of the pupils. His gaze was completely blank and unresponsive. There were the tiniest beginnings of tears.

"Ben, you're exhausted. We've been here for eight hours, and look at you. You've got to lie down."

After a moment, with the stupor starting to lift, Ben swallowed hard and ran a dry tongue over his lips. "I'd forgotten," he said hoarsely. "I'd forgotten what it had been like. I'd forgotten how bad those days had been."

"Yes, they were. Come with me, Ben."

Although he was able to rise, he had to lean on Judy for support. She put an arm about his waist, feeling the cold clamminess of his body, and struggled with him into the living room. There, gently coaxing, she got him to lie down on the couch and rest his head on a pillow. Then she sat at his side, facing him and tenderly wiping away the sweat.

"There's only one more Scroll," she whispered. "Just one more. And then it'll be all over."

Ben closed his eyes, forcing the tears to run off his face and into his ears. A small whimpering sound started in his throat and gradually grew into harsh sobs. "We were waiting for the Messiah," he cried. "We waited and waited. He said he was coming back. He *promised—*"

"Ben . . ."

"I'm not Ben!" he shouted suddenly, and smacked her hand out of the way. "I am David ben Jonah. And I'm a Jew. The Messiah *will* come and Zion *will* be re-established, as it was prophesied in the old books."

Judy did not move. She gazed down at him steadily, determined not to become frightened.

After a minute Ben ran his hands over his face and muttered, "I'm sorry. Forgive me. It was the strain, the tension . . ."

"I know," she said softly.

Wiping the tears away, he now turned his full attention to Judy, to the concern in her eyes, to the loving way she watched over him. He said, "We were there for a while, weren't we? We were back in Jerusalem."

She nodded.

"And you were with me all the while." He reached out a shaky hand and stroked her long hair. "I was aware of you every minute at my side, and it made me glad. You wonder, don't you, Judith, what this is all about."

"Yes."

"And so do I, but it was not revealed to me, the purpose of all this. It was meant to be and so we shall accept it. Soon my last Scroll will come, and it is indeed the last one, and then it will be revealed to us what God has planned."

Judy straightened up and looked away. Her eyes wandered about the darkness of the room, straining to see something that was not there. She recalled what it had felt like to spend a time in Jerusalem, to be at the side of a man she loved, to bind herself completely to a faith that she knew was the very essence of all beliefs.

It was at this moment that Judy experienced a revelation. It became clear to her in that instant, as Ben's hand caressed her hair and his voice spoke soothingly to her, that while the night before she had sought frantically for a way to bring Ben back to himself, tonight she was not sure she wanted to.

Looking down at him, at the face that was Ben's but at the eyes that were another man's, she knew that although she had loved him too much last night to let him become David, tonight she loved him too much to turn him back.

"You're happy, aren't you?" she whispered, already knowing the answer.

"Yes, I am."

Then how can I wish Ben's torment on you again? cried her mind. Isn't it less cruel to leave you in this state?

"Judith, there are tears in your eyes."

"No, no. It's eyestrain. Eight hours—" She stood abruptly and backed away from the couch.

To love this man and to remain with him meant only one thing: that she too would have to give up reality and share the insanity with him.

"I need some coffee—" Judy said in a tight voice, and dashed away to the kitchen.

There, in the darkness, pressed against the wall, she faced head on the decision she would have to make. There was going to be no way of staying with Ben and suffering his lunacy without herself becoming a part of it.

And as she gaped into the darkness, the visions came back. The flash of palm trees, and dusty roads, and narrow streets. The sound of hawkers in the marketplace, the smell of Jerusalem in the summer, the taste of watered wine.

It would be so easy . . .

Judy snapped herself out of it and turned on the light. That her own sanity, her own grip on reality was rapidly dissipating was no longer a question. All that remained now was the decision: to allow it to happen, or run away now and never come back.

There was no time to ponder it, for Judy was suddenly distracted from her reverie by sounds coming from another room. She stepped out of the kitchen and looked around.

The bedroom light was on. She walked cautiously toward it and came to a halt in the doorway. Ben was rummaging through the drawers in the dresser.

"What are you looking for?" she asked.

"The passport."

"Passport?"

"Ben has a passport, but I don't remember where I put it."

Judy went to stand at his side and frowned at him. "What do you want your passport for?"

Without looking up, he muttered, "To get to Israel."

Her eyes flew open. "Israel!"

"It's in here somewhere." And he started lifting out heaps of clothes and dumping them on the floor.

"Ben." She put a hand on his arm. "Ben, why do you want to go to Israel?"

He didn't answer. His gestures became more hurried, more frantic. "I know it's in here!"

"Ben, answer me!" she shouted.

Finally he straightened, and the look Judy saw in his eyes—the fury and the rage—startled her. "To go to Israel!" he shouted back. "There will be a revolt and I must be with them. I cannot remain here in this foreign land while my brothers are slain by the foe."

"Slain! Oh God, Ben, listen to me!"

He went back to rifling through the drawer. Judy seized his arm and cried, "But you can't go to Israel! There's nothing for you there. That war took place two thousand years ago. It's over, Ben. It's *over.*"

Twice he tried to shake her hand free, and the third time he grabbed her hand and flung it away. "Don't stand in my way, woman!"

"But, Ben—"

Judy tried to seize him again, this time with both hands, and as she did so, Ben suddenly turned on her, grabbed her by the shoulders and flung her violently from him. Judy fell back, caught her foot on the bed and crashed to the floor. Sprawled at his feet, she gaped up at him in astonishment.

In the next instant Ben froze. He became rooted to the spot and stared down in disbelief. Then, without a word, he dropped down to one knee and spread out his hands in a gesture of helplessness. "What have I done?" he whispered.

Judy did not move but stayed as she was, her body trembling, her lips slightly parted.

Ben continued to stare at her, his face all bewilderment and confusion. "The one person whom I have loved above all else, the woman I have held dearer to me than myself and whom I once placed above the Torah . . ." His voice grew thick and heavy.

Ben looked down at his hands, trying to understand what was happening. And while he knelt before the mute girl, he was overcome with a violent sexual desire. And he knew it to be a thousand times greater than what he had felt that day in the orchard—years ago. It overwhelmed him, this terrible burning, the sudden craving to drive himself once again into Sarah, to forsake once more the laws of the Torah and the bond of Saul's friendship. Suddenly, on his knees before her as she watched him with the tremblings of a sparrow, Ben wanted to relive that sublime afternoon of long ago and to put everything from his mind other than the possession of this woman.

But I must not, his mind argued, for she is not a free woman, and I am not a free man. It is direct transgression of God's Law and profanes my friendship with Saul. And yet . . .

He continued to stare at his hands, forced himself to look down, for he knew that if he but once raised his gaze to Sarah, he would become lost in the depths of her eyes.

"Ben," whispered a tiny voice. It was as weak and frail as the body it came from, spoken by the woman he had so obscenely pushed away from himself.

He did not reply. As shudders of passion now racked his body, the tormented man fought with the best of his will against the intense desire that burned in him.

Then another gentle whisper. "David . . ." It was a coax. A sweetly compelling, timid invitation.

Finally, weakened, he raised his eyes to hers. Seeing that small pale face and the long black hair made his heart nearly burst. After a difficult swallow, Ben managed a feeble voice. "We must not, Sarah dearest. That one time should never have been . . ."

There was an infinite sadness in her eyes, a sorrow that perplexed him. It was as though she wanted him and yet was waging a private struggle of her own; one which he had no knowledge of.

Yet how could he know? That in her deep love for Ben, and knowing she could never have Ben, she was willing to give herself to David. For the desire to have Ben, she would offer herself to a stranger and pretend to be another woman.

"It has been so long," she whispered, reaching out.

He caught her hand and pressed her fingertips to his lips. There was a thunderous roar in his ears. All sensibility seemed to leave him. In one smooth gesture, Ben swept her off the floor and carried her in his powerful arms to the bed, where he gently laid her down.

"Sarah, don't cry," he murmured in puzzlement. "I will leave you if it is your wish—"

But her small hand reached out for his and he felt how feverish she was. Again his devotion to Saul and the rigors of the Torah stayed David before another move, so that he towered over her in one second of indecision.

Judy looked up at him imploringly, as bewildered as he. She felt her own sexual desire overcome all other emotions, and wrestled with her own purgatory of doubt.

Then, capitulating at last, she murmured, "If not Ben, then David . . ." and to the man standing over her she said, "Now, my dearest, while we have this hour."

He was upon her in an instant, unleashed by his own desperation, and kissing her mouth with a violence that shocked them both. Judy tasted the salt of her tears mingling with the taste of his tongue. She felt his mouth devour hers, and tried to quell the sobs in her throat.

The assault Ben made upon her manifested the anguish of David ben Jonah, and a powerful love that had waited two thousand years to become incarnate.

CHAPTER SEVENTEEN

·····>·——◆>◉<◆——·<·····

For the next two days they dwelt neither in the present nor in the past, but existed in a twilight realm which they had created for their own needs out of their own futility. Ben was patient in his wait for the thirteenth Scroll. He sat quietly in those long hours, staring in silence at the collection of papyrus fragments he had accumulated from John Weatherby and would linger over each photograph as if reliving a sweet memory.

Judy was less sure of herself, although now resigned to a force that was too great to fight. She loved Ben/David to a point of no longer caring what was going to happen to them, or worrying about the future, for—she believed—just as everything that had happened thus far was meant to be, so would their tomorrows come to pass in an inevitability that could not be changed.

They made love three more times after that, and each encounter was as explosive as that first. As they lay in each other's arms late into the night, taking comfort in feeling one another's warm nakedness, Ben murmured quietly in an ancient dialect of Hebrew about the wonders of Jerusalem and the optimism of his time.

"I was wrong," he said in the ancient tongue, which Judy was able, for the most part, to understand. "I was wrong to try to go to Israel. For to take up arms and fight the enemy is an act of faithlessness before God. Has He not promised to send the Messiah, the Anointed One, to deliver Israel from oppression? In my weakness I became impatient and would have questioned the judgment of God. You were right, my love, to have tried to stop me."

Judy curled herself against his body, resting her head on his chest. There was no more beautiful hour than this, to lie in Ben's embrace and entertain the visions his gentle voice conjured: of walks along the lakeshore in Galilee; of the red anemone blooming in the spring-time; of the joy of a plentiful olive crop; of the peace and tran-quillity on a Judea hilltop. She wanted the moment to last forever.

But it did not.

On Saturday afternoon the mailman knocked on their door with a registered envelope from Israel.

After they read the note from Weatherby—something about pub-lishers and museums and official announcement—Ben and Judy sat at the desk to translate the last Scroll.

He seemed unperturbed and unhurried, indeed almost desirous of drawing the moment out, while Judy on the other hand was appre-hensive. She stared at the inner envelope in fascination, her mind alive with wildly flying questions.

What will happen to us now, once the last Scroll is read?

She looked at Ben, saw that peaceful expression on his face which she had come to recognize as the inner tranquillity of David. Wher-ever Benjamin Messer had been sent to, wherever the troubled and guilt-ridden mind of Ben had been buried, the man at her side was now a happier person for it. And that was all she wanted.

But what if, she wondered in a nagging fear, what if the Scrolls were his slender link with the identity he had assumed? And what if, because this is the last one or because of what it might say, that frail thread is broken?

In the ensuing four years, strife in the city increased immeas-urably.

The day Procurator Gessius Florus plundered the Temple Treasury was the day hundreds of Jews rose up in arms. To quell the uprising, the Procurator dispatched Roman troops throughout the city, brutal men who went to any lengths to keep down insurrection, and as a consequence, many Jews were killed and wounded. As news of this event spread throughout the country, more and more organized bands of Zealots rose up against the overlords, and slew the Romans wherever they found them.

Where there had once been occasional ambushes and sabotage, there was now open warfare.

Emperor Nero dispatched his best general, Vespasian, to put an end to the Revolt, and a great deal of battle was done in all the towns of Judea, Syria and Idumea. Because of its location in the path of the Roman onslaught, Galilee was hardest hit and suffered terrible damage. My brothers left their families to join with the rebel forces, and I am told they died fighting for Zion.

What happened to my mother and father, I will never know.

In that time, Jerusalem was boiling with fear and hatred and a taste for blood, but the fighting was minimal. We stood and waited to see what would become of the outlying cities, as Rome marched through them and toward us.

We are told of many acts of valor in those battles, thousands of Jews, only half of them Zealots, fighting with what they had to restore the supremacy of Israel.

Yet I knew in my heart that they were wrong, for it would be the King of Israel who would unfetter our bonds, and he had not yet returned to us.

I explained this to Saul, who, coming to our house late one night, pressed a sword into my hand, saying: The hour has come for you to arm yourself, brother!

But I refused the weapon and said: Were I to arm myself now and strike out against the foe, then it would be as a sign of faithlessness before God. I believe the Messiah will come; I believe in God's promise to His children; and I believe that on that day, the new King of Israel will set us free.

You are a stiff-necked fool, said Saul. And it hurt me deeply.

So it was that my brother and I became sorely divided.

News of Emperor Nero's death at Rome sent Vespasian back to take part in the civil upheaval which took place over the vacant throne, yet we in the East were given no respite, for he sent in his place his son Titus, a cruel and hard-driven man.

With the vanquishing of each town in the country and with the drawing nearer of the Roman machine, Jerusalem grew more afraid.

Our brothers who dwelt in the monastery by the Sea of Salt abandoned their home and dispersed throughout the land, and it was told to us that they had hidden their sacred scrolls in jars deep in the caves around the Sea. This was so that the Word of God would be preserved against the heathen conqueror, and so that the monks could return one day and bring them again to the light.

The hour of Jerusalem drew nigh. And as the ravaged survivors of Tiberias and Jotapata and Caesarea swarmed into Jerusalem for shelter, and as we heard tales of the might and fierceness of the Romans, I saw that it was time to take my wife and my slaves into the safety of the walls, to return to our farm when the danger was past.

Rebekah was tearful, but she was brave, and I was proud of her for it. We took only what we needed and secured the rest in storage, thinking we would return soon.

Miriam welcomed us into her house, where, with other members of the Poor, and with Jacob and Philip and Matthew, Rebekah and I shared our worldly goods and spent our days in prayer.

We never saw our farm again.

Vespasian became Emperor of Rome and his son Titus finally arrived at Jerusalem.

I cannot describe the cold fear that gripped our hearts at the sight of the Roman legions. There were tens of thousands of them marching toward the city and it was at that moment, as I stood looking down from the Temple toward the Mount of Olives, that I knew these were the Last Days.

It was at this time that a sorrowful thing occurred within the city. After seeing the immensity of the Roman strength, separated from us only by the Kedron, many citizens voiced a wish to surrender now and thus save themselves. Yet the Zealots would not allow it, for they believed these were the Last Days prophesied in the Scriptures, and that theirs was a duty to God. And so the people of Jerusalem became divided. The leaders of the city, the Sadducees and the Pharisees, believed that the Romans would not attack and that a peaceful accord would be reached. We of the Poor believed that prayer was the answer, and that God, seeing our faith, would deliver the Messiah to us. So Jerusalem became divided, and we were not a united front against the foe.

The day came when, growing weary of this standoff and anxious for decisive action, Titus ordered all land within the vicinity to be leveled and thus the Kedron ravine filled in. So it was that a cohort of Romans felled every tree, tore down every fence and leveled every building up to the base of the walls. This was how my farm was destroyed, and I watched the flames reach the sky until nothing remained to burn.

The next move of Titus was to build a huge ramp. He chose the best place for his assault opposite the tomb of John Hyrcanus, since here the first line of ramparts was on lower ground and thus an easy approach to the third wall, through which he intended to capture the Antonia, the upper town, and therefore the Temple.

Yet even so, even with the enemy so close in our proximity, did the strife continue within the city. As more and more people panicked and wanted to desert to the Romans, it was the powerful Zealots who were in command and they would allow for no surrender.

I could not believe the growing cataclysm my eyes beheld, as Jew fought Jew in the streets of Jerusalem, while outside the wall the Romans waited like vultures.

It was a sad time for all, and no man knew peace. Rather than have a single Jew give himself up to the enemy, Zealots slew him in the street as a warning against other attempts. For they had become fanatics. These zealous men, so fiery in their belief of a supreme Zion, grew to be lunatics when driven into a corner by Rome. We were all trapped and we knew we would be slaughtered, and so it was that these radical Jews became twisted in their ideals. While there were those of us who would have preferred a peaceful slavery, the Zealots chose death before dishonor.

Jerusalem would not unite against the enemy. And whether or not this would have helped, I do not know, for it quickly turned into a nightmare of astonishing proportions. Not a man among us could possibly have foreseen the calamity that was soon to befall us, and when we became truly aware of the seriousness of our situation, it was too late.

I prayed with my brothers of the Poor until my knees were callused. Titus and his men built their ramp up to the Antonia Fortress. Divided factions of Jews fought among themselves within the city.

And a worse enemy—far worse than I or my brothers or Titus or the Zealots could ever have anticipated—began to creep insidiously into the city.

And it was because of this enemy—not the rivaling Jews nor the Romans in the Kedron, but this last adversary which began its own war against us—that the days of Jerusalem were numbered.

For no man can stop the march of Famine.

The fighting became a daily thing, although restricted to the walls.

Again Saul tried to press me to carry a weapon, but I would not, for I believed God would save us before Rome breached the walls, and I could not show signs of faithlessness in His judgment.

Saul said: While you pray on your knees for your Messiah to come, courageous Jews are losing their lives to Roman spears. Haven't you seen? Haven't you heard? There is Jewish blood on the walls of the city and their cries ring out to the distant hills. Where is your Messiah!

And I replied: God will choose the Hour.

These were our last words together and they caused me great pain. Saul was a good rabbi and the best of Jews; where was his faith in God?

As Titus' ramp grew steadily each day, and as Jerusalem began to feel the first pangs of hunger, many citizens chose to flee through the gates on their own accord. In running to the enemy, they were saving their lives, but that was short-lived.

For a few crafty men sought to take their treasure with them on their flight and so swallowed as many gold coins at they could before scaling the walls and dropping down amidst the

Romans. At first the defectors were treated sanely and given asylum, but after a Roman soldier spotted an old Jew picking gold coins out of his own feces, word rapidly spread through all the camps that the fugitives had swallowed their money.

And so it was that on that terrible night, and every night thereafter, all the Jews who were in the Roman camps were slit open while yet alive and had their entrails examined for gold.

I can still hear the sounds of those slaughtered that night, my son, as their cries were carried on the wind and over the city. Those poor wretches who, in their ignorance and lack of faith, had run to the enemy to save themselves had ended by suffering the most abominable of fates. Perhaps four thousand were slain that night, men, women and even babies, slit open by Roman soldiers because of man's insatiable greed for gold. And of that multitude slain, my son, by hundreds of legionnaires, it is said that the treasure found amounted to no more than six pieces of gold.

I tried not to give in to despair, as so many around me had. The famine was rapidly gaining victory over the city as the grain ran low and the water supply dried up. We of the Poor were more fortunate than others, for those of us who had plenty shared with those who had none. We prayed daily for the Messiah to return, as he had promised forty years ago. The time he had spoken of was here; these were the Last Days.

The fighting grew worse, both within and without. Those Jews who continued to fly over the wall and thus take their chances with the Romans were crucified on the hilltops and left to hang for days as a warning by Titus. He wanted us to surrender the city, and we would not.

Those of us, tens of thousands of us, who stayed in the city found famine on our doorstep. And when we ventured into the streets, we were besieged by starving maniacs who tore us to pieces for one hidden piece of bread.

How quickly sanity leaves in the face of starvation!

Titus surrounded the city and needed to fight only a little, for he would let hunger wage his war for him.

As the weeks went by and hope diminished, we of the Poor prayed incessantly for the Messiah to come and deliver us. It would be this afternoon, or this evening, or tomorrow morning, and then we would hear the trumpets of the Lord and know we were saved.

In all this time, Rebekah never left my side. Miriam's house grew crowded, filled with families whose homes were no longer safe. We tried to feed everyone, but it was a meager supply. And still we sang the hymns of the New Covenant and expected to find Yeshua among us.

Sarah and Jonathan worked hard to nurse the sick and the wounded and to bolster the faith of those who were weakening. She helped dispense the mystical medicines which the monks of the Sea of Salt concocted at their monastery and which Jacob and the Twelve used in their healing arts. And I loved her more in these times than ever before, even though she had grown pale and thin and looked twice her age. Sarah never once questioned the judgment of God as so many others were now doing, and I thought of her as a saint among women.

Now the moment has come for to speak of the saddest time of all.

Word reached our house that Saul had been wounded and that he lay in the house of a friend in the Lower City. The boy who had brought the message was no more than Jonathan's age, a mere stripling whose tunic was shredded and whose eyes bespoke the horrors they had seen. He fell upon the small round of bread we gave him and choked on the cup of water. When I saw this, I became alarmed, for I knew that Saul must also be without food.

So I wrapped my own small ration and tucked it into my girdle, along with a pouch of white powder which Jacob often gave in small amounts for the relief of pain. I told Rebekah of my errand, but not Sarah, for I did not want her to know the bad news of her husband. Then I struck out into the evening.

Was it possible I could have prepared myself for the shock that met me in the streets? How blind I had been! How ignorant of the true plight of our city! While I had knelt for months on the floor of Miriam's house, praying to God and keeping heart with my brethren, Jerusalem had become a graveyard.

Swollen corpses lay about, giving up such a stench that, had my belly not been so empty, I would have vomited. Wretched creatures that had once been respectable citizens now poked about in the gutters, searching for bits of cow dung to eat and scavenging the bodies of the dead. All about me I saw hollow faces, gaunt and sunken as though risen from graves. Skeletal women held dead babes to their withered breasts. Wild dogs tore apart the weak and defenseless who lay by the wayside.

I was smitten as if by a club, and realized that in these past months what Saul had said was true, and that I had turned my back upon my fellow man.

I did not pass unscathed. Several times, passing by dark alleys, I was beset upon by wild things who clawed at my clothes and reeked of decay. Yet I was stronger than they, stronger indeed than ten of them, for I had eaten, if only a little, these past days while they had none. And so I was able, with some struggle, to fight off my assailants and somehow make it to the hiding place of Saul.

He lay upon the stone floor with two friends at his side. The only light in the death-like darkness came from the moon, which shone silvery through a small window high overhead. I do not know what place this was, but it smelled foul of urine and putrefaction. The two men who sat at his side were like those sunken-eyed ghosts that haunted the streets and needed only a place to lie down and die. They were dressed in rags, as was my dear Saul, filthy beyond belief and bespattered with blood. Seeing me, they rose without a word and left us.

I hovered over my friend for some time before falling to my knees next to him, so stunned was I at his appearance. Where was the handsome, laughing man I had for so long called brother? Who was this wasted wretch that barely breathed and lay in his own filth?

I could not fight back the tears. Forcing a smile, sweet Saul said: You should not have come to me, brother, for it is dangerous outside. You were safe in your house, at least for a while longer.

I was wrong! I cried in anguish. How blind I was. That first day you came to me I should have taken the sword, for then your death would not be for naught! Jerusalem will lose, Saul, and we will be lost forever!

But he shook his head, saying: No, my brother, it is I who was wrong and you were right. There will be a Messiah who comes to Israel one day and Zion will rule again. But this was not the day. When I took up the sword, David, I put aside my faith in God. It is you, through your prayers, who has kept the Covenant with Him. In my vanity I thought that I could save Jerusalem with my own hand. I pressed the judgment of God and sought to force His move. But now I see that we cannot know the Hour the Lord intends for His people. We can only wait and pray and show Him our worthiness.

You, my brother David, are worthy above all men, while I am not. And it is because of me and others like me, who showed a faithlessness in God, that the Day of the Messiah has been pushed back. Had I, too, prayed with you as I should have done—

Saul fell into a fit of coughing and spitting, and it frightened me.

Then, still smiling through his agony, he whispered: I have loved you above all else, my brother, and use my last breath to make one request of you.

I could not reply, but only wept.

He said: Take care of Sarah and Jonathan in my stead. I do not know where they are now, I have lost them. Seek them out and, somehow, save them from the fate that awaits them beyond the wall. I could not bear that the Romans should lay hands upon them. Promise me, David, that you will protect them!

And I promised Saul I would guard them with my own life.

And now, he whispered, there is one more thing I will tell you. I tell you this because I am dying and you will live, and I tell you because I love you. I have known for many years, David, that you love Sarah. This is because you are my brother and we have no secrets. I have seen it in your eyes and I have seen it in hers. You have loved one another since the day I first introduced you, and you continue to love one another to this hour. I do not hold it against you, nor did I ever, for Sarah is a good woman, I see what you see in her; and you are a good man, I know why she loves you.

Yet, I suspect, dear brother, that you do not know about

Jonathan. Indeed, Sarah is not aware that I know about him, but believes that she alone has kept the secret all these years. But a man knows these things, just as you must now know.

That Jonathan is your son.

Ben collapsed on the desk. He wept aloud, soaking the photograph with his tears, while Judy cried silently, her hand gently on his shoulder.

A long time passed before they were able to move on to the next fragment, and when they did, Ben no longer wrote the translation on paper, but instead read it out loud as he went.

How can this be? I cried.

Saul said: If you will but open your eyes, you will see yourself in Jonathan. He was born two months early, and yet you did not realize this, my sweet obtuse friend. I knew then that you had known Sarah and that she had not been a virgin. At first I was hurt, but I loved her so and loved you so, that I overcame the hurt and looked upon Jonathan as my own.

But when I am dead, Sarah will tell him the truth, that you are his father, and Jonathan will look for you.

Seek them out now, David, before it is too late!

Saul died in my arms with that same smile on his lips, and I envied him from that moment on.

But death never comes to him who seeks it, and although I wandered blindly through the streets unarmed, and carried still a piece of bread in my girdle, I passed unmolested.

When I returned to the house of Miriam—or what was left of it—I stood before it like a man walking in death. I was beyond all sensibilities and could feel no emotion to see the house in complete ruins.

Oh, the carnage! How can such innocents be the victims of such rapine! Who would slaughter defenseless women and children, mutilate them so, and assault them so obscenely as this!

Had I been of my own mind at that moment, I would have flown into an insane rage. But I could not. So dull had the last few hours made me that all I could do was survey the destruction and brutality about me. These sweet gentle Jews, whose only crime had been to wait for their Saviour, had been slaughtered for their few scraps of bread. And it had not been the Roman enemy that had done this thing, but fellow Jews.

Dear Rebekah, her red hair mingling with the red blood oozing from her head, lay beneath the body of Matthew, who must have tried to fight to defend her.

And were you not the one, dear Matthew, who often said that those who live by the sword shall die by it?

How wrong you were! How wrong you all were!

I blindly stumbled through the rubble and over the bodies of my dear brothers and sisters, but did not find Sarah and Jonathan. If they had fled, where could they have gone to? For there was no safety anywhere in the city.

So I knelt and said a simple prayer. There was nothing more I could do here, the battle was lost. And taking a last look at the bodies of my wife and friends, I felt a flood of hatred and anger surge through my being, bringing bitterness to my mouth like poison. So I stood upon this mass grave, shook my fist heavenward, and with greater resolve than I had ever known before, cursed the God of Abraham for all time.

I spent the next hours, those before dawn, searching for Sarah and Jonathan. But they were nowhere to be found.

Who knows what happened to them? What nefarious fate had befallen them. I could only pray that they were now dead and no longer witness to all this.

And so it happened that, in the last hour before dawn, as Titus' troops were making their final efforts to break over the walls, I came upon the house of a man I knew.

I had often seen him at Miriam's. He was a good Jew and a Pharisee who believed in the return of the Messiah. There were many gathered with him inside, huddled in the darkness, their eyes bulging in fear. Recognizing me, he invited me in.

He said: We have left one round of bread for all of us, and some sacrificial wine which we had hidden. We are going to celebrate communion now and pray. Will you join us?

I said that I would, and because I had once been a student at the Temple, offered to lead them in the prayer.

I broke the small round of bread into tiny morsels and passed it out to the congregation, saying: This bread symbolizes the body of the Messiah who will one day share communion with us.

Then I poured their last wine into a few cups, and as I did so, looked around at their faces. They were sorry, starving things with eyes that stared in bewilderment. And seeing them, I saw again the bodies of Rebekah and Jacob and Philip and all the others who had once been as hopeful as these. Then I remembered the pouch of white powder in my girdle, which I had intended for Saul, and while they could not see, emptied the whole of the powder into the cups. Then I passed out the wine so that each might drink, and I said: This wine symbolizes the blood of the Saviour who will one day share communion with us.

And the man whose house this was, after drinking the poison, said: Will you not share in this with us, brother?

And I replied: I will drink from my Master's cup.

He gave me a puzzled look and died peacefully a moment later.

There were eighty-nine of them in that house, from a very old man ranging down to a child of six. And every one was dead before I returned to the chill air of early morning.

How long I roamed the streets, stumbling over corpses, slipping in the ooze, I do not know. And how I came to pass unharmed, I do not know, except that possibly the Lord was meting His judgment upon me in this way. If death is merciful, then living is capital punishment. And such was the sentence for my crime, to live out my days beneath the burden of guilt for what I had done.

It was in the stark, biting air of dawn that the revelation came to me. And when I realized what my true crime had been that night, I knew that I was a man condemned to oblivion.

For my crime had not been in killing those eighty-nine back in that house, but in *robbing them of their last chance to see the Messiah*.

I fell to my knees on the cobblestones and tore my clothes and cried aloud.

Because I, David ben Jonah, had ceased for a night to believe in the coming of the Messiah, I had denied those gentle people their last few hours of hope! While they yet lived, he might yet have come. Just because I had lost faith, did not mean the Messiah would never come.

And that, my son, was your father's abominable crime, the wretched deed that has exiled him from the community of mankind.

I beat my fists upon the ground until they bled, and gashed stones against my face and chest. But there would be no dying for David ben Jonah. Not after the unforgivable crime he had committed against eighty-nine Nazarenes.

I knew in the next moment what I was to do, for it was as if I was no longer in command of myself, but following the lead of an unseen force.

I had to leave Jerusalem. It was not to be my privilege to die just yet, for the very God whom I had cursed now sought His revenge upon me.

The idea came to my mind how to escape; this was God's plan, and I followed it without protest.

To escape from Jerusalem I had to pass through the gates and into the Roman forces. And to pass safely through the enemy camps which surrounded the city, I could go only one way: as a leper.

The plan came to me as if in a dream, for I was in no wise anxious for my safety or my life—indeed I wished for death—and yet it came to me that I should escape the city in this manner, and so I knew it to be God's plan.

According to the Thirteenth Chapter of the Third Book of Moses, I rent my clothes, laid my head bare and put a covering over my mouth and upper lip. Then I walked through the streets and cried out: Unclean! Unclean! as it is written in the Law.

When I neared the Gennath Gate and was not far from the Hasmonean Palace, I saw that people turned away from me. I walked as if in a dream, unhurried and uncaring, for all life had gone from me and my body was made of wood, and yet the path was cleared for me. No one dared hinder me, and the doorway was opened by the Zealots who guarded it. They were a coarse and haggard mob with unkempt beards and clothes smeared in blood. They regarded me with contempt and made scurrilous remarks as I passed.

When the door closed behind me, I saw the formidable camps of the Romans before me, their rows of tents and early-morning fires as far as the eye could see. I called out: Unclean! Unclean! and passed through them. As I wandered toward the Damascus road, a pair of unsavory soldiers eyes me suspiciously and brandished their newly honed swords. As they spoke a common dialect of Greek, I was able to understand what they said of me, and it was this:

The one wanted to slit me open and search my bowels for gold, but the other feared to come near me. The first said that I might only be in disguise, but the other argued that he was not willing to take the chance.

And so it was that I went unharmed to the Damascus road, for not even Romans will touch a leper.

How long I walked, I will never know, but the way is long from Jerusalem to Galilee, and I saw the sun rise and set many times. After a while, because of need of food, I abandoned my leper guise and went about the countryside as a begger. An ear of corn here, a crust of bread there, and some water from an occasional well. And all about me I saw the destruction caused by Rome.

And as I walked, I came to realize that I was an even lowlier, more despicable creature than I had thought before, for in my easy escape from Jerusalem and my aimless journey toward the north, I had forgotten about Sarah and Jonathan. And in so doing had broken my promise to a dying friend.

Whatever horrors Sarah and Jonathan were suffering, it was because of me, for if I had been a man of my word I would have saved them along with myself . . .

I somehow made it to Magdala—how, I will never know. There was a force other than myself guiding me, for if it had been me alone, I would have lain down at the roadside and died long ago. But my survival was not my own wish, nor was this destination. And yet here I came, to my father's empty house, and to a village that had known war and plunder.

I took these Scrolls from the deserted synagogue, for I knew then what my purpose must be. The Lord God had saved me for one reason only, and that was to record on paper all that has happened. Again, why this is, I do not know. But just as it was in the plan of the Lord that you should be my son, Jonathan, so it must also be in His plan that you should know in detail the life of your father.

And I have given it to you. Maybe, if Sarah tells you the truth, you will come and seek me out. And in searching will find these Scrolls. And remember, my son, it is God Who judges; not you. And it was also God Who preordained the fate that befell Jerusalem.

For the Prophet Isaiah said: Behold, the Lord maketh the earth empty, and maketh it waste, and turneth it upside down, and scattereth abroad the inhabitants thereof. The land shall be utterly emptied and utterly spoiled, for the Lord has spoken this word. In the city is left desolation and the gate is smitten with destruction.

Always remember, my son, that you are a Jew, just as I am a Jew, just as my father was a Jew. You will continue to wait for the Messiah, as I know Sarah will teach you, and now I must warn you: look not to Rome. We in Jerusalem were the ones who knew the Master in his life, and we are gone now. Simon is dead, Jacob is dead, all of the Twelve are dead. There no longer exists a man who knew him.

In your youth and innocence I fear you will turn your eyes to the Gentiles, for they, too, use the word Messiah. But always remember, my son, that they have only imitated us. While Jerusalem waited for a man, Rome awaits a dream.

Always remember this parable: There once grew a strong and mighty tree which one day dropped a seed to the ground. Out of it grew a new shoot. One day, lightning struck the big tree and razed it until nothing remained. The new shoot, which had not been touched, continued to grow, yet it is separate from the parent and grows a different way.

Someday, when it is grown, a man will walk by and say:

"Here stands a mighty tree," not knowing that in a spot not far away there once stood a mightier one.

Hear O Israel, the Lord Our God, the Lord is One God! Can it be that there is some worthiness left in David ben Jonah to warrant the mercy of the God of Abraham? Surely I am dreaming! Surely this is a day of days! Have I gone mad or have I this morning spoken with my old friend Salmonides, who appeared like a ghost from the past! And the incredible tale he told me!

The old Greek, so happy to see me, actually threw himself at the feet of this wretched man and claimed to have been searching for me.

In my utter amazement I told him that I was a man to be despised and that I awaited the judgment of the Lord upon me, and so my death.

Then this arrogant fellow said: Then you have miscalculated your God, master, or possibly He is too busy destroying Jerusalem and has forgotten His appointment with you, for you are not going to die and you are not a man to be despised. There are those who love you.

And he went on with his incredible tale, of escaping in the night from Jerusalem, of bribing his way through the lines with the fortune he had earned from me all these years, and of bringing with him two other lives.

And how could I believe my eyes when I next saw Sarah and Jonathan standing before me?

Ben let out a cry, fell from the chair and landed on the floor with a crash. His body trembled violently and jerked as if in the grips of a seizure. When Judy, at once on her knees beside him, tried to lift him up, he murmured, "No . . . there's more. I . . . must read . . ."

Copious amounts of sweat ran from his ashen face. His eyes were wide and staring. He seemed oblivious of the girl who struggled with him, seemed unaware that he got somehow to his feet and leaned on the desk for support. Ben's shirt was drenched. He breathed heavily as if he had run for miles.

"Must finish . . . must read . . ."

"You have to stop, Ben, you're making yourself ill!"

The sound of her voice made him stop shaking, and he turned to look at her in a most curious way. "Judy," he whispered. Then he fell back into the chair and held his face in his hands.

Kneeling before him, Judy wiped away the streams of sweat that poured off his face and neck. She was weak herself, pale and exhausted. Together they had suffered the ordeal of Jerusalem.

"Judy . . ." he said into his hands. "I remember it. I remember all of it."

"Remember what?"

Finally he looked up at her. His eyes were icy blue and full of wonder. "I remember thinking I was David. I remember *being* David. Oh God, what happened to me? What happened to us?"

Her lips moved, but no words came out.

Then, after another long silence, Ben said a little sadly, "It's all over. David's gone."

"Oh, Ben—" She shuddered with relief.

"I don't know how I can tell, but I can. And I can't explain it to you. Maybe someday we'll figure it all out. I wonder . . ." Ben took hold of her hands and looked long into her eyes. "How did you figure into it, Judy? Would it have happened if I hadn't met you? Were you a cause of it, or merely a catalyst?"

She stared back up at him. They were back at the very beginning again, where they were four weeks ago.

"Was David ever really here?" murmured Ben. "Or was it me all along? And those coincidences . . ." He took Judy's face in his hands, kissed her mouth and murmured, "I love you."

She smiled and kissed him back.

"I want to figure this out, Judy. I want to understand what happened. Later, we'll sit down and go over the Scrolls again, and see if we can't find some clue, some key to the whole thing. I . . . I'm not the same man any more. David changed me. Do you suppose maybe it would have happened someday . . . anyway?"

"I don't know, Ben."

"I have to find myself all over again, Judy. But you can help me this time." He kissed her again, lingeringly. "And now . . . there's a little more to read. And then . . ."

"And then?"

"We can type up a decent translation and send it to Weatherby. Things are going to start happening fast and we want to be ready. Come on, let's see what David's last words were."

So together they read the last lines of the last fragment.

Now that I have told Jonathan the story in person, I cannot bring myself to destroy these Scrolls or to wash the papyrus clean, for they are still a part of me, and still my legacy. But to whom? To future generations?

And so, just as I have safely put away my first twelve Scrolls, now I will wrap this one and carefully secrete it with the rest. And if a Jew should find them in some distant time, is he not, after all, my son?